D0256925

EVERYMAN,

I WILL GO WITH THEE,

AND BE THY GUIDE,

IN THY MOST NEED

TO GO BY THY SIDE

✳

EVERYMAN'S POCKET CLASSICS

CAT
STORIES

EDITED BY DIANA SECKER TESDELL

EVERYMAN'S POCKET CLASSICS

Alfred A. Knopf New York London Toronto

THIS IS A BORZOI BOOK
PUBLISHED BY ALFRED A. KNOPF

This selection by Diana Secker Tesdell first published in
Everyman's Library, 2011
Copyright © 2011 by Everyman's Library
A list of acknowledgments to copyright owners appears at the back
of this volume.

All rights reserved. Published in the United States by Alfred A. Knopf,
a division of Random House, Inc., New York, and in Canada by
Random House of Canada Limited, Toronto. Distributed by
Random House, Inc., New York. Published in the United Kingdom
by Everyman's Library, Northburgh House, 10 Northburgh Street,
London EC1V 0AT, and distributed by Random House (UK) Ltd.

US website: www.randomhouse.com/everymans

ISBN: 978-0-307-70089-6 (US)
978-1-84159-610-5 (UK)

A CIP catalogue reference for this book is available from the
British Library

Library of Congress Cataloging-in-Publication Data
Cat stories / edited by Diana Secker Tesdell.
p.   cm.—(Everyman's pocket classics)
"This is a Borzoi book"
ISBN 978-0-307-70089-6 (hardcover: alk. paper)   1. Cats—Fiction.
2. Cats—Anecdotes.   I. Tesdell, Diana Secker.
PN6120.95.C3C36   2011   2011016382
808.83'93629752—dc23   CIP

Typography by Peter B. Willberg
Typeset in the UK by AccComputing, North Barrow, Somerset
Printed and bound in Germany by GGP Media GmbH, Pössneck

CAT
STORIES

Contents

7

FANCIFUL FELINES

PEOPLE AND THEIR CATS

'What does it mean to love an animal, a pet, in my case a cat, in the fierce, entire, and unambivalent way that some of us do?'
— ALICE ADAMS, 'The Islands'

ALICE ADAMS

THE ISLANDS

WHAT DOES IT mean to love an animal, a pet, in my case a cat, in the fierce, entire, and unambivalent way that some of us do? I really want to know this. Does the cat (did the cat) represent some person, a parent, or a child? some part of one's self? I don't think so – and none of the words or phrases that one uses for human connections sounds quite right: 'crazy about,' 'really liked,' 'very fond of' – none of those describes how I felt and still feel about my cat. Many years ago, soon after we got the cat (her name was Pink), I went to Rome with my husband, Andrew, whom I really liked; I was crazy about Andrew, and very fond of him too. And I have a most vivid memory of lying awake in Rome, in the pretty bed in its deep alcove, in the nice small hotel near the Borghese Gardens – lying there, so fortunate to be in Rome, with Andrew, and missing Pink, a small striped cat with no tail – missing Pink unbearably. Even blaming Andrew for having brought me there, although he loved her too, almost as much as I did. And now Pink has died, and I cannot accept or believe in her death, any more than I could believe in Rome. (Andrew also died, three years ago, but this is not his story.)

A couple of days after Pink died (this has all been recent), I went to Hawaii with a new friend, Slater. It had not been planned that way; I had known for months that Pink was slowly failing (she was nineteen), but I did not expect her to die. She just suddenly did, and then I went off to 'the islands,' as my old friend Zoe Pinkerton used to call them, in her nasal, moneyed voice. I went to Hawaii as planned, which interfered with my proper mourning for Pink. I feel as though those islands interposed themselves between her death and me. When I needed to be alone, to absorb her death, I was over there with Slater.

Slater is a developer; malls and condominium complexes all over the world. Andrew would not have approved of Slater, and sometimes I don't think I do either. Slater is tall and lean, red-haired, a little younger than I am, and very attractive, I suppose, although on first meeting Slater I was not at all drawn to him (which I have come to think is one of the reasons he found me so attractive, calling me the next day, insisting on dinner that night; he was probably used to women who found him terrific, right off). But I thought Slater talked too much about money, or just talked too much, period.

Later on, when I began to like him a little better (I was flattered by all that attention, is the truth), I thought that Slater's very differences from Andrew should be a good sign. You're supposed to look for opposites, not reproductions, I read somewhere.

Andrew and I had acquired Pink from Zoe, a very rich alcoholic, at that time a new neighbor of ours in Berkeley. Having met Andrew down in his bookstore, she invited us to what turned out to be a very long Sunday-lunch party in her splendidly decked and viewed new Berkeley hills house. Getting to know some of the least offensive neighbors, is how she probably thought of it. Her style was harsh, abrasive; anything for a laugh was surely one of her mottoes, but she was pretty funny, fairly often. We saw her around when she first moved to Berkeley (from Ireland: a brief experiment

14

that had not worked out too well). And then she met Andrew in his store, and found that we were neighbors, and she invited us to her party, and Andrew fell in love with a beautiful cat. 'The most beautiful cat I ever saw,' he told Zoe, and she was, soft and silver, with great blue eyes. The mother of Pink.

'Well, you're in luck,' Zoe told us. 'That's Molly Bloom, and she just had five kittens. They're all in a box downstairs, in my bedroom, and you get to choose any one you want. It's your door prize for being such a handsome couple.'

Andrew went off to look at the kittens, and then came back up to me. 'There's one that's really great,' he said. 'A tail-less wonder. Must be part Manx.'

As in several Berkeley hills houses, Zoe's great sprawl of a bedroom was downstairs, with its own narrow deck, its view of the bay and the bridge, and of San Francisco. The room was the most appalling mess I had ever seen. Clothes, papers, books, dirty glasses, spilled powder, more clothes dumped everywhere. I was surprised that my tidy, somewhat censorious husband even entered, and that he was able to find the big wicker basket (filled with what looked to be discarded silk under-things, presumably clean) in which five very tiny kittens mewed and tried to rise and stalk about on thin, uncertain legs.

The one that Andrew had picked was gray striped, a tabby, with a stub of a tail, very large eyes, and tall ears. I agreed that she was darling, how great it would be to have a cat again; our last cat, Lily, who was sweet and pretty but undistinguished, had died some years ago. And so Andrew and I went back upstairs and told Zoe, who was almost very drunk, that we wanted the one with no tail.

'Oh, Stubs,' she rasped. 'You don't have to take that one. What are you guys, some kind of Berkeley bleeding hearts?

15

You can have a whole cat.' And she laughed, delighted as always with her own wit.

No, we told her. We wanted that particular cat. We liked her best.

Aside from seeing the cats – our first sight of Pink! – the best part of Zoe's lunch was her daughter, Lucy, a shy, pretty, and very gentle young woman – as opposed to the other guests, a rowdy, oil-rich group, old friends of Zoe's from Texas.

'What a curious litter,' I remarked to Andrew, walking home up Mann to our considerably smaller house. 'All different. Five different patterns of cat.'

'Five fathers.' Andrew had read a book about this, I could tell. Andrew read everything. 'It's called multiple insemination, and occurs fairly often in cats. It's theoretically possible in humans, but they haven't come across any instances.' He laughed, really pleased with this lore.

'It's sure something to think about.'

'Just don't.'

Andrew. An extremely smart, passionate, selfish, and generous man, a medium-successful bookstore owner. A former academic: he left teaching in order to have more time to read, he said. Also (I thought) he much preferred being alone in his store to the company of students or, worse, of other professors – a loner, Andrew. Small and almost handsome, competitive, a gifted tennis player, mediocre pianist. Gray hair and gray-green eyes. As I have said, I was crazy about Andrew (usually). I found him funny and interestingly observant, sexy and smart. His death was more grievous to me than I can (or will) say.

'You guys don't have to take Stubs; you can have a whole

cat all your own.' Zoe Pinkerton on the phone, a few days later. Like many alcoholics, she tended to repeat herself, although in Zoe's case some vast Texas store of self-confidence may have fueled her repetitions.

And we in our turn repeated: we wanted the little one with no tail.

Zoe told us that she would bring 'Stubs' over in a week or so; then the kittens would be old enough to leave Molly Bloom.

Andrew: 'Molly Bloom indeed.'

I: 'No wonder she got multiply inseminated.'

Andrew: 'Exactly.'

We both, though somewhat warily, liked Zoe. Or we were both somewhat charmed by her. For one thing, she made it clear that she thought we were great. For another, she was smart; she had read even more than Andrew had.

A very small woman, she walked with a swagger; her laugh was loud, and liberal. I sometimes felt that Pink was a little like Zoe – a tiny cat with a high, proud walk; a cat with a lot to say.

In a couple of weeks, then, Zoe called, and she came over with this tiny tailless kitten under her arm. A Saturday afternoon. Andrew was at home, puttering in the garden like the good Berkeley husband that he did not intend to be.

Zoe arrived in her purple suede pants and a vivid orange sweater (this picture is a little poignant; fairly soon after that the booze began to get the better of her legs, and she stopped taking walks at all). She held out a tiny kitten, all huge gray eyes and pointed ears. A kitten who took one look at us and began to purr; she purred for several days, it seemed, as she walked all over our house and made it her own. This is absolutely the best place I've ever been, she seemed to say, and you are the greatest people – you are my people.

From the beginning, then, our connection with Pink seemed like a privilege; automatically we accorded her rights that poor Lily would never have aspired to.

She decided to sleep with us. In the middle of the night there came a light soft plop on our bed, which was low and wide, and then a small sound, *mmrrr*, a little announcement of her presence. 'Littlest announcer,' said Andrew, and we called her that, among her other names. Neither of us ever mentioned locking her out.

Several times in the night she would leave us and then return, each time with the same small sound, the littlest announcement.

In those days, the early days of Pink, I was doing a lot of freelance editing for local small presses, which is to say that I spent many waking hours at my desk. Pink assessed my habits early on, and decided to make them her own; or perhaps she decided that she too was an editor. In any case she would come up to my lap, where she would sit, often looking up with something to say. She was in fact the only cat I have ever known with whom a sort of conversation was possible; we made sounds back and forth at each other, very politely, and though mine were mostly nonsense syllables, Pink seemed pleased.

Pink was her main name, about which Zoe Pinkerton was very happy. 'Lordy, no one's ever named a cat for me before.' But Andrew and I used many other names for her. I had an idea that Pink liked a new name occasionally; maybe we all would? In any case we called her a lot of other, mostly P-starting names: Peppercorn, Pipsy Doodler, Poipu Beach. This last was a favorite place of Zoe's, when she went out to 'the islands.' Pink seemed to like all those names; she regarded us both with her great gray eyes – especially me; she was always mostly my cat.

Worried about raccoons and Berkeley free-roaming dogs, we decided early on that Pink was to be a house cat, for good. She was not expendable. But Andrew and I liked to take weekend trips, and after she came to live with us we often took Pink along. She liked car travel right away; settled on the seat between us, she would join right in whenever we broke what had been a silence – not interrupting, just adding her own small voice, a sort of soft clear mew.

This must have been in the early seventies; we talked a lot about Nixon and Watergate. 'Mew if you think he's guilty,' Andrew would say to Pink, who always responded satisfactorily.

Sometimes, especially on summer trips, we would take Pink out for a semiwalk; our following Pink is what it usually amounted to, as she bounded into some meadow grass, with miniature leaps. Once, before I could stop her, she suddenly raced ahead – to a chipmunk. I was horrified. But then she raced back to me with the chipmunk in her mouth, and after a tiny shake she let him go, and the chipmunk ran off, unscathed. (Pink had what hunters call a soft mouth. Of course she did.)

We went to Rome and I missed her, very much; and we went off to the Piazza Argentina and gave a lot of lire to the very old woman there who was feeding all those mangy, half-blind cats. In honor of Pink.

I hope that I am not describing some idealized 'perfect' adorable cat, because Pink was never that. She was entirely herself, sometimes cross and always independent. On the few occasions when I swatted her (very gently), she would hit me right back, a return swat on the hand – though always with sheathed claws.

I like to think that her long life with us, and then just with me, was a very happy one. Her version, though, would undoubtedly state that she was perfectly happy until Black and Brown moved in.

Another Berkeley lunch. A weekday, and all the women present work, and have very little time, and so this getting together seems a rare treat. Our hostess, a diminutive and brilliant art historian, announces that her cat, Parsley, is extremely pregnant. 'Honestly, any minute,' she laughs, and this is clearly true; the poor burdened cat, a brown Burmese, comes into the room, heavy and uncomfortable and restless. Searching.

A little later, in the midst of serving our many-salad lunch, the hostess says that the cat is actually having her kittens now, in the kitchen closet. We all troop out into the kitchen to watch.

The first tiny sac-enclosed kitten to barrel out is a black one, instantly vigorous, eager to stand up and get on with her life. Then three more come at intervals; it is harder to make out their colors.

'More multiple insemination,' I told Andrew that night.

'It must be rife in Berkeley, like everyone says.'

'It was fascinating, watching them being born.'

'I guess, if you like obstetrics.'

A month or so later the art historian friend called with a very sad story; she had just been diagnosed as being very clearly allergic to cats. 'I thought I wasn't feeling too well, but I never thought it could be the cats. I know you already have that marvelous Pink, but do you think – until I find someone to take them? Just the two that are left?'

Surprisingly, Andrew, when consulted, said, 'Well, why not? Be entertainment for old Pink; she must be getting pretty bored with just us.'

We did not consult Pink, who hated those cats on sight.

But Andrew was right away crazy about them, especially the black one (maybe he had wanted a cat of his own?). We called them, of course, Black and Brown. They were two Burmese females, or semi-Burmese, soon established in our house and seeming to believe that they lived there.

Black was (she is) the more interesting and aggressive of the two. And from the first she truly took to Pink, exhibiting the sort of clear affection that admits of no rebuff.

We had had Pink spayed as soon as she was old enough, after one quite miserable heat. And now Black and Brown seemed to come into heat consecutively, and to look to Pink for relief. She raged and scratched at them as they, alternatively, squirmed and rubbed toward her. Especially Brown, who gave all the signs of a major passion for Pink. Furious, Pink seemed to be saying, Even if I were the tomcat that you long for, I would never look at you.

Black and Brown were spayed, and relations among the cats settled down to a much less luridly sexual pattern. Black and Brown both liked Pink and wished to be close to her, which she would almost never permit. She refused to eat with them, haughtily waiting at mealtimes until they were through.

It is easy for me to imagine Black and Brown as people, as women. Black would be a sculptor, I think, very strong, moving freely and widely through the world. Unmarried, no children. Whereas Brown would be a very sweet and pretty, rather silly woman, adored by her husband and sons.

But I do not imagine Pink as a person at all. I only see her as herself. A cat.

Zoe was going to move to Hawaii, she suddenly said. 'Somewhere on Kauai, natch, and probably Poipu, if those grubby developers have kept their hands off anything there.' Her hatchet laugh. 'But I like the idea of living on the islands, away from it all. And so does Gordon. You guys will have to come and visit us there. Bring Pink, but not those other two strays.'

'Gordon' was a new beau, just turned up from somewhere in Zoe's complex Dallas childhood. With misgivings, but I think mostly goodwill, we went over to meet him, to hear about all these new plans.

Gordon was dark and pale and puffy, great black blotches under his narrow, dishonest eyes, a practiced laugh. Meeting him, I right off thought, They're not going to Hawaii; they're not going anywhere together.

Gordon did not drink at all that day, although I later heard that he was a famous drunk. But occasionally he chided Zoe, who as usual was belting down vodka on ice. 'Now Baby,' he kept saying. (Strident, striding Zoe – Baby?) 'Let's go easy on the sauce. Remember what we promised?' (We?)

At which Zoe laughed long and loud, as though her drinking were a good joke that we all shared.

A week or so after that Zoe called and said she was just out of the hospital. 'I'm not in the greatest shape in the world,' she said – and after that there was no more mention of Gordon, nor of a move to Hawaii.

And not very long after that Zoe moved down to Santa Barbara. She had friends there, she said.

Pink by now was in some cat equivalent to middle age. Still quite small, still playful at times, she was almost always talkative. She disliked Black and Brown, but sometimes I would find her nestled against one of them, usually Black, in sleep. I had a clear sense that I was not supposed to know about this occasional rapport, or whatever. Pink still came up to my lap as I worked, and she slept on our bed at night, which we had always forbidden Black and Brown to do.

We bought a new, somewhat larger house, farther up in the hills. It had stairs, and the cats ran happily up and down, and they seemed to thrive, like elderly people who benefit from a new program of exercise.

Andrew got sick, a terrible swift-moving cancer that killed him within a year, and for a long time I did very little but grieve. I sometimes saw friends, and I tried to work. There was a lot to do about Andrew's bookstore, which I sold, but mostly I stayed at home with my cats, all of whom were now allowed to sleep with me on that suddenly too-wide bed.

Pink at that time chose to get under the covers with me. In a peremptory way she would tap at my cheek or my forehead, demanding to be taken in. This would happen several times in the course of the night, which was not a great help to my already fragile pattern of sleep, but it never occurred to me to deny her. And I was always too embarrassed to mention this to my doctor when I complained of lack of sleep.

And then after several years I met Slater, at a well-meaning friend's house. Although as I have said I did not much like him at first, I was struck by his nice dark-red hair, and by his extreme directness – Andrew had a tendency to be vague; it was sometimes hard to get at just what he meant. Not so with Slater, who was very clear – immediately clear about the fact that he liked me a lot, and wanted us to spend time together. And so we became somewhat involved, Slater and I, despite certain temperamental obstacles, including the fact that he does not much like cats.

And eventually we began to plan a trip to Hawaii, where Slater had business to see to.

* * *

Pink as an old cat slept more and more, and her high-assed strut showed sometimes a slight arthritic creak. Her voice got appreciably louder; no longer a littlest announcer, her statements were loud and clear (I have to admit, it was not the most attractive sound). It seems possible that she was getting a little deaf. When I took her to the vet, a sympathetic, tall, and handsome young Japanese woman, she always said, 'She sure doesn't look her age—' at which both Pink and I preened.

The vet, Dr Ino, greatly admired the stripes below Pink's neck, on her breast, which looked like intricate necklaces. I admired them too (and so had Andrew).

Needless to say, the cats were perfectly trained to the sandbox, and very dainty in their habits. But at a certain point I began to notice small accidents around the house, from time to time. Especially when I had been away for a day or two. It seemed a punishment, cat turds in some dark corner. But it was hard to fix responsibility, and I decided to blame all three – and to take various measures like the installation of an upstairs sandbox, which helped. I did think Pink was getting a little old for all those stairs.

Since she was an old cat I sometimes, though rarely, thought of the fact that Pink would die. Of course she would, eventually – although at times (bad times: the weeks and months around Andrew's illness and death) I melodramatically announced (more or less to myself) that Pink's death would be the one thing I could not bear. 'Pink has promised to outlive me,' I told several friends, and almost believed.

At times I even felt that we were the same person-cat, that we somehow inhabited each other. In a way I still do feel that – if I did not, her loss would be truly unbearable.

I worried about her when I went away on trips. I would

always come home, come into my house, with some little apprehension that she might not be there. She was usually the last of the three cats to appear in the kitchen, where I stood confused among baggage, mail, and phone messages. I would greet Black and Brown, and then begin to call her – 'Pink, Pink?' – until, very diffident and proud, she would stroll unhurriedly toward me, and I would sweep her up into my arms with foolish cries of relief, and of love. *Ah, my darling old Pink.*

As I have said, Slater did not particularly like cats; he had nothing against them, really, just a general indifference. He eventually developed a fondness for Brown, believing that she liked him too, but actually Brown is a whore among cats; she will purr and rub up against anyone who might feed her. Whereas Pink was always discriminating, in every way, and fussy. Slater complained that one of the cats deposited small turds on the bathmat in the room where he sometimes showered, and I am afraid that this was indeed old Pink, both angry and becoming incontinent.

One night at dinner at my house, when Slater and I, alone, were admiring my view of the bay and of romantic San Francisco, all those lights, we were also talking about our trip to Hawaii. Making plans. He had been there before and was enthusiastic.

Then the phone rang, and it was Lucy, daughter of Zoe, who told me that her mother had died the day before, in Santa Barbara. 'Her doctor said it was amazing she'd lived so long. All those years of booze.'

'I guess. But Lucy, it's so sad, I'm so sorry.'

'I know.' A pause. 'I'd love to see you sometime. How's old Pink?'

'Oh, Pink's fine,' I lied.

Coming back to the table, I explained as best I could about Zoe Pinkerton, how we got Pink. I played it all down, knowing his feelings about cats. But I thought he would like the multiple-insemination part, and he did – as had Andrew. (It is startling when two such dissimilar men, Andrew, the somewhat dreamy book person, and Slater, the practical man, get so turned on by the same dumb joke.)

'So strange that we're going to Poipu,' I told Slater. 'Zoe always talked about Poipu.' As I said this I knew it was not the sort of coincidence that Slater would find remarkable.

'I'm afraid it's changed a lot,' he said, quite missing the point. 'The early developers have probably knocked hell out of it. The greedy competition.'

So much for mysterious ways.

Two days before we were to go to Hawaii, in the morning Pink seemed disoriented, unsure when she was in her sandbox, her feeding place. Also, she clearly had some bad intestinal disorder. She was very sick, but still in a way it seemed cruel to take her to the vet, whom I somehow knew could do nothing for her. However, at last I saw no alternative.

She (Dr Ino, the admirable vet) found a large hard mass in Pink's stomach, almost certainly cancer. Inoperable. 'I just can't reverse what's wrong with her,' the doctor told me, with great sadness. And succinctness: I saw what she meant. I was so terribly torn, though: Should I bring Pink home for a few more days – whatever was left to her – although she was so miserable, so embarrassed at her own condition?

I chose not to do that (although I still wonder, I still am torn). And I still cannot think of those last moments of Pink. Whose death I chose.

I wept on and off for a couple of days. I called some close

friends who would have wanted to know about Pink, I thought; they were all most supportively kind (most of my best friends love cats).

And then it was time to leave for Hawaii.

Sometimes, during those days of packing and then flying to Hawaii, I thought it odd that Pink was not more constantly on my mind, even odd that I did not weep more than I did. Now, though, looking back on that trip and its various aftermaths, I see that in fact I was thinking about Pink all that time, that she was totally in charge, as she always had been.

We stayed in a pretty condominium complex, two-story white buildings with porches and decks, and everywhere sweeping green lawns, and flowers. A low wall of rocks, a small coarsely sanded beach, and the vast and billowing sea.

Ours was a second-floor unit, with a nice wide balcony for sunset drinks, or daytime sunning. And, looking down from that balcony one night, our first, I saw the people in the building next door, out on the grass beside what must have been their kitchen, *feeding their cats*. They must have brought along these cats, two supple gray Siamese, and were giving them their supper. I chose not to mention this to Slater, I thought I could imagine his reaction, but in the days after that, every time we walked past that building I slowed my pace and looked carefully for the cats, and a couple of times I saw them. Such pretty cats, and very friendly, for Siamese. Imagine: traveling to Hawaii with your cats – though I was not at all sure that I would have wanted Black and Brown along, nice as they are, and pretty.

Another cat event (there were four in all) came as we drove from Lihue back to Poipu, going very slowly over those very sedate tree- and flower-lined streets, with their decorous, spare houses. Suddenly I felt – we felt – a sort of thump, and Slater, looking startled, slowed down even further and looked back.

'Lord God, that was a cat,' he said.

'A cat?'

'She ran right out into the car. And then ran back.'

'Are you sure? She's all right?'

'Absolutely. Got a good scare though.' Slater chuckled.

But you might have killed a cat, I did not say. And for a moment I wondered if he actually had, and lied, saying the cat was okay. However, Slater would never lie to spare my feelings, I am quite sure of that.

The third cat happening took place as we drove down a winding, very steep mountain road (we had been up to see the mammoth gorges cut into the island, near its western edge). On either side of the road was thick green jungle growth – and suddenly, there among the vines and shrubs, I saw a small yellow cat staring out, her eyes lowered. Frightened. Eyes begging.

Slater saw her too, and even he observed, 'Good Lord, people dumping off animals to starve. It's awful.'

'You're sure she doesn't live out there? a wilderness cat?'

'I don't think so.' Honest Slater.

We did not talk then or later about going back to rescue that cat – not until the next day, when he asked me what I would like to do and I said, 'I'd like to go back for that cat.' He assumed I was joking, and I guess I mostly was. There were too many obvious reasons not to save that particular cat, including the difficulty of finding her again. But I remembered her face; I can see it still, that expression of much-resented dependence. It was a way even Pink looked, very occasionally.

* * *

28

Wherever we drove, through small neat impoverished 'native' settlements (blocks of houses that Slater and his cohorts planned to buy, and demolish, to replace with fancy condos), with their lavish flowers all restrained into tiny beds, I kept looking at the yards, and under the houses. I wanted to see a cat, or some cats (I wanted to see Pink again). Realizing what I was doing, I continued to do it, to strain for the sight of a cat.

The fourth and final cat event took place as we walked home from dinner one night, in the flower-scented, corny-romantic Hawaiian darkness. To our left was the surging black sea and to our right large tamed white shrubbery, and a hotel swimming pool, glistening darkly under feeble yellow floodlights. And then quite suddenly, from nowhere, a small cat appeared in our path, shyly and uncertainly arching her back against a bush. A black cat with some yellow tortoise markings, a long thin curve of a tail.

'He looks just like your Pink, doesn't he?' Slater actually said this, and I suppose he believed it to be true.

'What – Pink? But her tail – Jesus, didn't you even see my cat?'

I'm afraid I went on in this vein, sporadically, for several days. But it did seem so incredible, not remembering Pink, my elegantly striped, my tailless wonder. (It is also true that I was purposefully using this lapse, as one will, in a poor connection.)

I dreaded going home with no Pink to call out to as I came in the door. And the actuality was nearly as bad as my imaginings of it: Black and Brown, lazy and affectionate, glad to see me. And no Pink, with her scolding *hauteur*, her long-delayed yielding to my blandishments.

*   *   *

I had no good pictures of Pink, and to explain this odd fact
I have to admit that I am very bad about snapshots; I have
never devised a really good way of storing and keeping them,
and tend rather to enclose any interesting ones in letters to
people who might like them, to whom they would have some
meaning. And to shove the others into drawers, among old
letters and other unclassifiable mementos.

I began then to scour my house for Pink pictures, looking
everywhere. In an album (Andrew and I put together a couple
of albums, early on) I found a great many pictures of Pink
as a tiny, tall-eared, brand-new kitten, stalking across a
padded window seat, hiding behind an oversized Boston
fern – among all the other pictures from those days: Zoe
Pinkerton, happy and smoking a long cigarette and almost
drunk, wearing outrageous colors, on the deck of her house.
And Andrew and I, young and very happy, silly, snapped by
someone at a party. Andrew in his bookstore, horn-rimmed
and quirky. Andrew uncharacteristically working in our
garden. Andrew all over the place.

But no middle-year or recent pictures of Pink. I had in
fact (I then remembered) sent the most recent shots of Pink
to Zoe; it must have been just before she (Zoe) died, with
a silly note about old survivors, something like that. It
occurred to me to get in touch with Lucy, Zoe's daughter,
to see if those pictures had turned up among Zoe's 'effects,'
but knowing the chaos in which Zoe had always lived
(and doubtless died) I decided that this would be tactless,
unnecessary trouble. And I gave up looking for pictures.

Slater called yesterday to say that he is going back to Hawaii,
a sudden trip. Business. I imagine that he is about to finish
the ruination of all that was left of Zoe's islands. He certainly

did not suggest that I come along, nor did he speak specifically of our getting together again, and I rather think that he, like me, has begun to wonder what we were doing together in the first place. It does seem to me that I was drawn to him for a very suspicious reason, his lack of resemblance to Andrew: Whyever should I seek out the opposite of a person I truly loved?

But I do look forward to some time alone now. I will think about Pink – I always feel her presence in my house, everywhere. Pink, stalking and severe, ears high. Pink, in my lap, raising her head with some small soft thing to say.

And maybe, since Black and Brown are getting fairly old now too, I will think about getting another new young cat. Maybe, with luck, a small gray partially Manx, with no tail at all, and beautiful necklaces.

MAEVE BRENNAN

I SEE YOU, BIANCA

MY FRIEND NICHOLAS is about the only person I know who has no particular quarrel with the city as it is these days. He thinks New York is all right. It isn't that he is any better off than the rest of us. His neighborhood, like all our neighborhoods, is falling apart, with too many buildings half up and half down, and too many temporary sidewalks, and too many doomed houses with big X's on their windows. The city has been like that for years now, uneasy and not very reasonable, but in all the shakiness Nicholas has managed to keep a fair balance. He was born here, in a house on 114th Street, within sight of the East River, and he trusts the city. He believes anyone with determination and patience can find a nice place to live and have the kind of life he wants here. His own apartment would look much as it does whether he lived in Rome or Brussels or Manchester. He has a floor through – two rooms made into one long room with big windows at each end, in a very modest brownstone, a little pre-Civil War house on East Twelfth Street near Fourth Avenue. His room is a spacious oblong of shadow and light – he made it like that, cavernous and hospitable – and it looks as though not two but ten or twenty rooms had contributed their best angles and their best corners and their best-kept secrets of depths and mood to it. Sometimes it seems to be the anteroom to many other rooms, and sometimes it seems to be the extension of many other rooms. It is like a telescope and at the same time it is like what you see through a telescope. What it is like, more than anything, is a private room hidden backstage in a very busy theater where the season is in full swing. The ceiling, mysteriously, is covered in stamped tin. At night the patterned ceiling seems to move with the flickering shadows, and in the daytime an occasional shadow drifts slowly across the tin as though it were searching for a permanent refuge. But there is no permanence here – there is only the valiant illusion of a permanence that is hardly more substantial than the shadow that touches it. The house is to be torn down. Nicholas has his apartment by the month, no lease and no assurance that he will still be here a year or even three months from now. Sometimes the furnace breaks down in the dead of winter, and then there is a very cold spell for a few days until the furnace is repaired – the landlord is too sensible to buy a new furnace for a house that may vanish overnight. When anything gets out of order inside the apartment, Nicholas repairs it himself. (He thinks about the low rent he pays and not about the reason for the low rent.) When a wall or a ceiling has to be painted, he paints it. When the books begin to pile up on the floor, he puts up more shelves to join the shelves that now cover most of one long wall from the floor to the ceiling. He builds a cabinet to hide a bad spot in the end wall. The two old rooms, his one room, never had such attention as they are getting in their last days.

The house looks north and Nicholas has the second floor, with windows looking north onto Twelfth Street and south onto back yards and the backs and sides of other houses and buildings. The neighborhood is a kind of no man's land, bleak in the daytime and forbidding at night, very near to the Village but not part of the Village, and not a part, either, of the Lower East Side. Twelfth Street at that point is very narrow and noisy. Elderly buildings that are not going to last much longer stand side by side with the enormous, blank façades of nearly new apartment houses, and there is a constant caravan of quarrelsome, cumbersome traffic moving toward the comparative freedom of Fourth Avenue. To his right Nicholas looks across the wide, stunted expanse of Fourth Avenue, where the traffic rolls steadily uptown. Like many exceedingly ugly parts of the city, Fourth Avenue is at its best in the rain, especially in the rain at night, when the whole scene, buildings, cars, and street, streams with such a black and garish intensity that it is beautiful, as long as one is safe from it — very safe, with both feet on the familiar floor of a familiar room filled with books, records, living plants, pictures and drawings, a tiny piano, chairs and tables and mirrors, and a long desk and a bed. All that is familiar is inside, and all the discontent is outside, and Nicholas can stand at his windows and look out on the noise and confusion with the cheerful interest of one who contemplates a puzzle he did not create and is not going to be called upon to solve. From the top of a tall filing cabinet near him, Bianca, his small white cat, also gazes at the street. It is afternoon now, and the sun is shining, and Bianca is there on the cabinet, looking out, only to be near Nicholas and to see what he sees. But she sees nothing.

What is that out there?

That is a view, Bianca.

And what is a view?

A view is where we are not. Where we are is never a view.

Bianca is interested only in where she is, and what she can see and hope to touch with her nose and paws. She looks down at the floor. She knows it well – the polished wood and the small rugs that are arranged here and there. She knows the floor – how safe it is, always there to catch her when she jumps down, and always very solid and familiar under her paws when she is getting ready to jump up. She likes to fly through the air, from a bookcase on one side of the room to a table on the other side, flying across the room without even looking at the floor and without making a sound. But whether she looks at it or not, she knows the floor is always there, the dependable floor, all over the apartment. Even in the bathroom, under the old-fashioned bathtub, and even under the bed, and under the lowest shelf in the kitchen, Bianca finds the well-known floor that has been her ground – her playground and her proving ground – during all of her three years of life.

Nicholas has been standing and staring at rowdy Twelfth Street for a long time now, and Bianca, rising, stretching, and yawning on top of the filing cabinet, looks down at the floor and sees a patch of sunlight there. She jumps down and walks over to the patch of sun and sits in it. Very nice in the sun, and Bianca sinks slowly down until she is lying full length in the warmth. The hot strong light makes her fur whiter and denser. She is drowsy now. The sun that draws the color from her eyes, making them empty and bright, has also drawn all resistance from her bones, and she grows limp and flattens out into sleep. She is very flat there on the shining floor – flat and blurred – a thin cat with soft white fur and a blunt, patient Egyptian head. She sleeps peacefully on her side, with her front paws crossed and her back paws placed neatly one behind the other, and from time to time her tail twitches impatiently in her dream. But the dream is too frail to hold her, and she sinks through it and continues to sink until she lies motionless in the abyss of deepest sleep. There is glittering dust in the broad ray that shines on her, and now Bianca is dust-colored, paler and purer than white, and so weightless that she seems about to vanish, as though she were made of the radiance that pours down on her and must go when it goes.

Bianca is sleeping not far from Nicholas's bed, which is wide and low and stands sideways against the wall. Behind the wall at that point is a long-lost fireplace, hidden away years before Nicholas took the apartment. But he has a second fireplace in the back part of the long room, and although it stopped working years ago, it was left open, and Nicholas has made a garden in it, a conservatory. The plants stand in tiers in the fireplace and on the floor close around it, and they flourish in the perpetual illumination of an electric bulb hidden in the chimney. Something is always in bloom. There are an ivy geranium, a rose geranium, and plain geraniums in pink and white. Then there are begonias, and feathery ferns, and a white violet, and several unnamed infant plants starting their lives in tiny pots. The jug for watering them all stands on the floor beside them, and it is kept full because Bianca likes to drink from it and occasionally to play with it, dipping in first one paw and then the other. She disturbs the water so that she can peer down into it and see the strange new depths she has created. She taps the leaves of the plants and then sits watching them. Perhaps she hopes they will hit back.

Also in this back half is Nicholas's kitchen, which is complete and well furnished, and separated from the rest of the room by a high counter. The kitchen gets the full light of one of the two windows that give him his back view. When he looks directly across, he sees the blank side wall of an old warehouse and, above, the sky. Looking straight down, he sees a neglected patch, a tiny wasteland that was once the garden of this house. It is a pathetic little spot of ground, hidden and forgotten and closed in and nearly sunless, but there is still enough strength in the earth to receive and nourish a stray ailanthus tree that sprouted there and grew unnoticed until it reached Nicholas's window. Nobody saw the little tree grow past the basement and the first floor because nobody lives down there, but once it touched the sill of Nicholas's room he welcomed it as though it were home at last after having delayed much too long on the way. He loved the tree and carried on about it as though he had been given the key to his inheritance, or a vision of it. He leaned out of the window and touched the leaves, and then he got out on the fire escape and hung over it, making sure it was healthy. He photographed it, and took a leaf, to make a drawing of it. And the little ailanthus, New York's hardship tree, changed at his touch from an overgrown weed to a giant fern of extraordinary importance. From the kitchen counter, Bianca watched, purring speculatively. Her paws were folded under her chest and her tail was curled around her. She was content. Watching Nicholas at the ailanthus was almost as good as watching him at the stove. When he climbed back into the room she continued to watch the few leaves that were high enough to appear, trembling, at the edge of the sill. Nicholas stood and looked at her, but she ignored him. As she stared toward the light her eyes grew paler, and as they grew paler they grew more definite. She looked very alert, but still she ignored him. He wanted to annoy her. He shouted at her. 'Bianca!' he shouted. 'I see you!' Bianca narrowed her eyes. 'I see you!' Nicholas yelled. 'I see you, Bianca. I *see* you, Bianca. I see you. I see you. I SEE you!' Then he was silent, and after a minute Bianca turned her head and looked at him, but only to show there was no contest – her will was stronger, why did he bother? – and then she looked away. She had won. She always did.

* * *

In the summer it rains – sudden summer rain that hammers against the windowpanes and causes the ailanthus to stagger and shiver in gratitude for having enough water for once in its life. What a change in the weather, as the heavy breathless summer lifts to reveal a new world of freedom – free air, free movement, clean streets and clean roofs and easy sleep. Bianca stares at the rain as it streams down the glass of the window. One drop survives the battering and rolls, all in one piece, down the pane. Bianca jumps for it, and through the glass she catches it, flattening it with her paw so that she can no longer see it. Then she looks at her chilled paw and, finding it empty, she begins to wash it, chewing irritably at it. But one paw leads to another, and she has four of them. She washes industriously. She takes very good care of her only coat. She is never idle, with her grooming to do, and her journeys to take, and then she attends on Nicholas. He is in and out of the apartment a good deal, and she often waits for him at the head of the stairs, so that he will see her first thing when he opens the door from the outside. When he is in the apartment she stays near him. If she happens to be on one of her journeys when he gets home, she appears at the window almost before he has taken off his coat. She goes out a good deal, up and down the fire escape and up and down the inside stairs that lead to the upper apartment and the roof. She wanders. Nicholas knows about it. He likes to think that she is free.

Bianca and the ailanthus provide Nicholas with the extra dimension all apartment dwellers long for. People who have no terraces and no gardens long to escape from their own four walls, but not to wander far. They only want to step outside for a minute. They stand outside their apartment houses on summer nights and during summer days. They stand around in groups or they sit together on the front steps of their buildings, taking the air and looking around at the street. Sometimes they carry a chair out, so that an old person can have a little outing. They lean out of their windows, with their elbows on the sills, and look into the faces of their neighbors at their windows on the other side of the street, all of them escaping from the rooms they live in and that they are glad to have but not to be closed up in. It should not be a problem, to have shelter without being shut away. The windowsills are safety hatches into the open, and so are the fire escapes and the roofs and the front stoops. Bianca and the ailanthus make Nicholas's life infinitely spacious. The ailanthus casts its new green light into his room, and Bianca draws a thread of his life all around the outside of the house and all around the inside, up and down the stairs. Where else does she go? Nobody knows. She has never been seen to stray from the walls of the house. Nicholas points out to his friends that it is possible to keep a cat in an apartment and still not make a prisoner of her. He says disaster comes only to those who attract it. He says Bianca is very smart, and that no harm will come to her.

She likes to sit on the windowsills of the upper-floor tenants, but she never visits any of them unless they invite her in. She also likes to sit in the ruins of the garden Nicholas once kept on the roof. She watched him make the garden there. It was a real garden and grew well, until the top-floor tenant began to complain bitterly about his leaking ceiling. Even plants hardy enough to thrive in a thin bed of city dust and soot need watering. Nicholas still climbs to the roof, not to mourn his garden – it was an experiment, and he does not regret it – but to look about at the Gulliver world he lives in: the new buildings too tall for the streets they stand in and the older, smaller buildings out of proportion to everything except the past that will soon absorb them. From the street, or from any window, the city often seems like a place thrown up without regard for reason, and haunted by chaos. But from any rooftop the city comes into focus. The roof is in proportion to the building beneath it, and from any roof it can easily be seen that all the other roofs, and their walls, are in proportion to each other and to the city. The buildings are tightly packed together, without regard to size or height, and light and shadow strike across them so that the scene changes every minute. The struggle for space in Manhattan creates an oceanic uproar in the air above the streets, and every roof turns into a magic carpet just as soon as someone is standing on it.

Nicholas climbs to the roof by his fire escape, but when he leaves the roof to go back to his apartment he goes down through the house, down three flights to his own landing, or all the way down to the street floor. He likes the house and he likes to walk around in it. Bianca follows him. She likes to be taken for a walk. She likes to walk around the downstairs hall, where the door is that gives onto the street. It is an old hall, old and cramped, the natural entrance to the family place this house once was. To the left as you enter from the street there are two doors opening into what were once the sitting-room and the dining-room. The doors are always locked now – there are no tenants there. The hall is narrow, and it is cut in half by the stairs leading up to Nicholas's landing. Under the stairs, beside the door that leads down into the basement, there is a mysterious cubbyhole, big enough for galoshes, or wine bottles, or for a very small suitcase. Nobody knows what the cubbyhole was made for, but Bianca took it for one of her hiding places, and it was there Nicholas first looked for her when he realized he had not seen her all day – which is to say for about ten hours. He was certain she was in the cubbyhole, and that she wanted to be coaxed out. He called her from the landing, and then he went downstairs, calling her, and then he knelt down and peered into the dark little recess. Bianca was not there, and she was not on the roof, or under the bed, or down at the foot of the ailanthus trying to climb up, and she was not anywhere. Bianca was gone. She was nowhere to be found. She was nowhere.

There is no end to Bianca's story because nobody knows what happened to her. She has been gone for several months now. Nicholas has given up putting advertisements in the paper, and he took down all the little cards he put up in the cleaner's and in the grocery store and in the drugstore and the flower shop and the shoeshine parlor. He has stopped watching for her in the street. At first he walked through the street whispering her name, and then one night he found himself yelling for her. He was furious with her. He said to himself that if she turned up at that moment he would kill her. He would certainly not be glad to see her. All he wanted was, one way or another, to know whether she was alive or dead. But there was no word from Bianca, and no word from anyone with actual news of her, although the phone rang constantly with people who thought they had seen her, so that he spent a good many hours running around the neighborhood in answer to false reports. It was no good. She was gone. He reminded himself that he hadn't really wanted a cat. He had only taken Bianca because a friend of his, burdened with too many kittens, pleaded with him. He finds himself wondering what happened to Bianca, but he wonders less and less. Now, he tells himself, she has shrunk so that she is little more than an occasional irritation in his mind. He does not really miss her very much. After all, she brought nothing into the apartment with her except her silence. She was very quiet and not especially playful. She

44

liked to roll and turn and paw the air in the moonlight, but otherwise she was almost sedate. But whatever she was, she is gone now, and Nicholas thinks that if he only knew for sure what happened to her he would have forgotten her completely by this time.

DAMON RUNYON

LILLIAN

WHAT I ALWAYS SAY is that Wilbur Willard is nothing but a very lucky guy, because what is it but luck that has been teetering along Forty-ninth Street one cold snowy morning when Lillian is mer-owing around the sidewalk looking for her mamma?

And what is it but luck that has Wilbur Willard all mulled up to a million, what with him having been sitting out a few seidels of Scotch with a friend by the name of Haggerty in an apartment over on Fifty-ninth Street? Because if Wilbur Willard is not mulled up, he will see Lillian as nothing but a little black cat, and give her plenty of room, for everybody knows that black cats are terribly bad luck, even when they are only kittens.

But being mulled up like I tell you, things look very different to Wilbur Willard, and he does not see Lillian as a little black kitten scrabbling around in the snow. He sees a beautiful leopard, because a copper by the name of O'Hara, who is walking past about then, and who knows Wilbur Willard, hears him say:

'Oh, you beautiful leopard!'

The copper takes a quick peek himself, because he does not wish any leopards running around his beat, it being against the law, but all he sees, as he tells me afterwards, is this rumpot ham, Wilbur Willard, picking up a scrawny little black kitten and shoving it in his overcoat pocket, and he also hears Wilbur say:

49

'Your name is Lillian.'

Then Wilbur teeters on up to his room on the top floor of an old fleabag on Eighth Avenue that is called the Hotel de Brussels, where he lives quite a while, because the management does not mind actors, the management of the Hotel de Brussels being very broad-minded indeed.

There is some complaint this same morning from one of Wilbur's neighbors, an old burlesque doll by the name of Minnie Madigan, who is not working since Abraham Lincoln is assassinated, because she hears Wilbur going on in his room about a beautiful leopard, and calls up the clerk to say that an hotel which allows wild animals is not respectable. But the clerk looks in on Wilbur and finds him playing with nothing but a harmless-looking little black kitten, and nothing comes of the old doll's beef, especially as nobody ever claims the Hotel de Brussels is respectable anyway, or at least not much.

Of course when Wilbur comes out from under the ether next afternoon he can see Lillian is not a leopard, and in fact Wilbur is quite astonished to find himself in bed with a little black kitten, because it seems Lillian is sleeping on Wilbur's chest to keep warm. At first Wilbur does not believe what he sees, and puts it down to Haggerty's Scotch, but finally he is convinced, and so he puts Lillian in his pocket, and takes her over to the Hot Box night club and gives her some milk, of which it seems Lillian is very fond.

Now where Lillian comes from in the first place of course nobody knows. The chances are somebody chucks her out of a window into the snow, because people are always chucking kittens, and one thing and another, out of windows in New York. In fact, if there is one thing this town has plenty of, it is kittens, which finally grow up to be cats, and go snooping around ash cans, and mer-owing on roofs, and keeping people from sleeping good.

Personally, I have no use for cats, including kittens, because I never see one that has any too much sense, although I know a guy by the name of Pussy McGuire who makes a first-rate living doing nothing but stealing cats, and some-times dogs, and selling them to old dolls who like such things for company. But Pussy only steals Persian and Angora cats, which are very fine cats, and of course Lillian is no such cat as this. Lillian is nothing but a black cat, and nobody will give you a dime a dozen for black cats in this town, as they are generally regarded as very bad jinxes.

Furthermore, it comes out in a few weeks that Wilbur Willard can just as well name her Herman, or Sidney, as not, but Wilbur sticks to Lillian, because this is the name of his partner when he is in vaudeville years ago. He often tells me about Lillian Withington when he is mulled up, which is more often than somewhat, for Wilbur is a great hand for drinking Scotch, or rye, or bourbon, or gin, or whatever else there is around for drinking, except water. In fact, Wilbur Willard is a high-class drinking man, and it does no good to tell him it is against the law to drink in this country, because it only makes him mad, and he says to the dickens with the law, only Wilbur Willard uses a much rougher word than dickens.

'She is like a beautiful leopard,' Wilbur says to me about Lillian Withington. 'Black-haired, and black-eyed, and all ripply, like a leopard I see in an animal act on the same bill at the Palace with us once. We are headliners then,' he says, 'Willard and Withington, the best singing and dancing act in the country.

'I pick her up in San Antonia, which is a spot in Texas,' Wilbur says. 'She is not long out of a convent, and I just lose my old partner, Mary McGee, who ups and dies on me of pneumonia down there. Lillian wishes to go on the stage, and joins out with me. A natural-born actress with a great voice. But like a leopard,' Wilbur says. 'Like a leopard. There is cat in her, no doubt of this, and cats and women are both ungrateful. I love Lillian Withington. I wish to marry her. But she is cold to me. She says she is not going to follow the stage all her life. She says she wishes money, and luxury, and a fine home and of course a guy like me cannot give a doll such things.

'I wait on her hand and foot,' Wilbur says. 'I am her slave. There is nothing I will not do for her. Then one day she walks in on me in Boston very cool and says she is quitting me. She says she is marrying a rich guy there. Well, naturally it busts up the act and I never have the heart to look for another partner, and then I get to belting that old black bottle around, and now what am I but a cabaret performer?'

Then sometimes he will bust out crying, and sometimes I will cry with him, although the way I look at it, Wilbur gets a pretty fair break, at that, in getting rid of a doll who wishes things he cannot give her. Many a guy in this town is tangled up with a doll who wishes things he cannot give her, but who keeps him tangled up just the same and busting himself trying to keep her quiet.

Wilbur makes pretty fair money as an entertainer in the Hot Box, though he spends most of it for Scotch, and he is not a bad entertainer, either. I often go to the Hot Box when I am feeling blue to hear him sing 'Melancholy Baby' and 'Moonshine Valley' and other sad songs which break my heart. Personally, I do not see why any doll cannot love Wilbur, especially if they listen to him sing such songs as 'Melancholy Baby' when he is mulled up good, because he is a tall, nice-looking guy with long eyelashes, and sleepy brown eyes, and his voice has a low moaning sound that usually goes very big with the dolls. In fact, many a doll does do some pitching to Wilbur when he is singing in the Hot Box, but somehow Wilbur never gives them a tumble, which I suppose is because he is thinking of Lillian Withington.

Well, after he gets Lillian, the black kitten, Wilbur seems to find a new interest in life, and Lillian turns out to be right cute, and not bad-looking after Wilbur gets her fed up good. She is blacker than a yard up a chimney, with not a white spot on her, and she grows so fast that by and by Wilbur cannot carry her in his pocket anymore, so he puts a collar on her and leads her round. So Lillian becomes very well known on Broadway, what with Wilbur taking her many places, and finally she does not even have to be led around by Wilbur, but follows him like a pooch. And in all the Roaring Forties there is no pooch that cares to have any truck with Lillian, for she will leap aboard them quicker than you can say scat, and scratch and bite them until they are very glad indeed to get away from her.

But of course the pooches in the Forties are mainly nothing but Chows, and Pekes, and Poms, or little woolly white poodles, which are led around by blonde dolls, and are not fit to take their own part against a smart cat. In fact, Wilbur Willard is finally not on speaking terms with any doll that owns a pooch between Times Square and Columbus Circle, and they are all hoping that both Wilbur and Lillian will go lay down and die somewhere. Furthermore, Wilbur has a couple of battles with guys who also belong to the dolls, but Wilbur is no sucker in a battle if he is not mulled up too much and leg-weary.

After he is through entertaining people in the Hot Box, Wilbur generally goes around to any speakeasies which may still be open, and does a little off-hand drinking on top of what he already drinks down in the Hot Box, which is plenty, and although it is considered very risky in this town to mix Hot Box liquor with any other, it never seems to bother Wilbur. Along towards daylight he takes a couple of bottles of Scotch over to his room in the Hotel de Brussels and uses them for a nightcap, so by the time Wilbur Willard is ready to slide off to sleep he has plenty of liquor of one kind and another inside him, and he sleeps pretty.

Of course nobody on Broadway blames Wilbur so very much for being such a rumpot, because they know about him loving Lillian Withington, and losing her, and it is considered a reasonable excuse in this town for a guy to do some drinking when he loses a doll, which is why there is so much drinking here, but it is a mystery to one and all how Wilbur stands off all this liquor without croaking. The cemeteries are full of guys who do a lot less drinking than Wilbur, but he never even seems to feel extra rough, or if he does he keeps it to himself and does not go around saying it is the kind of liquor you get nowadays.

He costs some of the boys around Mindy's plenty of dough one winter, because he starts in doing most of his drinking after hours in Good Time Charley's speakeasy, and the boys lay a price of four to one against him lasting until spring, never figuring a guy can drink very much of Good Time Charley's liquor and keep on living. But Wilbur Willard does it just the same, so everybody says the guy is naturally superhuman, and lets it go at that.

Sometimes Wilbur drops into Mindy's with Lillian following him on the look-out for pooches, or riding on his shoulder if the weather is bad, and the two of them will sit with us for hours chewing the rag about one thing and another. At such times Wilbur generally has a bottle on his hip and takes a shot now and then, but of course this does not come under the head of serious drinking with him. When Lillian is with Wilbur she always lays as close to him as she can get and anybody can see that she seems to be very fond of Wilbur and that he is very fond of her, although he sometimes forgets himself and speaks of her as a beautiful leopard. But of course this is only a slip of the tongue, and anyway if Wilbur gets any pleasure out of thinking Lillian is a leopard, it is nobody's business but his own.

'I suppose she will run away from me someday,' Wilbur says, running his hand over Lillian's back until her fur crackles. 'Yes, although I give her plenty of liver and catnip, and one thing and another, and all my affection, she will probably give me the shake. Cats are like women, and women are like cats. They are both very ungrateful.'

'They are both generally bad luck,' Big Nig, the crap shooter, says. 'Especially cats, and most especially black cats.'

Many other guys tell Wilbur about black cats being bad luck, and advise him to slip Lillian into the North River some night with a sinker on her, but Wilbur claims he already has all the bad luck in the world when he loses Lillian Withington, and that Lillian, the cat, cannot make it any worse, so he goes on taking extra good care of her, and Lillian goes on getting bigger and bigger, until I commence thinking maybe there is some St Bernard in her.

Finally I commence to notice something funny about Lillian. Sometimes she will be acting very loving towards Wilbur, and then again she will be very unfriendly to him, and will spit at him, and snatch at him with her claws, very hostile. It seems to me that she is all right when Willard is mulled up, but is as sad and fretful as he is himself when he is only a little bit mulled. And when Lillian is sad and fretful she makes it very tough indeed on the pooches in the neighborhood of the Brussels.

In fact, Lillian takes to pooch-hunting, sneaking off when Wilbur is getting his rest, and running pooches bow-legged, especially when she finds one that is not on a leash. A loose pooch is just naturally cherry pie for Lillian.

Well, of course, this causes great indignation among the dolls who own the pooches, particularly when Lillian comes home one day carrying a Peke as big as she is herself by the scruff of the neck, and with a very excited blonde doll following her and yelling bloody murder outside Wilbur Willard's door when Lillian pops into Wilbur's room through a hole he cuts in the door for her, still lugging the Peke. But it seems that instead of being mad at Lillian and giving her a pasting for such goings-on, Wilbur is somewhat pleased, because he happens to be still in a fog when Lillian arrives with the Peke, and is thinking of Lillian as a beautiful leopard.

'Why,' Wilbur says, 'this is devotion indeed. My beautiful leopard goes off into the jungle and fetches me an antelope for dinner.'

Now of course there is no sense whatever to this, because a Peke is certainly not anything like an antelope, but the blonde doll outside Wilbur's door hears Wilbur mumble, and gets the idea that he is going to eat her Peke for dinner and the squawk she puts up is very terrible. There is plenty of trouble around the Brussels in chilling the blonde doll's beef over Lillian snagging her Peke, and what is more the blonde doll's ever-loving guy, who turns out to be a tough Ginney bootlegger by the name of Gregorio, shows up at the Hot Box the next night and wishes to put the slug on Wilbur Willard.

But Wilbur rounds him up with a few drinks and by singing 'Melancholy Baby' to him, and before he leaves the Ginney gets very sentimental towards Wilbur, and Lillian, too, and wishes to give Wilbur five bucks to let Lillian grab the Peke again, if Lillian will promise not to bring it back. It seems Gregorio does not really care for the Peke, and is only acting quarrelsome to please the blonde doll and make her think he loves her dearly.

But I can see Lillian is having different moods, and finally I ask Wilbur if he notices it.

'Yes,' he says, very sad, 'I do not seem to be holding her love. She is getting very fickle. A guy moves on to my floor at the Brussels the other day with a little boy, and Lillian becomes very fond of this kid at once. In fact, they are great friends. Ah, well,' Wilbur says, 'cats are like women. Their affection does not last.'

I happen to go over to the Brussels a few days later to explain to a guy by the name of Crutchy, who lives on the same floor as Wilbur Willard, that some of our citizens do not like his face and that it may be a good idea for him to leave town, especially if he insists on bringing ale into their territory, and I see Lillian out in the hall with a youngster which I judge is the kid Wilbur is talking about. This kid is maybe three years old, and very cute, what with black hair, and black eyes, and he is wooling Lillian around the hall in a way that is most surprising, for Lillian is not such a cat as will stand for much wooling around, not even from Wilbur Willard.

I am wondering how anybody comes to take such a kid to a joint like the Brussels, but I figure it is some actor's kid, and that maybe there is no mamma for it. Later I am talking to Wilbur about this, and he says:

'Well, if the kid's old man is an actor, he is not working at it. He sticks close to his room all the time, and he does not allow the kid to go anywhere but in the hall, and I feel sorry for the little guy, which is why I allow Lillian to play with him.'

Now it comes on a very cold spell, and a bunch of us are sitting in Mindy's along towards five o'clock in the morning when we hear fire engines going past. By and by in comes a guy by the name of Kansas, who is named Kansas because he comes from Kansas, and who is a crap shooter by trade.

'The old Brussels is on fire,' this guy Kansas says.

'She is always on fire,' Big Nig says, meaning there is always plenty of hot stuff going on around the Brussels.

About this time who walks in but Wilbur Willard, and anybody can see he is just naturally floating. The chances are he comes from Good Time Charley's, and he is certainly carrying plenty of pressure. I never see Wilbur Willard mulled up more. He does not have Lillian with him, but then he never takes Lillian to Good Time Charley's, because Charley hates cats.

'Hey, Wilbur,' Big Nig says, 'your joint, the Brussels, is on fire.'

'Well,' Wilbur says, 'I am a little firefly, and I need a light. Let us go where there is fire.'

The Brussels is only a few blocks from Mindy's, and there is nothing else to do just then, so some of us walk over to Eighth Avenue with Wilbur teetering along ahead of us. The old shack is certainly roaring good when we get in sight of it, and the firemen are tossing water into it, and the coppers have the fire lines out to keep the crowd back, although there is not much of a crowd at such an hour in the morning.

'Is it not beautiful?' Wilbur Willard says, looking up at the flames. 'Is it not like a fairy palace all lighted up this way?'

You see, Wilbur does not realize the joint is on fire, although guys and dolls are running out of it every which way, most of them half-dressed, or not dressed at all, and the firemen are getting out the life nets in case anybody wishes to hop out of the windows.

'It is certainly beautiful,' Wilbur says. 'I must get Lillian so she can see this.'

And before anybody has time to think, there is Wilbur Willard walking into the front door of the Brussels as if nothing happens. The firemen and the coppers are so astonished all they can do is holler at Wilbur, but he pays no attention whatever. Well, naturally everybody figures Wilbur is a gone gosling, but in about ten minutes he comes walking out of this same door through the fire and smoke as cool as you please, and he has Lillian in his arms.

'You know,' Wilbur says, coming over to where we are standing with our eyes popping out, 'I have to walk all the way up to my floor because the elevators seem to be out of commission. The service is getting terrible in this hotel. I will certainly make a strong beef to the management about it as soon as I pay something on my account.'

Then what happens but Lillian lets out a big mer-ow, and hops out of Wilbur's arms and skips past the coppers and the firemen with her back all humped up and the next thing anybody knows she is tearing through the front door of the old hotel and making plenty of speed.

'Well, well,' Wilbur says, looking much surprised, 'there goes Lillian.'

And what does this daffy Wilbur Willard do but turn and go marching back into the Brussels again, and by this time the smoke is pouring out of the front doors so thick he is out of sight in a second. Naturally he takes the coppers and firemen by surprise, because they are not used to guys walking in and out of fires on them.

This time anybody standing around will lay you plenty of odds – two and a half and maybe three to one – that Wilbur never shows up again, because the old Brussels is now just popping with fire and smoke from the lower windows, although there does not seem to be quite so much fire in the upper story. Everybody seems to be out of the joint, and even the firemen are fighting the blaze from the outside because the Brussels is so old and ramshackly there is no sense in them risking the floors.

I mean everybody is out of the joint except Wilbur Willard and Lillian, and we figure they are getting a good frying somewhere inside, although Feet Samuels is around offering to take thirteen to five for a few small bets that Lillian comes out okay, because Feet claims that a cat has nine lives and that is a fair bet at the price.

Well, up comes a swell-looking doll all heated up about something and pushing and clawing her way through the crowd up to the ropes and screaming until you can hardly hear yourself think, and about this same minute everybody hears a voice going ai-lee-hi-hee-hoo, like a Swiss yodeler, which comes from the roof of the Brussels, and looking up what do we see but Wilbur Willard standing up there on the edge of the roof, high above the fire and smoke, and yodeling very loud.

Under one arm he has a big bundle of some kind, and under the other he has the little kid I see playing in the hall with Lillian. As he stands up there going ai-lee-hi-hee-hoo, the swell-dressed doll near us begins yipping louder than Wilbur is yodeling, and the firemen rush over under him with a life net.

Wilbur lets go another ai-lee-hi-hee-hoo, and down he comes all spraddled out, with the bundle and the kid, but he hits the net sitting down and bounces up and back again for a couple of minutes before he finally settles. In fact, Wilbur is enjoying the bouncing, and the chances are he will be bouncing yet if the firemen do not drop their hold on the net and let him fall to the ground.

Then Wilbur steps out of the net, and I can see the bundle is a rolled-up blanket with Lillian's eyes peeking out of one end. He still has the kid under the other arm with his head stuck out in front, and his legs stuck out behind, and it does not seem to me that Wilbur is handling the kid as careful as he is handling Lillian. He stands there looking at the firemen with a very sneering look, and finally he says:

'Do not think you can catch me in your net unless I wish to be caught. I am a butterfly, and very hard to overtake.'

Then all of a sudden the swell dressed doll who is doing so much hollering, piles on top of Wilbur and grabs the kid from him and begins hugging and kissing it.

'Wilbur,' she says, 'God bless you, Wilbur, for saving my baby! Oh, thank you, Wilbur, thank you! My wretched husband kidnaps and runs away with him, and it is only a few hours ago that my detectives find out where he is.'

Wilbur gives the doll a funny look for about half a minute and starts to walk away, but Lillian comes wiggling out of the blanket, looking and smelling pretty much singed up, and the kid sees Lillian and begins hollering for her, so Wilbur finally hands Lillian over to the kid. And not wishing to leave Lillian, Wilbur stands around somewhat confused, and the doll gets talking to him, and finally they go away together, and as they go Wilbur is carrying the kid, and the kid is carrying Lillian, and Lillian is not feeling so good from her burns.

Furthermore, Wilbur is probably more sober than he ever is before in years at this hour in the morning, but before they go I get a chance to talk some to Wilbur when he is still rambling somewhat, and I make out from what he says that the first time he goes to get Lillian he finds her in his room and does not see hide or hair of the little kid and does not even think of him, because he does not know what room the kid is in, anyway, having never noticed such a thing.

But the second time he goes up, Lillian is sniffing at the

crack under the door of a room down the hall from Wilbur's and Wilbur says he seems to remember seeing a trickle of something like water coming out of the crack.

'And,' Wilbur says, 'as I am looking for a blanket for Lillian, and it will be a bother to go back to my room, I figure I will get one out of this room. I try the knob but the door is locked, so I kick it in, and walk in to find the room full of smoke, and fire is shooting through the windows very lovely, and when I grab a blanket off the bed for Lillian, what is under the blanket but the kid?

'Well,' Wilbur says, 'the kid is squawking, and Lillian is mer-owing, and there is so much confusion generally that it makes me nervous, so I figure we better go up on the roof and let the stink blow off us, and look at the fire from there. It seems there is a guy stretched out on the floor of the room alongside an upset table between the door and the bed. He has a bottle in one hand, and he is dead. Well, naturally there is no percentage in lugging a dead guy along, so I take Lillian and the kid and go up on the roof, and we just naturally fly off like humming-birds. Now I must get a drink,' Wilbur says. 'I wonder if anybody has anything on their hip?'

Well, the papers are certainly full of Wilbur and Lillian the next day, especially Lillian, and they are both great heroes.

But Wilbur cannot stand the publicity very long, because he never has any time to himself for his drinking, what with the scribes and the photographers hopping on him every few minutes wishing to hear his story, and to take more pictures of him and Lillian, so one night he disappears, and Lillian disappears with him.

About a year later it comes out that he marries his old doll, Lillian Withington-Harmon, and falls into a log of dough, and what is more he cuts out the liquor and becomes quite a useful citizen one way and another. So everybody has to admit that black cats are not always bad luck, although I say Wilbur's case is a little exceptional because he does not start out knowing Lillian is a black cat, but thinking she is a leopard.

I happen to run into Wilbur one day all dressed up in good clothes and jewelry and chucking quite a swell.

'Wilbur,' I say to him, 'I often think how remarkable it is the way Lillian suddenly gets such an attachment for the little kid and remembers about him being in the hotel and leads you back there a second time to the right room. If I do not see this come off with my own eyes, I will never believe a cat has brains enough to do such a thing, because I consider cats extra dumb.'

'Brains nothing,' Wilbur says. 'Lillian does not have brains enough to grease a gimlet. And what is more, she has no more attachment for the kid than a jack rabbit. The time has come,' Wilbur says, 'to expose Lillian. She gets a lot of credit which is never coming to her. I will now tell you about Lillian, and nobody knows this but me.

'You see,' Wilbur says, 'when Lillian is a little kitten I always put a little Scotch in her milk, partly to help make her good and strong, and partly because I am never no hand to drink alone, unless there is nobody with me. Well, at first Lillian does not care so much for this Scotch in her milk, but finally she takes a liking to it, and I keep making her toddy stronger until in the end she will lap up a good big snort without any milk for a chaser, and yell for more. In fact, I suddenly realize that Lillian becomes a rumpot, just like I am in those days, and simply must have her grog, and it is when she is good and rummed up that Lillian goes off snatching Pekes, and acting tough generally.

'Now,' Wilbur says, 'the time of the fire is about the time I get home every morning and give Lillian her schnapps. But

63

when I go into the hotel and get her the first time I forget to Scotch her up, and the reason she runs back into the hotel is because she is looking for her shot. And the reason she is sniffing at the kid's door is not because the kid is in there but because the trickle that is coming through the crack under the door is nothing but Scotch that is running out of the bottle in the dead guy's hand. I never mention this before because I figure it may be a knock to a dead guy's memory,' Wilbur says. 'Drinking is certainly a disgusting thing, especially secret drinking.'

'But how is Lillian getting along these days?' I ask Wilbur Willard.

'I am greatly disappointed in Lillian,' he says. 'She refuses to reform when I do, and the last I hear of her she takes up with Gregorio, the Ginney bootlegger, who keeps her well Scotched up all the time so she will lead his blonde doll's Peke a dog's life.'

DORIS LESSING

AN OLD WOMAN
AND HER CAT

HER NAME WAS Hetty, and she was born with the twentieth century. She was seventy when she died of cold and malnutrition. She had been alone for a long time, since her husband had died of pneumonia in a bad winter soon after the Second World War. He had not been more than middle-aged. Her four children were now middle-aged, with grown children. Of these descendants one daughter sent her Christmas cards, but otherwise she did not exist for them. For they were all respectable people, with homes and good jobs and cars. And Hetty was not respectable. She had always been a bit strange, these people said, when mentioning her at all.

When Fred Pennefather, her husband, was alive and the children just growing up, they all lived much too close and uncomfortable in a Council flat in that part of London which is like an estuary, with tides of people flooding in and out: they were not half a mile from the great stations of Euston, St Pancras and King's Cross. The blocks of flats were pioneers in that area, standing up grim, grey, hideous, among many acres of little houses and gardens, all soon to be demolished so that they could be replaced by more tall grey blocks. The Pennefathers were good tenants, paying their rent, keeping out of debt; he was a building worker, 'steady', and proud of it. There was no evidence then of Hetty's future dislocation from the normal, unless it was that she very often slipped down for an hour or so to the platforms where the locomotives drew in and ground out again. She liked the smell of it all, she said. She liked to see people moving about, 'coming and going from all those foreign places'. She meant Scotland, Ireland, the North of England. These visits into the din, the smoke, the massed swirling people were for her a drug, like other people's drinking or gambling. Her husband teased her, calling her a gypsy. She was in fact part gypsy, for her mother had been one, but had chosen to leave her people and marry a man who lived in a house. Fred Pennefather liked his wife for being different from the run of the women he knew; and had married her because of it, but her children were fearful that her gypsy blood might show itself in worse ways than haunting railway stations. She was a tall woman with a lot of glossy black hair, a skin that tanned easily, and dark strong eyes. She wore bright colours, and enjoyed quick tempers and sudden reconciliations. In her prime she attracted attention, was proud and handsome. All this made it inevitable that the people in those streets should refer to her as 'that gypsy woman'. When she heard them, she shouted back that she was none the worse for that.

After her husband died and the children married and left, the Council moved her to a small flat in the same building. She got a job selling food in a local store, but found it boring. There seem to be traditional occupations for middle-aged women living alone, the busy and responsible part of their lives being over. Drink. Gambling. Looking for another husband. A wistful affair or two. That's about it. Hetty went through a period of, as it were, testing out all these, like hobbies, but tired of them. While still earning her small wage as a saleswoman, she began a trade in buying and selling secondhand clothes. She did not have a shop of her own, but bought clothes from householders, and sold these to stalls and the secondhand shops. She adored doing this. It was a passion. She gave up her respectable job and forgot all about her love of trains and travellers. Her room was always full of bright bits of cloth, a dress that had a pattern she fancied and did not want to sell, strips of beading, old furs, embroidery, lace. There were street traders among the people in the flats, but there was something in the way Hetty went about it that lost her friends. Neighbours of twenty or thirty years' standing said she had gone queer, and wished to know her no longer. But she did not mind. She was enjoying herself too much, particularly the moving about the streets with her old perambulator, in which she crammed what she was buying or selling. She liked the gossiping, the bargaining, the wheedling from householders. It was this last which – and she knew this quite well, of course – the neighbours objected to. It was the thin edge of the wedge. It was begging. Decent people did not beg. She was no longer decent.

Lonely in her tiny flat, she was there as little as possible, always preferring the lively streets. But she had after all to spend some time in her room, and one day she saw a kitten lost and trembling in a dirty corner, and brought it home to the block of flats. She was on a fifth floor. While the kitten was growing into a large strong tom, he ranged about that conglomeration of staircases and lifts and many dozens of flats, as if the building were a town. Pets were not actively persecuted by the authorities, only forbidden and then tolerated. Hetty's life from the coming of the cat became more sociable, for the beast was always making friends with somebody in the cliff that was the block of flats across the court, or not coming home for nights at a time, so that she had to go and look for him and knock on doors and ask, or returning home kicked and limping, or bleeding after a fight with his kind. She made scenes with the kickers, or the owners of the enemy cats, exchanged cat lore with cat lovers, was always having to bandage and nurse her poor Tibby. The cat was soon a scarred warrior with fleas, a torn ear, and a ragged look to him. He was a multi-coloured cat and his eyes were small and yellow. He was a long way down the scale from the delicately coloured, elegantly shaped pedigree cats. But he was independent, and often caught himself pigeons when he could no longer stand the tinned cat food, or the bread and packet gravy Hetty fed him, and he purred and nestled when she grabbed him to her bosom at those times she suffered loneliness. This happened less and less. Once she had realized that her children were hoping that she would leave them alone because the old rag trader was an embarrassment to them, she accepted it, and a bitterness that always had wild humour in it only welled up at times like Christmas. She sang or chanted to the cat: 'You nasty old beast, filthy old cat, nobody wants you, do they Tibby, no, you're just an alley tom, just an old stealing cat, hey Tibs, Tibs, Tibs.'

The building teemed with cats. There were even a couple of dogs. They all fought up and down the grey cement corridors. There were sometimes dog and cat messes which someone had to clear up, but which might be left for days and weeks as part of neighbourly wars and feuds. There were many complaints. Finally an official came from the Council to say that the ruling about keeping animals was going to be enforced. Hetty, like others, would have to have her cat destroyed. This crisis coincided with a time of bad luck for her. She had had 'flu; had not been able to earn money, had found it hard to get out for her pension, had run into debt. She owed a lot of back rent, too. A television set she had hired and was not paying for attracted the visits of a television representative. The neighbours were gossiping that Hetty had 'gone savage'. This was because the cat had brought up the stairs and along the passageways a pigeon he had caught, shedding feathers and blood all the way; a woman coming in to complain found Hetty plucking the pigeon to stew it, as she had done with others, sharing the meal with Tibby.

'You're filthy,' she would say to him, setting the stew down to cool in his dish. 'Filthy old thing. Eating that dirty old pigeon. What do you think you are, a wild cat? Decent cats don't eat dirty birds. Only those old gypsies eat wild birds.'

One night she begged help from a neighbour who had a car, and put into the car herself, the television set, the cat, bundles of clothes, and the pram. She was driven across London to a room in a street that was a slum because it was waiting to be done up. The neighbour made a second trip to bring her bed and her mattress, which were tied to the roof of the car, a chest of drawers, an old trunk, saucepans. It was in this way that she left the street in which she had lived for thirty years, nearly half her life.

She set up house again in one room. She was frightened to go near 'them' to re-establish pension rights and her identity, because of the arrears of rent she had left behind, and because of the stolen television set. She started trading again, and the little room was soon spread, like her last, with a rainbow of colours and textures and lace and sequins. She cooked on a single gas ring and washed in the sink. There was no hot water unless it was boiled in saucepans. There were several old ladies and a family of five children in the house, which was condemned.

She was in the ground floor back, with a window which opened on to a derelict garden, and her cat was happy in a hunting ground that was a mile around this house where his mistress was so splendidly living. A canal ran close by, and in the dirty city-water were islands which a cat could reach by leaping from moored boat to boat. On the islands were rats and birds. There were pavements full of fat London pigeons. The cat was a fine hunter. He soon had his place in the hierarchies of the local cat population and did not have to fight much to keep it. He was a strong male cat, and fathered many litters of kittens.

In that place Hetty and he lived five happy years. She was trading well, for there were rich people close by to shed what the poor needed to buy cheaply. She was not lonely, for she made a quarrelling but satisfying friendship with a woman on the top floor, a widow like herself who did not see her children either. Hetty was sharp with the five children, complaining about their noise and mess, but she slipped them bits of money and sweets after telling their mother that 'she was a fool to put herself out for them, because they wouldn't appreciate it'. She was living well, even without her pension. She sold the television set and gave herself and her friend upstairs some day-trips to the coast, and bought a small radio. She never read books or magazines. The truth was that she could not write or read, or only so badly it was no pleasure to her. Her cat was all reward and no cost, for he fed himself, and continued to bring in pigeons for her to cook and eat, for which in return he claimed milk.

'Greedy Tibby, you greedy *thing*, don't think I don't know, oh yes I do, you'll get sick eating those old pigeons, I do keep telling you that, don't I?'

At last the street was being done up. No longer a uniform, long, disgraceful slum, houses were being bought by the middle-class people. While this meant more good warm clothes for trading – or begging, for she still could not resist the attraction of getting something for nothing by the use of her plaintive inventive tongue, her still-flashing handsome eyes – Hetty knew, like her neighbours, that soon this house with its cargo of poor people would be bought for improvement.

In the week Hetty was seventy years old came the notice that was the end of this little community. They had four weeks to find somewhere else to live.

Usually, the shortage of housing being what it is in London – and everywhere else in the world, of course – these people would have had to scatter, fending for themselves. But the fate of this particular street was attracting attention, because a municipal election was pending. Homelessness among the poor was finding a focus in this street which was a perfect symbol of the whole area, and indeed the whole city, half of it being fine converted tasteful houses, full of people who spent a lot of money, and half being dying houses tenanted by people like Hetty.

As a result of speeches by councillors and churchmen, local authorities found themselves unable to ignore the victims of this redevelopment. The people in the house Hetty was in were visited by a team consisting of an unemployment officer, a social worker, and a rehousing officer. Hetty, a strong gaunt old woman wearing a scarlet wool suit she had found among her cast-offs that week, a black knitted tea-cosy on her head, and black buttoned Edwardian boots too big for her, so that she had to shuffle, invited them into her room. But although all were well used to the extremes of poverty, none wished to enter the place, but stood in the doorway and made her this offer: that she should be aided to get her pension – why had she not claimed it long ago? – and that she, together with the four other old ladies in the house, should move to a Home run by the Council out in the northern suburbs. All these women were used to, and enjoyed, lively London, and while they had no alternative but to agree, they fell into a saddened and sullen state. Hetty agreed too. The last two winters had set her bones aching badly, and a cough was never far away. And while perhaps she was more of an urban soul even than the others, since she had walked up and down so many streets with her old perambulator loaded with rags and laces, and since she knew so intimately London's texture and taste, she minded least of all the idea of a new home 'among green fields'. There were, in fact, no fields near the promised Home, but for some reason all the old ladies had chosen to bring out this old song of a phrase, as if it belonged to their situation, that of old women not far off death. 'It will be nice to be near green fields again,' they said to each other over cups of tea.

The housing officer came to make final arrangements. Hetty Pennefather was to move with the others in two weeks' time. The young man, sitting on the very edge of the only chair in the crammed room, because it was greasy and he suspected it had fleas or worse in it, breathed as lightly as he could because of the appalling stink: there was a lavatory in the house, but it had been out of order for three days, and it was just the other side of a thin wall. The whole house smelled.

The young man, who knew only too well the extent of the misery due to lack of housing, who knew how many old people abandoned by their children did not get the offer to spend their days being looked after by the authorities, could not help feeling that this wreck of a human being could count herself lucky to get a place in this 'Home', even if it was – and he knew and deplored the fact – an institution in which the old were treated like naughty and dim-witted children until they had the good fortune to die.

But just as he was telling Hetty that a van would be coming to take her effects and those of the other four old ladies, and that she need not take anything more with her than her clothes 'and perhaps a few photographs', he saw what he had thought was a heap of multi-coloured rags get up and put its ragged gingery-black paws on the old woman's skirt. Which today was a cretonne curtain covered with pink and red roses that Hetty had pinned around her because she liked the pattern.

'You can't take that cat with you,' he said automatically. It was something he had to say often, and knowing what misery the statement caused, he usually softened it down. But he had been taken by surprise.

Tibby now looked like a mass of old wool that has been matting together in dust and rain. One eye was permanently half-closed, because a muscle had been ripped in a fight. One ear was vestigial. And down a flank was a hairless slope with a thick scar on it. A cat-hating man had treated Tibby as he treated all cats, to a pellet from his airgun. The resulting wound had taken two years to heal. And Tibby smelled.

No worse, however, than his mistress, who sat stiffly still, bright-eyed with suspicion, hostile, watching the well-brushed tidy young man from the Council.

'How old is that beast?'

'Ten years, no, only eight years, he's a young cat about five years old,' said Hetty, desperate.

'It looks as if you'd do him a favour to put him out of his misery,' said the young man.

When the official left, Hetty had agreed to everything. She was the only one of the old women with a cat. The others had budgerigars or nothing. Budgies were allowed in the Home.

She made her plans, confided in the others, and when the van came for them and their clothes and photographs and budgies, she was not there, and they told lies for her. 'Oh we don't know where she can have gone, dear,' the old women repeated again and again to the indifferent van driver. 'She was here last night, but she did say something about going to her daughter in Manchester.' And off they went to die in the Home.

Hetty knew that when houses have been emptied for re-development they may stay empty for months, even years. She intended to go on living in this one until the builders moved in.

It was a warm autumn. For the first time in her life she lived like her gypsy forebears, and did not go to bed in a room in a house like respectable people. She spent several nights, with Tibby, sitting crouched in a doorway of an empty house two doors from her own. She knew exactly when the police would come around, and where to hide herself in the bushes of the overgrown shrubby garden.

As she had expected, nothing happened in the house, and she moved back in. She smashed a back windowpane so that Tibby could move in and out without her having to unlock the front door for him, and without leaving a window suspiciously open. She moved to the top back room and left it every morning early, to spend the day in the streets with her pram and her rags. At night she kept a candle glimmering low down on the floor. The lavatory was still out of order, so she used a pail on the first floor, instead, and secretly emptied it at night into the canal, which in the day was full of pleasure boats and people fishing.

Tibby brought her several pigeons during that time.

'Oh you are a clever puss, Tibby, Tibby! Oh you're clever, you are. You know how things are, don't you, you know how to get around and about.'

The weather turned very cold; Christmas came and went. Hetty's cough came back, and she spent most of her time under piles of blankets and old clothes, dozing. At night she watched the shadows of the candle flame on floor and ceiling – the windowframes fitted badly, and there was a draught.

Twice tramps spent the night in the bottom of the house and she heard them being moved on by the police. She had to go down to make sure the police had not blocked up the broken window the cat used, but they had not. A blackbird had flown in and had battered itself to death trying to get out. She plucked it, and roasted it over a fire made with bits of floorboard in a baking pan: the gas of course had been cut off. She had never eaten very much, and was not frightened that some dry bread and a bit of cheese was all that she had eaten during her sojourn under the heap of clothes. She was cold, but did not think about that much. Outside there was slushy brown snow everywhere. She went back to her nest thinking that soon the cold spell would be over and she could get back to her trading. Tibby sometimes got into the pile with her, and she clutched the warmth of him to her. 'Oh you clever cat, you clever old thing, looking after yourself, aren't you? That's right my ducky, that's right my lovely.'

And then, just as she was moving about again, with snow gone off the ground for a time but winter only just begun, in January, she saw a builder's van draw up outside, a couple of men unloading their gear. They did not come into the house: they were to start work next day. By then Hetty, her cat, her pram piled with clothes and her two blankets, were gone. She also took a box of matches, a candle, an old saucepan and a fork and spoon, a tin-opener, a candle and a rat-trap. She had a horror of rats.

About two miles away, among the homes and gardens of amiable Hampstead, where live so many of the rich, the intelligent and the famous, stood three empty, very large houses. She had seen them on an occasion, a couple of years before, when she had taken a bus. This was a rare thing for her, because of the remarks and curious looks provoked by her mad clothes, and by her being able to appear at the same time such a tough battling old thing and a naughty child. For the older she got, this disreputable tramp, the more there strengthened in her a quality of fierce, demanding childishness. It was all too much of a mixture; she was uncomfortable to have near.

She was afraid that 'they' might have rebuilt the houses, but there they still stood, too tumbledown and dangerous to be of much use to tramps, let alone the armies of London's homeless. There was no glass left anywhere. The flooring at ground level was mostly gone, leaving small platforms and juts of planking over basements full of water. The ceilings were crumbling. The roofs were going. The houses were like bombed buildings.

But on the cold dark of a late afternoon she pulled the pram up the broken stairs and moved cautiously around the frail boards of a second-floor room that had a great hole in it right down to the bottom of the house. Looking into it was like looking into a well. She held a candle to examine the state of the walls, here more or less whole, and saw that rain and wind blowing in from the window would leave one corner dry. Here she made her home. A sycamore tree screened the gaping window from the main road twenty yards away. Tibby, who was cramped after making the journey under the clothes piled in the pram, bounded down and out and vanished into neglected undergrowth to catch his supper. He returned fed and pleased, and seemed happy to stay clutched in her hard thin old arms. She had come to watch for his return after hunting trips, because the warm purring bundle of bones and fur did seem to allay, for a while, the permanent ache of cold in her bones.

Next day she sold her Edwardian boots for a few shillings – they were fashionable again – and bought a loaf and some bacon scraps. In a corner of the ruins well away from the one she had made her own, she pulled up some floorboards, built a fire, and toasted bread and the bacon scraps. Tibby had brought in a pigeon, and she roasted that, but not very efficiently. She was afraid of the fire catching and the whole mass going up in flames; she was afraid too of the smoke showing and attracting the police. She had to keep damping down the fire, and so the bird was bloody and unappetizing, and in the end Tibby got most of it. She felt confused, and discouraged, but thought it was because of the long stretch of winter still ahead of her before spring could come. In fact, she was ill. She made a couple of attempts to trade and earn money to feed herself before she acknowledged she was ill. She knew she was not yet dangerously ill, for she had been that in her life, and would have been able to recognize the cold listless indifference of a real last-ditch illness. But all her bones ached, and her head ached, and she coughed more than she ever had. Yet she still did not think of herself as suffering particularly from the cold, even in that sleety January weather. She had never, in all her life, lived in a properly heated place, had never known a really warm home, not even when she lived in the Council flats. Those flats had electric fires, and the family had never used them, for the sake of economy, except in very bad spells of cold. They piled clothes on to themselves, or went to bed early. But she did know that to keep herself from dying now she could not treat the cold with her usual indifference. She knew she must eat. In the comparatively dry corner of the windy room, away from the gaping window through which snow and sleet were drifting, she made another nest – her last. She had found a piece of plastic sheeting in the rubble, and she laid that down first, so that the damp would not strike up. Then she spread her two blankets over that. Over them were heaped the mass of old clothes. She wished she had another piece of plastic to

79

put on top, but she used sheets of newspaper instead. She heaved herself into the middle of this, with a loaf of bread near to her hand. She dozed, and waited, and nibbled bits of bread, and watched the snow drifting softly in. Tibby sat close to the old blue face that poked out of the pile and put up a paw to touch it. He miaowed and was restless, and then went out into the frosty morning and brought in a pigeon. This the cat put, still struggling and fluttering a little, close to the old woman. But she was afraid to get out of the pile in which the heat was being made and kept with such difficulty. She really could not climb out long enough to pull up more splinters of plank from the floors, to make a fire, to pluck the pigeon, to roast it. She put out a cold hand to stroke the cat.

'Tibby, you old thing, you brought it for me then, did you? You did, did you? Come here, come in here . . .' But he did not want to get in with her. He miaowed again, pushed the bird closer to her. It was now limp and dead.

'You have it then. You eat it. I'm not hungry, thank you Tibby.'

But the carcase did not interest him. He had eaten a pigeon before bringing this one up to Hetty. He fed himself well. In spite of his matted fur, and his scars and his half-closed yellow eye, he was a strong healthy cat.

At about four the next morning there were steps and voices downstairs. Hetty shot out of the pile and crouched behind a fallen heap of plaster and beams, now covered with snow, at the end of the room near the window. She could see through the hole in the floorboards down to the first floor, which had collapsed entirely, and through it to the ground floor. She saw a man in a thick overcoat and muffler and leather gloves holding a strong torch to illuminate a thin bundle of clothes lying on the floor. She saw that this bundle was a sleeping man or woman. She was indignant – *her* home

80

was being trespassed upon. And she was afraid because she had not been aware of this other tenant of the ruin. Had he, or she, heard her talking to the cat? And where was the cat? If he wasn't careful he would be caught, and that would be the end of him. The man with a torch went off and came back with a second man. In the thick dark far below Hetty was a small cave of strong light, which was the torchlight. In this space of light two men bent to lift the bundle, carried it out across the danger-traps of fallen and rotting boards that made gangplanks over the water-filled basements. One man was holding the torch in the hand that supported the dead person's feet, and the light jogged and lurched over trees and grasses: the corpse was being taken through the shrubberies to a car.

There are men in London who, between the hours of two and five in the morning – when the real citizens are asleep, who should not be disturbed by such unpleasantness as the corpses of the poor – make the rounds of all the empty, rotting houses they know about, to collect the dead, and to warn the living that they ought not to be there at all, inviting them to one of the official Homes or lodgings for the homeless.

Hetty was too frightened to get back into her warm heap. She sat with the blankets pulled around her, and looked through gaps in the fabric of the house, making out shapes and boundaries and holes and puddles and mounds of rubble, as her eyes, like her cat's, became accustomed to the dark.

She heard scuffling sounds and knew they were rats. She had meant to set the trap, but the thought of her friend Tibby, who might catch his paw, had stopped her. She sat up until the morning light came in grey and cold, after nine. Now she did know herself to be very ill and in danger, for she had lost all the warmth she had huddled into her bones under the rags. She shivered violently. She was shaking herself apart with shivering. In between spasms she drooped limp and exhausted. Through the ceiling above her – but it was not a ceiling, only a cobweb of slats and planks – she could see into a dark cave which had been a garret, and through the roof above that, the grey sky, teeming with incipient rain. The cat came back from where he had been hiding, and sat crouched on her knees, keeping her stomach warm, while she thought out her position. These were her last clear thoughts. She told herself that she would not last out until spring unless she allowed 'them' to find her, and take her to hospital. After that, she would be taken to a Home.

But what would happen to Tibby, her poor cat? She rubbed the old beast's scruffy head with the ball of her thumb and muttered: 'Tibby, Tibby, they won't get you, no, you'll be all right, yes, I'll look after you.'

Towards midday, the sun oozed yellow through miles of greasy grey cloud, and she staggered down the rotting stairs, to the shops. Even in those London streets, where the extraordinary has become usual, people turned to stare at a tall gaunt woman, with a white face that had flaming red patches on it, and blue compressed lips, and restless black eyes. She wore a tightly buttoned man's overcoat, torn brown woollen mittens, and an old fur hood. She pushed a pram loaded with old dresses and scraps of embroidery and torn jerseys and shoes, all stirred into a tight tangle, and she kept pushing this pram up against people as they stood in queues, or gossiped, or stared into windows, and she muttered: 'Give me your old clothes darling, give me your old pretties, give Hetty something, poor Hetty's hungry.' A woman gave her a handful of small change, and Hetty bought a roll filled with tomato and lettuce. She did not dare go into a café, for even in her confused state she knew she would offend, and would probably be asked to leave. But she begged a cup of tea at a street stall, and when the hot sweet liquid flooded through her she felt she might survive the winter. She bought a carton of milk and pushed the pram back through the slushy snowy street to the ruins.

Tibby was not there. She urinated down through the gap in the boards, muttering, 'A nuisance, that old tea,' and wrapped herself in a blanket and waited for the dark to come.

Tibby came in later. He had blood on his foreleg. She had heard scuffling and she knew that he had fought a rat, or several, and had been bitten. She poured the milk into the tilted saucepan and Tibby drank it all.

She spent the night with the animal held against her chilly bosom. They did not sleep, but dozed off and on. Tibby would normally be hunting, the night was his time, but he had stayed with the old woman now for three nights.

Early next morning they again heard the corpse removers among the rubble on the ground floor, and saw the beams of the torch moving on wet walls and collapsed beams. For a moment the torchlight was almost straight on Hetty, but no one came up: who could believe that a person could be desperate enough to climb those dangerous stairs, to trust those crumbling splintery floors, and in the middle of winter?

Hetty had now stopped thinking of herself as ill, of the degrees of her illness, of her danger – of the impossibility of her surviving. She had cancelled out in her mind the presence of winter and its lethal weather, and it was as if spring were nearly here. She knew that if it had been spring when she had had to leave the other house, she and the cat could have lived here for months and months, quite safely and comfortably. Because it seemed to her an impossible and even a silly thing that her life, or, rather, her death, could

83

depend on something so arbitrary as builders starting work on a house in January rather than in April, she could not believe it: the fact would not stay in her mind. The day before she had been quite clear-headed. But today her thoughts were cloudy, and she talked and laughed aloud. Once she scrambled up and rummaged in her rags for an old Christmas card she had got four years before from her good daughter.

In a hard harsh angry grumbling voice she said to her four children that she needed a room of her own now that she was getting on. 'I've been a good mother to you,' she shouted to them before invisible witnesses – former neighbours, welfare workers, a doctor. 'I never let you want for anything, never! When you were little you always had the best of everything! You can ask anybody; go on, ask them, then!'

She was restless and made such a noise that Tibby left her and bounded on to the pram and crouched watching her. He was limping, and his foreleg was rusty with blood. The rat had bitten deep. When the daylight came, he left Hetty in a kind of sleep, and went down into the garden where he saw a pigeon feeding on the edge of the pavement. The cat pounced on the bird, dragged it into the bushes, and ate it all, without taking it up to his mistress. After he had finished eating, he stayed hidden, watching the passing people. He stared at them intently with his blazing yellow eye, as if he were thinking, or planning. He did not go into the old ruin and up the crumbling wet stairs until late – it was as if he knew it was not worth going at all.

He found Hetty, apparently asleep, wrapped loosely in a blanket, propped sitting in a corner. Her head had fallen on her chest, and her quantities of white hair had escaped from a scarlet woollen cap, and concealed a face that was flushed a deceptive pink – the flush of coma from cold. She was not yet dead, but she died that night. The rats came up the walls and along the planks and the cat fled down and away from them, limping still into the bushes.

Hetty was not found for a couple of weeks. The weather changed to warm, and the man whose job it was to look for corpses was led up the dangerous stairs by the smell. There was something left of her, but not much.

As for the cat, he lingered for two or three days in the thick shrubberies, watching the passing people and beyond them, the thundering traffic of the main road. Once a couple stopped to talk on the pavement, and the cat, seeing two pairs of legs, moved out and rubbed himself against one of the legs. A hand came down and he was stroked and patted for a little. Then the people went away.

The cat saw he would not find another home, and he moved off, nosing and feeling his way from one garden to another, through empty houses, finally into an old churchyard. This graveyard already had a couple of stray cats in it, and he joined them. It was the beginning of a community of stray cats going wild. They killed birds, and the field mice that lived among the grasses, and they drank from puddles. Before winter had ended the cats had had a hard time of it from thirst, during the two long spells when the ground froze and there was snow and no puddles and the birds were hard to catch because the cats were so easy to see against the clean white. But on the whole they managed quite well. One of the cats was female, and soon there were a swarm of wild cats, as wild as if they did not live in the middle of a city surrounded by streets and houses. This was just one of half a dozen communities of wild cats living in that square mile of London.

Then an official came to trap the cats and take them away. Some of them escaped, hiding till it was safe to come back again. But Tibby was caught. He was not only getting old and stiff – he still limped from the rat's bite – but he was friendly, and did not run away from the man, who had only to pick him up in his arms.

'You're an old soldier, aren't you?' said the man. 'A real tough one, a real old tramp.'

It is possible that the cat even thought that he might be finding another human friend and a home.

But it was not so. The haul of wild cats that week numbered hundreds, and while if Tibby had been younger a home might have been found for him, since he was amiable, and wished to be liked by the human race, he was really too old, and smelly and battered. So they gave him an injection and, as we say, 'put him to sleep'.

SAKI

TOBERMORY

IT WAS A CHILL, rain washed afternoon of a late August day, that indefinite season when partridges are still in security or cold storage, and there is nothing to hunt – unless one is bounded on the north by the Bristol Channel, in which case one may lawfully gallop after fat red stags. Lady Blemley's house-party was not bounded on the north by the Bristol Channel, hence there was a full gathering of her guests round the tea-table on this particular afternoon. And, in spite of the blankness of the season and the triteness of the occasion, there was no trace in the company of that fatigued restlessness which means a dread of the pianola and a subdued hankering for auction bridge. The undisguised open-mouthed attention of the entire party was fixed on the homely negative personality of Mr Cornelius Appin. Of all her guests, he was the one who had come to Lady Blemley with the vaguest reputation. Some one had said he was 'clever', and he had got his invitation in the moderate expectation, on the part of his hostess, that some portion at least of his cleverness would be contributed to the general entertainment. Until tea-time that day she had been unable to discover in what direction, if any, his cleverness lay. He was neither a wit nor a croquet champion, a hypnotic force nor a begetter of amateur theatricals. Neither did his exterior suggest the sort of man in whom women are willing to pardon a generous measure of mental deficiency. He had subsided into mere Mr Appin, and the Cornelius seemed a piece of transparent baptismal bluff. And now he was claiming to have launched on the world a discovery beside which the invention of gunpowder, of the printing-press, and of steam locomotion were inconsiderable trifles. Science had made bewildering strides in many directions during recent decades, but this thing seemed to belong to the domain of miracle rather than to scientific achievement.

'And do you really ask us to believe,' Sir Wilfrid was saying, 'that you have discovered a means for instructing animals in the art of human speech, and that dear old Tobermory has proved your first successful pupil?'

'It is a problem at which I have worked for the last seventeen years,' said Mr Appin, 'but only during the last eight or nine months have I been rewarded with glimmerings of success. Of course I have experimented with thousands of animals, but latterly only with cats, those wonderful creatures which have assimilated themselves so marvellously with our civilization while retaining all their highly developed feral instincts. Here and there among cats one comes across an outstanding superior intellect, just as one does among the ruck of human beings, and when I made the acquaintance of Tobermory a week ago I saw at once that I was in contact with a "Beyond-cat" of extraordinary intelligence. I had gone far along the road to success in recent experiments; with Tobermory, as you call him, I have reached the goal.'

Mr Appin concluded his remarkable statement in a voice which he strove to divest of a triumphant inflection. No one said 'Rats,' though Clovis's lips moved in a monosyllabic contortion which probably invoked those rodents of disbelief.

'And do you mean to say,' asked Miss Resker, after a slight pause, 'that you have taught Tobermory to say and understand easy sentences of one syllable?'

'My dear Miss Resker,' said the wonder-worker patiently, 'one teaches little children and savages and backward adults in that piecemeal fashion; when one has once solved the problem of making a beginning with an animal of highly developed intelligence one has no need for those halting methods. Tobermory can speak our language with perfect correctness.'

This time Clovis very distinctly said, 'Beyond rats!' Sir Wilfrid was more polite, but equally sceptical.

'Hadn't we better have the cat in and judge for ourselves?' suggested Lady Blemley.

Sir Wilfrid went in search of the animal, and the company settled themselves down to the languid expectation of witnessing some more or less adroit drawing-room ventriloquism.

In a minute Sir Wilfrid was back in the room, his face white beneath its tan and his eyes dilated with excitement.

'By Gad, it's true!'

His agitation was unmistakably genuine, and his hearers started forward in a thrill of awakened interest.

Collapsing into an armchair he continued breathlessly: 'I found him dozing in the smoking-room and called out to him to come for his tea. He blinked at me in his usual way, and I said, "Come on, Toby; don't keep us waiting"; and, by Gad! he drawled out in a most horribly natural voice that he'd come when he dashed well pleased! I nearly jumped out of my skin!'

Appin had preached to absolutely incredulous hearers; Sir Wilfrid's statement carried instant conviction. A Babel-like chorus of startled exclamation arose, amid which the scientist sat mutely enjoying the first fruit of his stupendous discovery.

In the midst of the clamour Tobermory entered the room

and made his way with velvet tread and studied unconcern across to the group seated round the tea-table.

A sudden hush of awkwardness and constraint fell on the company. Somehow there seemed an element of embarrassment in addressing on equal terms a domestic cat of acknowledged dental ability.

'Will you have some milk, Tobermory?' asked Lady Blemley in a rather strained voice.

'I don't mind if I do,' was the response, couched in a tone of even indifference. A shiver of suppressed excitement went through the listeners, and Lady Blemley might be excused for pouring out the saucerful of milk rather unsteadily.

'I'm afraid I've spilt a good deal of it,' she said apologetically.

'After all, it's not my Axminster,' was Tobermory's rejoinder.

Another silence fell on the group, and then Miss Resker, in her best district-visitor manner, asked if the human language had been difficult to learn. Tobermory looked squarely at her for a moment and then fixed his gaze serenely on the middle distance. It was obvious that boring questions lay outside his scheme of life.

'What do you think of human intelligence?' asked Mavis Pellington lamely.

'Of whose intelligence in particular?' asked Tobermory coldly.

'Oh, well, mine for instance,' said Mavis, with a feeble laugh.

'You put me in an embarrassing position,' said Tobermory, whose tone and attitude certainly did not suggest a shred of embarrassment. 'When your inclusion in this house-party was suggested Sir Wilfrid protested that you were the most brainless woman of his acquaintance, and that there was a wide distinction between hospitality and the care of the feeble-minded. Lady Blemley replied that your lack of brain-power was the precise quality which had earned you your invitation, as you were the only person she could think of who might be idiotic enough to buy their old car. You know, the one they call "The Envy of Sisyphus", because it goes quite nicely up-hill if you push it.'

Lady Blemley's protestations would have had greater effect if she had not casually suggested to Mavis only that morning that the car in question would be just the thing for her down at her Devonshire home.

Major Barfield plunged in heavily to effect a diversion.

'How about your carryings-on with the tortoise-shell puss up at the stables, eh?'

The moment he had said it every one realized the blunder.

'One does not usually discuss these matters in public,' said Tobermory frigidly. 'From a slight observation of your ways since you've been in this house I should imagine you'd find it inconvenient if I were to shift the conversation on to your own little affairs.'

The panic which ensued was not confined to the Major.

'Would you like to go and see if cook has got your dinner ready?' suggested Lady Blemley hurriedly, affecting to ignore the fact that it wanted at least two hours to Tobermory's dinner-time.

'Thanks,' said Tobermory, 'not quite so soon after my tea. I don't want to die of indigestion.'

'Cats have nine lives, you know,' said Sir Wilfrid heartily.

'Possibly,' answered Tobermory; 'but only one liver.'

'Adelaide!' said Mrs Cornett, 'do you mean to encourage that cat to go out and gossip about us in the servants' hall?'

The panic had indeed become general. A narrow ornamental balustrade ran in front of most of the bedroom windows at the Towers, and it was recalled with dismay that this had formed a favourite promenade for Tobermory at all hours, whence he could watch the pigeons – and heaven knew what else besides. If he intended to become reminiscent in his present outspoken strain the effect would be something more than disconcerting. Mrs Cornett, who spent much time at her toilet table, and whose complexion was reputed to be of a nomadic though punctual disposition, looked as ill at ease as the Major. Miss Scrawen, who wrote fiercely sensuous poetry and led a blameless life, merely displayed irritation; if you are methodical and virtuous in private you don't necessarily want every one to know it. Bertie van Tahn, who was so depraved at seventeen that he had long ago given up trying to be any worse, turned a dull shade of gardenia white, but he did not commit the error of dashing out of the room like Odo Finsberry, a young gentleman who was understood to be reading for the Church and who was possibly disturbed at the thought of scandals he might hear concerning other people. Clovis had the presence of mind to maintain a composed exterior; privately he was calculating how long it would take to procure a box of fancy mice through the agency of the *Exchange and Mart* as a species of hush-money.

Even in a delicate situation like the present, Agnes Resker could not endure to remain too long in the background.

'Why did I ever come down here?' she asked dramatically.

Tobermory immediately accepted the opening.

'Judging by what you said to Mrs Cornett on the croquet-lawn yesterday, you were out for food. You described the Blemleys as the dullest people to stay with that you knew, but said they were clever enough to employ a first-rate cook; otherwise they'd find it difficult to get any one to come down a second time.'

'There's not a word of truth in it! I appeal to Mrs Cornett—' exclaimed the discomfited Agnes.

'Mrs Cornett repeated your remark afterwards to Bertie van Tahn,' continued Tobermory, 'and said, "That woman is a regular Hunger Marcher; she'd go anywhere for four square meals a day," and Bertie van Tahn said—'

At this point the chronicle mercifully ceased. Tobermory had caught a glimpse of the big yellow Tom from the Rectory working his way through the shrubbery towards the stable wing. In a flash he had vanished through the open French window.

With the disappearance of his too brilliant pupil Cornelius Appin found himself beset by a hurricane of bitter upbraiding, anxious inquiry, and frightened entreaty. The responsibility for the situation lay with him, and he must prevent matters from becoming worse. Could Tobermory impart his dangerous gift to other cats? was the first question he had to answer. It was possible, he replied, that he might have initiated his intimate friend the stable puss into his new accomplishment, but it was unlikely that his teaching could have taken a wider range as yet.

'Then,' said Mrs Cornett, 'Tobermory may be a valuable cat and a great pet; but I'm sure you'll agree, Adelaide, that both he and the stable cat must be done away with without delay.'

'You don't suppose I've enjoyed the last quarter of an hour, do you?' said Lady Blemley bitterly. 'My husband and I are very fond of Tobermory – at least, we were before this horrible accomplishment was infused into him; but now, of course, the only thing is to have him destroyed as soon as possible.'

'We can put some strychnine in the scraps he always gets at dinner-time,' said Sir Wilfrid, 'and I will go and drown the stable cat myself. The coachman will be very sore at losing his pet, but I'll say a very catching form of mange has broken out in both cats and we're afraid of its spreading to the kennels.'

'But my great discovery!' expostulated Mr Appin; 'after all my years of research and experiment—'

'You can go and experiment on the short-horns at the farm, who are under proper control,' said Mrs Cornett, 'or the elephants at the Zoological Gardens. They're said to be highly intelligent, and they have this recommendation, that they don't come creeping about our bedrooms and under chairs, and so forth.'

An archangel ecstatically proclaiming the Millennium, and then finding that it clashed unpardonably with Henley and would have to be indefinitely postponed, could hardly have felt more crestfallen than Cornelius Appin at the reception of his wonderful achievement. Public opinion, however, was against him – in fact, had the general voice been consulted on the subject it is probable that a strong minority vote would have been in favour of including him in the strychnine diet.

Defective train arrangements and a nervous desire to see matters brought to a finish prevented an immediate dispersal of the party, but dinner that evening was not a social success. Sir Wilfrid had had rather a trying time with the stable cat and subsequently with the coachman. Agnes Resker ostentatiously limited her repast to a morsel of dry toast, which she bit as though it were a personal enemy; while Mavis Pellington maintained a vindictive silence throughout the meal. Lady Blemley kept up a flow of what she hoped was conversation, but her attention was fixed on the doorway. A plateful of carefully dosed fish scraps was in readiness on the sideboard, but sweets and savoury and dessert went their way, and no Tobermory appeared either in the dining-room or kitchen.

The sepulchral dinner was cheerful compared with the subsequent vigil in the smoking-room. Eating and drinking had at least supplied a distraction and cloak to the prevailing embarrassment. Bridge was out of the question in the general tension of nerves and tempers, and after Odo Finsberry had given a lugubrious rendering of 'Mélisande in the Wood' to a frigid audience, music was tacitly avoided. At eleven the servants went to bed, announcing that the small window in the pantry had been left open as usual for Tobermory's private use. The guests read steadily through the current batch of magazines, and fell back gradually on the 'Badminton Library' and bound volumes of *Punch*. Lady Blemley made periodic visits to the pantry, returning each time with an expression of listless depression which forestalled questioning.

At two o'clock Clovis broke the dominating silence.

'He won't turn up tonight. He's probably in the local newspaper office at the present moment, dictating the first instalment of his reminiscences. Lady What's-her-name's book won't be in it. It will be the event of the day.'

Having made this contribution to the general cheerfulness, Clovis went to bed. At long intervals the various members of the house-party followed his example.

The servants taking round the early tea made a uniform announcement in reply to a uniform question. Tobermory had not returned.

Breakfast was, if anything, a more unpleasant function than dinner had been, but before its conclusion the situation was relieved. Tobermory's corpse was brought in from the shrubbery, where a gardener had just discovered it. From the bites on his throat and the yellow fur which coated his claws it was evident that he had fallen in unequal combat with the big Tom from the Rectory.

By midday most of the guests had quitted the Towers, and after lunch Lady Blemley had sufficiently recovered her spirits to write an extremely nasty letter to the Rectory about the loss of her valuable pet.

Tobermory had been Appin's one successful pupil, and he was destined to have no successor. A few weeks later an elephant in the Dresden Zoological Garden, which had shown no previous signs of irritability, broke loose and killed an Englishman who had apparently been teasing it. The victim's name was variously reported in the papers as Oppin and Eppelin, but his front name was faithfully rendered Cornelius.

'If he was trying German irregular verbs on the poor beast,' said Clovis, 'he deserved all he got.'

P. G. WODEHOUSE

CATS WILL
BE CATS

THERE HAD FALLEN upon the bar-parlour of the Angler's Rest one of those soothing silences which from time to time punctuate the nightly feasts of Reason and flows of Soul in that cosy resort. It was broken by a Whisky and Splash.

'I've been thinking a lot,' said the Whisky and Splash, addressing Mr Mulliner, 'about that cat of yours, that Webster.'

'Has Mr Mulliner got a cat named Webster?' asked a Small Port who had just rejoined our little circle after an absence of some days.

The Sage of the bar-parlour shook his head smilingly.

'Webster,' he said, 'did not belong to me. He was the property of the Dean of Bolsover who, on being raised to a bishopric and sailing from England to take up his episcopal duties at his See of Bongo-Bongo in West Africa, left the animal in the care of his nephew, my cousin Edward's son Lancelot, the artist. I was telling these gentlemen the other evening how Webster for a time completely revolutionized Lancelot's life. His early upbringing at the Deanery had made him austere and censorious, and he exerted on my cousin's son the full force of a powerful and bigoted personality. It was as if Savonarola or some minor prophet had suddenly been introduced into the carefree, Bohemian atmosphere of the studio.'

'He stared at Lancelot and unnerved him,' explained a Pint of Bitter.

'He made him shave daily and knock off smoking,' added a Lemon Sour.

'He thought Lancelot's fiancée, Gladys Bingley, worldly,' said a Rum and Milk, 'and tried to arrange a match between him and a girl called Brenda Carberry-Pirbright.'

'But one day,' concluded Mr Mulliner, 'Lancelot discovered that the animal, for all its apparently rigid principles, had feet of clay and was no better than the rest of us. He happened to drop a bottle of alcoholic liquor and the cat drank deeply of its contents and made a sorry exhibition of itself, with the result that the spell was, of course, instantly broken. What aspect of the story of Webster,' he asked the Whisky and Splash, 'has been engaging your thoughts?'

'The psychological aspect,' said the Whisky and Splash. 'As I see it, there is a great psychological drama in this cat. I visualize his higher and lower selves warring. He has taken the first false step, and what will be the issue? Is this new, demoralizing atmosphere into which he has been plunged to neutralize the pious teachings of early kittenhood at the Deanery? Or will sound churchmanship prevail and keep him the cat he used to be?'

'If,' said Mr Mulliner, 'I am right in supposing that you want to know what happened to Webster at the conclusion of the story I related the other evening, I can tell you. There was nothing that you could really call a war between his higher and lower selves. The lower self won hands down. From the moment when he went on that first majestic toot this once saintly cat became a Bohemian of Bohemians. His days started early and finished late, and were a mere welter of brawling and loose gallantry. As early as the end of the second week his left ear had been reduced through incessant gang-warfare to a mere tattered scenario and his battle-cry had become as familiar to the denizens of Bott Street, Chelsea, as the yodel of the morning milkman.'

The Whisky and Splash said it reminded him of some great Greek tragedy. Mr Mulliner said yes, there were points of resemblance.

'And what,' enquired the Rum and Milk, 'did Lancelot think of all this?'

'Lancelot,' said Mr Mulliner, 'had the easy live and let live creed of the artist. He was indulgent towards the animal's excesses. As he said to Gladys Bingley one evening, when she was bathing Webster's right eye in a boric solution, cats will be cats. In fact, he would scarcely have given a thought to the matter had there not arrived one morning from his uncle a wireless message, dispatched in mid-ocean, announcing that he had resigned his bishopric for reasons of health and would shortly be back in England once more. The communication ended with the words: "All my best to Webster." '

If you recall the position of affairs between Lancelot and the Bishop of Bongo-Bongo, as I described them the other night (said Mr Mulliner), you will not need to be told how deeply this news affected the young man. It was a bomb-shell. Lancelot, though earning enough by his brush to support himself, had been relying on touching his uncle for that extra bit which would enable him to marry Gladys Bingley. And when he had been placed *in loco parentis* to Webster, he had considered this touch a certainty. Surely, he told himself, the most ordinary gratitude would be sufficient to cause his uncle to unbelt.

But now what?

'You saw that wireless,' said Lancelot, agitatedly discussing the matter with Gladys. 'You remember the closing words: "All my best to Webster." Uncle Theodore's first act on landing in England will undoubtedly be to hurry here for a sacred reunion with this cat. And what will he find? A feline plug-ugly. A gangster. The Big Shot of Bott Street. Look at the animal now,' said Lancelot, waving a distracted hand at the cushion where it lay. 'Run your eye over him. I ask you!'

Certainly Webster was not a natty spectacle. Some tough cats from the public-house on the corner had recently been trying to muscle in on his personal dust-bin, and, though he had fought them off, the affair had left its mark upon him. A further section had been removed from his already abbreviated ear, and his once sleek flanks were short of several patches of hair. He looked like the late Legs Diamond after a social evening with a few old friends.

'What,' proceeded Lancelot, writhing visibly, 'will Uncle Theodore say on beholding that wreck? He will put the entire blame on me. He will insist that it was I who dragged that fine spirit down into the mire. And phut will go any chance I ever had of getting into his ribs for a few hundred quid for honeymoon expenses.'

Gladys Bingley struggled with a growing hopelessness.

'You don't think a good wig-maker could do something?'

'A wig-maker might patch on a little extra fur,' admitted Lancelot, 'but how about that ear?'

'A facial surgeon?' suggested Gladys.

Lancelot shook his head.

'It isn't merely his appearance,' he said. 'It's his entire personality. The poorest reader of character, meeting Webster now, would recognize him for what he is – a hard egg and a bad citizen.'

'When do you expect your uncle?' asked Gladys, after a pause.

'At any moment. He must have landed by this time. I can't understand why he has not turned up.'

At this moment there sounded from the passage outside the *plop* of a letter falling into the box attached to the front door. Lancelot went listlessly out. A few moments later Gladys heard him utter a surprised exclamation, and he came hurrying back, a sheet of note-paper in his hand.

'Listen to this,' he said. 'From Uncle Theodore.'

'Is he in London?'

'No. Down in Hampshire, at a place called Widdrington Manor. And the great point is that he does not want to see Webster yet.'

'Why not?'

'I'll read you what he says.'

And Lancelot proceeded to do so, as follows:

> 'Widdrington Manor,
> 'Bottleby-in-the-Vale,
> 'Hants.
>
> 'MY DEAR LANCELOT,
>
> 'You will doubtless be surprised that I have not hastened to greet you immediately upon my return to these shores. The explanation is that I am being entertained at the above address by Lady Widdrington, widow of the late Sir George Widdrington, C.B.E., and her mother, Mrs Pulteney-Banks, whose acquaintance I made on shipboard during my voyage home.
>
> 'I find our English countryside charming after the somewhat desolate environment of Bongo-Bongo, and am enjoying a pleasant and restful visit. Both Lady Widdrington and her mother are kindness itself, especially the former, who is my constant companion on every country ramble. We have a strong bond in our mutual love of cats.
>
> 'And this, my dear boy, brings me to the subject of

Webster. As you can readily imagine, I am keenly desirous of seeing him once more and noting all the evidences of the loving care which, I have no doubt, you have lavished upon him in my absence, but I do not wish you to forward him to me here. The fact is, Lady Widdrington, though a charming woman, seems entirely lacking in discrimination in the matter of cats. She owns and is devoted to a quite impossible orange-coloured animal of the name of Percy, whose society could not but prove distasteful to one of Webster's high principles. When I tell you that only last night this Percy was engaging in personal combat – quite obviously from the worst motives – with a large tortoiseshell beneath my very window, you will understand what I mean.

'My refusal to allow Webster to join me here is, I fear, puzzling my kind hostess, who knows how greatly I miss him, but I must be firm.

'Keep him, therefore, my dear Lancelot, until I call in person, when I shall remove him to the quiet rural retreat where I plan to spend the evening of my life.

'With every good wish to you both,
'Your affectionate uncle,
'THEODORE.'

Gladys Bingley had listened intently to this letter, and as Lancelot came to the end of it she breathed a sigh of relief.

'Well, that gives us a bit of time,' she said.

'Yes,' agreed Lancelot. 'Time to see if we can't awake in this animal some faint echo of its old self-respect. From today Webster goes into monastic seclusion. I shall take him round to the vet's, with instructions that he be forced to lead the simple life. In those pure surroundings, with no temptations, no late nights, plain food and a strict milk diet, he may become himself again.'

' "The Man Who Came Back",' said Gladys.

'Exactly,' said Lancelot.

And so for perhaps two weeks something approaching tranquillity reigned once more in my cousin Edward's son's studio in Bott Street, Chelsea. The veterinary surgeon issued encouraging reports. He claimed a distinct improvement in Webster's character and appearance, though he added that he would still not care to meet him at night in a lonely alley. And then one morning there arrived from his Uncle Theodore a telegram which caused the young man to knit his brows in bewilderment.

It ran thus:

'On receipt of this come immediately Widdrington Manor prepared for indefinite visit period Circumstances comma I regret to say comma necessitate innocent deception semicolon so will you state on arrival that you are my legal representative and have come to discuss important family matters with me period Will explain fully when see you comma but rest assured comma my dear boy comma that would not ask this were it not absolutely essential period Do not fail me period Regards to Webster.'

Lancelot finished reading this mysterious communication, and looked at Gladys with raised eyebrows. There is unfortunately in most artists a material streak which leads them to place an unpleasant interpretation on telegrams like this. Lancelot was no exception to the rule.

'The old boy's been having a couple,' was his verdict.

Gladys, a woman and therefore more spiritual, demurred.

'It sounds to me,' she said, 'more as if he had gone off his onion. Why should he want you to pretend to be a lawyer?'

'He says he will explain fully.'

'And how *do* you pretend to be a lawyer?'

Lancelot considered.

'Lawyers cough dryly, I know that,' he said. 'And then I suppose one would put the tips of the fingers together a good deal and talk about Rex *v.* Biggs Ltd and torts and malfeasances and so forth. I think I could give a reasonably realistic impersonation.'

'Well, if you're going, you'd better start practising.'

'Oh, I'm going all right,' said Lancelot. 'Uncle Theodore is evidently in trouble of some kind, and my place is by his side. If all goes well, I might be able to bite his ear before he sees Webster. About how much ought we to have in order to get married comfortably?'

'At least five hundred.'

'I will bear it in mind,' said Lancelot, coughing dryly and putting the tips of his fingers together.

Lancelot had hoped, on arriving at Widdrington Manor, that the first person he met would be his Uncle Theodore, explaining fully. But when the butler ushered him into the drawing-room only Lady Widdrington, her mother Mrs Pulteney-Banks, and her cat Percy were present. Lady Widdrington shook hands, Mrs Pulteney-Banks bowed from the arm-chair in which she sat swathed in shawls, but when Lancelot advanced with the friendly intention of tickling the cat Percy under the right ear, he gave the young man a cold, evil look out of the corner of his eye and, backing a pace, took an inch of skin off his hand with one well-judged swipe of a steel-pronged paw.

Lady Widdrington stiffened.

'I'm afraid Percy does not like you,' she said in a distant voice.

'They know, they know!' said Mrs Pulteney-Banks darkly. She knitted and purled a moment, musing. 'Cats are cleverer than we think,' she added.

Lancelot's agony was too keen to permit him even to cough dryly. He sank into a chair and surveyed the little company with watering eyes.

They looked to him a hard bunch. Of Mrs Pulteney-Banks he could see little but a cocoon of shawls, but Lady Widdrington was right out in the open, and Lancelot did not like her appearance. The chatelaine of Widdrington Manor was one of those agate-eyed, purposeful, tweed-clad women of whom rural England seems to have a monopoly. She was not unlike what he imagined Queen Elizabeth must have been in her day. A determined and vicious specimen. He marvelled that even a mutual affection for cats could have drawn his gentle uncle to such a one.

As for Percy, he was pure poison. Orange of body and inky-black of soul, he lay stretched out on the rug, exuding arrogance and hate. Lancelot, as I have said, was tolerant of toughness in cats, but there was about this animal none of Webster's jolly, whole-hearted, swashbuckling rowdiness. Webster was the sort of cat who would charge, roaring and ranting, to dispute with some rival the possession of a decaying sardine, but there was no more vice in him than in the late John L. Sullivan. Percy, on the other hand, for all his sleek exterior, was mean and bitter. He had no music in his soul, and was fit for treasons, stratagems and spoils. One could picture him stealing milk from a sick tabby.

Gradually the pain of Lancelot's wound began to abate, but it was succeeded by a more spiritual discomfort. It was plain to him that the recent episode had made a bad impression on the two women. They obviously regarded him with suspicion and dislike. The atmosphere was frigid, and conversation proceeded jerkily. Lancelot was glad when the dressing-gong sounded and he could escape to his room.

He was completing the tying of his tie when the door opened and the Bishop of Bongo-Bongo entered.

'Lancelot, my boy!' said the Bishop.

'Uncle!' cried Lancelot.

They clasped hands. More than four years had passed since these two had met, and Lancelot was shocked at the other's appearance. When last he had seen him, at the dear old deanery, his Uncle Theodore had been a genial, robust man who wore his gaiters with an air. Now, in some subtle way, he seemed to have shrunk. He looked haggard and hunted. He reminded Lancelot of a rabbit with a good deal on its mind.

The Bishop had moved to the door. He opened it and glanced along the passage. Then he closed it and tip-toeing back, spoke in a cautious undertone.

'It was good of you to come, my dear boy,' he said.

'Why, of course I came,' replied Lancelot heartily. 'Are you in trouble of some kind, Uncle Theodore?'

'In the gravest trouble,' said the Bishop, his voice a mere whisper. He paused for a moment. 'You have met Lady Widdrington?'

'Yes.'

'Then when I tell you that, unless ceaseless vigilance is exercised, I shall undoubtedly propose marriage to her, you will appreciate my concern.'

Lancelot gaped.

'But why do you want to do a potty thing like that?'

The Bishop shivered.

'I do not want to do it, my boy,' he said. 'Nothing is further from my wishes. The salient point, however, is that Lady Widdrington and her mother want me to do it, and you must have seen for yourself that they are strong, determined women. I fear the worst.'

He tottered to a chair and dropped into it, shaking. Lancelot regarded him with affectionate pity.

'When did this start?' he asked.

'On board ship,' said the Bishop. 'Have you ever made an ocean voyage, Lancelot?'

'I've been to America a couple of times.'

'That can scarcely be the same thing,' said the Bishop, musingly. 'The transatlantic trip is so brief, and you do not get those nights of tropic moon. But even on your voyages to America you must have noticed the peculiar attitude towards the opposite sex induced by the salt air.'

'They all look good to you at sea,' agreed Lancelot.

'Precisely,' said the Bishop. 'And during a voyage, especially at night, one finds oneself expressing oneself with a certain warmth which even at the time one tells oneself is injudicious. I fear that on board the liner with Lady Widdrington, my dear boy, I rather let myself go.'

Lancelot began to understand.

'You shouldn't have come to her house,' he said.

'When I accepted the invitation, I was, if I may use a figure of speech, still under the influence. It was only after I had been here some ten days that I awoke to the realization of my peril.'

'Why didn't you leave?'

The Bishop groaned softly.

'They would not permit me to leave. They countered every excuse. I am virtually a prisoner in this house, Lancelot. The other day I said that I had urgent business with my legal adviser and that this made it imperative that I should proceed instantly to the metropolis.'

'That should have worked,' said Lancelot.

'It did not. It failed completely. They insisted that I invite my legal adviser down here where my business could be discussed in the calm atmosphere of the Hampshire countryside. I endeavoured to reason with them, but they were firm. You do not know how firm women can be,' said the Bishop, shivering, 'till you have placed yourself in my unhappy position. How well I appreciate now that powerful image of Shakespeare's – the one about grappling with hoops of steel. Every time I meet Lady Widdrington, I can feel those hoops drawing me ever closer to her. And the woman repels me even as that cat of hers repels me. Tell me, my boy, to turn for an instant to a pleasanter subject, how is my dear Webster?'

Lancelot hesitated.

'Full of beans,' he said.

'He is on a diet?' asked the Bishop anxiously. 'The doctor has ordered vegetarianism?'

'Just an expression,' explained Lancelot, 'to indicate robustness.'

'Ah!' said the Bishop, relieved. 'And what disposition have you made of him in your absence? He is in good hands, I trust?'

'The best,' said Lancelot. 'His host is the ablest veterinary in London – Doctor J. G. Robinson of 9 Bott Street, Chelsea, a man not only skilled in his profession but of the highest moral tone.'

'I knew I could rely on you to see that all was well with him,' said the Bishop emotionally. 'Otherwise, I should have shrunk from asking you to leave London and come here – strong shield of defence though you will be to me in my peril.'

'But what use can I be to you?' said Lancelot, puzzled.

'The greatest,' the Bishop assured him. 'Your presence will be invaluable. You must keep the closest eye upon Lady Widdrington and myself; and whenever you observe us wandering off together – she is assiduous in her efforts to induce me to visit the rose-garden in her company, for example – you must come hurrying up and detach me with the ostensible purpose of discussing legal matters. By these means we may avert what I had come to regard as the inevitable.'

'I understand thoroughly,' said Lancelot. 'A jolly good scheme. Rely on me.'

'The ruse I have outlined,' said the Bishop regretfully, 'involves, as I hinted in my telegram, a certain innocent deception, but at times like this one cannot afford to be too nice in one's methods. By the way, under what name did you make your appearance here?'

'I used my own.'

'I would have preferred Polkinghorne or Gooch or Withers,' said the Bishop pensively. 'They sound more legal. However, that is a small matter. The essential thing is that I may rely on you to – er – to—?'

'To stick around?'

'Exactly. To adhere. From now on, my boy, you must be my constant shadow. And if, as I trust, our efforts are rewarded, you will not find me ungrateful. In the course of a lifetime I have contrived to accumulate no small supply of this world's goods, and if there is any little venture or enterprise for which you require a certain amount of capital—'

'I am glad,' said Lancelot, 'that you brought this up, Uncle Theodore. As it so happens, I am badly in need of five hundred pounds – and could, indeed, do with a thousand.'

The Bishop grasped his hand.

'See me through this ordeal, my dear boy,' he said, 'and

you shall have it. For what purpose do you require this money?'

'I want to get married.'

'Ugh!' said the Bishop, shuddering strongly. 'Well, well,' he went on, recovering himself, 'it is no affair of mine. No doubt you know your own mind best. I must confess, however, that the mere mention of the holy state occasions in me an indefinable sinking feeling. But then, of course, you are not proposing to marry Lady Widdrington.'

'And nor,' cried Lancelot heartily, 'are you, uncle – not while I'm around. Tails up, Uncle Theodore, tails up!'

'Tails up!' repeated the Bishop dutifully, but he spoke the words without any real ring of conviction in his voice.

It was fortunate that, in the days which followed, my cousin Edward's son Lancelot was buoyed up not only by the prospect of collecting a thousand pounds, but also by a genuine sympathy and pity for a well-loved uncle. Otherwise, he must have faltered and weakened.

To a sensitive man – and all artists are sensitive – there are few things more painful than the realization that he is an unwelcome guest. And not even if he had had the vanity of a Narcissus could Lancelot have persuaded himself that he was *persona grata* at Widdrington Manor.

The march of civilization has done much to curb the natural ebullience of woman. It has brought to her the power of self-restraint. In emotional crises nowadays women seldom give physical expression to their feelings; and neither Lady Widdrington nor her mother, the aged Mrs Pulteney-Banks, actually struck Lancelot or spiked him with a knitting-needle. But there were moments when they seemed only by a miracle of strong will to check themselves from such manifestations of dislike.

As the days went by, and each day the young man skilfully broke up a promising *tête-à-tête*, the atmosphere grew more tense and electric. Lady Widdrington spoke dreamily of the excellence of the train service between Bottleby-in-the-Vale and London, paying a particularly marked tribute to the 8.45 a.m. express. Mrs Pulteney-Banks mumbled from among her shawls of great gowks – she did not specify more exactly, courteously refraining from naming names – who spent their time idling in the country (where they were not wanted) when their true duty and interest lay in the metropolis. The cat Percy, by word and look, continued to affirm his low opinion of Lancelot.

And, to make matters worse, the young man could see that his principal's *morale* was becoming steadily lowered. Despite the uniform success of their manoeuvres, it was evident that the strain was proving too severe for the Bishop. He was plainly cracking. A settled hopelessness had crept into his demeanour. More and more had he come to resemble a rabbit who, fleeing from a stoat, draws no cheer from the reflection that he is all right so far, but flings up his front paws in a gesture of despair, as if to ask what profit there can be in attempting to evade the inevitable.

And, at length, one night when Lancelot had switched off his light and composed himself for sleep, it was switched on again and he perceived his uncle standing by the bedside, with a haggard expression on his fine features

At a glance Lancelot saw that the good old man had reached breaking-point.

'Something the matter, uncle?' he asked.

'My boy,' said the Bishop, 'we are undone.'

'Oh, surely not?' said Lancelot, as cheerily as his sinking heart would permit.

'Undone,' repeated the Bishop hollowly. 'Tonight Lady

Widdrington specifically informed me that she wishes you to leave the house.'

Lancelot drew in his breath sharply. Natural optimist though he was, he could not minimize the importance of this news.

'She has consented to allow you to remain for another two days, and then the butler has instructions to pack your belongings in time for the eight-forty-five express.'

'H'm!' said Lancelot.

'H'm, indeed,' said the Bishop. 'This means that I shall be left alone and defenceless. And even with you sedulously watching over me it has been a very near thing once or twice. That afternoon in the summer-house!'

'And that day in the shrubbery,' said Lancelot. There was a heavy silence for a moment.

'What are you going to do?' asked Lancelot.

'I must think ... think,' said the Bishop. 'Well, good night, my boy.'

He left the room with bowed head, and Lancelot, after a long period of wakeful meditation, fell into a fitful slumber.

From this he was aroused some two hours later by an extraordinary commotion somewhere outside his room. The noise appeared to proceed from the hall, and, donning a dressing-gown, he hurried out.

A strange spectacle met his eyes. The entire numerical strength of Widdrington Manor seemed to have assembled in the hall. There was Lady Widdrington in a mauve *négligé*, Mrs Pulteney-Banks in a system of shawls, the butler in pyjamas, a footman or two, several maids, the odd-job man, and the boy who cleaned the shoes. They were gazing in manifest astonishment at the Bishop of Bongo-Bongo, who stood, fully clothed, near the front door, holding in one hand an umbrella, in the other a bulging suit-case.

In a corner sat the cat, Percy, swearing in a quiet undertone.

As Lancelot arrived the Bishop blinked and looked dazedly about him.

'Where am I?' he said.

Willing voices informed him that he was at Widdrington Manor, Bottleby-in-the-Vale, Hants, the butler going so far as to add the telephone number.

'I think,' said the Bishop, 'I must have been walking in my sleep.'

'Indeed?' said Mrs Pulteney-Banks, and Lancelot could detect the dryness in her tone.

'I am sorry to have been the cause of robbing the household of its well-earned slumber,' said the Bishop nervously. 'Perhaps it would be best if I now retired to my room.'

'Quite,' said Mrs Pulteney-Banks, and once again her voice crackled dryly.

'I'll come and tuck you up,' said Lancelot.

'Thank you, my boy,' said the Bishop.

Safe from observation in his bedroom, the Bishop sank wearily on the bed, and allowed the umbrella to fall hopelessly to the floor.

'It is Fate,' he said. 'Why struggle further?'

'What happened?' asked Lancelot.

'I thought matters over,' said the Bishop, 'and decided that my best plan would be to escape quietly under cover of the night. I had intended to wire to Lady Widdrington on the morrow that urgent matters of personal importance had necessitated a sudden visit to London. And just as I was getting the front door open I trod on that cat.'

'Percy?'

'Percy,' said the Bishop bitterly. 'He was prowling about in the hall, on who knows what dark errand. It is some small satisfaction to me in my distress to recall that I must have flattened out his tail properly. I came down on it with my full weight, and I am not a slender man. Well,' he said, sighing drearily, 'this is the end. I give up. I yield.'

'Oh, don't say that, uncle.'

'I do say that,' replied the Bishop, with some asperity. 'What else is there to say?'

It was a question which Lancelot found himself unable to answer. Silently he pressed the other's hand, and walked out.

In Mrs Pulteney-Banks's room, meanwhile, an earnest conference was taking place.

'Walking in his sleep, indeed!' said Mrs Pulteney-Banks.

Lady Widdrington seemed to take exception to the older woman's tone.

'Why shouldn't he walk in his sleep?' she retorted.

'Why should he?'

'Because he was worrying.'

'Worrying!' sniffed Mrs Pulteney-Banks.

'Yes, worrying,' said Lady Widdrington, with spirit. 'And I know why. You don't understand Theodore as I do.'

'As slippery as an eel,' grumbled Mrs Pulteney-Banks. 'He was trying to sneak off to London.'

'Exactly,' said Lady Widdrington. 'To his cat. You don't understand what it means to Theodore to be separated from his cat. I have noticed for a long time that he was restless and ill at ease. The reason is obvious. He is pining for Webster. I know what it is myself. That time when Percy was lost for two days I nearly went off my head. Directly after breakfast tomorrow I shall wire to Doctor Robinson of Bott Street, Chelsea, in whose charge Webster now is, to send him down here by the first train. Apart from anything else, he will be nice company for Percy.'

'Tchah!' said Mrs Pulteney-Banks.

'What do you mean, Tchah?' demanded Lady Widdrington.

'I mean Tchah,' said Mrs Pulteney-Banks.

An atmosphere of constraint hung over Widdrington Manor throughout the following day. The natural embarrassment of the Bishop was increased by the attitude of Mrs Pulteney-Banks, who had contracted a habit of looking at him over her zareba of shawls and sniffing meaningly. It was with relief that towards the middle of the afternoon he accepted Lancelot's suggestion that they should repair to the study and finish up what remained of their legal business.

The study was on the ground floor, looking out on pleasant lawns and shrubberies. Through the open window came the scent of summer flowers. It was a scene which should have soothed the most bruised soul, but the Bishop was plainly unable to draw refreshment from it. He sat with his head in his hands, refusing all Lancelot's well-meant attempts at consolation.

'Those sniffs!' he said, shuddering, as if they still rang in his ears. 'What meaning they held! What a sinister significance!'

'She may just have got a cold in the head,' urged Lancelot.

'No. The matter went deeper than that. They meant that that terrible old woman saw through my subterfuge last night. She read me like a book. From now on there will be added vigilance. I shall not be permitted out of their sight, and the end can be only a question of time. Lancelot, my boy,' said the Bishop, extending a trembling hand pathetically towards his nephew, 'you are a young man on the threshold of life. If you wish that life to be a happy one, always remember this: when on an ocean voyage, never visit the boat-deck after dinner. You will be tempted. You will say to yourself that the lounge is stuffy and that the cool breezes will correct that replete feeling which so many of us experience after the evening meal ... you will think how pleasant it must be up there, with the rays of the moon turning the waves to molten silver ... but don't go, my boy, don't go!'

'Right-ho, uncle,' said Lancelot soothingly.

The Bishop fell into a moody silence.

'It is not merely,' he resumed, evidently having followed some train of thought, 'that, as one of Nature's bachelors, I regard the married state with alarm and concern. It is the peculiar conditions of my tragedy that render me distraught. My lot once linked to that of Lady Widdrington, I shall never see Webster again.'

'Oh, come, uncle. This is morbid.'

The Bishop shook his head.

'No,' he said. 'If this marriage takes place, my path and Webster's must divide. I could not subject that pure cat to life at Widdrington Manor, a life involving, as it would, the constant society of the animal Percy. He would be contaminated. You know Webster, Lancelot. He has been your companion – may I not almost say your mentor? – for months. You know the loftiness of his ideals.'

For an instant, a picture shot through Lancelot's mind – the picture of Webster, as he had seen him only a brief while since – standing in the yard with the backbone of a herring in his mouth, crooning a war-song at the alley cat from whom he had stolen the *bonne-bouche*. But he replied without hesitation.

'Oh, rather.'

'They are very high.'

'Extremely high.'

'And his dignity,' said the Bishop. 'I deprecate a spirit of pride and self-esteem, but Webster's dignity was not tainted with those qualities. It rested on a clear conscience and the knowledge that, even as a kitten, he had never permitted his feet to stray. I wish you could have seen Webster as a kitten, Lancelot.'

'I wish I could, uncle.'

'He never played with balls of wool, preferring to sit in the shadow of the cathedral wall, listening to the clear singing of the choir as it melted on the sweet stillness of the summer day. Even then you could see that deep thoughts exercised his mind. I remember once . . .'

But the reminiscence, unless some day it made its appearance in the good old man's memoirs, was destined to be lost to the world. For at this moment the door opened and the butler entered. In his arms he bore a hamper, and from this hamper there proceeded the wrathful ejaculations of a cat who has had a long train-journey under constricted conditions and is beginning to ask what it is all about.

'Bless my soul!' cried the Bishop, startled.

A sickening sensation of doom darkened Lancelot's soul. He had recognized that voice. He knew what was in that hamper.

'Stop!' he exclaimed. 'Uncle Theodore, don't open that hamper!'

But it was too late. Already the Bishop was cutting the strings with a hand that trembled with eagerness. Chirruping noises proceeded from him. In his eyes was the wild gleam seen only in the eyes of cat-lovers restored to their loved one.

'Webster!' he called in a shaking voice.

And out of the hamper shot Webster, full of strange oaths. For a moment he raced about the room, apparently searching for the man who had shut him up in the thing, for there was flame in his eye. Becoming calmer, he sat down and began to lick himself, and it was then for the first time that the Bishop was enabled to get a steady look at him.

Two weeks' residence at the vet's had done something for Webster, but not enough. Not, Lancelot felt agitatedly, nearly enough. A mere fortnight's seclusion cannot bring back fur to lacerated skin; it cannot restore to a chewed ear that extra inch which makes all the difference. Webster had gone to Doctor Robinson looking as if he had just been caught in machinery of some kind, and that was how, though in a very slightly modified degree, he looked now. And at the sight of him the Bishop uttered a sharp, anguished cry. Then, turning on Lancelot, he spoke in a voice of thunder.

'So this, Lancelot Mulliner, is how you have fulfilled your sacred trust!'

Lancelot was shaken, but he contrived to reply.

'It wasn't my fault, uncle. There was no stopping him.'

'Pshaw!'

'Well, there wasn't,' said Lancelot. 'Besides, what harm is there in an occasional healthy scrap with one of the neighbours? Cats will be cats.'

'A sorry piece of reasoning,' said the Bishop, breathing heavily.

'Personally,' Lancelot went on, though speaking dully, for he realized how hopeless it all was, 'if I owned Webster, I should be proud of him. Consider his record,' said Lancelot, warming a little as he proceeded. 'He comes to Bott Street without so much as a single fight under his belt, and, despite this inexperience, shows himself possessed of such genuine natural talent that in two weeks he has every cat for streets around jumping walls and climbing lamp-posts at the mere sight of him. I wish,' said Lancelot, now carried away by his theme, 'that you could have seen him clean up a puce-coloured Tom from Number Eleven. It was the finest sight

I have ever witnessed. He was conceding pounds to this animal, who, in addition, had a reputation extending as far afield as the Fulham Road. The first round was even, with the exchanges perhaps a shade in favour of his opponent. But when the gong went for Round Two . . .'

The Bishop raised his hand. His face was drawn.

'Enough!' he cried. 'I am inexpressibly grieved. I . . .'

He stopped. Something had leaped upon the windowsill at his side, causing him to start violently. It was the cat Percy who, hearing a strange feline voice, had come to investigate.

There were days when Percy, mellowed by the influence of cream and the sunshine, could become, if not agreeable, at least free from active venom. Lancelot had once seen him actually playing with a ball of paper. But it was evident immediately that this was not one of those days. Percy was plainly in evil mood. His dark soul gleamed from his narrow eyes. He twitched his tail to and fro, and for a moment stood regarding Webster with a hard sneer.

Then, wiggling his whiskers, he said something in a low voice.

Until he spoke, Webster had apparently not observed his arrival. He was still cleaning himself after the journey. But, hearing this remark, he started and looked up. And, as he saw Percy, his ears flattened and the battle-light came into his eye.

There was a moment's pause. Cat stared at cat. Then, swishing his tail to and fro, Percy repeated his statement in a louder tone. And from this point, Lancelot tells me, he could follow the conversation word for word as easily as if he had studied cat-language for years.

This, he says, is how the dialogue ran:

WEBSTER: Who, me?
PERCY: Yes, you.

WEBSTER: A what?

PERCY: You heard.

WEBSTER: Is that so?

PERCY: Yeah.

WEBSTER: Yeah?

PERCY: Yeah. Come on up here and I'll bite the rest of your ear off.

WEBSTER: Yeah? You and who else?

PERCY: Come on up here. I dare you.

WEBSTER (*flushing hotly*): You do, do you? Of all the nerve! Of all the crust! Why, I've eaten better cats than you before breakfast.

(*to Lancelot*)

Here, hold my coat and stand to one side. Now, then!

And, with this, there was a whizzing sound and Webster had advanced in full battle-order. A moment later, a tangled mass that looked like seventeen cats in close communion fell from the windowsill into the room.

A cat-fight of major importance is always a spectacle worth watching, but Lancelot tells me that, vivid and stimulating though this one promised to be, his attention was riveted not upon it, but upon the Bishop of Bongo-Bongo.

In the first few instants of the encounter the prelate's features had betrayed no emotion beyond a grievous alarm and pain. 'How art thou fallen from Heaven, oh Lucifer, Son of Morning,' he seemed to be saying as he watched his once blameless pet countering Percy's onslaught with what had the appearance of being about sixteen simultaneous legs. And then, almost abruptly, there seemed to awake in him at the same instant a passionate pride in Webster's prowess and that sporting spirit which lies so near the surface in all of us. Crimson in the face, his eyes gleaming with partisan enthusiasm, he danced round the combatants, encouraging his nominee with word and gesture.

'Capital! Excellent! Ah, stoutly struck, Webster!'

'Hook him with your left, Webster!' cried Lancelot.

'Precisely!' boomed the Bishop.

'Soak him, Webster!'

'Indubitably!' agreed the Bishop. 'The expression is new to me, but I appreciate its pith and vigour. By all means, soak him, my dear Webster.'

And it was at this moment that Lady Widdrington, attracted by the noise of battle, came hurrying into the room. She was just in time to see Percy run into a right swing and bound for the windowsill, closely pursued by his adversary. Long since Percy had begun to realize that, in inviting this encounter, he had gone out of his class and come up against something hot. All he wished for now was flight. But Webster's hat was still in the ring, and cries from without told that the battle had been joined once more on the lawn.

Lady Widdrington stood appalled. In the agony of beholding her pet so manifestly getting the loser's end she had forgotten her matrimonial plans. She was no longer the calm, purposeful woman who intended to lead the Bishop to the altar if she had to use chloroform; she was an outraged cat-lover, and she faced him with blazing eyes.

'What,' she demanded, 'is the meaning of this?'

The Bishop was still labouring under obvious excitement.

'That beastly animal of yours asked for it, and did Webster give it to him!'

'Did he!' said Lancelot. 'That corkscrew punch with the left!'

'That sort of quick upper-cut with the right!' cried the Bishop.

'There isn't a cat in London that could beat him.'

'In London?' said the Bishop warmly. 'In the whole of England. O admirable Webster!'

Lady Widdrington stamped a furious foot.

'I insist that you destroy that cat!'

'Which cat?'

'That cat,' said Lady Widdrington, pointing.

Webster was standing on the windowsill. He was panting slightly, and his ear was in worse repair than ever, but on his face was the satisfied smile of a victor. He moved his head from side to side, as if looking for the microphone through which his public expected him to speak a modest word or two.

'I demand that that savage animal be destroyed,' said Lady Widdrington.

The Bishop met her eye steadily.

'Madam,' he replied, 'I shall sponsor no such scheme.'

'You refuse?'

'Most certainly I refuse. Never have I esteemed Webster so highly as at this moment. I consider him a public benefactor, a selfless altruist. For years every right-thinking person must have yearned to handle that inexpressibly abominable cat of yours as Webster has just handled him, and I have no feelings towards him but those of gratitude and admiration. I intend, indeed, personally and with my own hands to give him a good plate of fish.'

Lady Widdrington drew in her breath sharply.

'You will not do it here,' she said.

She pressed the bell.

'Fotheringay,' she said in a tense, cold voice, as the butler appeared, 'the Bishop is leaving us tonight. Please see that his bags are packed for the six-forty-one.'

She swept from the room. The Bishop turned to Lancelot with a benevolent smile.

'It will just give me nice time,' he said, 'to write you that cheque, my boy.'

He stooped and gathered Webster into his arms, and Lancelot, after one quick look at them, stole silently out. This sacred moment was not for his eyes.

CATS AND
THEIR PEOPLE

*'He and the Cat looked at each other across that impassable
barrier of silence which has been set between man and beast from
the creation of the world.'*
— MARY E. WILKINS FREEMAN, 'The Cat'

RUDYARD KIPLING

THE CAT THAT WALKED BY HIMSELF

HEAR AND ATTEND and listen; for this befell and behappened and became and was, O my Best Beloved, when the Tame animals were wild. The Dog was wild, and the Horse was wild, and the Cow was wild, and the Sheep was wild, and the Pig was wild – as wild as wild could be – and they walked in the Wet Wild Woods by their wild lones. But the wildest of all the wild animals was the Cat. He walked by himself, and all places were alike to him.

Of course the Man was wild too. He was dreadfully wild. He didn't even begin to be tame till he met the Woman, and she told him that she did not like living in his wild ways. She picked out a nice dry Cave, instead of a heap of wet leaves, to lie down in; and she strewed clean sand on the floor; and she lit a nice fire of wood at the back of the Cave; and she hung a dried wild-horse skin, tail-down, across the opening of the Cave; and she said, 'Wipe your feet, dear, when you come in, and now we'll keep house.'

That night, Best Beloved, they ate wild sheep roasted on the hot stones, and flavoured with wild garlic and wild pepper; and wild duck stuffed with wild rice and wild fenugreek and wild coriander; and marrow-bones of wild oxen; and wild cherries, and wild grenadillas. Then the Man went to sleep in front of the fire ever so happy; but the Woman sat up, combing her hair. She took the bone of the shoulder of mutton – the big flat blade-bone – and she looked at the wonderful marks on it, and she threw more wood on the fire, and she made a Magic. She made the First Singing Magic in the world.

Out in the Wet Wild Woods all the wild animals gathered together where they could see the light of the fire a long way off, and they wondered what it meant.

Then Wild Horse stamped with his wild foot and said, 'O my Friends and O my Enemies, why have the Man and the Woman made that great light in that great Cave, and what harm will it do us?'

Wild Dog lifted up his wild nose and smelled the smell of the roast mutton, and said, 'I will go up and see and look, and say; for I think it is good. Cat, come with me.'

'Nenni!' said the Cat. 'I am the Cat who walks by himself, and all places are alike to me. I will not come.'

'Then we can never be friends again,' said Wild Dog, and he trotted off to the Cave. But when he had gone a little way the Cat said to himself, 'All places are alike to me. Why should I not go too and see and look and come away at my own liking?' So he slipped after Wild Dog softly, very softly, and hid himself where he could hear everything.

When Wild Dog reached the mouth of the Cave he lifted up the dried horse-skin with his nose and sniffed the beautiful smell of the roast mutton, and the Woman, looking at the blade-bone, heard him, and laughed, and said, 'Here comes the first. Wild Thing out of the Wild Woods, what do you want?'

Wild Dog said, 'O my Enemy and Wife of my Enemy, what is this that smells so good in the Wild Woods?'

Then the Woman picked up a roasted mutton-bone and threw it to Wild Dog, and said, 'Wild Thing out of the Wild Woods, taste and try.' Wild Dog gnawed the bone, and it was more delicious than anything he had ever tasted, and he said, 'O my Enemy and Wife of my Enemy, give me another.'

The Woman said, 'Wild Thing out of the Wild Woods, help my Man to hunt through the day and guard this Cave at night, and I will give you as many roast bones as you need.'

'Ah!' said the Cat, listening. 'This is a very wise Woman, but she is not so wise as I am.'

Wild Dog crawled into the Cave and laid his head on the Woman's lap, and said, 'O my Friend and Wife of my Friend, I will help your Man to hunt through the day, and at night I will guard your Cave.'

'Ah!' said the Cat, listening. 'That is a very foolish Dog.' And he went back through the Wet Wild Woods waving his wild tail, and walking by his wild lone. But he never told anybody.

When the Man waked up he said, 'What is Wild Dog doing here?' And the Woman said, 'His name is not Wild Dog any more, but the First Friend, because he will be our friend for always and always and always. Take him with you when you go hunting.'

Next night the Woman cut great green armfuls of fresh grass from the water-meadows, and dried it before the fire, so that it smelt like new-mown hay, and she sat at the mouth of the Cave and plaited a halter out of horse-hide, and she looked at the shoulder-of-mutton bone – at the big broad blade-bone – and she made a Magic. She made the Second Singing Magic in the world.

Out in the Wild Woods all the wild animals wondered what had happened to Wild Dog, and at last Wild Horse stamped with his foot and said, 'I will go and see and say why Wild Dog has not returned. Cat, come with me.'

'Nenni!' said the Cat. 'I am the Cat who walks by himself, and all places are alike to me. I will not come.' But all the same he followed Wild Horse softly, very softly, and hid himself where he could hear everything.

When the Woman heard Wild Horse tripping and stumbling on his long mane, she laughed and said, 'Here comes the second. Wild Thing out of the Wild Woods, what do you want?'

Wild Horse said, 'O my Enemy and Wife of my Enemy, where is Wild Dog?'

The Woman laughed, and picked up the blade-bone and looked at it, and said, 'Wild Thing out of the Wild Woods, you did not come here for Wild Dog, but for the sake of this good grass.'

And Wild Horse, tripping and stumbling on his long mane, said, 'That is true; give it me to eat.'

The Woman said, 'Wild Thing out of the Wild Woods, bend your wild head and wear what I give you, and you shall eat the wonderful grass three times a day.'

'Ah,' said the Cat, listening, 'this is a clever Woman, but she is not so clever as I am.'

Wild Horse bent his wild head, and the Woman slipped the plaited hide halter over it, and Wild Horse breathed on the Woman's feet and said, 'O my Mistress, and Wife of my Master, I will be your servant for the sake of the wonderful grass.'

'Ah,' said the Cat, listening, 'that is a very foolish Horse.' And he went back through the Wet Wild Woods, waving his wild tail and walking by his wild lone. But he never told anybody.

When the Man and the Dog came back from hunting, the Man said, 'What is Wild Horse doing here?' And the Woman said, 'His name is not Wild Horse any more, but the First Servant, because he will carry us from place to place for always and always and always. Ride on his back when you go hunting.'

Next day, holding her wild head high that her wild horns

should not catch in the wild trees, Wild Cow came up to the Cave, and the Cat followed, and hid himself just the same as before; and everything happened just the same as before; and the Cat said the same things as before; and when Wild Cow had promised to give her milk to the Woman every day in exchange for the wonderful grass, the Cat went back through the Wet Wild Woods waving his wild tail and walking by his wild lone, just the same as before. But he never told anybody. And when the Man and the Horse and the Dog came home from hunting and asked the same questions same as before, the Woman said, 'Her name is not Wild Cow any more, but the Giver of Good Food. She will give us the warm white milk for always and always and always, and I will take care of her while you and the First Friend and the First Servant go hunting.'

Next day the Cat waited to see if any other Wild Thing would go up to the Cave, but no one moved in the Wet Wild Woods, so the Cat walked there by himself; and he saw the Woman milking the Cow, and he saw the light of the fire in the Cave, and he smelt the smell of the warm white milk.

Cat said, 'O my Enemy and Wife of my Enemy, where did Wild Cow go?'

The Woman laughed and said, 'Wild Thing out of the Wild Woods, go back to the Woods again, for I have braided up my hair, and I have put away the magic blade-bone, and we have no more need of either friends or servants in our Cave.'

Cat said, 'I am not a friend, and I am not a servant. I am the Cat who walks by himself, and I wish to come into your Cave.'

Woman said, 'Then why did you not come with First Friend on the first night?'

Cat grew very angry and said, 'Has Wild Dog told tales of me?'

Then the Woman laughed and said, 'You are the Cat who walks by himself, and all places are alike to you. You are neither a friend nor a servant. You have said it yourself. Go away and walk by yourself in all places alike.'

Then Cat pretended to be sorry and said, 'Must I never come into the Cave? Must I never sit by the warm fire? Must I never drink the warm white milk? You are very wise and very beautiful. You should not be cruel even to a Cat.'

Woman said, 'I knew I was wise, but I did not know I was beautiful. So I will make a bargain with you. If ever I say one word in your praise, you may come into the Cave.'

'And if you say two words in my praise?' said the Cat.

'I never shall,' said the Woman, 'but if I say two words in your praise, you may sit by the fire in the Cave.'

'And if you say three words?' said the Cat.

'I never shall,' said the Woman, 'but if I say three words in your praise, you may drink the warm white milk three times a day for always and always and always.'

Then the Cat arched his back and said, 'Now let the Curtain at the mouth of the Cave, and the Fire at the back of the Cave, and the Milk-pots that stand beside the Fire, remember what my Enemy and the Wife of my Enemy has said.' And he went away through the Wet Wild Woods waving his wild tail and walking by his wild lone.

That night when the Man and the Horse and the Dog came home from hunting, the Woman did not tell them of the bargain that she had made with the Cat, because she was afraid that they might not like it.

Cat went far and far away and hid himself in the Wet Wild Woods by his wild lone for a long time till the Woman forgot all about him. Only the Bat – the little upside-down

Bat – that hung inside the Cave knew where Cat hid; and every evening Bat would fly to Cat with news of what was happening.

One evening Bat said, 'There is a Baby in the Cave. He is new and pink and fat and small, and the Woman is very fond of him.'

'Ah,' said the Cat, listening, 'but what is the Baby fond of?'

'He is fond of things that are soft and tickle,' said the Bat. 'He is fond of warm things to hold in his arms when he goes to sleep. He is fond of being played with. He is fond of all those things.'

'Ah,' said the cat, listening, 'then my time has come.'

Next night Cat walked through the Wet Wild Woods and hid very near the cave till morning-time, and Man and Dog and Horse went hunting. The Woman was busy cooking that morning, and the Baby cried and interrupted. So she carried him outside the Cave and gave him a handful of pebbles to play with. But still the Baby cried.

Then the Cat put out his paddy-paw and patted the Baby on the cheek, and it cooed; and the Cat rubbed against its fat knees and tickled it under its fat chin with his tail. And the Baby laughed; and the Woman heard him and smiled.

Then the Bat – the little upside-down Bat – that hung in the mouth of the Cave said, 'O my Hostess and Wife of my Host and Mother of my Host's Son, a Wild Thing from the Wild Woods is most beautifully playing with your Baby.'

'A blessing on that Wild Thing whoever he may be,' said the Woman, straightening her back, 'for I was a busy woman this morning and he has done me a service.'

That very minute and second, Best Beloved, the dried horse-skin Curtain that was stretched tail-down at the mouth of the Cave fell down – *woosh!* – because it remembered the bargain she had made with the Cat; and when the

Woman went to pick it up – lo and behold! – the Cat was sitting quite comfy inside the Cave.

'O my Enemy and Wife of my Enemy and Mother of my Enemy,' said the Cat, 'it is I: for you have spoken a word in my praise, and now I can sit within the Cave for always and always and always. But still I am the Cat who walks by himself, and all places are alike to me.'

The Woman was very angry, and shut her lips tight and took up her spinning-wheel and began to spin.

But the Baby cried because the Cat had gone away, and the Woman could not hush it, for it struggled and kicked and grew black in the face.

'O my Enemy and Wife of my Enemy and Mother of my Enemy,' said the cat, 'take a strand of the thread that you are spinning and tie it to your spinning-whorl and drag it along the floor, and I will show you a Magic that shall make your Baby laugh as loudly as he is now crying.'

'I will do so,' said the Woman, 'because I am at my wits' end; but I will not thank you for it.'

She tied the thread to the little clay spindle-whorl and drew it across the floor, and the Cat ran after it and patted it with his paws and rolled head over heels, and tossed it backward over his shoulder and chased it between his hind legs and pretended to lose it, and pounced down upon it again, till the Baby laughed as loudly as it had been crying, and scrambled after the Cat and frolicked all over the Cave till it grew tired and settled down to sleep with the Cat in its arms.

'Now,' said Cat, 'I will sing the Baby a song that shall keep him asleep for an hour.' And he began to purr, loud and low, low and loud, till the Baby fell fast sleep. The Woman smiled as she looked down upon the two of them, and said, 'That was wonderfully done. No question but you are very clever, O Cat.'

That very minute and second, Best Beloved, the smoke of the Fire at the back of the Cave came down in clouds from the roof – *puff!* – because it remembered the bargain she had made with the Cat; and when it had cleared away – lo and behold! – the Cat was sitting quite comfy close to the fire.

'O my Enemy and Wife of my Enemy and Mother of my Enemy,' said the Cat, 'it is I: for you have spoken a second word in my praise, and now I can sit by the warm fire at the back of the Cave for always and always and always. But still I am the Cat who walks by himself, and all places are alike to me.'

Then the Woman was very very angry, and let down her hair and put more wood on the fire and brought out the broad blade-bone of the shoulder of mutton and began to make a Magic that should prevent her from saying a third word in praise of the Cat. It was not a Singing Magic, Best Beloved, it was a Still Magic; and by and by the Cave grew so still that a little wee-wee mouse crept out of a corner and ran across the floor.

'O my Enemy and Wife of my Enemy and Mother of my Enemy,' said the Cat, 'is that little mouse part of your Magic?'

'Ouh! Chee! No indeed!' said the Woman, and she dropped the blade-bone and jumped upon the footstool in front of the fire and braided up her hair very quick for fear that the mouse should run up it.

'Ah,' said the Cat, watching, 'then the mouse will do me no harm if I eat it?'

'No,' said the Woman, braiding up her hair, 'eat it quickly and I will ever be grateful to you.'

Cat made one jump and caught the little mouse, and the Woman said, 'A hundred thanks. Even the First Friend is not quick enough to catch little mice as you have done. You must be very wise.'

That moment and second, O Best Beloved, the Milk-pot that stood by the fire cracked in two pieces – *ffft!* – because it remembered the bargain she had made with the Cat; and when the Woman jumped down from the footstool – lo and behold! – the Cat was lapping up the warm white milk that lay in one of the broken pieces.

'O my Enemy and Wife of my Enemy and Mother of my Enemy,' said the Cat, 'it is I: for you have spoken three words in my praise, and now I can drink the warm white milk three times a day for always and always and always. But *still* I am the Cat who walks by himself, and all places are alike to me.'

Then the Woman laughed and set the Cat a bowl of the warm white milk and said, 'O Cat, you are as clever as a man, but remember that your bargain was not made with the Man or the Dog, and I do not know what they will do when they come home.'

'What is that to me?' said the Cat. 'If I have my place in the Cave by the fire and my warm white milk three times a day I do not care what the Man or the Dog can do.'

That evening when the Man and the Dog came into the Cave, the Woman told them all the story of the bargain, while the Cat sat by the fire and smiled. Then the Man said, 'Yes, but he has not made a bargain with *me* or with all proper Men after me.' Then he took off his two leather boots and he took up his little stone axe (that makes three) and he fetched a piece of wood and a hatchet (that is five altogether), and he set them out in a row and he said, 'Now we will make *our* bargain. If you do not catch mice when you are in the Cave for always and always and always, I will throw these five things at you whenever I see you, and so shall all proper Men do after me.'

'Ah,' said the Woman, listening, 'this is a very clever Cat, but he is not so clever as my Man.'

The Cat counted the five things (and they looked very knobby) and he said, 'I will catch mice when I am in the Cave for always and always and always; but *still* I am the Cat who walks by himself, and all places are alike to me.'

'Not when I am near,' said the Man. 'If you had not said that last I would have put all these things away for always and always and always; but now I am going to throw my two boots and my little stone axe (that makes three) at you whenever I meet you. And so shall all proper Men do after me!'

Then the Dog said, 'Wait a minute. He has not made a bargain with *me* or with all proper Dogs after me.' And he showed his teeth and said, 'If you are not kind to the Baby while I am in the Cave for always and always and always, I will hunt you till I catch you, and when I catch you I will bite you. And so shall all proper Dogs do after me.'

'Ah,' said the Woman, listening, 'this is a very clever Cat, but he is not so clever as the Dog.'

Cat counted the Dog's teeth (and they looked very pointed) and he said, 'I will be kind to the Baby while I am in the Cave, as long as he does not pull my tail too hard, for always and always and always. But *still* I am the Cat that walks by himself, and all places are alike to me!'

'Not when I am near,' said the Dog. 'If you had not said that last I would have shut my mouth for always and always and always; but *now* I am going to hunt you up a tree whenever I meet you. And so shall all proper Dogs do after me.'

Then the Man threw his two boots and his little stone axe (that makes three) at the Cat, and the Cat ran out of the Cave and the Dog chased him up a tree; and from that day to this, Best Beloved, three proper Men out of five will always throw things at a Cat whenever they meet him, and all proper Dogs will chase him up a tree. But the Cat keeps his side of the bargain too. He will kill mice, and he will be kind to Babies when he is in the house, just as long as they do not pull his tail too hard. But when he has done that, and between times, and when the moon gets up and night comes, he is the Cat that walks by himself, and all places are alike to him. Then he goes out to the Wet Wild Woods or up the Wet Wild Trees or on the Wet Wild Roofs, waving his wild tail and walking by his wild lone.

MARY E. WILKINS FREEMAN

THE CAT

THE SNOW WAS falling, and the Cat's fur was stiffly pointed with it, but he was imperturbable. He sat crouched, ready for the death-spring, as he had sat for hours. It was night – but that made no difference – all times were as one to the Cat when he was in wait for prey. Then too, he was under no constraint of human will, for he was living alone that winter. Nowhere in the world was any voice calling him; on no hearth was there a waiting dish. He was quite free except for his own desires, which tyrannized over him when unsatisfied as now. The Cat was very hungry – almost famished, in fact. For days the weather had been very bitter, and all the feebler wild things which were his prey by inheritance, the born serfs to his family, had kept, for the most part, in their burrows and nests, and the Cat's long hunt had availed him nothing. But he waited with the inconceivable patience and persistency of his race; besides, he was certain. The Cat was a creature of absolute convictions, and his faith in his deductions never wavered. The rabbit had gone in there between those low-hung pine boughs. Now her little doorway had before it a shaggy curtain of snow, but in there she was. The Cat had seen her enter, so like a swift grey shadow that even his sharp and practised eyes had glanced back for the substance following, and then she was gone. So he sat down and waited, and he waited still in the white night, listening angrily to the north wind starting in the upper heights of the mountains with distant screams, then swelling into an awful crescendo of rage, and swooping down with furious white wings of snow like a flock of fierce eagles into the valleys and ravines. The Cat was on the side of a mountain, on a wooded terrace. Above him a few feet away towered the rock ascent as steep as the wall of a cathedral. The Cat had never climbed it – trees were the ladders to his heights of life. He had often looked with wonder at the rock, and miauled bitterly and resentfully as man does in the face of a forbidding Providence. At his left was the sheer precipice. Behind him, with a short stretch of woody growth between, was the frozen perpendicular wall of a mountain stream. Before him was the way to his home. When the rabbit came out she was trapped; her little cloven feet could not scale such unbroken steeps. So the Cat waited. The place in which he was looked like a maelstrom of the wood. The tangle of trees and bushes clinging to the mountain-side with a stern clutch of roots, the prostrate trunks and branches, the vines embracing everything with strong knots and coils of growth, had a curious effect, as of things which had whirled for ages in a current of raging water, only it was not water, but wind, which had disposed everything in circling lines of yielding to its fiercest points of onset. And now over all this whirl of wood and rock and dead trunks and branches and vines descended the snow. It blew down like smoke over the rock-crest above; it stood in a gyrating column like some death-wraith of nature, on the level, then it broke over the edge of the precipice, and the Cat cowered before the fierce backward set of it. It was as if ice needles pricked his skin through his beautiful thick fur, but he never faltered and never once cried. He had nothing to gain from crying, and everything to lose; the rabbit would hear him cry and know he was waiting.

It grew darker and darker, with a strange white smother, instead of the natural blackness of night. It was a night of storm and death superadded to the night of nature. The mountains were all hidden, wrapped about, overawed, and tumultuously overborne by it, but in the midst of it waited, quite unconquered, this little, unswerving, living patience and power under a little coat of grey fur.

A fiercer blast swept over the rock, spun on one mighty foot of whirlwind athwart the level, then was over the precipice.

Then the Cat saw two eyes luminous with terror, frantic with the impulse of flight, he saw a little, quivering, dilating nose, he saw two pointing ears, and he kept still, with every one of his fine nerves and muscles strained like wires. Then the rabbit was out – there was one long line of incarnate flight and terror – and the Cat had her.

Then the Cat went home, trailing his prey through the snow.

The Cat lived in the house which his master had built, as rudely as a child's block-house, but staunchly enough. The snow was heavy on the low slant of its roof, but it would not settle under it. The two windows and the door were made fast, but the Cat knew a way in. Up a pine-tree behind the house he scuttled, though it was hard work with his heavy rabbit, and was in his little window under the eaves, then down through the trap to the room below, and on his master's bed with a spring and a great cry of triumph, rabbit and all. But his master was not there; he had been gone since early fall and it was now February. He would not return until spring, for he was an old man, and the cruel cold of the mountains clutched at his vitals like a panther, and he had gone to the village to winter. The Cat had known for a long time that his master was gone, but his reasoning was always sequential and circuitous; always for him what had been would be, and the more easily for his marvellous waiting powers so he always came home expecting to find his master.

When he saw that he was still gone, he dragged the rabbit off the rude couch which was the bed to the floor, put one little paw on the carcass to keep it steady, and began gnawing with head to one side to bring his strongest teeth to bear.

It was darker in the house than it had been in the wood, and the cold was as deadly, though not so fierce. If the Cat had not received his fur coat unquestioningly of Providence, he would have been thankful that he had it. It was a mottled grey, white on the face and breast, and thick as fur could grow.

The wind drove the snow on the windows with such force that it rattled like sleet, and the house trembled a little. Then all at once the Cat heard a noise, and stopped gnawing his rabbit and listened, his shining green eyes fixed upon a window. Then he heard a hoarse shout, a halloo of despair and entreaty; but he knew it was not his master come home, and he waited, one paw still on the rabbit. Then the halloo came again, and then the Cat answered. He said all that was essential quite plainly to his own comprehension. There was in his cry of response inquiry, information, warning, terror, and finally, the offer of comradeship; but the man outside did not hear him, because of the howling of the storm.

Then there was a great battering pound at the door, then another, and another. The Cat dragged his rabbit under the bed. The blows came thicker and faster. It was a weak arm which gave them, but it was nerved by desperation. Finally the lock yielded, and the stranger came in. Then the Cat, peering from under the bed, blinked with a sudden light, and his green eyes narrowed. The stranger struck a match and looked about. The Cat saw a face wild and blue with hunger and cold, and a man who looked poorer and older than his poor old master, who was an outcast among men for his poverty and lowly mystery of antecedents; and he heard a muttered, unintelligible voicing of distress from the harsh piteous mouth. There was in it both profanity and prayer, but the Cat knew nothing of that.

The stranger braced the door which he had forced, got some wood from the stock in the corner, and kindled a fire in the old stove as quickly as his half-frozen hands would allow. He shook so pitiably as he worked that the Cat under the bed felt the tremor of it. Then the man, who was small and feeble and marked with the scars of suffering which he had pulled down upon his own head, sat down in one of the old chairs and crouched over the fire as if it were the one love and desire of his soul, holding out his yellow hands like yellow claws, and he groaned. The Cat came out from under the bed and leaped up on his lap with the rabbit. The man gave a great shout and start of terror, and sprang, and the Cat slid clawing to the floor, and the rabbit fell inertly, and the man leaned, gasping with fright, and ghastly, against the wall. The Cat grabbed the rabbit by the slack of its neck and dragged it to the man's feet. Then he raised his shrill, insistent cry, he arched his back high, his tail was a splendid waving plume. He rubbed against the man's feet, which were bursting out of their torn shoes.

The man pushed the Cat away, gently enough, and began searching about the little cabin. He even climbed painfully the ladder to the loft, lit a match, and peered up in the darkness with straining eyes. He feared lest there might be a man, since there was a cat. His experience with men had not been pleasant, and neither had the experience of men been pleasant with him. He was an old wandering Ishmael among his kind; he had stumbled upon the house of a brother, and the brother was not at home, and he was glad.

He returned to the Cat, and stooped stiffly and stroked his back, which the animal arched like the spring of a bow.

Then he took up the rabbit and looked at it eagerly by the

firelight. His jaws worked. He could almost have devoured it raw. He fumbled – the Cat close at his heels – around some rude shelves and a table, and found, with a grunt of self-gratulation, a lamp with oil in it. That he lighted; then he found a frying-pan and a knife, and skinned the rabbit, and prepared it for cooking, the Cat always at his feet.

When the odour of the cooking flesh filled the cabin, both the man and the Cat looked wolfish. The man turned the rabbit with one hand and stooped to pat the Cat with the other. The Cat thought him a fine man. He loved him with all his heart, though he had known him such a short time, and though the man had a face both pitiful and sharply set at variance with the best of things.

It was a face with the grimy grizzle of age upon it, with fever hollows in the cheeks, and the memories of wrong in the dim eyes, but the Cat accepted the man unquestioningly and loved him. When the rabbit was half cooked, neither the man nor the Cat would wait any longer. The man took it from the fire, divided it exactly in halves, gave the Cat one, and took the other himself. Then they ate.

Then the man blew out the light, called the Cat to him, got on the bed, drew up the ragged coverings, and fell asleep with the Cat in his bosom.

The man was the Cat's guest all the rest of the winter, and winter is long in the mountains. The rightful owner of the little hut did not return until May. All that time the Cat toiled hard, and he grew rather thin himself, for he shared everything except mice with his guest; and sometimes game was wary, and the fruit of patience of days was very little for two. The man was ill and weak, however, and unable to eat much, which was fortunate, since he could not hunt for himself. All day long he lay on the bed, or else sat crouched over the fire. It was a good thing that fire-wood was ready at hand for the picking up, not a stone's-throw from the door, for that he had to attend to himself.

The Cat foraged tirelessly. Sometimes he was gone for days together, and at first the man used to be terrified, thinking he would never return; then he would hear the familiar cry at the door, and stumble to his feet and let him in. Then the two would dine together, sharing equally; then the Cat would rest and purr, and finally sleep in the man's arms.

Towards spring the game grew plentiful; more wild little quarry were tempted out of their homes, in search of love as well as food. One day the Cat had luck – a rabbit, a partridge, and a mouse. He could not carry them all at once, but finally he had them together at the house door. Then he cried, but no one answered. All the mountain streams were loosened, and the air was full of the gurgle of many waters, occasionally pierced by a bird-whistle. The trees rustled with a new sound to the spring wind; there was a flush of rose and gold-green on the breasting surface of a distant mountain seen through an opening in the wood. The tips of the bushes were swollen and glistening red, and now and then there was a flower, but the Cat had nothing to do with flowers. He stood beside his booty at the house door, and cried and cried with his insistent triumph and complaint and pleading, but no one came to let him in. Then the cat left his little treasures at the door, and went around to the back of the house to the pine-tree, and was up the trunk with a wild scramble, and in through his little window, and down through the trap to the room, and the man was gone.

The Cat cried again – that cry of the animal for human companionship which is one of the sad notes of the world; he looked in all the corners; he sprang to the chair at the window and looked out; but no one came. The man was gone and he never came again.

The Cat ate his mouse out on the turf beside the house; the rabbit and the partridge he carried painfully into the house, but the man did not come to share them. Finally, in the course of a day or two, he ate them up himself, then he slept a long time on the bed, and when he waked the man was not there.

Then the Cat went forth to his hunting-grounds again, and came home at night with a plump bird, reasoning with his tireless persistency in expectancy that the man would be there; and there was a light in the window, and when he cried his old master opened the door and let him in.

His master had strong comradeship with the Cat, but not affection. He never patted him like that gentler outcast, but he had a pride in him and an anxiety for his welfare, though he had left him alone all winter without scruple. He feared lest some misfortune might have come to the Cat, though he was so large of his kind, and a mighty hunter. Therefore, when he saw him at the door in all the glory of his glossy winter coat, his white breast and face shining like snow in the sun, his own face lit up with welcome, and the Cat embraced his feet with his sinuous body vibrant with rejoicing purrs.

The Cat had his bird to himself, for his master had his own supper already cooking on the stove. After supper the Cat's master took his pipe, and sought a small store of tobacco which he had left in his hut over winter. He had thought often of it; that and the Cat seemed something to come home to in the spring. But the tobacco was gone; not a dust left. The man swore a little in a grim monotone, which made the profanity lose its customary effect. He had been, and was, a hard drinker; he had knocked about the world until the marks of its sharp corners were on his very soul, which was thereby callused, until his very sensibility to loss was dulled. He was a very old man.

He searched for the tobacco with a sort of dull combativeness of persistency; then he stared with stupid wonder around the room. Suddenly many features struck him as being changed. Another stove-lid was broken; an old piece of carpet was tucked up over a window to keep out the cold; his fire-wood was gone. He looked and there was no oil left in his can. He looked at the covering on his bed; he took them up, and again he made that strange remonstrant noise in his throat. Then he looked again for his tobacco.

Finally he gave it up. He sat down beside the fire, for May in the mountains is cold; he held his empty pipe in his mouth, his rough forehead knitted, and he and the Cat looked at each other across that impassable barrier of silence which has been set between man and beast from the creation of the world.

WALTER DE LA MARE

BROOMSTICKS

MISS CHAUNCEY'S CAT, Sam, had been with her many years before she noticed anything unusual, anything *disturbing*, in his conduct. Like most cats who live under the same roof with but one or two humans, he had always been more sagacious than cats of a common household. He had learned Miss Chauncey's ways. He acted, that is, as nearly like a small mortal dressed up in a hairy coat as one could expect a cat to act. He was what is called an 'intelligent' cat.

But though Sam had learned much from Miss Chauncey, I am bound to say that Miss Chauncey had learned very little from Sam. She was a kind indulgent mistress; she could sew, and cook, and crochet, and make a bed, and read and write and cipher a little. And when she was a girl she used to sing 'Kathleen Mavourneen' to the piano. Sam, of course, could do nothing of this kind.

But then, Miss Chauncey could no more have caught and killed a mouse or a blackbird with her five naked fingers than she could have been Pope of Rome. Nor could she run up a six-foot brick wall, or leap clean from the hearth-mat in her parlor on to the shelf of her chimneypiece without disturbing a single ornament, or even tinkle one crystal glass-drop against another. Unlike Sam, she could not find her way in the dark, or by her sense of smell; or keep in good health by merely nibbling grass in the garden. If, moreover, as a little girl she had been held up by her feet and hands two or three feet above the ground and then dropped, she would have at once fallen plump on her back, whereas when Sam was only

159

a three-months-old, he could have managed to twist clean about in the air in twelve inches and come down on his four feet as firm as a table.

While Sam, then, had learned a good deal from Miss Chauncey, she had learned nothing from him. And even if she had been willing to be taught, it is doubtful if she would ever have proved even a promising pupil. What is more, she knew much less about Sam than he knew about his mistress – until, at least, that afternoon when she was doing her hair in the glass. And then she could hardly believe her own eyes. It was a moment that completely changed her views about Sam – and nothing after that experience was ever quite the same again.

Sam had always been a fine upstanding creature, his fur jet-black and silky, his eyes a lambent green, even in sunshine, and at night a-glow like green topazes. He was now full seven years of age, and had an unusually powerful miaou. Living as he did quite alone with Miss Chauncey at Post Houses, it was natural that he should become her constant companion. For Post Houses was a singularly solitary house, standing almost in the middle of Haggurdsdon Moor, just where two wandering byways cross each other like the half-closed blades of a pair of shears or scissors.

It was a mile and a half from its nearest neighbor, Mr Cullings, the carrier; and yet another quarter of a mile from the village of Haggurdsdon. Its roads were extremely ancient. They had been sheep-tracks long before the Romans came to England and had cut *their* roads from shore to shore. But for many years past few travelers or carts or even sheep with their shepherd came Miss Chauncey's way. You could have gazed from her windows for hours together, even on a summer's day, without seeing so much as a tinker's barrow or a gipsy's van.

Post Houses, too, was perhaps the ugliest house there ever was. Its four corners stood straight up on the moor like a house of nursery bricks. From its flat roof on a clear day the eye could see for miles across the moor, Mr Cullings' cottage being out of sight in a shallow hollow. It had belonged to Miss Chauncey's ancestors for numbers of generations. Many people in Haggurdsdon indeed called it Chauncey's. And though in a great wind it was almost as full of noises as an organ, though it was a cold barn in winter and though another branch of the family had as far back as the 'seventies gone to live in the Isle of Wight, Miss Chauncey still remained faithful to its four walls. In fact she loved the ugly old place, for she had lived in it ever since she was a little girl with knickerbockers showing under her skirts and pale-blue ribbon shoulder knots.

This fact alone made Sam's conduct the more reprehensible, for never cat had kinder mistress. Miss Chauncey herself was now about sixty years of age – fifty-three years older than Sam. She was five foot ten-and-a-half inches in height. On week-days she wore black alpaca, and on Sundays a watered silk. Her large round steel spectacles straddling across her high nose gave her a look of being keen as well as cold. But truly she was neither. For even so stupid a man as Mr Cullings could take her in over the cartage charge of a parcel – just by looking tired or sighing as he glanced at his rough-haired, knock-kneed mare. And there was the warmest of hearts under her stiff bodice.

Being so far from the village, milk and cream were a little difficult, of course. But Miss Chauncey could deny Sam nothing – in reason. She paid a whole sixpence a week to a little girl called Susan Ard who brought these dainties from the nearest farm. They were dainties indeed, for though the grasses on Haggurdsdon Moor were of dark sour green, the cows that grazed on it gave an uncommonly rich milk, and Sam flourished on it. Mr Cullings called once a week on his round, and had a standing order to bring with him a few sprats or fresh herrings, or any other toothsome fish that was in season. Miss Chauncey would not even withhold her purse from expensive whitebait, if no other cheaper fish were procurable. And Mr Cullings would eye Sam fawning about his cartwheel, or gloating up at his dish, and say, ''Ee be a queer animal, shure enough; 'ee be a wunnerful queer animal, 'ee be.'

As for Miss Chauncey herself, she was a niggardly eater, though much attached to her tea. She made her own bread and cookies. On Saturday a butcher-boy drove up in a striped apron. Besides which she was a wonderful manager. Her cupboards were full of homemade jams and bottled fruits and dried herbs – everything of that kind, for Post Houses had a nice long strip of garden behind it, surrounded by a high old yellow brick wall.

Quite early in life Sam, of course, had learned to know his mealtime – though how he 'told' it was known only to himself, for he never appeared even to glance at the face of the grandfather's clock on the staircase. He was punctual, particularly in his toilet, and a prodigious sleeper. He had learned to pull down the latch of the back door, if, in the months when an open window was not to be found, he wished to go out. Indeed at last he preferred the latch. He never slept on Miss Chauncey's patchwork quilt, unless his own had been placed over it. He was particular almost to a foppish degree in his habits, and he was no thief. He had a mew on one note to show when he wanted something to eat; a mew a semitone or two higher if he wanted drink (that is, cold water, for which he had a great taste); and yet another mew – gentle and sustained – when he wished, so to speak, to converse with his mistress.

Not, of course, that the creature talked *English*, but he liked to sit up on one chair by the fireside, especially in the kitchen – for he was no born parlor-cat – and to look up at the glinting glasses of Miss Chauncey's spectacles, and then down awhile at the fire-flames (drawing his claws in and out as he did so, and purring the while), almost as if he might be preaching a sermon, or reciting a poem.

But this was in the happy days when all seemed well. This was in the days when Miss Chauncey's mind was innocent of all doubts and suspicions. Like others of his kind, too, Sam delighted to lie in the window and idly watch the birds in the apple-trees – tits and bullfinches and dunnocks – or to crouch over a mouse-hole for hours together. Such were his amusements (for he never ate his mice) while Miss Chauncey with cap and broom, duster and dishclout, went about her housework. But he also had a way of examining things in which cats are not generally interested. He as good as told Miss Chauncey one afternoon that a hole was coming in her parlor carpet. For he walked to and fro and back and forth with his tail up, until she attended to him. And he certainly warned her, with a yelp like an Amazonian monkey, when a red-hot coal had set her kitchen mat on fire.

He would lie or sit with his whiskers to the North before noonday, and due South afterwards. In general his manners were perfection. But occasionally when she called him, his face would appear to knot itself into a frown – at any rate to assume a low sullen look, as if he expostulated 'Why must you be interrupting me, Madam, when I am thinking of something else?' And now and then, Miss Chauncey fancied he would deliberately secrete himself or steal out and in of Post Houses unbeknown.

Miss Chauncey, too, would sometimes find him trotting from room to room as if on a visit of inspection. On his fifth birthday he had brought an immense mouse and laid it beside the patent toe-cap of her boot, as she sat knitting by the fire. She smiled and nodded merrily at him, as usual, but on this occasion he had looked at her intently, and then deliberately shook his head. After that, he never paid the smallest attention to mouse or mouse-hole or mousery, and Miss Chauncey was obliged to purchase a cheese-bait trap, else she would have been overrun.

Almost any domestic cat may do things of this nature, and of course all this was solely on Sam's domestic side. For he shared a house with Miss Chauncey and, like any two beings that lived together, he was bound to keep up certain appearances. He met her half-way, as the saying goes. When, however, he was 'on his own,' he was no longer Miss Chauncey's Sam, he was no longer merely the cat at Post Houses, but just *himself*. He went back, that is, to his own free independent life; to his own private habits.

Then the moor on which he roved was his own country, and the humans and their houses on it were no more to him in his wild, privy existence than molehills or badgers' earths, or rabbits' mounds, are to us. On this side of his life his mistress knew practically nothing. She did not consider it. She supposed that Sam behaved like other cats, though it was evident that at times he went far abroad, for he now and then brought home a Cochin China chick, and the nearest Cochin China fowls were at the vicarage, a good four miles off. Sometimes of an evening, too, when Miss Chauncey was taking a little walk herself, she would see him – a swiftly-moving black speck – far along the road, hastening home. And there was more purpose expressed in his gait and appearance than ever Mr Cullings showed!

It was pleasant to observe, too, when he came within miaouing distance how his manner changed. He turned at once from being a Cat into being a Domestic Cat. He was instantaneously no longer the Feline Adventurer, the Nocturnal Marauder and Haunter of Haggurdsdon Moor (though Miss Chauncey would not have so expressed it), but simply his mistress's spoiled pet, Sam. She loved him dearly. But, as again with human beings who are accustomed to live together, she did not *think* very much about him. It could not but be a shock then that latish afternoon, when without the slightest warning Miss Chauncey discovered that Sam was deliberately deceiving her!

She was brushing her thin brown front hair before her looking-glass. And this moment it hung down over her face like a fine loose veil. And as she always mused of other things when she was brushing her hair, she was somewhat absent-minded the while. Then suddenly on raising her eyes behind this mesh of hair, she perceived not only that Sam's reflection was in sight of the looking-glass, but that something a little mysterious was happening. Sam was sitting up as if to beg. There was nothing in that. It had been a customary feat of his since he was six months old. Still, for what might he be begging, no one by?

Now the window to the right of the chintz-valanced dressing-table was open at the top. Without, it was beginning to grow dark. All Haggurdsdon Moor lay hushed and still in the evening's coming gloom. And apart from begging when there was nothing to beg for, Sam seemed, so to speak, to be gesticulating with his paws. He appeared, that is, to be making signs, just as if there were someone or something looking in at the window at him from out of the air – which was quite impossible. And there was a look upon his face that certainly Miss Chauncey had never seen before.

She stayed a moment with her hair-brush uplifted, her long lean arm at an angle with her head. On seeing this, Sam

165

had instantly desisted from these motions. He had dropped to his fours again, and was now apparently composing himself for another nap. No; this too was a pretense, for presently as she watched, he turned restlessly about so that his whiskers were once again due South. His backward part toward the window, he was now gazing straight in front of him out of a far from friendly face. Far indeed from friendly for a creature that has lived with you ever since he opened the eyes of his first kittenhood.

As if he had read her thoughts, Sam at that moment lifted his head to look at his mistress; she withdrew her eyes to the glass only in the nick of time and when she turned from her toilet there sat he – so serene in appearance, so puss-like, so ordinary once more that Miss Chauncey could scarcely believe anything whatever had been amiss. Had her eyes deluded her – her glass? Was that peculiar motion of Sam's fore-paws (almost as if he were knitting), was that wide excited stare only due to the fact that he was catching what was, to her, an invisible fly?

Miss Chauncey having now neatly arranged her 'window-curtains' – the sleek loops of hair she wore on either side her high forehead – glanced yet again at the window. Nothing there but the silence of the moor; nothing there but the faint pricking of a star as the evening darkened.

Sam's cream was waiting on the hearthrug in the parlor as usual at five o'clock. The lamp was lit. The red blinds were drawn. The fire crackled in the grate. There they sat, these two; the walls of the four-cornered house beside the crossroads rising up above them like a huge oblong box under the immense starry sky that saucered in the wide darkness of the moor.

And while she so sat – with Sam there, seemingly fast asleep – Miss Chauncey was thinking. What had occurred in the bedroom that early evening had reminded her of other odd little bygone happenings. Trifles she had scarcely noticed but which now returned clearly to memory. How often in the past, for example, Sam at this hour would be sitting as if fast asleep (as now) his paws tucked neatly in, looking much like a stout alderman after a high dinner. And then suddenly, without warning, as if a distant voice had called him, he would leap to his feet and run straight out of the room. And somewhere in the house – door ajar or window agape, he would find his egress and be up and away into the night. This had been a common thing to happen.

Once, too, Miss Chauncey had found him squatting on his hindquarters on the window-ledge of a little room that had been entirely disused since her fair little Cousin Milly had stayed at Post Houses when Miss Chauncey was a child of eight. She had cried out at sight of him, 'You foolish Sam, you! Come in, sir. You will be tumbling out of the window next!' And she remembered as if it were yesterday that though at this he had stepped gingerly in at once from his dizzy perch, he had not looked at her. He had passed her without a sign.

On moonlight evenings, too – why, you could never be sure where he was. You could never be sure from what errand he had *returned*. Was she sure indeed where he was on *any* night? The longer she reflected, the deeper grew her doubts and misgivings. This night, at any rate, Miss Chauncey determined to keep watch. But she was not happy in doing so. She hated all manner of spying. They were old companions, Sam and she; and she, without him, in bleak Post Houses, would be sadly desolate. She loved Sam dearly. None the less, the spectacle of that afternoon haunted her, and it would be wiser to know all that there was to be known, even if for Sam's sake only.

Now Miss Chauncey always slept with her bedroom door ajar. She had slept so ever since her nursery days. Being a rather timid little girl, she liked in those far-away times to hear the grown-up voices downstairs and the spoons and forks clinking. As for Sam, he always slept in his basket beside her fireplace. Every morning there he would be, though on some mornings Miss Chauncey's eyes would open gently to find herself gazing steadily into his pale-green ones as he stood on his hind-paws, resting his front ones on her bed-side, and looking up into her face. 'Time for your milk, Sam?' his mistress would murmur. And Sam would mew, as distantly almost as a seagull in the height of the sky.

Tonight, however, Miss Chauncey only pretended to fall asleep. It was difficult, however, to keep wholly awake, and she was all but drowsing off when there came a faint squeak from the hinge of her door, and she realized that Sam was gone out. After waiting a moment or two, she struck a match. Yes, there was his empty basket in the dark silent room, and presently from far away – from the steeple at Haggurdsdon Village – came the knolling of midnight.

Miss Chauncey placed the dead end of the match in the saucer of her candlestick, and at that moment fancied she heard a faint *whssh* at her window, as of a sudden gust or scurry of wind, or the wings of a fast-flying bird – of a wild goose. It even reminded Miss Chauncey of half-forgotten Guy Fawkes Days and of the sound the stick of a rocket makes as it sweeps down through the air while its green and ruby lights die out in the immense heavens above. Miss Chauncey gathered up her long legs in the bed, drew on the flannel dressing-gown that always hung on her bed-rail, and lifting back the blind an inch or two, looked out of the window.

It was a high starry night, and a brightening in the sky above the roof seemed to betoken there must be a moon over the backward parts of the house. Even as she watched, a streak of pale silver descended swiftly out of the far spaces of the heavens where a few large stars were gathered as if in the shape of a sickle. It was a meteorite; and at that very instant Miss Chauncey fancied she heard a faint remote dwindling *whssh* in the air. Was *that* a meteor too? Could she have been deceived? Was she being deceived in everything? She drew back.

And then, as if in deliberate and defiant answer, out of the distance, from what appeared to be the extreme end of her long garden, where grew a tangle of sloe bushes, there followed a prolonged and as if half-secret caterwaul; very low-contralto, one might say – *Meearou-rou-rou-rou-rou.*

Heaven forbid! Was *that* Sam's tongue? The caterwauling ceased. Yet still Miss Chauncey could not suppress a shudder. She knew Sam's voice of old. But surely not that! Surely not that!

Strange and immodest, too, though it was to hear herself in that solitary place calling out in the dead of night, she none the less at once opened the window and summoned Sam by name. There was no response. The trees and bushes of the garden stood motionless; their faint shadows on the ground revealing how small a moon was actually in the sky, and how low it hung towards its setting. The vague undulations of the moor stretched into the distance. Not a light to be seen except those of the firmament. Again, and yet again, Miss Chauncey cried 'Sam, Sam! Come away in! Come away in, sir, you bad creature!' Not a sound. Not the least stir of leaf or blade of grass.

When, after so broken a night, Miss Chauncey awoke a little late the next morning, the first thing her eyes beheld when she sat up in bed was Sam – couched as usual in his basket. It was a mystery, an uneasy one. After supping up his morning bowl, he slept steadily on until noonday. This happened to be the day of the week when Miss Chauncey made bread. On and on, she steadily kneaded the dough with her knuckled hands, glancing ever and again towards the motionless creature. With fingers clotted from the great earthenware bowl, she stood over him at last for a few moments, and looked at him closely.

He was lying curled round with his whiskered face to one side towards the fire. And it seemed to Miss Chauncey that she had never noticed before that faint peculiar grin on his face. 'Sam!' she cried sharply. An eye instantly opened, fiercely green as if a mouse had squeaked. He stared at her for an instant; then the lid narrowed. The gaze slunk away a little, but Sam began to purr.

The truth of it is, all this was making Miss Chauncey exceedingly unhappy. Mr Cullings called that afternoon with a basket of some fine comely young sprats. 'Them'll wake his Royal Highness up,' he said. 'They'm fresh as daisies. Lor, m'm, what a Nero that beast be!'

'Cats *are* strange creatures, Mr Cullings,' replied Miss Chauncey reflectively, complacently, supposing that Mr Cullings had misplaced an *h* and had meant to say *an hero*. And Sam himself, with uplifted tail, and as if of the same opinion, was rubbing his head gently against her boot.

Mr Cullings eyed her closely. 'Why, yes, they be,' he said. 'What I says is, is that as soon as they're out of sight, you are out of their mind. There's no more gratitood nor affection in a cat than in a pump. Though so far as the pump is concerned, the gratitood should be on our side. I knew a Family of Cats once what fairly druv their mistress out of house and home.'

'But you wouldn't have a cat *only* a pet?' said Miss Chauncey faintly; afraid to ask for further particulars of the peculiar occurrence.

'Why no, m'm,' said the carrier. 'As the Lord made 'em, so they be. But I'll be bound they could tell some knotty stories if they had a human tongue in their heads!'

Sam had ceased caressing his mistress's foot, and was looking steadily at Mr Cullings, his hair roughed a little about the neck and shoulders. And the carrier looked back.

'No, m'm. We wouldn't keep 'em,' he said at last, 'if they was *four* times that size. Or, not for long!'

Having watched Mr Cullings' little cart bowl away into the distance, Miss Chauncey returned into the house, more disturbed than ever. Nor did her uneasiness abate when Sam refused even to sniff at his sprats. Instead, he crawled under a low table in the kitchen, behind the old seaman's chest in which Miss Chauncey kept her kindling-wood. She fancied she heard his claws working in the wood now and again; once he seemed to be expressing his natural feelings in what vulgar people with little sympathy for animals describe as 'swearing'.

Her caressing 'Sams', at any rate, were all in vain. His only reply was a kind of sneeze which uncomfortably resembled 'spitting'. Miss Chauncey's feelings had already been hurt. It was now her mind that suffered. Something the carrier had said, or the way he had said it, or the peculiar look she had noticed on his face when he was returning Sam's stare in the porch, haunted her thoughts. She was no longer young; was she becoming fanciful? Or must she indeed conclude that for weeks past Sam had been steadily deceiving her, or at any rate concealing his wanderings and his interests? What nonsense! Worse still: – Was she now so credulous as to believe that Sam had in actual fact been making signals – and secretly, behind her back – to some confederate that must either have been up in the sky, or in the moon!

Whether or not, Miss Chauncey determined to keep a sharper eye on him, if for his own sake only. She would at least make sure that he did not leave the house that night. But then: why not? she asked herself. Why shouldn't the creature choose his own hour and season? Cats, like owls, *see* best in the dark. They go best a-mousing in the dark, and may prefer the dark for their private, social, and even public affairs. Post Houses, after all, was only rather more than two miles from Haggurdsdon Village, and there were cats there in plenty. Poor fellow, her own dumb human company must sometimes be dull enough!

Such were Miss Chauncey's reflections; and as if to re-assure her, Sam himself at that moment serenely entered the room and leapt up on to the empty chair beside her tea-table. As if, too, to prove that he had thought better of his evil temper, or to insinuate that there had been nothing amiss between himself and Mr Cullings, he was licking his chops, and there was no mistaking the odor of fish which he brought in with him from his saucer.

'So you have thought better of it, my boy?' thought Miss Chauncey, though she did not utter the words aloud. And yet as she returned his steady feline gaze, she realized how difficult it was to read the intelligence behind those eyes. You might say that, Sam being only a cat, there was no meaning in them at all. But Miss Chauncey knew she couldn't have said it if such eyes had looked out of a *human* shape at her! She would have been acutely alarmed.

Unfortunately, and almost as if Sam had overheard his mistress's speculations regarding possible cat friends in the Village, there came at that moment a faint warbling mew beneath the open window. In a flash Sam was out of his chair and over the window-ledge, and Miss Chauncey rose only just in time to see him in infuriated pursuit of a slim sleek tortoise-shell creature that had evidently come to Post Houses in hope of a friendlier reception, and was now fleeing in positive fear of its life.

Sam returned from his chase as fresh as paint, and Miss Chauncey was horrified to detect – caught up between the claws of his right foot – a tuft or two of tortoise-shell fur, which, having composed himself by the fire, he promptly removed by licking.

Still pondering on these disquieting events, Miss Chauncey took her usual evening walk in the garden. Candytuft and Virginia stock were blossoming along the shell-lined path, and roses were already beginning to blow on the high brick wall which shut off her narrow strip of land from the vast lap of the moor. Having come to the end of the path, Miss Chauncey pushed on a little farther than usual, to where the grasses grew more rampant, and where wild headlong weeds raised their heads beneath her few lichenous apple trees. Still farther down – for hers was a long, though narrow, garden – there grew straggling bushes of sloe, spiny white-thorn. These had blossomed there indeed in the moor's bleak springs long before Post Houses had raised its chimney-pots into the sky. Here, too, flourished a dense drift of dead nettles – their sour odor haunting the air.

And it was in this forlorn spot that – like Robinson Crusoe before her – Miss Chauncey was suddenly brought to a standstill by the sight of what appeared to be nothing else than a strange footprint in the mould. Nearby the footprint, moreover, showed what might be the impression of a walking-cane or possibly of something stouter and heavier – a crutch. Could she again be deceived? The footprint, it was true, was unlike most human footprints, the heel sunk low, the toe square. Might it be accidental? *Was* it a footprint?

Miss Chauncey glanced up across the bushes toward the house. It loomed gaunt and forbidding in the moorland dusk. And she fancied she could see, though the evening light might be deceiving her, the cowering shape of Sam looking out at her from the kitchen-window. To be watched! To be herself spied upon – and watched.

But then, of course, Sam was always watching her. What oddity was there in that? Where else would his sprats come from, his cream, his saucer of milk, his bowl of fresh well-water? Nevertheless Miss Chauncey returned to her parlor gravely discomposed.

It was an uncommonly still evening, and as she went from room to room locking the windows, she noticed there was already a moon in the sky. She eyed it with misgiving. And at last bedtime came, and when Sam, as usual, after a lick or two had composed himself in his basket, Miss Chauncey, holding the key almost challengingly within view, deliber-ately locked her bedroom door.

When she awoke next morning Sam was sleeping in his basket as usual, and during the day-time he kept pretty closely to the house. So, too, on the Wednesday and the Thursday. It was not until the following Friday that having occasion to go into an upper bedroom that had no fireplace, and being followed as usual by Sam, Miss Chauncey detected the faint rank smell of soot in the room. No chimney, and a smell of soot! She turned rapidly on her companion; he had already left the room.

And when that afternoon she discovered a black sooty smear upon her own patchwork quilt, she realized not only that her suspicions had been justified, but that for the first time in his life Sam had deliberately laid himself down there in her absence. At this act of sheer defiance, she was no longer so much hurt as exceedingly angry. There was no doubt now.

Sam was deliberately defying her. No two companions could share a house on such terms as these. He must be taught a lesson.

That evening in full sight of the creature, having locked her bedroom door, she stuffed a large piece of mattress ticking into the mouth of her chimney and pulled down the register. Having watched these proceedings, Sam rose from his basket, and with an easy spring, leapt up on to the dressing-table. Beyond the window, the moor lay almost as bright as day. Ignoring Miss Chauncey, the creature squatted there steadily and openly staring into the empty skies, for a whole stretch of them was visible from where he sat.

Miss Chauncey proceeded to make her toilet for the night, trying in vain to pretend that she was entirely uninterested in what the animal was at. Faint sounds – not exactly mew-ings or growlings – but a kind of low inward caterwauling, hardly audible, was proceeding from his throat. But whatever these sounds might mean, Sam himself can have been the only listener. There was not a sign or movement at the window or in the world without. And then Miss Chauncey promptly drew down the blind. At this Sam at once raised his paw for all the world as if he were about to protest, and then, apparently thinking better of it, he pretended instead that the action had been only for the purpose of commencing his nightly wash.

Long after her candle had been extinguished, Miss Chauncey lay listening. Every stir and movement in the quiet darkness could be clearly followed. First there came a furtive footing and tapping at the register of the fireplace, so closely showing what was happening that Miss Chauncey could positively see in her imagination Sam on the hearth-stone, erecting himself there upon his hind-legs, vainly attempting to push the obstacle back.

175

This being in vain, he appeared to have dropped back on to his fours. Then came a pause. Had he given up his intention? No; now he was at the door, pawing, gently scratching. Then a leap, even towards the handle; but one only – the door was locked. Retiring from the door, he now sprang lightly again on to the dressing-table. What now was he at? By covertly raising her head a little from her pillow, Miss Chauncey could see him with paw thrust out, gently drawing back the blind from the moon-flooded window-pane. And even while she listened and watched, she heard yet again – and yet again – the faint *whssh* as of a wild swan cleaving the air; and then what might have been the cry of a bird, but which to Miss Chauncey's ears resembled a shrill cackle of laughter. At this Sam hastily turned from the window and without the least attempt at concealment pounced clean from the dressing-table on to the lower rail of her bed.

This unmannerly conduct could be ignored no longer. Poor Miss Chauncey raised herself in her sheets, pulled her night-cap a little closer down over her ears, and thrusting out her hand towards the chair beside the bed, struck a match and relit her candle. It was with a real effort that she then slowly turned her head and faced her night-companion. His hair was bristling about his body as if he had had an electric shock. His whiskers stood out at stiff angles with his jaws. He looked at least twice his usual size, and his eyes blazed in his head, as averting his face from her regard he gave vent to a low sustained *Miariou-rou-rou!*

'I say you shall *not*,' cried Miss Chauncey at the creature. At the sound of her words, he turned slowly and confronted her. And it seemed that until that moment Miss Chauncey had never actually seen Sam's countenance as in actual fact it really was. It was not so much the grinning tigerish look

176

it wore, but the sullen assurance upon it of what he wanted and that he meant to get it.

All thought of sleep was out of the question. Miss Chauncey could be obstinate too. The creature seemed to shed an influence on the very air which she could hardly resist. She rose from her bed and thrusting on her slippers made her way to the window. Once more a peculiar inward cry broke out from the bed-rail. She raised the blind and the light of the moon from over the moor swept in upon her little apartment. And when she turned to remonstrate with her pet at his ingratitude, and at all this unseemliness and the deceit of his ways, there was something so menacing and pitiless in his aspect that Miss Chauncey hesitated no more.

'Well, mark me!' she cried in a trembling voice, 'go out of the *door* you shan't. But if you enjoy soot, soot it shall be.'

With that she thrust back the register with the poker, and drew down the bundle of ticking with the tongs. And before the fit of coughing caused by the consequent smotheration that followed had ceased, the lithe black shape had sprung from the bed-rail, and with a scramble was into the hearth, over the fire-bars, up the chimney, and away.

Trembling from head to foot, Miss Chauncey sat down on a cane rocking-chair that stood nearby to reflect what next she must be doing. *Wh-ssh! Wh-ssh!* Again at the window came that mysterious rushing sound, but now the flurrying murmur as of a rocket shooting up with its fiery train of sparks thinning into space, rather than the sound of its descending stick. And then in the hush that followed, there sounded yet again, like a voice from the foot of the garden – a caterwauling piercing and sonorous enough to arouse the sleeping cocks in the Haggurdsdon hen-roosts and for miles around. Out of the distance their chanticleering broke shrill on the night air; to be followed a moment afterwards by the tardy clang of midnight from the church steeple. Then once more silence; utter quiet. Miss Chauncey returned to her bed, but that night she slept no more.

Her mind overflowed with unhappy thoughts. Her faith in Sam was gone. Far worse she had lost faith even in her affection for him. To have wasted that! – all the sprats, all the whitebait in the wide seas were as nothing by comparison. That Sam had wearied of her company was at least beyond question. It shamed her to think how much this meant to her – a mere animal! But she knew what was gone; knew how dull and spiritless in future the day's round would seem – the rising, the housework, the meals, a clean linen collar – the long, slow afternoon, forsaken and companionless! The solitary tea, her candle, prayers, bed – on and on. In what wild company was her cat Sam now? At her own refusal to face that horrid question it was as if she had heard the hollow clanging slam of an immense iron door.

Next morning – still ruminating on these strange events, grieved to the heart at this dreadful rift between herself and one who had been her honest companion of so many years; ashamed, too, that Sam should have had his way with her when she had determined not to allow him to go out during the night – the next morning Miss Chauncey, as if merely to take a little exercise, once again ventured down to the foot of her garden. A faint, blurred mark (such as she had seen on the previous evening) in the black mould of what *might* be a footprint is nothing very much.

But now – in the neglected patch beyond the bushes of white-thorn and bramble – there was no doubt in the world appeared the marks of many. And surely no cats' paw-prints these! Of what use, too, to a cat could a crutch or a staff be? A staff or crutch which – to judge from the impression it had left in the mould – must have been at least as thick as a broomstick.

More disquieted and alarmed than ever over this fresh mystery, Miss Chauncey glanced up and back towards the chimney-pots of the house, clearly and sharply fretted against the morning light of the eastern skies. And she realized what perils even so sure-footed a creature as Sam had faced when he skirred up out of the chimney in his wild effort to emerge into the night. Having thus astonishingly reached the rim of the chimney-pot – the burning stars above and the wilderness of the moor spread out far beneath and around him – he must have leaped from the top of the pot to a narrow brick ledge not three inches wide. Thence on to the peak of the roof and thence down a steep slippery slope of slates to a leaden gutter.

And how then? The thick tod of ivy matting the walls of the house reached hardly more than half-way up. Could Sam actually have plunged from gutter to tod? The very thought of such peril drew Miss Chauncey's steps towards the house again, in the sharpest anxiety to assure herself that he was still in the land of the living.

And lo and behold, when she was but half-way on her journey, she heard a succession of frenzied cries and catcalls in the air from over the moor. Hastily placing a flower-pot by the wall, she stood on tiptoe and peered over. And even now, at this very moment, in full sight across the nearer slope of the moor she descried her Sam, not now in chase of a fool ishly trustful visitor, but hotly pursued by what appeared to be the complete rabblement of Haggurdsdon's cats. Sore spent though he showed himself to be, Sam was keeping his distance. Only a few lank tabby gibs, and what appeared to be a gray-ginger Manx (unless he was an ordinary cat with his tail chopped off) were close behind.

'Sam! Sam!' Miss Chauncey cried, and yet again, 'Sam!' but

in her excitement and anxiety her foot slipped on the flower-pot and in an instant the feline chase had fallen out of sight. Gathering herself together again, she clutched a long besom or garden broom that was leaning against the wall, and rushed down to the point at which she judged Sam would make his entrance into the garden. She was not mistaken, nor an instant too soon. With a bound he was up and over, and in three seconds the rabble had followed in frenzied pursuit.

What came after Miss Chauncey could never very clearly recall. She could but remember plying her besom with might and main amid the rabble and mêlée of animals, while Sam, no longer a fugitive, turned on his enemies and fought them cat for cat. None the less, it was by no means an easy victory. And had not the over-fatted cur from the butcher's in Haggurdsdon – which had long since started in pursuit of this congregation of his enemies – had he not at last managed to overtake them, the contest might very well have had a tragic ending. But at the sound of his baying and at sight of the cur's teeth snapping at them as he vainly attempted to surmount the wall, Sam's enemies turned and fled in all directions. And faint and panting, Miss Chauncey was able to fling down her besom and to lean for a brief respite against the trunk of a tree.

At last she opened her eyes again. 'Well, Sam,' she managed to mutter at last, 'we got the best of them, then?'

But to her amazement she found herself uttering these friendly words into a complete vacancy. The creature was nowhere to be seen. His cream disappeared during the day, however, and by an occasional rasping sound Miss Chauncey knew that he once more lay hidden in his dingy resort behind the kindling-wood box. And there she did not disturb him.

Not until tea-time of the following day did Sam reappear. And then – after attending to his hurts – it was merely to sit with face towards the fire, sluggish and sullen and dumb as a dog. It was not Miss Chauncey's 'place' to make advances, she thought. She took no notice of the beast except to rub in a little hog's fat on the raw places of his wounds. She was rejoiced to find, however, that he kept steadily to Post Houses for the next few days, though her dismay was re-awakened at hearing on the third night a more dismal wailing and wauling than ever from the sloe-bushes, even while Sam himself sat motionless beside the fire. His ears twitched, his fur seemed to bristle; he sneezed or spat, but remained otherwise motionless.

When Mr Cullings called again, Sam at once hid himself in the coal-cellar, but gradually his manners toward Miss Chauncey began to recover their usual suavity. And within a fortnight after the full-moon, the two of them had almost returned to their old friendly companionship. He was healed, sleek, confident and punctual. No intruder of his species had appeared from Haggurdsdon. The night noises had ceased; Post Houses to all appearances – apart from its strange ugliness – was as peaceful and calm as any other solitary domicile in the United Kingdom.

But alas and alas. With the very first peeping of the crescent moon, Sam's mood and habits began to change again. He mooched about with a sly and furtive eye. And when he fawned on her, purring and clawing, the whole look of him was full of deceit. If Miss Chauncey chanced softly to enter the room wherein he sat, he would at once leap down from the window at which he had been perched as if in the attempt to prove that he had *not* been looking out of it. And once, towards evening, though she was no spy, she could not but pause at the parlor door. She had peeped through its crack as it stood ajar. And there on the hard sharp back of an old prie-dieu chair that had belonged to her pious great-aunt Jemima, there sat Sam on his hindquarters. And without the least doubt in the world he was vigorously signalling to some observer outside with his forepaws. Miss Chauncey turned away sick at heart.

From that hour on Sam more and more steadily ignored and flouted his mistress, was openly insolent, shockingly audacious. Mr Cullings gave her small help indeed. 'If I had a cat, m'm, what had manners like that, after all your kindness, fresh fish and all every week, and cream, as I understand, not skim, I'd – I'd give him away.'

'To whom?' said Miss Chauncey shortly.

'Well,' said the carrier, 'I don't know as how I'd much mind to who. Just a home, m'm.'

'He seems to have no friends in the Village,' said Miss Chauncey in as light a tone as she could manage.

'When they're as black as that, with them saucer eyes, you can never tell,' said Mr Cullings. 'There's that old trollimog what lives in Hogges Bottom. She's got a cat that might be your Sam's twin.'

'Indeed no, he has the mange,' said Miss Chauncey, loyal to the end. The carrier shrugged his shoulders, climbed into his cart, and bowled away off over the moor. And Miss Chauncey returning into the house, laid the platter of silvery sprats on the table, sat down and burst into tears.

It was, then, in most ways a fortunate thing that the very next morning – three complete days, that is, before the next full-moontide – she received a letter from her sister-in-law in Shanklin, in the Isle of Wight, entreating her to pay them a long visit.

'My dear Emma, you must sometimes be feeling very lonely (it ran), shut up in that great house so far from any neighbors. We often think of you, and particularly these last few days. It's nice to have that Sam of yours for company, but after all, as George says, a pet is only a pet. And we do all think it's high time you took a little holiday with us. I am looking out of my window at this moment. The sea is as calm as a mill-pond, a solemn beautiful blue. The fishing boats are coming in with their brown sails. This is the best time of the year with us, because as it's not yet holy-day-time there are few of those horrid visitors to be seen, and no crowds. George says you *must* come. He joins with me in his love as would Maria if she weren't out shopping, and will meet you at the station in the trap. Emmie is now free of her cough, only whooping when the memory takes her and never sick. And we shall all be looking forward to seeing you in a few days.'

At this kindness, and with all her anxieties, Miss Chauncey all but broke down. When the butcher drove up in his cart an hour or two afterwards, he took a telegram for her back to the Village, and on the Monday her box was packed and all that remained was to put Sam in his basket in preparation for the journey. But I am bound to say it took more than the persuasion of his old protectress to accomplish this. Indeed Mr Cullings had actually to hold the creature with his gloved hands and none too gently, while Miss Chauncey pressed down the lid and pushed the skewer in to hold it close.

'What's done's dumned done!' said the carrier, as he rubbed a pinch of earth into his scratches. 'But what I say is, better done forever. Mark my words, m'm!'

Miss Chauncey took a shilling out of her large leather purse; but made no reply.

Indeed all this trouble proved at last in vain. Thirty miles distant from Haggurdsdon, at Blackmoor Junction, Miss Chauncey had to change trains. Her box and Sam's basket were placed together on the station platform beside half-a-dozen empty milkcans and some fowls in a crate, and Miss Chauncey went to enquire of the station-master to make sure of her platform.

It was the furious panic-stricken cackling of these fowls that brought her hastily back to her belongings, only to find that by hook or by crook Sam had managed to push the skewer of the basket out of its cane loops. The wicker lid yawned open – the basket was empty. Indeed one poor gaping hen, its life fluttering away from its helpless body, was proof not only of Sam's prowess but of his cowardly ferocity.

A few days afterwards, as Miss Chauncey sat in the very room to which her sister-in-law had referred in her invitation, looking over the placid surface of the English Channel, the sun gently shining in the sky, there came a letter from Mr Cullings. It was in pencil and written upon the back of a baker's bag:

'Dear Madam, i take the libberty of riteing you in referense to the Animall as how i helped put in is bawskit which has cum back returned empty agenn by rail me having okashun to cart sum hop powles from Haggurdsdon late at nite ov Sunday. I seez him squattin at the parlor windy grimasin out at me fit to curdle your blood in your vanes and lights at the upper windies and a yowling and screetching such as i never hopes to hear agen in a Christian lokalety. And that ole wumman from Hogges Botom sitting in the porch mi own vew being that there is no good in the place and the Animall be bewitched. Mr Flint the fyshmunger agrees with me as how now only last mesures is of any use and as i have said afore i am wiling to take over the house the rent if so be being low and moddrate considering of the bad name it as in these parts around Haggurdsdon. I remain dear madam waitin your orders and oblidge yours truely William Cullings.'

To look at Miss Chauncey you might have supposed she was a strong-minded woman. You might have supposed that this uncivil reference to the bad name her family house had won for itself would have mortified her beyond words. Whether or not, she neither showed this letter to her sister-in-law nor for many days together did she even answer it. Sitting on the Esplanade, and looking out to sea, she brooded on and on in the warm, salt, yet balmy air. It was a distressing problem. But 'No, he must go his own way,' she sighed to herself at last; 'I have done my best for him.'

What is more, Miss Chauncey never returned to Post Houses. She sold it at last, house and garden and for a pitiful sum, to the carrier, Mr Cullings. By that time Sam had vanished, had been never seen again.

Not that Miss Chauncey was faithless of memory. Whenever the faint swish of a seagull's wing sounded in the air above her head; or the crackling of an ascending rocket for the amusement of the visitors broke the silence of the nearer heavens over the sea; whenever even she became conscious of the rustling frou-frou of her Sunday watered silk gown as she sallied out to church from the neat little villa she now rented on the Shanklin Esplanade — she never noticed such things without being instantly transported back in imagination to her bedroom at Post Houses, to see again that strange deluded animal, once her Sam, squatting there on her patchwork counterpane, and as it were knitting with his forepaws the while he stood erect upon his hind.

PATRICIA HIGHSMITH

MING'S BIGGEST PREY

MING WAS RESTING comfortably on the foot of his mistress's bunk, when the man picked him up by the back of the neck, stuck him out on the deck and closed the cabin door. Ming's blue eyes widened in shock and brief anger, then nearly closed again because of the brilliant sunlight. It was not the first time Ming had been thrust out of the cabin rudely, and Ming realized that the man did it when his mistress, Elaine, was not looking.

The sailboat now offered no shelter from the sun, but Ming was not yet too warm. He leapt easily to the cabin roof and stepped on to the coil of rope just behind the mast. Ming liked the rope coil as a couch, because he could see everything from the height, the cup shape of the rope protected him from strong breezes, and also minimized the swaying and sudden changes of angle of the *White Lark*, since it was more or less the center point. But just now the sail had been taken down, because Elaine and the man had eaten lunch, and often they had a siesta afterward, during which time, Ming knew, that the man didn't like him in the cabin. Lunchtime was all right. In fact, Ming had just lunched on delicious grilled fish and a bit of lobster. Now, lying in a relaxed curve on the coil of rope, Ming opened his mouth in a great yawn, then with his slant eyes almost closed against the strong sunlight, gazed at the beige hills and the white and pink houses and hotels that circled the bay of Acapulco. Between the

White Lark and the shore where people plashed inaudibly, the sun twinkled on the water's surface like thousands of tiny electric lights going on and off. A water-skier went by, skimming up white spray behind him. Such activity! Ming half dozed, feeling the heat of the sun sink into his fur. Ming was from New York, and he considered Acapulco a great improvement over his environment in the first weeks of his life. He remembered a sunless box with straw on the bottom, three or four other kittens in with him, and a window behind which giant forms paused for a few moments, tried to catch his attention by tapping, then passed on. He did not remember his mother at all. One day a young woman who smelled of something pleasant came into the place and took him away – away from the ugly, frightening smell of dogs, of medicine and parrot dung. Then they went on what Ming now knew was an airplane. He was quite used to airplanes now and rather liked them. On airplanes he sat on Elaine's lap, or slept on her lap, and there were always tidbits to eat if he was hungry.

Elaine spent much of the day in a shop in Acapulco, where dresses and slacks and bathing suits hung on all the walls. This place smelled clean and fresh, there were flowers in pots and in boxes out front, and the floor was of cool blue and white tile. Ming had perfect freedom to wander out into the patio behind the shop, or to sleep in his basket in a corner. There was more sunlight in front of the shop, but mischievous boys often tried to grab him if he sat in front, and Ming could never relax there.

Ming liked best lying in the sun with his mistress on one of the long canvas chairs on their terrace at home. What Ming did not like were the people she sometimes invited to their house, people who spent the night, people by the score who stayed up very late eating and drinking, playing the gramophone or the piano – people who separated him from Elaine. People who stepped on his toes, people who sometimes picked him up from behind before he could do anything about it, so that he had to squirm and fight to get free, people who stroked him roughly, people who closed a door somewhere, locking him in. *People!* Ming detested people. In all the world, he liked only Elaine. Elaine loved him and understood him.

Especially this man called Teddie Ming detested now. Teddie was around all the time lately. Ming did not like the way Teddie looked at him, when Elaine was not watching. And sometimes Teddie, when Elaine was not near, muttered something which Ming knew was a threat. Or a command to leave the room. Ming took it calmly. Dignity was to be preserved. Besides, wasn't his mistress on his side? The man was the intruder. When Elaine was watching, the man sometimes pretended a fondness for him, but Ming always moved gracefully but unmistakably in another direction.

Ming's nap was interrupted by the sound of the cabin door opening. He heard Elaine and the man laughing and talking. The big red-orange sun was near the horizon.

'Ming!' Elaine came over to him. 'Aren't you getting *cooked*, darling? I thought you were *in*!'

'So did I!' said Teddie.

Ming purred as he always did when he awakened. She picked him up gently, cradled him in her arms, and took him below into the suddenly cool shade of the cabin. She was talking to the man, and not in a gentle tone. She set Ming down in front of his dish of water, and though he was not thirsty, he drank a little to please her. Ming did feel addled by the heat, and he staggered a little.

Elaine took a wet towel and wiped Ming's face, his ears and his four paws. Then she laid him gently on the bunk that smelled of Elaine's perfume but also of the man whom Ming detested.

Now his mistress and the man were quarreling, Ming could tell from the tone. Elaine was staying with Ming, sitting on the edge of the bunk. Ming at last heard the splash that meant Teddie had dived into the water. Ming hoped he stayed there, hoped he drowned, hoped he never came back. Elaine wet a bathtowel in the aluminum sink, wrung it out, spread it on the bunk, and lifted Ming on to it. She brought water, and now Ming was thirsty, and drank. She left him to sleep again while she washed and put away the dishes. These were comfortable sounds that Ming liked to hear.

But soon there was another *plash* and *plop*, Teddie's wet feet on the deck, and Ming was awake again.

The tone of quarreling recommenced. Elaine went up the few steps on to the deck. Ming, tense but with his chin still resting on the moist bathtowel, kept his eyes on the cabin door. It was Teddie's feet that he heard descending. Ming lifted his head slightly, aware that there was no exit behind him, that he was trapped in the cabin. The man paused with a towel in his hands, staring at Ming.

Ming relaxed completely, as he might do preparatory to a yawn, and this caused his eyes to cross. Ming then let his tongue slide a little way out of his mouth. The man started to say something, looked as if he wanted to hurl the wadded towel at Ming, but he wavered, whatever he had been going to say never got out of his mouth, and he threw the towel in the sink, then bent to wash his face. It was not the first time Ming had let his tongue slide out at Teddie. Lots of people laughed when Ming did this, if they were people at a party, for instance, and Ming rather enjoyed that. But Ming sensed that Teddie took it as a hostile gesture of some kind, which was why Ming did it deliberately to Teddie, whereas among other people, it was often an accident when Ming's tongue slid out.

The quarreling continued. Elaine made coffee. Ming began to feel better, and went on deck again, because the sun had now set. Elaine had started the motor, and they were gliding slowly towards the shore. Ming caught the song of birds, the odd screams, like shrill phrases, of certain birds that cried only at sunset. Ming looked forward to the adobe house on the cliff that was his and his mistress's home. He knew that the reason she did not leave him at home (where he would have been more comfortable) when she went on the boat, was because she was afraid that people might trap him, even kill him. Ming understood. People had tried to grab him from almost under Elaine's eyes. Once he had been suddenly hauled away in a cloth bag, and though fighting as hard as he could, he was not sure he would have been able to get out, if Elaine had not hit the boy herself and grabbed the bag from him.

Ming had intended to jump up on the cabin roof again, but after glancing at it, he decided to save his strength, so he crouched on the warm, gently sloping deck with his feet tucked in, and gazed at the approaching shore. Now he could hear guitar music from the beach. The voices of his mistress and the man had come to a halt. For a few moments, the loudest sound was the *chug-chug-chug* of the boat's motor. Then Ming heard the man's bare feet climbing the cabin steps. Ming did not turn his head to look at him, but his ears twitched back a little, involuntarily. Ming looked at the water just the distance of a short leap in front of him and below him. Strangely, there was no sound from the man behind him. The hair on Ming's neck prickled, and Ming glanced over his right shoulder.

At that instant, the man bent forward and rushed at Ming with his arms outspread.

Ming was on his feet at once, darting straight towards the man, which was the only direction of safety on the rail-less deck, and the man swung his left arm and cuffed Ming in the chest. Ming went flying backwards, claws scraping the deck, but his hind legs went over the edge. Ming clung with his front feet to the sleek wood which gave him little hold, while his hind legs worked to heave him up, worked at the side of the boat which sloped to Ming's disadvantage.

The man advanced to shove a foot against Ming's paws, but Elaine came up the cabin steps just then.

'What's happening? *Ming!*'

Ming's strong hind legs were getting him on to the deck little by little. The man had knelt as if to lend a hand. Elaine had fallen on to her knees also, and had Ming by the back of the neck now.

Ming relaxed, hunched on the deck. His tail was wet.

'He fell overboard!' Teddie said. 'It's true, he's groggy. Just lurched over and fell when the boat gave a dip.'

'It's the sun. Poor *Ming!*' Elaine held the cat against her breast, and carried him into the cabin. 'Teddie – could you steer?'

The man came down into the cabin. Elaine had Ming on the bunk and was talking softly to him. Ming's heart was still beating fast. He was alert against the man at the wheel, even though Elaine was with him. Ming was aware that they had entered the little cove where they always went before getting off the boat.

Here were the friends and allies of Teddie, whom Ming detested by association, although these were merely Mexican boys. Two or three boys in shorts called 'Señor Teddie!' and offered a hand to Elaine to climb on to the dock, took the rope attached to the front of the boat, offered to carry '*Ming! – Ming!*' Ming leapt on to the dock himself and crouched, waiting for Elaine, ready to dart away from any other hand that might reach for him. And there were several brown hands making a rush for him, so that Ming had to keep jumping aside. There were laughs, yelps, stomps of bare feet on wooden boards. But there was also the reassuring voice of Elaine, warning them off. Ming knew she was busy carrying off the plastic satchels, locking the cabin door. Teddie with the aid of one of the Mexican boys was stretching the canvas over the cabin now. And Elaine's sandaled feet were beside Ming. Ming followed her as she walked away. A boy took the things Elaine was carrying, then she picked Ming up.

They got into the big car without a roof that belonged to Teddie, and drove up the winding road towards Elaine's and Ming's house. One of the boys was driving. Now the tone in which Elaine and Teddie were speaking was calmer, softer. The man laughed. Ming sat tensely on his mistress's lap. He could feel her concern for him in the way she stroked him and touched the back of his neck. The man reached out to put his fingers on Ming's back, and Ming gave a low growl that rose and fell and rumbled deep in his throat.

'Well, well,' said the man, pretending to be amused, and took his hand away.

Elaine's voice had stopped in the middle of something she was saying. Ming was tired, and wanted nothing more than to take a nap on the big bed at home. The bed was covered with a red and white striped blanket of thin wool.

Hardly had Ming thought of this, when he found himself in the cool, fragrant atmosphere of his own home, being lowered gently on to the bed with the soft woolen cover. His mistress kissed his cheek, and said something with the word hungry in it. Ming understood, at any rate. He was to tell her when he was hungry.

Ming dozed, and awakened at the sound of voices on the terrace a couple of yards away, past the open glass doors. Now it was dark. Ming could see one end of the table, and could tell from the quality of the light that there were candles on the table. Concha, the servant who slept in the house, was clearing the table. Ming heard her voice, then the voices of Elaine and the man. Ming smelled cigar smoke. Ming jumped to the floor and sat for a moment looking out of the door towards the terrace. He yawned, then arched his back and stretched, and limbered up his muscles by digging his claws into the thick straw carpet. Then he slipped out to the right on the terrace and glided silently down the long stairway of broad stones to the garden below. The garden was like a jungle or a forest. Avocado trees and mango trees grew as high as the terrace itself, there were bougainvillea against the wall, orchids in the trees, and magnolias and several camellias which Elaine had planted. Ming could hear birds twittering and stirring in their nests. Sometimes he climbed trees to get at their nests, but tonight he was not in the mood, though he was no longer tired. The voices of his mistress and the man disturbed him. His mistress was not a friend of the man's tonight, that was plain.

Concha was probably still in the kitchen, and Ming decided to go in and ask her for something to eat. Concha liked him. One maid who had not liked him had been dismissed by Elaine. Ming thought he fancied barbecued pork. That was what his mistress and the man had eaten tonight. The breeze blew fresh from the ocean, ruffling Ming's fur slightly. Ming felt completely recovered from the awful experience of nearly falling into the sea.

Now the terrace was empty of people. Ming went left,

back into the bedroom, and was at once aware of the man's presence, though there was no light on and Ming could not see him. The man was standing by the dressing table, opening a box. Again involuntarily Ming gave a low growl which rose and fell, and Ming remained frozen in the position he had been in when he first became aware of the man, his right front paw extended for the next step. Now his ears were back, he was prepared to spring in any direction, although the man had not seen him.

'*Ssss-st!* Damn you!' the man said in a whisper. He stamped his foot, not very hard, to make the cat go away.

Ming did not move at all. Ming heard the soft rattle of the white necklace which belonged to his mistress. The man put it into his pocket, then moved to Ming's right, out of the door that went into the big living-room. Ming now heard the clink of a bottle against glass, heard liquid being poured. Ming went through the same door and turned left towards the kitchen.

Here he meowed, and was greeted by Elaine and Concha. Concha had her radio turned on to music.

'Fish? – Pork. He likes pork,' Elaine said, speaking the odd form of words which she used with Concha.

Ming, without much difficulty, conveyed his preference for pork, and got it. He fell to with a good appetite. Concha was exclaiming 'Ah-eee-ee!' as his mistress spoke with her, spoke at length. Then Concha bent to stroke him, and Ming put up with it, still looking down at his plate, until she left off and he could finish his meal. Then Elaine left the kitchen. Concha gave him some of the tinned milk, which he loved, in his now empty saucer, and Ming lapped this up. Then he rubbed himself against her bare leg by way of thanks, and went out of the kitchen, made his way cautiously into the living-room en route to the bedroom. But now Elaine and the man were out on the terrace. Ming had just entered the bedroom, when he heard Elaine call:

'Ming? Where are you?'

Ming went to the terrace door and stopped, and sat on the threshold.

Elaine was sitting sideways at the end of the table, and the candlelight was bright on her long fair hair, on the white of her trousers. She slapped her thigh, and Ming jumped on to her lap.

The man said something in a low tone, something not nice.

Elaine replied something in the same tone. But she laughed a little.

Then the telephone rang.

Elaine put Ming down, and went into the living-room towards the telephone.

The man finished what was in his glass, muttered something at Ming, then set the glass on the table. He got up and tried to circle Ming, or to get him towards the edge of the terrace, Ming realized, and Ming also realized that the man was drunk – therefore moving slowly and a little clumsily. The terrace had a parapet about as high as the man's hips, but it was broken by grills in three places, grills with bars wide enough for Ming to pass through, though Ming never did, merely looked through the grills sometimes. It was plain to Ming that the man wanted to drive him through one of the grills, or grab him and toss him over the terrace parapet. There was nothing easier for Ming than to elude him. Then the man picked up a chair and swung it suddenly, catching Ming on the hip. That had been quick, and it hurt. Ming took the nearest exit, which was down the outside steps that led to the garden.

The man started down the steps after him. Without reflecting, Ming dashed back up the few steps he had come, keeping close to the wall which was in shadow. The man hadn't seen him, Ming knew. Ming leapt to the terrace parapet, sat down and licked a paw once to recover and collect himself. His heart beat fast as if he were in the middle of a fight. And hatred ran in his veins. Hatred burned his eyes as he crouched and listened to the man uncertainly climbing the steps below him. The man came into view.

Ming tensed himself for a jump, then jumped as hard as he could, landing with all four feet on the man's right arm near the shoulder. Ming clung to the cloth of the man's white jacket, but they were both falling. The man groaned. Ming hung on. Branches crackled. Ming could not tell up from down. Ming jumped off the man, became aware of direction and of the earth too late, and landed on his side. Almost at the same time, he heard the thud of the man hitting the ground, then of his body rolling a little way, then there was silence. Ming had to breathe fast with his mouth open until his chest stopped hurting. From the direction of the man, he could smell drink, cigar, and the sharp odor that meant fear. But the man was not moving.

Ming could now see quite well. There was even a bit of moonlight. Ming headed for the steps again, had to go a long way through the bush, over stones and sand, to where the steps began. Then he glided up and arrived once more upon the terrace.

Elaine was just coming on to the terrace.

'Teddie?' she called. Then she went back into the bedroom where she turned on a lamp. She went into the kitchen. Ming followed her. Concha had left the light on, but Concha was now in her own room, where the radio played.

Elaine opened the front door.

The man's car was still in the driveway, Ming saw. Now Ming's hip had begun to hurt, or now he had begun to notice it. It caused him to limp a little. Elaine noticed this, touched his back, and asked him what was the matter. Ming only purred.

'Teddie? – Where are you?' Elaine called.

She took a torch and shone it down into the garden, down among the great trunks of the avocado trees, among the orchids and the lavender and pink blossoms of the bougain-villeas. Ming, safe beside her on the terrace parapet, followed the beam of the torch with his eyes and purred with content. The man was not below here, but below and to the right. Elaine went to the terrace steps and carefully, because there was no rail here, only broad steps, pointed the beam of the light downward. Ming did not bother looking. He sat on the terrace where the steps began.

'Teddie!' she said. *'Teddie!'* Then she ran down the steps.

Ming still did not follow her. He heard her draw in her breath. Then she cried:

'Concha!'

Elaine ran back up the steps.

Concha had come out of her room. Elaine spoke to Concha. Then Concha became excited. Elaine went to the telephone, and spoke for a short while, then she and Concha went down the steps together. Ming settled himself with his paws tucked under him on the terrace, which was still faintly warm from the day's sun. A car arrived. Elaine came up the steps, and went and opened the front door. Ming kept out of the way on the terrace, in a shadowy corner, as three or four strange men came out on the terrace and tramped down the steps. There was a great deal of talk below, noises of feet, breaking of bushes, and then the smell of all of them mounted the steps, the smell of tobacco, sweat, and the familiar smell of blood. The man's blood. Ming was pleased, as he was pleased when he killed a bird and created this smell

of blood under his own teeth. This was big prey. Ming, unnoticed by any of the others, stood up to his full height as
the group passed with the corpse, and inhaled the aroma of
his victory with a lifted nose.

Then suddenly the house was empty. Everyone had gone,
even Concha. Ming drank a little water from his bowl in the
kitchen, then went to his mistress's bed, curled against the
slope of the pillows, and fell fast asleep. He was awakened by
the *rr-rr-r* of an unfamiliar car. Then the front door opened,
and he recognized the step of Elaine and then Concha. Ming
stayed where he was. Elaine and Concha talked softly for a
few minutes. Then Elaine came into the bedroom. The lamp
was still on. Ming watched her slowly open the box on her
dressing table, and into it she let fall the white necklace that
made a little clatter. Then she closed the box. She began to
unbutton her shirt, but before she had finished, she flung
herself on the bed and stroked Ming's head, lifted his left paw
and pressed it gently so that the claws came forth.

'Oh, Ming – Ming,' she said.

Ming recognized the tones of love.

EDGAR ALLAN POE

THE BLACK CAT

FOR THE MOST wild yet most homely narrative which I am about to pen, I neither expect nor solicit belief. Mad indeed would I be to expect it, in a case where my very senses reject their own evidence. Yet, mad am I not – and very surely do I not dream. But tomorrow I die, and today I would unburden my soul. My immediate purpose is to place before the world, plainly, succinctly, and without comment, a series of mere household events. In their consequences, these events have terrified – have tortured – have destroyed me. Yet I will not attempt to expound them. To me, they have presented little but horror – to many they will seem less terrible than *baroques*. Hereafter, perhaps, some intellect may be found which will reduce my phantasm to the commonplace – some intellect more calm, more logical, and far less excitable than my own, which will perceive, in the circumstances I detail with awe, nothing more than an ordinary succession of very natural causes and effects.

From my infancy I was noted for the docility and humanity of my disposition. My tenderness of heart was even so conspicuous as to make me the jest of my companions. I was especially fond of animals, and was indulged by my parents with a great variety of pets. With these I spent most of my time, and never was so happy as when feeding and caressing them. This peculiarity of character grew with my growth, and, in my manhood, I derived from it one of my principal sources of pleasure. To those who have cherished an affection for a faithful and sagacious dog, I need hardly be at the trouble of explaining the nature or the intensity of the gratification thus derivable. There is something in the unselfish and self-sacrificing love of a brute, which goes directly to the heart of him who has had frequent occasion to test the paltry friendship and gossamer fidelity of mere *Man*.

I married early, and was happy to find in my wife a disposition not uncongenial with my own. Observing my partiality for domestic pets, she lost no opportunity of procuring those of the most agreeable kind. We had birds, gold-fish, a fine dog, rabbits, a small monkey, and a *cat*.

This latter was a remarkably large and beautiful animal, entirely black, and sagacious to an astonishing degree. In speaking of his intelligence, my wife, who at heart was not a little tinctured with superstition, made frequent allusion to the ancient popular notion, which regarded all black cats as witches in disguise. Not that she was ever *serious* upon this point – and I mention the matter at all for no better reason than that it happens, just now, to be remembered.

Pluto – this was the cat's name – was my favorite pet and playmate. I alone fed him, and he attended me wherever I went about the house. It was even with difficulty that I could prevent him from following me through the streets.

Our friendship lasted, in this manner, for several years, during which my general temperament and character – through the instrumentality of the Fiend Intemperance – had (I blush to confess it) experienced a radical alteration for the worse. I grew, day by day, more moody, more irritable, more regardless of the feelings of others. I suffered myself to use intemperate language to my wife. At length, I even offered her personal violence. My pets, of course, were made to feel the change in my disposition. I not only neglected, but ill-used them. For Pluto, however, I still retained sufficient regard to restrain me from maltreating him, as I made no scruple of maltreating the rabbits, the monkey, or even the dog, when, by accident, or through affection, they came in my way. But my disease grew upon me – for what disease is like Alcohol! – and at length even Pluto, who was now becoming old, and consequently somewhat peevish – even Pluto began to experience the effects of my ill temper.

One night, returning home, much intoxicated, from one of my haunts about town, I fancied that the cat avoided my presence. I seized him; when, in his fright at my violence, he inflicted a slight wound upon my hand with his teeth. The fury of a demon instantly possessed me. I knew myself no longer. My original soul seemed, at once, to take its flight from my body; and a more than fiendish malevolence, gin-nurtured, thrilled every fibre of my frame. I took from my waistcoat-pocket a penknife, opened it, grasped the poor beast by the throat, and deliberately cut one of its eyes from the socket! I blush, I burn, I shudder, while I pen the damn-able atrocity.

When reason returned with the morning – when I had slept off the fumes of the night's debauch – I experienced a sentiment half of horror, half of remorse, for the crime of which I had been guilty; but it was, at best, a feeble and equi-vocal feeling, and the soul remained untouched. I again plunged into excess, and soon drowned in wine all memory of the deed.

In the meantime the cat slowly recovered. The socket of the lost eye presented, it is true, a frightful appearance, but he no longer appeared to suffer any pain. He went about the house as usual, but, as might be expected, fled in extreme terror at my approach. I had so much of my old heart left, as to be at first grieved by this evident dislike on the part of a creature which had once so loved me. But this feeling soon gave place to irritation. And then came, as if to my final and irrevocable overthrow, the spirit of PERVERSENESS. Of this spirit philosophy takes no account. Yet I am not more sure that my soul lives, than I am that perverseness is one of the primitive impulses of the human heart – one of the indivisible primary faculties, or sentiments, which give direction to the character of Man. Who has not, a hundred times, found himself committing a vile or a stupid action, for no other reason than because he knows he should *not*? Have we not a perpetual inclination, in the teeth of our best judgment, to violate that which is *Law*, merely because we understand it to be such? This spirit of perverseness, I say, came to my final overthrow. It was this unfathomable longing of the soul *to vex itself* – to offer violence to its own nature – to do wrong for the wrong's sake only – that urged me to continue and finally to consummate the injury I had inflicted upon the unoffending brute. One morning, in cold blood, I slipped a noose about its neck and hung it to the limb of a tree; – hung it with the tears streaming from my eyes, and with the bitterest remorse at my heart; – hung it *because* I knew that it had loved me, and *because* I felt it had given me no reason of offense; – hung it *because* I knew that in so doing I was committing a sin – a deadly sin that would so jeopardize my immortal soul as to place it – if such a thing were possible – even beyond the reach of the infinite mercy of the Most Merciful and Most Terrible God.

On the night of the day on which this most cruel deed was done, I was aroused from sleep by the cry of fire. The curtains of my bed were in flames. The whole house was blazing. It was with great difficulty that my wife, a servant, and myself, made our escape from the conflagration. The destruction was complete. My entire worldly wealth was swallowed up, and I resigned myself thenceforward to despair.

I am above the weakness of seeking to establish a sequence of cause and effect, between the disaster and the atrocity. But I am detailing a chain of facts – and wish not to leave even a possible link imperfect. On the day succeeding the fire, I visited the ruins. The walls, with one exception, had fallen in. This exception was found in a compartment wall, not very thick, which stood about the middle of the house, and against which had rested the head of my bed. The plastering had here, in great measure, resisted the action of the fire – a fact which I attributed to its having been recently spread. About this wall a dense crowd were collected, and many persons seemed to be examining a particular portion of it with very minute and eager attention. The words 'strange!' 'singular!' and other similar expressions, excited my curiosity. I approached and saw, as if graven in *bas-relief* upon the white surface, the figure of a gigantic *cat*. The impression was given with an accuracy truly marvelous. There was a rope about the animal's neck.

When I first beheld this apparition – for I could scarcely regard it as less – my wonder and my terror were extreme. But at length reflection came to my aid. The cat, I remembered, had been hung in a garden adjacent to the house. Upon the alarm of fire, this garden had been immediately filled by the crowd – by some one of whom the animal must have been cut from the tree and thrown, through an open window, into my chamber. This had probably been done with the view of arousing me from sleep. The falling of other walls had compressed the victim of my cruelty into the substance of the freshly-spread plaster; the lime of which, with the flames, and the *ammonia* from the carcass, had then accomplished the portraiture as I saw it.

Although I thus readily accounted to my reason, if not altogether to my conscience, for the startling fact just detailed, it did not the less fail to make a deep impression upon my fancy. For months I could not rid myself of the phantasm of the cat; and, during this period, there came back into my spirit a half-sentiment that seemed, but was not, remorse. I went so far as to regret the loss of the animal, and to look about me, among the vile haunts which I now habitually frequented, for another pet of the same species, and of somewhat similar appearance, with which to supply its place.

One night as I sat, half stupefied, in a den of more than infamy, my attention was suddenly drawn to some black object, reposing upon the head of one of the immense hogsheads of gin, or of rum, which constituted the chief furniture of the apartment. I had been looking steadily at the top of this hogshead for some minutes, and what now caused me surprise was the fact that I had not sooner perceived the object thereupon. I approached it, and touched it with my hand. It was a black cat – a very large one – fully as large as Pluto, and closely resembling him in every respect but one. Pluto had not a white hair upon any portion of his body; but this cat had a large, although indefinite splotch of white, covering nearly the whole region of the breast.

Upon my touching him, he immediately arose, purred loudly, rubbed against my hand, and appeared delighted with my notice. This, then, was the very creature of which I was in search. I at once offered to purchase it of the landlord; but this person made no claim to it – knew nothing of it – had never seen it before.

I continued my caresses, and when I prepared to go home, the animal evinced a disposition to accompany me. I permitted it to do so; occasionally stooping and patting it as I proceeded. When it reached the house it domesticated itself at once, and became immediately a great favorite with my wife.

For my own part, I soon found a dislike to it arising within me. This was just the reverse of what I had anticipated; but – I know not how or why it was – its evident fondness for myself rather disgusted and annoyed me. By slow degrees these feelings of disgust and annoyance rose into the bitterness of hatred. I avoided the creature; a certain sense of shame, and the remembrance of my former deed of cruelty, preventing me from physically abusing it. I did not, for some weeks, strike, or otherwise violently ill use it; but gradually – very gradually – I came to look upon it with unutterable loathing, and to flee silently from its odious presence, as from the breath of a pestilence.

What added, no doubt, to my hatred of the beast, was the discovery, on the morning after I brought it home, that, like Pluto, it also had been deprived of one of its eyes. This circumstance, however, only endeared it to my wife, who, as I have already said, possessed, in a high degree, that humanity of feeling which had once been my distinguishing trait, and the source of many of my simplest and purest pleasures.

With my aversion to this cat, however, its partiality for myself seemed to increase. It followed my footsteps with a pertinacity which it would be difficult to make the reader comprehend. Whenever I sat, it would crouch beneath my chair, or spring upon my knees, covering me with its loathsome caresses. If I arose to walk it would get between my feet and thus nearly throw me down, or, fastening its long and sharp claws in my dress, clamber, in this manner, to my breast. At such times, although I longed to destroy it with a blow, I was yet withheld from so doing, partly by a memory of my former crime, but chiefly – let me confess it at once – by absolute *dread* of the beast.

This dread was not exactly a dread of physical evil – and yet I should be at a loss how otherwise to define it.

I am almost ashamed to own – yes, even in this felon's cell, I am almost ashamed to own – that the terror and horror with which the animal inspired me, had been heightened by one of the merest chimeras it would be possible to conceive. My wife had called my attention, more than once, to the character of the mark of white hair, of which I have spoken, and which constituted the sole visible difference between the strange beast and the one I had destroyed. The reader will remember that this mark, although large, had been originally very indefinite; but, by slow degrees – degrees nearly imperceptible, and which for a long time my reason struggled to reject as fanciful – it had, at length, assumed a rigorous distinctness of outline. It was now the representation of an object that I shudder to name – and for this, above all, I loathed, and dreaded, and would have rid myself of the monster *had I dared* – it was now, I say, the image of a hideous – of a ghastly thing – of the GALLOWS! – oh, mournful and terrible engine of Horror and of Crime – of Agony and of Death!

And now was I indeed wretched beyond the wretchedness of mere Humanity. And *a brute beast* – whose fellow I had contemptuously destroyed – *a brute beast* to work out for *me* – for me, a man fashioned in the image of the High God – so much of insufferable woe! Alas! neither by day nor by night knew I the blessing of rest any more! During the former the creature left me no moment alone, and in the latter I started hourly from dreams of unutterable fear to find the hot breath of *the thing* upon my face, and its vast weight – an incarnate nightmare that I had no power to shake off – incumbent eternally upon my *heart!*

Beneath the pressure of torments such as these the feeble remnant of the good within me succumbed. Evil thoughts became my sole intimates – the darkest and most evil of thoughts. The moodiness of my usual temper increased to hatred of all things and of all mankind; while from the sudden, frequent, and ungovernable outbursts of a fury to which I now blindly abandoned myself, my uncomplaining wife, alas, was the most usual and the most patient of sufferers.

One day she accompanied me, upon some household errand, into the cellar of the old building which our poverty compelled us to inhabit. The cat followed me down the steep stairs, and, nearly throwing me headlong, exasperated me to madness. Uplifting an axe, and forgetting in my wrath the childish dread which had hitherto stayed my hand, I aimed a blow at the animal, which, of course, would have proved instantly fatal had it descended as I wished. But this blow was arrested by the hand of my wife. Goaded by the interference into a rage more than demoniacal, I withdrew my arm from her grasp and buried the axe in her brain. She fell dead upon the spot without a groan.

This hideous murder accomplished, I set myself forthwith, and with entire deliberation, to the task of concealing the body. I knew that I could not remove it from the house, either by day or by night, without the risk of being observed by the neighbors. Many projects entered my mind. At one period I thought of cutting the corpse into minute fragments, and destroying them by fire. At another, I resolved to dig a grave for it in the floor of the cellar. Again, I deliberated about casting it in the well in the yard – about packing it in a box, as if merchandise, with the usual arrangements, and so getting a porter to take it from the house. Finally I hit upon what I considered a far better expedient than either of these. I determined to wall it up in the cellar, as the monks of the Middle Ages are recorded to have walled up their victims.

For a purpose such as this the cellar was well adapted. Its walls were loosely constructed, and had lately been plastered throughout with a rough plaster, which the dampness of the atmosphere had prevented from hardening. Moreover, in one of the walls was a projection, caused by a false chimney, or fireplace, that had been filled up and made to resemble the rest of the cellar. I made no doubt that I could readily displace the bricks at this point, insert the corpse, and wall the whole up as before, so that no eye could detect any thing suspicious.

And in this calculation I was not deceived. By means of a crowbar I easily dislodged the bricks, and, having carefully deposited the body against the inner wall, I propped it in that position, while with little trouble I relaid the whole structure as it originally stood. Having procured mortar, sand, and hair, with every possible precaution, I prepared a plaster which could not be distinguished from the old, and with this I very carefully went over the new brick-work. When I had finished, I felt satisfied that all was right. The wall did not present the slightest appearance of having been disturbed. The rubbish on the floor was picked up with the minutest care. I looked around triumphantly, and said to myself: 'Here at least, then, my labor has not been in vain.'

My next step was to look for the beast which had been the cause of so much wretchedness; for I had, at length, firmly resolved to put it to death. Had I been able to meet with it at the moment, there could have been no doubt of its fate; but it appeared that the crafty animal had been alarmed at the violence of my previous anger, and forbore to present itself in my present mood. It is impossible to describe or to imagine the deep, the blissful sense of relief which the absence of the detested creature occasioned in my bosom. It did not make its appearance during the night; and thus for one night, at least, since its introduction into the house, I soundly and tranquilly slept; aye, *slept* even with the burden of murder upon my soul.

The second and the third day passed, and still my tormentor came not. Once again I breathed as a freeman. The monster, in terror, had fled the premises for ever! I should behold it no more! My happiness was supreme! The guilt of my dark deed disturbed me but little. Some few inquiries had been made, but these had been readily answered. Even a search had been instituted – but of course nothing was to be discovered. I looked upon my future felicity as secured.

Upon the fourth day of the assassination, a party of the police came, very unexpectedly, into the house, and proceeded again to make rigorous investigation of the premises. Secure, however, in the inscrutability of my place of concealment, I felt no embarrassment whatever. The officers bade me accompany them in their search. They left no nook or corner unexplored. At length, for the third or fourth time, they descended into the cellar. I quivered not in a muscle. My heart beat calmly as that of one who slumbers in innocence. I walked the cellar from end to end. I folded my arms upon my bosom, and roamed easily to and fro. The police were thoroughly satisfied and prepared to depart. The glee at my heart was too strong to be restrained. I burned to say if but one word, by way of triumph, and to render doubly sure their assurance of my guiltlessness.

'Gentlemen,' I said at last, as the party ascended the steps, 'I delight to have allayed your suspicions. I wish you all health and a little more courtesy. By the bye, gentlemen, this – this is a very well-constructed house,' (in the rabid desire to say something easily, I scarcely knew what I uttered at all), – 'I may say an *excellently* well-constructed house. These walls – are you going, gentlemen? – these walls are solidly put together'; and here, through the mere frenzy of bravado, I rapped heavily with a cane which I held in my hand, upon that very portion of the brick-work behind which stood the corpse of the wife of my bosom.

But may God shield and deliver me from the fangs of the Arch-Fiend! No sooner had the reverberation of my blows sunk into silence, than I was answered by a voice from within the tomb! – by a cry, at first muffled and broken, like the sobbing of a child, and then quickly swelling into one long, loud, and continuous scream, utterly anomalous and in-human – a howl – a wailing shriek, half of horror and half of triumph, such as might have arisen only out of hell, con-jointly from the throats of the damned in their agony and of the demons that exult in the damnation.

Of my own thoughts it is folly to speak. Swooning, I stag-gered to the opposite wall. For one instant the party on the stairs remained motionless, through extremity of terror and awe. In the next a dozen stout arms were toiling at the wall. It fell bodily. The corpse, already greatly decayed and clotted with gore, stood erect before the eyes of the spectators. Upon its head, with red extended mouth and solitary eye of fire, sat the hideous beast whose craft had seduced me into mur-der, and whose informing voice had consigned me to the hangman. I had walled the monster up within the tomb.

NEIL GAIMAN

THE PRICE

TRAMPS AND VAGABONDS have marks they make on gate-posts and trees and doors, letting others of their kind know a little about the people who live at the houses and farms they pass on their travels. I think cats must leave similar signs; how else to explain the cats who turn up at our door through the year, hungry and flea-ridden and abandoned?

We take them in. We get rid of the fleas and the ticks, feed them, and take them to the vet. We pay for them to get their shots, and, indignity upon indignity, we have them neutered or spayed.

And they stay with us: for a few months, or for a year, or for ever.

Most of them arrive in summer. We live in the country, just the right distance out of town for the city dwellers to abandon their cats near us.

We never seem to have more than eight cats, rarely have less than three. The cat population of my house is currently as follows: Hermione and Pod, tabby and black respectively, the mad sisters who live in my attic office and do not mingle; Snowflake, the blue-eyed long-haired white cat, who lived wild in the woods for years before she gave up her wild ways for soft sofas and beds; and, last but largest, Furball, Snow-flake's cushionlike calico long-haired daughter, orange and black and white, whom I discovered as a tiny kitten in our garage one day, strangled and almost dead, her head poked through an old badminton net, and who surprised us all by not dying but instead growing up to be the best-natured cat I have ever encountered.

And then there is the black cat. Who has no other name than the Black Cat and who turned up almost a month ago. We did not realize he was going to be living here at first: he looked too well-fed to be a stray, too old and jaunty to have been abandoned. He looked like a small panther, and he moved like a patch of night.

One day, in the summer, he was lurking about our ramshackle porch: eight or nine years old, at a guess, male, greenish-yellow of eye, very friendly, quite unperturbable. I assumed he belonged to a neighboring farmer or household.

I went away for a few weeks, to finish writing a book, and when I came home he was still on our porch, living in an old cat bed one of the children had found for him. He was, however, almost unrecognizable. Patches of fur had gone, and there were deep scratches on his gray skin. The tip of one ear was chewed away. There was a gash beneath one eye, a slice gone from one lip. He looked tired and thin.

We took the Black Cat to the vet, where we got him some antibiotics, which we fed him each night, along with soft cat food.

We wondered who he was fighting. Snowflake, our beautiful white near-feral queen? Raccoons? A rat-tailed, fanged possum?

Each night the scratches would be worse – one night his side would be chewed up; the next it would be his underbelly, raked with claw marks and bloody to the touch.

When it got to that point, I took him down to the basement to recover beside the furnace and the piles of boxes. He was surprisingly heavy, the Black Cat, and I picked him up and carried him down there, with a cat basket, and a litter box, and some food and water. I closed the door behind me.

I had to wash the blood from my hands when I left the basement.

He stayed down there for four days. At first he seemed too weak to feed himself: a cut beneath one eye had rendered him almost one-eyed, and he limped and lolled weakly, thick yellow pus oozing from the cut in his lip.

I went down there every morning and every night, and I fed him and gave him antibiotics, which I mixed with his canned food, and I dabbed at the worst of the cuts, and spoke to him. He had diarrhea, and, although I changed his litter daily, the basement stank evilly.

The four days that the Black Cat lived in the basement were a bad four days in my house: the baby slipped in the bath and banged her head and might have drowned; I learned that a project I had set my heart on – adapting Hope Mirrlees's novel *Lud in the Mist* for the BBC – was no longer going to happen, and I realized that I did not have the energy to begin again from scratch, pitching it to other networks or to other media; my daughter left for summer camp and immediately began to send home a plethora of heart-tearing letters and cards, five or six each day, imploring us to bring her home; my son had some kind of fight with his best friend, to the point that they were no longer on speaking terms; and, returning home one night, my wife hit a deer that ran out in front of the car. The deer was killed, the car was left undriveable, and my wife sustained a small cut over one eye.

By the fourth day, the cat was prowling the basement, walking haltingly but impatiently between the stacks of books and comics, the boxes of mail and cassettes, of pictures and of gifts and of stuff. He mewed at me to let him out and, reluctantly, I did so.

He went back onto the porch and slept there for the rest of the day.

The next morning there were deep new gashes in his flanks, and clumps of black cat hair – his – covered the wooden boards of the porch.

Letters arrived that day from my daughter, telling us that camp was going better and she thought she could survive a few days; my son and his friend sorted out their problem, although what the argument was about – trading cards, computer games, *Star Wars*, or A Girl – I would never learn. The BBC executive who had vetoed *Lud in the Mist* was discovered to have been taking bribes (well, 'questionable loans') from an independent production company and was sent home on permanent leave: his successor, I was delighted to learn when she faxed me, was the woman who had initially proposed the project to me before leaving the BBC.

I thought about returning the Black Cat to the basement, but decided against it. Instead, I resolved to try and discover what kind of animal was coming to our house each night and from there to formulate a plan of action – to trap it, perhaps.

For birthdays and at Christmas, my family gives me gadgets and gizmos, pricy toys which excite my fancy but, ultimately, rarely leave their boxes. There is a food dehydrator and an electric carving knife, a breadmaking machine, and, last year's present, a pair of see-in-the-dark binoculars. On Christmas Day I had put the batteries into the binoculars and had walked about the basement in the dark, too impatient even to wait until nightfall, stalking a flock of imaginary starlings. (You were warned not to turn it on in the light: that would have damaged the binoculars and quite possibly your eyes as well.) Afterward I had put the device back into its box, and it sat there still, in my office, beside the box of computer cables and forgotten bits and pieces.

Perhaps, I thought, if the creature, dog or cat or raccoon or what-have-you, were to see me sitting on the porch, it would not come, so I took a chair into the box-and-coat-room, little larger than a closet, which overlooks the porch, and, when everyone in the house was asleep, I went out onto the porch and bade the Black Cat goodnight.

That cat, my wife had said, when he first arrived, *is a person*. And there was something very personlike in his huge leonine face: his broad black nose, his greenish-yellow eyes, his fanged but amiable mouth (still leaking amber pus from the right lower lip).

I stroked his head, and scratched him beneath the chin, and wished him well. Then I went inside and turned off the light on the porch.

I sat on my chair in the darkness inside the house with the see-in-the-dark binoculars on my lap. I had switched the binoculars on, and a trickle of greenish light came from the eyepieces.

Time passed, in the darkness.

I experimented with looking at the darkness with the binoculars, learning to focus, to see the world in shades of green. I found myself horrified by the number of swarming insects I could see in the night air: it was as if the night world were some kind of nightmarish soup, swimming with life. Then I lowered the binoculars from my eyes and stared out at the rich blacks and blues of the night, empty and peaceful and calm.

Time passed. I struggled to keep awake, found myself profoundly missing cigarettes and coffee, my two lost addictions. Either of them would have kept my eyes open. But before I had tumbled too far into the world of sleep and dreams, a yowl from the garden jerked me fully awake. I fumbled the binoculars to my eyes and was disappointed to see that it was merely Snowflake, the white cat, streaking across the front garden like a patch of greenish-white light.

She vanished into the woodland to the left of the house and was gone.

I was about to settle myself back down when it occurred to me to wonder what exactly had startled Snowflake so, and I began scanning the middle distance with the binoculars, looking for a huge raccoon, a dog, or a vicious possum. And there was indeed something coming down the driveway toward the house. I could see it through the binoculars, clear as day.

It was the Devil.

I had never seen the Devil before, and, although I had written about him in the past, if pressed would have confessed that I had no belief in him, other than as an imaginary figure, tragic and Miltonian. The figure coming up the driveway was not Milton's Lucifer. It was the Devil.

My heart began to pound in my chest, to pound so hard that it hurt. I hoped it could not see me, that, in a dark house, behind window glass, I was hidden.

The figure flickered and changed as it walked up the drive. One moment it was dark, bull-like, minotaurish, the next it was slim and female, and the next it was a cat itself, a scarred, huge gray-green wildcat, its face contorted with hate.

There are steps that lead up to my porch, four white wooden steps in need of a coat of paint (I knew they were white, although they were, like everything else, green through my binoculars). At the bottom of the steps, the Devil stopped and called out something that I could not understand, three, perhaps four words in a whining, howling language that must have been old and forgotten when Babylon was young; and, although I did not understand the words, I felt the hairs raise on the back of my head as it called.

And then I heard, muffled through the glass but still

audible, a low growl, a challenge, and – slowly, unsteadily – a black figure walked down the steps of the house, away from me, toward the Devil. These days the Black Cat no longer moved like a panther, instead he stumbled and rocked, like a sailor only recently returned to land.

The Devil was a woman, now. She said something soothing and gentle to the cat, in a tongue that sounded like French, and reached out a hand to him. He sank his teeth into her arm, and her lip curled, and she spat at him.

The woman glanced up at me then, and if I had doubted that she was the Devil before, I was certain of it now: the woman's eyes flashed red fire at me, but you can see no red through the night-vision binoculars, only shades of a green. And the Devil saw me through the window. It saw me. I am in no doubt about that at all.

The Devil twisted and writhed, and now it was some kind of jackal, a flat-faced, huge-headed, bull-necked creature, halfway between a hyena and a dingo. There were maggots squirming in its mangy fur, and it began to walk up the steps.

The Black Cat leapt upon it, and in seconds they became a rolling, writhing thing, moving faster than my eyes could follow.

All this in silence.

And then a low roar down the country road at the bottom of our drive, in the distance, lumbered a late-night truck, its blazing headlights burning bright as green suns through the binoculars. I lowered them from my eyes and saw only darkness, and the gentle yellow of headlights, and then the red of rear lights as it vanished off again into the nowhere at all.

When I raised the binoculars once more, there was nothing to be seen. Only the Black Cat on the steps, staring up into the air. I trained the binoculars up and saw something flying away – a vulture, perhaps, or an eagle – and then it flew beyond the trees and was gone.

I went out onto the porch, and picked up the Black Cat, and stroked him, and said kind, soothing things to him. He mewled piteously when I first approached him, but, after a while, he went to sleep on my lap, and I put him into his basket, and went upstairs to my bed, to sleep myself. There was dried blood on my T-shirt and jeans, the following morning.

That was a week ago.

The thing that comes to my house does not come every night. But it comes most nights: we know it by the wounds on the cat, and the pain I can see in those leonine eyes. He has lost the use of his front left paw, and his right eye has closed for good.

I wonder what we did to deserve the Black Cat. I wonder who sent him. And, selfish and scared, I wonder how much more he has to give.

FANCIFUL
FELINES

'The city of cats and the city of men exist one inside the other,
but they are not the same city.'
— ITALO CALVINO, 'The Garden of Stubborn Cats'

FRITZ LEIBER

SPACE-TIME FOR SPRINGERS

GUMMITCH WAS A superkitten as he knew very well, with an I.Q. of about 160. Of course, he didn't talk. But everybody knows that I.Q. tests based on language ability are very one-sided. Besides, he would talk as soon as they started setting a place for him at table and pouring him coffee. Ashurbanipal and Cleopatra ate horsemeat from pans on the floor and they didn't talk. Sissy sat at table but they didn't pour her coffee and she didn't talk – not one word. Father and Mother (whom Gummitch had nicknamed Old Horsemeat and Kitty-Come-Here) sat at table and poured each other coffee and they *did* talk. Q.E.D.

Meanwhile, he would get by very well on thought projection and intuitive understanding of all human speech – not even to mention cat patois, which almost any civilized animal could play by ear. The dramatic monologues and Socratic dialogues, the quiz and panel-show appearances, the felidological expedition to darkest Africa (where he would uncover the real truth behind lions and tigers), the exploration of the outer planets – all these could wait. The same went for the books for which he was ceaselessly accumulating material: *The Encyclopedia of Odors*, *Anthropofeline Psychology*, *Invisible Signs and Secret Wonders*, *Space-Time for Springers*, *Slit Eyes Look at Life*, et cetera. For the present it was enough to live existence to the hilt and soak up knowledge, missing no experience proper to his age level – to rush about with tail aflame.

So to all outward appearances Gummitch was just a

231

vividly normal kitten, as shown by the succession of nick-names he bore along the magic path that led from blue-eyed infancy toward puberty: Little One, Squawker, Portly, Bumble (for purring not clumsiness), Old Starved-to-Death, Fierso, Loverboy (affection not sex), Spook and Catnik. Of these only the last perhaps requires further explanation: the Russians had just sent Muttnik up after Sputnik, so that when one evening Gummitch streaked three times across the firmament of the living-room floor in the same direction, past the fixed stars of the humans and the comparatively slow-moving heavenly bodies of the two older cats, and Kitty-Come-Here quoted the line from Keats:

> Then felt I like some watcher of the skies
> When a new planet swims into his ken;

it was inevitable that Old Horsemeat would say, 'Ah – Catnik!'

The new name lasted all of three days, to be replaced by Gummitch, which showed signs of becoming permanent.

The little cat was on the verge of truly growing up, at least so Gummitch overheard Old Horsemeat comment to Kitty-Come-Here. A few short weeks, Old Horsemeat said, and Gummitch's fiery flesh would harden, his slim neck thicken, the electricity vanish from everything but his fur, and all his delightful kittenish qualities rapidly give way to the earth-bound single-mindedness of a tom. They'd be lucky, Old Horsemeat concluded, if he didn't turn completely surly like Ashurbanipal.

Gummitch listened to these predictions with gay uncon-cern and with secret amusement from his vantage point of superior knowledge, in the same spirit that he accepted so many phases of his outwardly conventional existence: the murderous sidelong looks he got from Ashurbanipal and Cleopatra as he devoured his own horsemeat from his own little tin pan, because they sometimes were given canned cat-food but he never; the stark idiocy of Baby, who didn't know the difference between a live cat and a stuffed teddy bear and who tried to cover up his ignorance by making goo-goo noises and poking indiscriminately at all eyes; the far more serious – because cleverly hidden – maliciousness of Sissy, who had to be watched out for warily – especially when you were alone – and whose retarded – even warped – development, Gummitch knew, was Old Horsemeat and Kitty-Come-Here's deepest, most secret, worry (more of Sissy and her evil ways soon); the limited intellect of Kitty-Come-Here, who despite the amounts of coffee she drank was quite as featherbrained as kittens are supposed to be and who firmly believed, for example, that kittens operated in the same space-time as other beings – that to get from *here* to *there* they had to cross the space *between* – and similar falla-cies; the mental stodginess of even Old Horsemeat, who although he understood quite a bit of the secret doctrine and talked intelligently to Gummitch when they were alone, nevertheless suffered from the limitations of his status – a rather nice old god but a maddeningly slow-witted one.

But Gummitch could easily forgive all this massed in-adequacy and downright brutishness in his felino-human household, because he was aware that he alone knew the real truth about himself and about other kittens and babies as well, the truth which was hidden from weaker minds, the truth that was as intrinsically incredible as the germ theory of disease or the origin of the whole great universe in the explosion of a single atom.

As a baby kitten Gummitch had believed that Old Horse-meat's two hands were hairless kittens permanently attached to the ends of Old Horsemeat's arms but having an independent life of their own. How he had hated and loved those two five-legged sallow monsters, his first playmates, comforters and battle-opponents!

Well, even that fantastic discarded notion was but a trifling fancy compared to the real truth about himself!

The forehead of Zeus split open to give birth to Minerva. Gummitch had been born from the waist-fold of a dirty old terrycloth bathrobe, Old Horsemeat's basic garment. The kitten was intuitively certain of it and had proved it to himself as well as any Descartes or Aristotle. In a kitten-size tuck of that ancient bathrobe the atoms of his body had gathered and quickened into life. His earliest memories were of snoozing wrapped in terrycloth, warmed by Old Horsemeat's heat. Old Horsemeat and Kitty-Come-Here were his true parents. The other theory of his origin, the one he heard Old Horsemeat and Kitty-Come-Here recount from time to time – that he had been the only surviving kitten of a litter abandoned next door, that he had had the shakes from vitamin deficiency and lost the tip of his tail and the hair on his paws and had to be nursed back to life and health with warm yellowish milk-and-vitamins fed from an eyedropper – that other theory was just one of those rationalizations with which mysterious nature cloaks the birth of heroes, perhaps wisely veiling the truth from minds unable to bear it, a rationalization as false as Kitty-Come-Here and Old Horsemeat's touching belief that Sissy and Baby were their children rather than the cubs of Ashurbanipal and Cleopatra.

The day that Gummitch had discovered by pure intuition the secret of his birth he had been filled with a wild instant excitement. He had only kept it from tearing him to pieces by rushing out to the kitchen and striking and devouring a fried scallop, torturing it fiendishly first for twenty minutes.

And the secret of his birth was only the beginning. His intellectual faculties aroused, Gummitch had two days later intuited a further and greater secret: since he was the child of humans he would, upon reaching this maturation date of which Old Horsemeat had spoken, turn not into a sullen tom but into a godlike human youth with reddish golden hair the color of his present fur. He would be poured coffee; and he would instantly be able to talk, probably in all languages. While Sissy (how clear it was now!) would at approximately the same time shrink and fur out into a sharp-clawed and vicious she-cat dark as her hair, sex and self-love her only concerns, fit harem-mate for Cleopatra, concubine to Ashurbanipal.

Exactly the same was true, Gummitch realized at once, for all kittens and babies, all humans and cats, wherever they might dwell. Metamorphosis was as much a part of the fabric of their lives as it was of the insects'. It was also the basic fact underlying all legends of werewolves, vampires and witches' familiars.

If you just rid your mind of preconceived notions, Gummitch told himself, it was all very logical. Babies were stupid, fumbling, vindictive creatures without reason or speech. What more natural than that they should grow up into mute, sullen, selfish beasts bent only on rapine and reproduction? While kittens were quick, sensitive, subtle, supremely alive. What other destiny were they possibly fitted for except to become the deft, word-speaking, book-writing, music-making, meat-getting-and-dispensing masters of the world? To dwell on the physical differences, to point out that kittens and men, babies and cats, are rather unlike in appearance and size, would be to miss the forest for the trees – very much as if an entomologist should proclaim metamorphosis a myth because his microscope failed to discover the wings of a butterfly in a caterpillar's slime or a golden beetle in a grub.

Nevertheless it was such a mind-staggering truth, Gummitch realized at the same time, that it was easy to understand why humans, cats, babies and perhaps most kittens were quite unaware of it. How safely to explain to a butterfly that he was once a hairy crawler, or to a dull larva that he will one day be a walking jewel? No, in such situations the delicate minds of man- and feline-kind are guarded by a merciful mass amnesia, such as Velikovsky has explained prevents us from recalling that in historical times the Earth was catastrophically bumped by the planet Venus operating in the manner of a comet before settling down (with a cosmic sigh of relief, surely!) into its present orbit.

This conclusion was confirmed when Gummitch in the first fever of illumination tried to communicate his great insight to others. He told it in cat patois, as well as that limited jargon permitted, to Ashurbanipal and Cleopatra and even, on the off chance, to Sissy and Baby. They showed no interest whatever, except that Sissy took advantage of his unguarded preoccupation to stab him with a fork.

Later, alone with Old Horsemeat, he projected the great new thoughts, staring with solemn yellow eyes at the old god, but the latter grew markedly nervous and even showed signs of real fear, so Gummitch desisted. ('You'd have sworn he was trying to put across something as deep as the Einstein theory or the doctrine of original sin,' Old Horsemeat later told Kitty-Come-Here.)

But Gummitch was a man now in all but form, the kitten reminded himself after these failures, and it was part of his destiny to shoulder secrets alone when necessary. He wondered if the general amnesia would affect him when he metamorphosed. There was no sure answer to this question, but he hoped not – and sometimes felt that there was reason for his hopes. Perhaps he would be the first true kitten-man, speaking from a wisdom that had no locked doors in it.

Once he was tempted to speed up the process by the use of drugs. Left alone in the kitchen, he sprang onto the table and started to lap up the black puddle in the bottom of Old Horsemeat's coffee cup. It tasted foul and poisonous and he withdrew with a little snarl, frightened as well as revolted. The dark beverage would not work its tongue-loosening magic, he realized, except at the proper time and with the proper ceremonies. Incantations might be necessary as well. Certainly unlawful tasting was highly dangerous.

The futility of expecting coffee to work any wonders by itself was further demonstrated to Gummitch when Kitty-Come-Here, wordlessly badgered by Sissy, gave a few spoonfuls to the little girl, liberally lacing it first with milk and sugar. Of course Gummitch knew by now that Sissy was destined shortly to turn into a cat and that no amount of coffee would ever make her talk, but it was nevertheless instructive to see how she spat out the first mouthful, drooling a lot of saliva after it, and dashed the cup and its contents at the chest of Kitty-Come-Here.

Gummitch continued to feel a great deal of sympathy for his parents in their worries about Sissy and he longed for the day when he would metamorphose and be able as an acknowledged man-child truly to console them. It was heartbreaking to see how they each tried to coax the little girl to talk, always attempting it while the other was absent, how they seized on each accidentally wordlike note in the few sounds she uttered and repeated it back to her hopefully, how they were more and more possessed by fears not so much of her retarded (they thought) development as of her increasingly obvious maliciousness, which was directed chiefly at Baby ... though the two cats and Gummitch bore their share. Once she had caught Baby alone in his crib and used the sharp corner of a block to dot Baby's large-domed lightly downed head with triangular red marks. Kitty-Come-Here had discovered her doing it, but the woman's first action had been to rub Baby's head to obliterate the marks so that Old Horsemeat wouldn't see them. That was the night Kitty-Come-Here hid the abnormal psychology books.

Gummitch understood very well that Kitty-Come-Here and Old Horsemeat, honestly believing themselves to be Sissy's parents, felt just as deeply about her as if they actually were and he did what little he could under the present circumstances to help them. He had recently come to feel a quite independent affection for Baby – the miserable little proto-cat was so completely stupid and defenseless – and so he unofficially constituted himself the creature's guardian, taking his naps behind the door of the nursery and dashing about noisily whenever Sissy showed up. In any case he realized that as a potentially adult member of a felino-human household he had his natural reponsibilities.

Accepting responsibilities was as much a part of a kitten's life, Gummitch told himself, as shouldering unsharable intuitions and secrets, the number of which continued to grow from day to day.

There was, for instance, the Affair of the Squirrel Mirror.

Gummitch had early solved the mystery of ordinary mirrors and of the creatures that appeared in them. A little observation and sniffing and one attempt to get behind the heavy wall-job in the living-room had convinced him that mirror beings were insubstantial or at least hermetically sealed into their other world, probably creatures of pure spirit, harmless imitative ghosts – including the silent Gummitch Double who touched paws with him so softly yet so coldly.

Just the same, Gummitch had let his imagination play with what would happen if one day, while looking into the mirror world, he should let loose his grip on his spirit and let it slip into the Gummitch Double while the other's spirit slipped into his body – if, in short, he should change places with the scentless ghost kitten. Being doomed to a life consisting wholly of imitation and completely lacking in opportunities to show initiative – except for the behind-the-scenes judgement and speed needed in rushing from one mirror to another to keep up with the real Gummitch – would be sickeningly dull, Gummitch decided, and he resolved to keep a tight hold on his spirit at all times in the vicinity of mirrors.

But that isn't telling about the Squirrel Mirror. One morning Gummitch was peering out the front bedroom window that overlooked the roof of the porch. Gummitch had already classified windows as semi-mirrors having two kinds of space on the other side: the mirror world and that harsh region filled with mysterious and dangerously organized-sounding noises called the outer world, into which grownup humans reluctantly ventured at intervals, donning special garments for the purpose and shouting loud farewells that were meant to be reassuring but achieved just the opposite effect. The coexistence of two kinds of space presented no paradox to the kitten who carried in his mind the 27-chapter outline of *Space-Time for Springers* – indeed, it constituted one of the minor themes of the book.

This morning the bedroom was dark and the outer world was dull and sunless, so the mirror world was unusually difficult to see. Gummitch was just lifting his face toward it, nose twitching, his front paws on the sill, when what should rear up on the other side, exactly in the space that the Gummitch Double normally occupied, but a dirty brown, narrow-visaged image with savagely low forehead, dark evil walleyes, and a huge jaw filled with shovel-like teeth.

Gummitch was enormously startled and hideously frightened. He felt his grip on his spirit go limp, and without volition he teleported himself three yards to the rear, making use of that faculty for cutting corners in space-time, traveling by space-warp in fact, which was one of his powers that Kitty-Come-Here refused to believe in and that even Old Horsemeat accepted only on faith.

Then, not losing a moment, he picked himself up by his furry seat, swung himself around, dashed downstairs at top speed, sprang to the top of the sofa, and stared for several seconds at the Gummitch Double in the wall-mirror – not relaxing a muscle strand until he was completely convinced that he was still himself and had not been transformed into the nasty brown apparition that had confronted him in the bedroom window.

'Now what do you suppose brought that on?' Old Horsemeat asked Kitty-Come-Here.

Later Gummitch learned that what he had seen had been a squirrel, a savage, nut-hunting being belonging wholly to the outer world (except for forays into attics) and not at all to the mirror one. Nevertheless he kept a vivid memory of his profound momentary conviction that the squirrel had taken the Gummitch Double's place and been about to take his own. He shuddered to think what would have happened if the squirrel had been actively interested in trading spirits with him. Apparently mirrors and mirror-situations, just as he had always feared, were highly conducive to spirit transfers. He filed the information away in the memory cabinet reserved for dangerous, exciting and possibly useful information, such as plans for climbing straight up glass (diamond-tipped claws!) and flying higher than the trees.

These days his thought cabinets were beginning to feel filled to bursting and he could hardly wait for the moment when the true rich taste of coffee, lawfully drunk, would permit him to speak.

He pictured the scene in detail: the family gathered in conclave at the kitchen table, Ashurbanipal and Cleopatra respectfully watching from floor level, himself sitting erect on chair with paws (or would they be hands?) lightly touching his cup of thin china, while Old Horsemeat poured the thin black steaming stream. He knew the Great Transformation must be close at hand.

At the same time he knew that the other critical situation in the household was worsening swiftly. Sissy, he realized now, was far older than Baby and should long ago have undergone her own somewhat less glamorous though equally necessary transformation (the first tin of raw horsemeat could hardly be as exciting as the first cup of coffee). Her time was long overdue. Gummitch found increasing horror in this mute vampirish being inhabiting the body of a rapidly growing girl, though inwardly equipped to be nothing but a most bloodthirsty she-cat. How dreadful to think of Old Horsemeat and Kitty-Come-Here having to care all their lives for such a monster! Gummitch told himself that if any opportunity for alleviating his parents' misery should ever present itself to him, he would not hesitate for an instant.

Then one night, when the sense of Change was so burstingly strong in him that he knew tomorrow must be the Day, but when the house was also exceptionally unquiet with boards creaking and snapping, taps adrip, and curtains mysteriously rustling at closed windows (so that it was clear that the many spirit worlds including the mirror one must be pressing very close), the opportunity came to Gummitch.

Kitty-Come-Here and Old Horsemeat had fallen into especially sound, drugged sleeps, the former with a bad cold, the latter with one unhappy highball too many (Gummitch knew he had been brooding about Sissy). Baby slept too, though with uneasy whimperings and joggings – moonlight shone full on his crib past a window shade which had whirringly rolled itself up without human or feline agency. Gummitch kept vigil under the crib, with eyes closed but with wildly excited mind pressing outward to every boundary of the house and even stretching here and there into the outerworld. On this night of all nights sleep was unthinkable.

Then suddenly he became aware of footsteps, footsteps so soft they must, he thought, be Cleopatra's.

No, softer than that, so soft they might be those of the Gummitch Double escaped from the mirror world at last and padding up toward him through the darkened halls. A ribbon of fur rose along his spine.

Then into the nursery Sissy came prowling. She looked slim as an Egyptian princess in her long thin yellow nightgown and as sure of herself, but the cat was very strong in her tonight, from the flat intent eyes to the dainty canine teeth slightly bared – one look at her now would have sent Kitty-Come-Here running for the telephone number she kept hidden, the telephone number of the special doctor – and Gummitch realized he was witnessing a monstrous suspension of natural law in that this being should be able to exist for a moment without growing fur and changing round pupils for slit eyes.

He retreated to the darkest corner of the room, suppressing a snarl.

Sissy approached the crib and leaned over Baby in the

moonlight, keeping her shadow off him. For a while she gloated. Then she began softly to scratch his cheek with a long hatpin she carried, keeping away from his eye, but just barely. Baby awoke and saw her and Baby didn't cry. Sissy continued to scratch, always a little more deeply. The moonlight glittered on the jeweled end of the pin.

Gummitch knew he faced a horror that could not be countered by running about or even spitting and screeching. Only magic could fight so obviously supernatural a manifestation. And this was also no time to think of consequences, no matter how clearly and bitterly etched they might appear to a mind intensely awake.

He sprang up onto the other side of the crib, not uttering a sound, and fixed his golden eyes on Sissy's in the moonlight. Then he moved forward straight at her evil face, stepping slowly, not swiftly, using his extraordinary knowledge of the properties of space *to walk straight through her hand and arm as they flailed the hatpin at him.* When his nose-tip finally paused a fraction of an inch from hers his eyes had not blinked once, and she could not look away. Then he unhesitatingly flung his spirit into her like a fistful of flaming arrows and he worked the Mirror Magic.

Sissy's moonlit face, feline and terrified, was in a sense the last thing that Gummitch, the real Gummitch-kitten, ever saw in this world. For the next instant he felt himself enfolded by the foul black blinding cloud of Sissy's spirit, which his own had displaced. At the same time he heard the little girl scream, very loudly but even more distinctly, '*Mommy!*'

That cry might have brought Kitty-Come-Here out of her grave, let alone from sleep merely deep or drugged. Within seconds she was in the nursery, closely followed by Old Horsemeat, and she had caught up Sissy in her arms and the little girl was articulating the wonderful word again and again, and miraculously following it with the command – there could be no doubt, Old Horsemeat heard it too – 'Hold me tight!'

Then Baby finally dared to cry. The scratches on his cheek came to attention and Gummitch, as he had known must happen, was banished to the basement amid cries of horror and loathing chiefly from Kitty-Come-Here.

The little cat did not mind. No basement would be one-tenth as dark as Sissy's spirit that now enshrouded him for always, hiding all the file drawers and the labels on all the folders, blotting out forever even the imagining of the scene of first coffee-drinking and first speech.

In a last intuition, before the animal blackness closed in utterly, Gummitch realized that the spirit, alas, is not the same thing as the consciousness and that one may lose – sacrifice – the first and still be burdened with the second.

Old Horsemeat had seen the hatpin (and hid it quickly from Kitty-Come-Here) and so he knew that the situation was not what it seemed and that Gummich was at the very least being made into a sort of scapegoat. He was quite apologetic when he brought the tin pans of food to the basement during the period of the little cat's exile. It was a comfort to Gummitch, albeit a small one. Gummitch told himself, in his new black halting manner of thinking, that after all a cat's best friend is his man.

From that night Sissy never turned back in her development. Within two months she had made three years' progress in speaking. She became an outstandingly bright, light-footed, high-spirited little girl. Although she never told anyone this, the moonlit nursery and Gummitch's magnified face were her first memories. Everything before that was inky blackness. She was always very nice to Gummitch in a careful sort of way. She could never stand to play the game 'Owl Eyes.'

After a few weeks Kitty-Come-Here forgot her fears and Gummitch once again had the run of the house. But by then the transformation Old Horsemeat had always warned about had fully taken place. Gummitch was a kitten no longer but an almost burly tom. In him it took the psychological form not of sullenness or surliness but an extreme dignity. He seemed at times rather like an old pirate brooding on treasures he would never live to dig up, shores of adventure he would never reach. And sometimes when you looked into his yellow eyes you felt that he had in him all the materials for the book *Slit Eyes Look at Life* – three or four volumes at least – although he would never write it. And that was natural when you come to think of it, for as Gummitch knew very well, bitterly well indeed, his fate was to be the only kitten in the world that did not grow up to be a man.

ITALO CALVINO

THE GARDEN OF STUBBORN CATS

Translated by William Weaver

THE CITY OF CATS and the city of men exist one inside the other, but they are not the same city. Few cats recall the time when there was no distinction: the streets and squares of men were also streets and squares of cats, and the lawns, courtyards, balconies, and fountains; you lived in a broad and various space. But for several generations now domestic felines have been prisoners of an uninhabitable city; the streets are uninterruptedly overrun by the mortal traffic of cat-crushing automobiles; in every square foot of terrain where once a garden extended or a vacant lot or the ruins of an old demolition, now condominiums loom up, welfare housing, brand-new skyscrapers; every entrance is crammed with parked cars; the courtyards, one by one, have been roofed by reinforced concrete and transformed into garages or movie houses or storerooms or workshops. And where a rolling plateau of low roofs once extended, copings, terraces, water tanks, balconies, skylights, corrugated-iron sheds, now one general superstructure rises wherever structures can rise; the intermediate differences in height, between the low ground of the street and the supernal heaven of the penthouses, disappear; the cat of a recent litter seeks in vain the itinerary of its fathers, the point from which to make the soft leap from balustrade to cornice to drainpipe, or for the quick climb on the roof tiles.

But in this vertical city, in this compressed city where all voids tend to fill up and every block of cement tends to mingle with other blocks of cement, a kind of countercity opens, a negative city, that consists of empty slices between wall and wall, of the minimal distances ordained by the building regulations between two constructions, between the rear of one construction and the rear of the next; it is a city of cavities, wells, air conduits, driveways, inner yards, accesses to basements, like a network of dry canals on a planet of stucco and tar, and it is through this network, grazing the walls, that the ancient cat population still scurries.

On occasion, to pass the time, Marcovaldo would follow a cat. It was during the work break, between noon and three, when all the personnel except Marcovaldo went home to eat, and he – who brought his lunch in his bag – laid his place among the packing cases in the warehouse, chewed his snack, smoked a half cigar, and wandered around, alone and idle, waiting for work to resume. In those hours, a cat that peeped in at a window was always welcome company, and a guide for new explorations. He had made friends with a tabby, well fed, a blue ribbon around its neck, surely living with some well-to-do family. This tabby shared with Marcovaldo the habit of an afternoon stroll right after lunch; and naturally a friendship sprang up.

Following his tabby friend, Marcovaldo had started looking at places as if through the round eyes of a cat and even if these places were the usual environs of his firm he saw them in a different light, as settings for cattish stories, with connections practicable only by light, velvety paws. Though from the outside the neighborhood seemed poor in cats, every day on his rounds Marcovaldo made the acquaintance of some new face, and a meow, a hiss, a stiffening of fur on an arched back was enough for him to sense ties and intrigues and rivalries among them. At those moments he thought he had already penetrated the secrecy of the felines' society; and then he felt himself scrutinized by pupils that became slits, under the surveillance of the antennae of taut whiskers, and all the cats around him sat impassive as sphinxes, the pink triangle of their noses convergent on the black triangles of their lips, and the only things that moved were the tips of the ears, with a vibrant jerk like radar. They reached the end of a narrow passage, between squalid blank walls; and, looking around, Marcovaldo saw that the cats that had led him this far had vanished, all of them together, no telling in which direction, even his tabby friend, and they had left him alone. Their realm had territories, ceremonies, customs that it was not yet granted to him to discover.

On the other hand, from the cat city there opened unsuspected peep-holes onto the city of men; and one day the same tabby led him to discover the great Biarritz Restaurant.

Anyone wishing to see the Biarritz Restaurant had only to assume the posture of a cat, that is, proceed on all fours. Cat and man, in this fashion, walked around a kind of dome, at whose foot some low, rectangular little windows opened. Following the tabby's example, Marcovaldo looked down. They were transoms through which the luxurious hall received air and light. To the sound of Gypsy violins, partridges and quails swirled by on silver dishes balanced by the white-gloved fingers of waiters in tailcoats. Or, more precisely, above the partridges and quails the dishes whirled, and above the dishes the white gloves, and poised on the waiters' patent-leather shoes, the gleaming parquet floor, from which hung dwarf potted palms and tablecloths and crystal and buckets like bells with the champagne bottle for their clapper: everything was turned upside down because Marcovaldo, for fear of being seen, wouldn't stick his head inside the window and confined himself to looking at the reversed reflection of the room in the tilted pane.

But it was not so much the windows of the dining-room as those of the kitchens that interested the cat: looking through the former you saw, distant and somehow trans-figured, what in the kitchens presented itself – quite concrete and within paw's reach – as a plucked bird or a fresh fish. And it was toward the kitchens, in fact, that the tabby wanted to lead Marcovaldo, either through a gesture of altruistic friend-ship or else because it counted on the man's help for one of its raids. Marcovaldo, however, was reluctant to leave his belvedere over the main room, first as he was fascinated by the luxury of the place, and then because something down there had riveted his attention. To such an extent that, overcoming his fear of being seen, he kept peeking in, with his head in the transom.

In the midst of the room, directly under that pane, there was a little glass fish tank, a kind of aquarium, where some fat trout were swimming. A special customer approached, a man with a shiny bald pate, black suit, black beard. An old waiter in tailcoat followed him, carrying a little net as if he were going to catch butterflies. The gentleman in black looked at the trout with a grave, intent air; then he raised one hand and with a slow, solemn gesture singled out a fish. The waiter dipped the net into the tank, pursued the appointed trout, captured it, headed for the kitchens, hold-ing out in front of him, like a lance, the net in which the fish wriggled. The gentleman in black, solemn as a magistrate who has handed down a capital sentence, went to take his seat and wait for the return of the trout, sautéed *à la meunière*.

If I found a way to drop a line from up here and make one of those trout bite, Marcovaldo thought, I couldn't be accused of theft; at worst, of fishing in an unauthorized place. And ignoring the meows that called him toward the kitchens, he went to collect his fishing tackle.

Nobody in the crowded dining-room of the Biarritz saw the long, fine line, armed with hook and bait, as it slowly dropped into the tank. The fish saw the bait, and flung themselves on it. In the fray one trout managed to bite the worm, and immediately it began to rise, rise, emerge from the water, a silvery flash, it darted up high, over the laid tables and the trolleys of hors d'œuvres, over the blue flames of the crêpes Suzette, until it vanished into the heavens of the transom.

Marcovaldo had yanked the rod with the brisk snap of the expert fisherman, so the fish landed behind his back. The trout had barely touched the ground when the cat sprang. What little life the trout still had was lost between the tabby's teeth. Marcovaldo, who had abandoned his line at that moment to run and grab the fish, saw it snatched from under his nose, hook and all. He was quick to put one foot on the rod, but the snatch had been so strong that the rod was all the man had left, while the tabby ran off with the fish, pulling the line after it. Treacherous kitty! It had vanished.

But this time it wouldn't escape him; there was that long line trailing after him and showing the way he had taken. Though he had lost sight of the cat, Marcovaldo followed the end of the line; there it was, running along a wall; it climbed a parapet, wound through a doorway, was swallowed up by a basement.... Marcovaldo, venturing into more and more cattish places, climbed roofs, straddled railings, always managed to catch a glimpse – perhaps only a second before it disappeared – of that moving trace that indicated the thief's path.

Now the line played out down a sidewalk, in the midst of the traffic, and Marcovaldo, running after it, almost managed to grab it. He flung himself down on his belly; there, he grabbed it! He managed to seize one end of the line before it slipped between the bars of a gate.

Beyond a half-rusted gate and two bits of wall buried under climbing plants, there was a little rank garden, with a small, abandoned-looking building at the far end of it. A carpet of dry leaves covered the path, and dry leaves lay everywhere under the boughs of the two plane trees, forming actually some little mounds in the yard. A layer of leaves was yellowing in the green water of a pool. Enormous buildings rose all around, skyscrapers with thousands of windows, like so many eyes trained disapprovingly on that little square patch with two trees, a few tiles, and all those yellow leaves, surviving right in the middle of an area of great traffic.

And in this garden, perched on the capitals and balustrades, lying on the dry leaves of the flower beds, climbing on the trunks of the trees or on the drainpipes, motionless on their four paws, their tails making a question mark, seated to wash their faces, there were tiger cats, black cats, white cats, calico cats, tabbies, Angoras, Persians, house cats and stray cats, perfumed cats and mangy cats. Marcovaldo realized he had finally reached the heart of the cats' realm, their secret island. And, in his emotion, he almost forgot his fish.

It had remained, that fish, hanging by the line from the branch of a tree, out of reach of the cats' leaps; it must have dropped from its kidnapper's mouth at some clumsy movement, perhaps as it was defended from the others, or perhaps displayed as an extraordinary prize. The line had got tangled, and Marcovaldo, tug as he would, couldn't manage to yank it loose. A furious battle had meanwhile been joined among the cats, to reach that unreachable fish, or rather, to win the right to try and reach it. Each wanted to prevent the others from leaping; they hurled themselves on one another, they tangled in midair, they rolled around clutching each other, and finally a general war broke out in a whirl of dry, crackling leaves.

After many futile yanks, Marcovaldo now felt the line was free, but he took care not to pull it: the trout would have fallen right in the midst of that infuriated scrimmage of felines.

It was at this moment that, from the top of the walls of the gardens, a strange rain began to fall: fishbones, heads, tails, even bits of lung and lights. Immediately the cats' attention was distracted from the suspended trout and they flung themselves on the new delicacies. To Marcovaldo, this seemed the right moment to pull the line and regain his fish. But, before he had time to act, from a blind of the little villa, two yellow, skinny hands darted out: one was brandishing scissors; the other, a frying pan. The hand with the scissors was raised above the trout, the hand with the frying pan was thrust under it. The scissors cut the line, the trout fell into the pan; hands, scissors, and pan withdrew, the blind closed – all in the space of a second. Marcovaldo was totally bewildered.

'Are you also a cat lover?' A voice at his back made him turn round. He was surrounded by little old women, some of them ancient, wearing old-fashioned hats on their heads; others, younger, but with the look of spinsters; and all were carrying in their hands or their bags packages of leftover meat or fish, and some even had little pans of milk. 'Will you help me throw this package over the fence, for those poor creatures?'

All the ladies, cat lovers, gathered at this hour around the garden of dry leaves to take food to their protégés.

'Can you tell me why they are all here, these cats?' Marcovaldo inquired.

'Where else could they go? This garden is all they have left! Cats come here from other neighborhoods, too, from miles and miles around. . . .'

'And birds, as well,' another lady added. 'They're forced to live by the hundreds and hundreds on these few trees. . . .'

255

'And the frogs, they're all in that pool, and at night they never stop croaking. . . . You can hear them even on the eighth floor of the buildings around here.'

'Who does this villa belong to anyway?' Marcovaldo asked. Now, outside the gate, there weren't just the cat-loving ladies but also other people: the man from the gas pump opposite, the apprentices from a mechanic's shop, the postman, the grocer, some passersby. And none of them, men and women, had to be asked twice; all wanted to have their say, as always when a mysterious and controversial subject comes up.

'It belongs to a marchesa. She lives there, but you never see her. . . .'

'She's been offered millions and millions, by developers, for this little patch of land, but she won't sell. . . .'

'What would she do with millions, an old woman all alone in the world? She wants to hold on to her house, even if it's falling to pieces, rather than be forced to move. . . .' 'It's the only undeveloped bit of land in the downtown area. . . . Its value goes up every year. . . . They've made her offers—'

'Offers! That's not all. Threats, intimidation, persecution . . . you don't know the half of it! Those contractors!'

'But she holds out. She's held out for years. . . .'

'She's a saint. Without her, where would those poor animals go?'

'A lot she cares about the animals, the old miser! Have you ever seen her give them anything to eat?'

'How can she feed the cats when she doesn't have food for herself? She's the last descendant of a ruined family!'

'She hates cats. I've seen her chasing them and hitting them with an umbrella!'

'Because they were tearing up her flower beds!'

'What flower beds? I've never seen anything in this garden but a great crop of weeds!'

Marcovaldo realized that with regard to the old marchesa opinions were sharply divided: some saw her as an angelic being, others as an egoist and a miser.

'It's the same with the birds; she never gives them a crumb!'

'She gives them hospitality. Isn't that plenty?'

'Like she gives the mosquitoes, you mean. They all come from here, from that pool. In the summertime the mosqui toes eat us alive, and it's all the fault of that marchesa!'

'And the mice? This villa is a mine of mice. Under the dead leaves they have their burrows, and at night they come out. . . .'

'As far as the mice go, the cats take care of them. . . .'

'Oh, you and your cats! If we had to rely on them. . . .'

'Why? Have you got something to say against cats?'

Here the discussion degenerated into a general quarrel.

'The authorities should do something: confiscate the villa!' one man cried.

'What gives them the right?' another protested.

'In a modern neighborhood like ours, a mouse nest like this . . . it should be forbidden. . . .'

'Why, I picked my apartment precisely because it over looked this little bit of green. . . .'

'Green, hell! Think of the fine skyscraper they could build here!'

Marcovaldo would have liked to add something of his own, but he couldn't get a word in. Finally, all in one breath, he exclaimed: 'The marchesa stole a trout from me!'

The unexpected news supplied fresh ammunition to the old woman's enemies, but her defenders exploited it as proof of the indigence to which the unfortunate noblewoman was reduced. Both sides agreed that Marcovaldo should go and knock at her door to demand an explanation.

It wasn't clear whether the gate was locked or unlocked; in any case, it opened, after a push, with a mournful creak. Marcovaldo picked his way among the leaves and cats, climbed the steps to the porch, knocked hard at the entrance.

At a window (the very one where the frying pan had appeared), the blind was raised slightly and in one corner a round, pale blue eye was seen, and a clump of hair dyed an undefinable color, and a dry skinny hand. A voice was heard, asking: 'Who is it? Who's at the door?' the words accompanied by a cloud smelling of fried oil.

'It's me, Marchesa. The trout man,' Marcovaldo explained. 'I don't mean to trouble you. I only wanted to tell you, in case you didn't know, that the trout was stolen from me, by that cat, and I'm the one who caught it. In fact the line—'

'Those cats! It's always those cats . . . ,' the marchesa said from behind the shutter, with a shrill, somewhat nasal voice. 'All my troubles come from the cats! Nobody knows what I go through! Prisoner night and day of those horrid beasts! And with all the refuse people throw over the walls, to spite me!'

'But my trout . . .'

'Your trout! What am I supposed to know about your trout!' The marchesa's voice became almost a scream, as if she wanted to drown out the sizzle of the oil in the pan, which came through the window along with the aroma of fried fish. 'How can I make sense of anything, with all the stuff that rains into my house?'

'I understand, but did you take the trout or didn't you?'

'When I think of all the damage I suffer because of the cats! Ah, fine state of affairs! I'm not responsible for anything!

I can't tell you what I've lost! Thanks to those cats, who've occupied house and garden for years! My life at the mercy of those animals! Go and find the owners! Make them pay damages! Damages? A whole life destroyed! A prisoner here, unable to move a step!'

'Excuse me for asking: but who's forcing you to stay?'

From the crack in the blind there appeared sometimes a round, pale blue eye, sometimes a mouth with two protruding teeth; for a moment the whole face was visible, and to Marcovaldo it seemed, bewilderingly, the face of a cat.

'They keep me prisoner, they do, those cats! Oh, I'd be glad to leave! What wouldn't I give for a little apartment all my own, in a nice clean modern building! But I can't go out.... They follow me, they block my path, they trip me up!' The voice became a whisper, as if to confide a secret. 'They're afraid I'll sell the lot.... They won't leave me.... won't allow me.... When the builders come to offer me a contract, you should see them, those cats! They get in the way, pull out their claws; they even chased a lawyer off! Once I had the contract right here, I was about to sign it, and they dived in through the window, knocked over the inkwell, tore up all the pages....'

All of a sudden Marcovaldo remembered the time, the shipping department, the boss. He tiptoed off over the dried leaves, as the voice continued to come through the slats of the blind, enfolded in that cloud apparently from the oil of a frying pan. 'They even scratched me.... I still have the scar.... All alone here at the mercy of these demons....'

Winter came. A blossoming of white flakes decked the branches and capitals and the cats' tails. Under the snow, the dry leaves dissolved into mush. The cats were rarely seen, the cat lovers even less; the packages of fishbones were consigned only to cats who came to the door. Nobody, for quite a while, had seen anything of the marchesa. No smoke came now from the chimneypot of the villa.

One snowy day, the garden was again full of cats, who had returned as if it were spring, and they were meowing as if on a moonlight night. The neighbors realized that something had happened; they went and knocked at the marchesa's door. She didn't answer: she was dead.

In the spring, instead of the garden, there was a huge building site that a contractor had set up. The steam shovels dug down to great depths to make room for the foundations, cement poured into the iron armatures, a very high crane passed beams to the workmen who were making the scaffoldings. But how could they go on with their work? Cats walked along all the planks, they made bricks fall and upset buckets of mortar, they fought in the midst of the piles of sand. When you started to raise an armature, you found a cat perched on the top of it, hissing fiercely. More treacherous pusses climbed onto the masons' backs as if to purr, and there was no getting rid of them. And the birds continued making their nests in all the trestles, the cab of the crane looked like an aviary. . . . And you couldn't dip up a bucket of water that wasn't full of frogs, croaking and hopping. . . .

ALGERNON BLACKWOOD

ANCIENT
SORCERIES

I

THERE ARE, it would appear, certain wholly unremarkable persons, with none of the characteristics that invite adventure, who yet once or twice in the course of their smooth lives undergo an experience so strange that the world catches its breath – and looks the other way! And it was cases of this kind, perhaps, more than any other, that fell into the widespread net of John Silence, the psychic doctor, and, appealing to his deep humanity, to his patience, and to his great qualities of spiritual sympathy, led often to the revelation of problems of the strangest complexity, and of the profoundest possible human interest.

Matters that seemed almost too curious and fantastic for belief he loved to trace to their hidden sources. To unravel a tangle in the very soul of things – and to release a suffering human soul in the process – was with him a veritable passion. And the knots he untied were, indeed, after passing strange.

The world, of course, asks for some plausible basis to which it can attach credence – something it can, at least, pretend to explain. The adventurous type it can understand: such people carry about with them an adequate explanation of their exciting lives, and their characters obviously drive them into the circumstances which produce the adventures. It expects nothing else from them, and is satisfied. But dull, ordinary folk have no right to out-of-the-way experiences, and the world having been led to expect otherwise, is disappointed with them, not to say shocked. Its complacent judgement has been rudely disturbed.

'Such a thing happened to *that* man!' it cries – 'a commonplace person like that! It is too absurd! There must be something wrong!'

Yet there could be no question that something did actually happen to little Arthur Vezin, something of the curious nature he described to Dr Silence. Outwardly or inwardly, it happened beyond a doubt, and in spite of the jeers of his few friends who heard the tale, and observed wisely that 'such a thing might perhaps have come to Iszard, that crack-brained Iszard, or to that odd fish Minski, but it could never have happened to commonplace little Vezin, who was fore-ordained to live and die according to scale.'

But, whatever his method of death was, Vezin certainly did not 'live according to scale' so far as this particular event in his otherwise uneventful life was concerned; and to hear him recount it, and watch his pale delicate features change, and hear his voice grow softer and more hushed as he proceeded, was to know the conviction that his halting words perhaps failed sometimes to convey. He lived the thing over again each time he told it. His whole personality became muffled in the recital. It subdued him more than ever, so that the tale became a lengthy apology for an experience that he deprecated. He appeared to excuse himself and ask your pardon for having dared to take part in so fantastic an episode. For little Vezin was a timid, gentle, sensitive soul, rarely able to assert himself, tender to man and beast, and almost constitutionally unable to say No, or to claim many things that should rightly have been his. His whole scheme of life seemed utterly remote from anything more exciting than missing a train or losing an umbrella on an omnibus. And when this curious event came upon him he was already more years beyond forty than his friends suspected or he cared to admit.

John Silence, who heard him speak of his experience more than once, said that he sometimes left out certain details and put in others; yet they were all obviously true. The whole scene was unforgettably cinematographed on to his mind. None of the details were imagined or invented. And when he told the story with them all complete, the effect was undeniable. His appealing brown eyes shone, and much of the charming personality, usually so carefully repressed, came forward and revealed itself. His modesty was always there, of course, but in the telling he forgot the present and allowed himself to appear almost vividly as he lived again in the past of his adventure.

He was on the way home when it happened, crossing northern France from some mountain trip or other where he buried himself solitary-wise every summer. He had nothing but an unregistered bag in the rack, and the train was jammed to suffocation, most of the passengers being unredeemed holiday English. He disliked them, not because they were his fellow-countrymen, but because they were noisy and obtrusive, obliterating with their big limbs and tweed clothing all the quieter tints of the day that brought him satisfaction and enabled him to melt into insignificance and forget that he was anybody. These English clashed about him like a brass band, making him feel vaguely that he ought to be more self-assertive and obstreperous, and that he did not claim insistently enough all kinds of things that he didn't want and that were really valueless, such as corner seats, windows up or down, and so forth.

So that he felt uncomfortable in the train, and wished the journey were over and he was back again living with his unmarried sister in Surbiton.

And when the train stopped for ten panting minutes at the little station in northern France, and he got out to stretch his legs on the platform, and saw to his dismay a further batch of the British Isles debouching from another train, it suddenly seemed impossible to him to continue the journey. Even *his* flabby soul revolted, and the idea of staying a night in the little town and going on next day by a slower, emptier train, flashed into his mind. The guard was already shouting '*en voiture*' and the corridor of his compartment was already packed when the thought came to him. And, for once, he acted with decision and rushed to snatch his bag.

Finding the corridor and steps impassable, he tapped at the window (for he had a corner seat) and begged the French-man who sat opposite to hand his luggage out to him, explaining in his wretched French that he intended to break the journey there. And this elderly Frenchman, he declared, gave him a look, half of warning, half of reproach, that to his dying day he could never forget; handed the bag through the window of the moving train; and at the same time poured into his ears a long sentence, spoken rapidly and low, of which he was able to comprehend only the last few words: '*à cause du sommeil et à cause des chats*'.

In reply to Dr Silence, whose singular psychic acuteness at once seized upon this Frenchman as a vital point in the adventure, Vezin admitted that the man had impressed him favourably from the beginning, though without being able to explain why. They had sat facing one another during the four hours of the journey, and though no conversation had passed between them – Vezin was timid about his stuttering French – he confessed that his eyes were being continually drawn to his face, almost, he felt, to rudeness, and that each, by a dozen nameless little politenesses and attentions, had evinced the desire to be kind. The men liked each other and their personalities did not clash, or would not have clashed had they chanced to come to terms of acquaintance. The Frenchman, indeed, seemed to have exercised a silent protective influence over the insignificant little Englishman, and without words or gestures betrayed that he wished him well and would gladly have been of service to him.

'And this sentence that he hurled at you after the bag?' asked John Silence, smiling that peculiarly sympathetic smile that always melted the prejudices of his patient, 'were you unable to follow it exactly?'

'It was so quick and low and vehement,' explained Vezin, in his small voice, 'that I missed practically the whole of it. I only caught the few words at the very end, because he spoke them so clearly, and his face was bent down out of the carriage window so near to mine.'

'"*À cause du sommeil et à cause des chats*"?' repeated Dr Silence, as though half speaking to himself.

'That's it exactly,' said Vezin; 'which, I take it, means something like "because of sleep and because of the cats", doesn't it?'

'Certainly, that's how I should translate it,' the doctor observed shortly, evidently not wishing to interrupt more than necessary.

'And the rest of the sentence – all the first part I couldn't understand, I mean – was a warning not to do something – not to stop in the town, or at some particular place in the town, perhaps. That was the impression it made on me.'

Then, of course, the train rushed off, and left Vezin standing on the platform alone and rather forlorn.

The little town climbed in straggling fashion up a sharp hill rising out of the plain at the back of the station, and was crowned by the twin towers of the ruined cathedral peeping over the summit. From the station itself it looked uninteresting and modern, but the fact was that the mediaeval position lay out of sight just beyond the crest. And once he reached the top and entered the old streets, he stepped clean out of modern life into a bygone century. The noise and bustle of the crowded train seemed days away. The spirit of this silent hill-town, remote from tourists and motor-cars, dreaming its own quiet life under the autumn sun, rose up and cast its spell upon him. Long before he recognized this spell he acted under it. He walked softly, almost on tiptoe, down the winding narrow streets where the gables all but met over his head, and he entered the doorway of the solitary inn with a deprecating and modest demeanour that was in itself an apology for intruding upon the place and disturbing its dream.

At first, however, Vezin said, he noticed very little of all this. The attempt at analysis came much later. What struck him then was only the delightful contrast of the silence and peace after the dust and noisy rattle of the train. He felt soothed and stroked like a cat.

'Like a cat, you said?' interrupted John Silence, quickly catching him up.

'Yes. At the very start I felt that.' He laughed apologetically. 'I felt as though the warmth and the stillness and the comfort made me purr. It seemed to be the general mood of the whole place – then.'

The inn, a rambling ancient house, the atmosphere of the old coaching days still about it, apparently did not welcome him too warmly. He felt he was only tolerated, he said. But it was cheap and comfortable, and the delicious cup of afternoon tea he ordered at once made him feel really very pleased with himself for leaving the train in this bold, original way. For to him it had seemed bold and original. He felt something of a dog. His room, too, soothed him with its dark panelling and low irregular ceiling, and the long sloping passage that led to it seemed the natural pathway to a real Chamber of Sleep – a little dim cubby hole out of the world where noise could not enter. It looked upon the courtyard at the back. It was all very charming, and made him think of himself as dressed in very soft velvet somehow, and the floors seemed padded, the walls provided with cushions. The sounds of the streets could not penetrate there. It was an atmosphere of absolute rest that surrounded him.

On engaging the two-franc room he had interviewed the only person who seemed to be about that sleepy afternoon, an elderly waiter with Dundreary whiskers and a drowsy courtesy, who had ambled lazily towards him across the stone yard; but on coming downstairs again for a little promenade in the town before dinner he encountered the proprietress herself. She was a large woman whose hands, feet, and features seemed to swim towards him out of a sea of person. They emerged, so to speak. But she had great dark, vivacious eyes that counteracted the bulk of her body, and betrayed the fact that in reality she was both vigorous and alert. When he first caught sight of her she was knitting in a low chair against the sunlight of the wall, and something at once made him see her as a great tabby cat, dozing, yet awake, heavily sleepy, and yet at the same time prepared for instantaneous action. A great mouser on the watch occurred to him.

She took him in with a single comprehensive glance that was polite without being cordial. Her neck, he noticed, was extraordinarily supple in spite of its proportions, for it turned so easily to follow him, and the head it carried bowed so very flexibly.

'But when she looked at me, you know,' said Vezin, with that little apologetic smile in his brown eyes, and that faintly deprecating gesture of the shoulders that was characteristic of him, 'the odd notion came to me that really she had intended to make quite a different movement, and that with a single bound she could have leaped at me across the width of that stone yard and pounced upon me like some huge cat upon a mouse.'

He laughed a little soft laugh, and Dr Silence made a note in his book without interrupting, while Vezin proceeded in a tone as though he feared he had already told too much and more than we could believe.

'Very soft, yet very active she was, for all her size and mass, and I felt she knew what I was doing even after I had passed and was behind her back. She spoke to me, and her voice was smooth and running. She asked if I had my luggage, and was comfortable in my room, and then added that dinner was at seven o'clock, and that they were very early people in this little country town. Clearly, she intended to convey that late hours were not encouraged.'

Evidently, she contrived by voice and manner to give him the impression that here he would be 'managed', that everything would be arranged and planned for him, and that he had nothing to do but fall into the groove and obey. No decided action or sharp personal effort would be looked for from him. It was the very reverse of the train. He walked quietly out into the street feeling soothed and peaceful. He realized that he was in a *milieu* that suited him and stroked him the right way. It was so much easier to be obedient. He began to purr again, and to feel that all the town purred with him.

About the streets of that little town he meandered gently, falling deeper and deeper into the spirit of repose that characterized it. With no special aim he wandered up and down, and to and fro. The September sunshine fell slantingly over the roofs. Down winding alleyways, fringed with tumbling gables and open casements, he caught fairylike glimpses of the great plain below, and of the meadows and yellow copses lying like a dream-map in the haze. The spell of the past held very potently here, he felt.

The streets were full of picturesquely garbed men and women, all busy enough, going their respective ways; but no one took any notice of him or turned to stare at his obviously English appearance. He was even able to forget that with his tourist appearance he was a false note in a charming picture, and he melted more and more into the scene, feeling delightfully insignificant and unimportant and unselfconscious. It was like becoming part of a softly coloured dream which he did not even realize to be a dream.

On the eastern side the hill fell away more sharply, and the plain below ran off rather suddenly into a sea of gathering shadows in which the little patches of woodland looked like islands and the stubble fields like deep water. Here he strolled along the old ramparts of ancient fortifications that once had been formidable, but now were only vision-like with their charming mingling of broken grey walls and wayward vine and ivy. From the broad coping on which he sat for a moment, level with the rounded tops of clipped plane trees, he saw the esplanade far below lying in shadow. Here and there a yellow sunbeam crept in and lay upon the fallen yellow leaves, and from the height he looked down and saw that the townsfolk were walking to and fro in the cool of the evening. He could just hear the sound of their slow footfalls, and the murmur of their voices floated up to him through the gaps between the trees. The figures looked like shadows as he caught glimpses of their quiet movements far below.

He sat there for some time pondering, bathed in the waves of murmurs and half-lost echoes that rose to his ears, muffled by the leaves of the plane trees. The whole town, and the little hill out of which it grew as naturally as an ancient wood, seemed to him like a being lying there half asleep on the plain and crooning to itself as it dozed.

And, presently, as he sat lazily melting into its dream, a sound of horns and strings and wood instruments rose to his ears, and the town band began to play at the far end of the crowded terrace below to the accompaniment of a very soft, deep-throated drum. Vezin was very sensitive to music, knew about it intelligently, and had even ventured, unknown to his friends, upon the composition of quiet melodies with low-running chords which he played to himself with the soft pedal when no one was about. And this music floating up through the trees from an invisible and doubtless very picturesque band of the townspeople wholly charmed him. He recognized nothing that they played, and it sounded as though they were simply improvising without a conductor. No definitely marked time ran through the pieces, which ended and began oddly after the fashion of wind through an Aeolian harp. It was part of the place and scene, just as the dying sunlight and faintly breathing wind were part of the scene and hour, and the mellow notes of old-fashioned plaintive horns, pierced here and there by the sharper strings, all half smothered by the continuous booming of the deep drum, touched his soul with a curiously potent spell that was almost too engrossing to be quite pleasant.

There was a certain queer sense of bewitchment in it all. The music seemed to him oddly unartificial. It made him think of trees swept by the wind, of night breezes singing among wires and chimney-stacks, or in the rigging of invisible ships; or – and the simile leaped up in his thoughts with a sudden sharpness of suggestion – a chorus of animals, of wild creatures, somewhere in desolate places of the world,

272

crying and singing as animals will, to the moon. He could fancy he heard the wailing, half-human cries of cats upon the tiles at night, rising and falling with weird intervals of sound, and this music, muffled by distance and the trees, made him think of a queer company of these creatures on some roof far away in the sky, uttering their solemn music to one another and the moon in chorus.

It was, he felt at the time, a singular image to occur to him, yet it expressed his sensation pictorially better than anything else. The instruments played such impossibly odd intervals, and the crescendos and diminuendos were so very suggestive of cat-land on the tiles at night, rising swiftly, dropping without warning to deep notes again, and all in such strange confusion of discords and accords. But, at the same time a plaintive sweetness resulted on the whole, and the discords of these half-broken instruments were so singular that they did not distress his musical soul like fiddles out of tune.

He listened a long time, wholly surrendering himself as his character was, and then strolled homewards in the dusk as the air grew chilly.

'There was nothing to alarm?' put in Dr Silence briefly.

'Absolutely nothing,' said Vezin; 'but you know it was all so fantastical and charming that my imagination was profoundly impressed. Perhaps, too,' he continued, gently explanatory, 'it was this stirring of my imagination that caused other impressions; for, as I walked back, the spell of the place began to steal over me in a dozen ways, though all intelligible ways. But there were other things I could not account for in the least, even then.'

'Incidents, you mean?'

'Hardly incidents, I think. A lot of vivid sensations crowded themselves upon my mind and I could trace them to no causes. It was just after sunset and the tumbled old buildings traced magical outlines against an opalescent sky of gold and red. The dusk was running down the twisted streets. All round the hill the plain pressed in like a dim sea, its level rising with the darkness. The spell of this kind of scene, you know, can be very moving, and it was so that night. Yet I felt that what came to me had nothing directly to do with the mystery and wonder of the scene.'

'Not merely the subtle transformations of the spirit that come with beauty,' put in the doctor, noticing his hesitation.

'Exactly,' Vezin went on, duly encouraged and no longer so fearful of our smiles at his expense. 'The impressions came from somewhere else. For instance, down the busy main street where men and women were bustling home from work, shopping at stalls and barrows, idly gossiping in groups, and all the rest of it, I saw that I aroused no interest and that no one turned to stare at me as a foreigner and stranger. I was utterly ignored, and my presence among them excited no special interest or attention.

'And then, quite suddenly, it dawned upon me with conviction that all the time this indifference and inattention were merely feigned. Everybody as a matter of fact was watching me closely. Every movement I made was known and observed. Ignoring me was all a pretence – an elaborate pretence.'

He paused a moment and looked at us to see if we were smiling, and then continued, reassured –

'It is useless to ask me how I noticed this, because I simply cannot explain it. But the discovery gave me something of a shock. Before I got back to the inn, however, another curious thing rose up strongly in my mind and forced my recognition of it as true. And this, too, I may as well say at once, was equally inexplicable to me. I mean I can only give you the fact, as fact it was to me.'

The little man left his chair and stood on the mat before the fire. His diffidence lessened from now onwards, as he lost himself again in the magic of the old adventure. His eyes shone a little already as he talked.

'Well,' he went on, his soft voice rising somewhat with his excitement, 'I was in a shop when it came to me first – though the idea must have been at work for a long time subconsciously to appear in so complete a form all at once. I was buying socks, I think,' he laughed, 'and struggling with my dreadful French, when it struck me that the woman in the shop did not care two pins whether I bought anything or not. She was indifferent whether she made a sale or did not make a sale. She was only pretending to sell.

'This sounds a very small and fanciful incident to build upon what follows. But really it was not small. I mean it was the spark that lit the line of powder and ran along to the big blaze in my mind.

'For the whole town, I suddenly realized, was something other than I so far saw it. The real activities and interests of the people were elsewhere and otherwise than appeared. Their true lives lay somewhere out of sight behind the scenes. Their busy-ness was but the outward semblance that masked their actual purposes. They bought and sold, and ate and drank, and walked about the streets, yet all the while the main stream of their existence lay somewhere beyond my ken, underground, in secret places. In the shops and at the stalls they did not care whether I purchased their articles or not; at the inn, they were indifferent to my staying or going; their life lay remote from my own, springing from hidden, mysterious sources, coursing out of sight, unknown. It was all a great elaborate pretence, assumed possibly for my benefit, or possibly for purposes of their own. But the main current of their energies ran elsewhere. I almost felt as an unwelcome foreign substance might be expected to feel when it has found its way into the human system and the whole body organizes itself to eject it or to absorb it. The town was doing this very thing to me.

'This bizarre notion presented itself forcibly to my mind as I walked home to the inn, and I began busily to wonder wherein the true life of this town could lie and what were the actual interests and activities of its hidden life.

'And, now that my eyes were partly opened, I noticed other things too that puzzled me, first of which, I think, was the extraordinary silence of the whole place. Positively, the town was muffled. Although the streets were paved with cobbles the people moved about silently, softly, with padded feet, like cats. Nothing made noise. All was hushed, subdued, muted. The very voices were quiet, low-pitched like purring. Nothing clamorous, vehement or emphatic seemed able to live in the drowsy atmosphere of soft dreaming that soothed this little hill-town into its sleep. It was like the woman at the inn – an outward repose screening intense inner activity and purpose.

'Yet there was no sign of lethargy or sluggishness anywhere about it. The people were active and alert. Only a magical and uncanny softness lay over them all like a spell.'

Vezin passed his hand across his eyes for a moment as though the memory had become very vivid. His voice had run off into a whisper so that we heard the last part with difficulty. He was telling a true thing obviously, yet something that he both liked and hated telling.

'I went back to the inn,' he continued presently in a louder voice, 'and dined. I felt a new strange world about me. My old world of reality receded. Here, whether I liked it or no, was something new and incomprehensible. I regretted having left the train so impulsively. An adventure was upon me, and I loathed adventures as foreign to my nature. Moreover, this was the beginning apparently of an adventure somewhere deep within me, in a region I could not check or measure, and a feeling of alarm mingled itself with my wonder – alarm for the stability of what I had for forty years recognized as my "personality".

'I went upstairs to bed, my mind teeming with thoughts that were unusual to me, and of rather a haunting description. By way of relief I kept thinking of that nice, prosaic noisy train and all those wholesome, blustering passengers. I almost wished I were with them again. But my dreams took me elsewhere. I dreamed of cats, and soft-moving creatures, and the silence of life in a dim muffled world beyond the senses.'

II

Vezin stayed on from day to day, indefinitely, much longer than he had intended. He felt in a kind of dazed, somnolent condition. He did nothing in particular, but the place fascinated him and he could not decide to leave. Decisions were always very difficult for him and he sometimes wondered how he had ever brought himself to the point of leaving the train. It seemed as though some one else must have arranged it for him, and once or twice his thoughts ran to the swarthy Frenchman who had sat opposite. If only he could have understood that long sentence ending so strangely with '*à cause du sommeil et à cause des chats*'. He wondered what it all meant.

Meanwhile the hushed softness of the town held him prisoner and he sought in his muddling, gentle way to find out where the mystery lay, and what it was all about. But his limited French and his constitutional hatred of active investigation made it hard for him to buttonhole anybody and ask questions. He was content to observe, and watch, and remain negative.

The weather held on calm and hazy, and this just suited him. He wandered about the town till he knew every street and alley. The people suffered him to come and go without let or hindrance, though it became clearer to him every day that he was never free himself from observation. The town watched him as a cat watches a mouse. And he got no nearer to finding out what they were all so busy with or where the main stream of their activities lay. This remained hidden. The people were as soft and mysterious as cats.

But that he was continually under observation became more evident from day to day.

For instance, when he strolled to the end of the town and entered a little green public garden beneath the ramparts and seated himself upon one of the empty benches in the sun, he was quite alone – at first. Not another seat was occupied; the little park was empty, the paths deserted. Yet, within ten minutes of his coming, there must have been fully twenty persons scattered about him, some strolling aimlessly along the gravel walks, staring at the flowers, and others seated on the wooden benches enjoying the sun like himself. None of them appeared to take any notice of him; yet he understood quite well they had all come there to watch. They kept him under close observation. In the street they had seemed busy enough, hurrying upon various errands; yet these were suddenly all forgotten and they had nothing to do but loll and laze in the sun, their duties unremembered. Five minutes after he left, the garden was again deserted, the seats vacant. But in the crowded street it was the same thing again; he was never alone. He was ever in their thoughts.

By degrees, too, he began to see how it was he was so

cleverly watched, yet without the appearance of it. The people did nothing *directly.* They behaved *obliquely.* He laughed in his mind as the thought thus clothed itself in words, but the phrase exactly described it. They looked at him from angles which naturally should have led their sight in another direction altogether. Their movements were oblique, too, so far as these concerned himself. The straight, direct thing was not their way evidently. They did nothing obviously. If he entered a shop to buy, the woman walked instantly away and busied herself with something at the farther end of the counter, though answering at once when he spoke, showing that she knew he was there and that this was only her way of attending to him. It was the fashion of the cat she followed. Even in the dining-room of the inn, the be-whiskered and courteous waiter, lithe and silent in all his movements, never seemed able to come straight to his table for an order or a dish. He came by zigzags, indirectly, vaguely, so that he appeared to be going to another table altogether, and only turned suddenly at the last moment, and was there beside him.

Vezin smiled curiously to himself as he described how he began to realize these things. Other tourists there were none in the hostel, but he recalled the figures of one or two old men, inhabitants, who took their *déjeuner* and dinner there, and remembered how fantastically they entered the room in similar fashion. First, they paused in the doorway, peering about the room, and then, after a temporary inspection, they came in, as it were, sideways, keeping close to the walls so that he wondered which table they were making for, and at the last minute making almost a little quick run to their particular seats. And again he thought of the ways and methods of cats.

Other small incidents, too, impressed him as all part of

this queer, soft town with its muffled, indirect life, for the way some of the people appeared and disappeared with extraordinary swiftness puzzled him exceedingly. It may have been all perfectly natural, he knew, yet he could not make it out how the alleys swallowed them up and shot them forth in a second of time when there were no visible doorways or openings near enough to explain the phenomenon. Once he followed two elderly women who, he felt, had been particularly examining him from across the street – quite near the inn this was – and saw them turn the corner a few feet only in front of him. Yet when he sharply followed on their heels he saw nothing but an utterly deserted alley stretching in front of him with no sign of a living thing. And the only opening through which they could have escaped was a porch some fifty yards away, which not the swiftest human runner could have reached in time.

And in just such sudden fashion people appeared, when he never expected them. Once when he heard a great noise of fighting going on behind a low wall, and hurried up to see what was going on, what should he see but a group of girls and women engaged in vociferous conversation which instantly hushed itself to the normal whispering note of the town when his head appeared over the wall. And even then none of them turned to look at him directly, but slunk off with the most unaccountable rapidity into doors and sheds across the yard. And their voices, he thought, had sounded so like, so strangely like, the angry snarling of fighting animals, almost of cats.

The whole spirit of the town, however, continued to evade him as something elusive, protean, screened from the outer world, and at the same time intensely, genuinely vital; and, since he now formed part of its life, this concealment puzzled and irritated him; more – it began rather to frighten him.

Out of the mists that slowly gathered about his ordinary surface thoughts, there rose again the idea that the inhabitants were waiting for him to declare himself, to take an attitude, to do this, or to do that; and that when he had done so they in their turn would at length make some direct response, accepting or rejecting him. Yet the vital matter concerning which his decision was awaited came no nearer to him.

Once or twice he purposely followed little processions or groups of the citizens in order to find out, if possible, on what purpose they were bent; but they always discovered him in time and dwindled away, each individual going his or her own way. It was always the same: he never could learn what their main interest was. The cathedral was ever empty, the old church of St Martin, at the other end of the town, deserted. They shopped because they had to, and not because they wished to. The booths stood neglected, the stalls unvisited, the little *cafés* desolate. Yet the streets were always full, the townsfolk ever on the bustle.

'Can it be,' he thought to himself, yet with a deprecating laugh that he should have dared to think anything so odd, 'can it be that these people are people of the twilight, that they live only at night their real life, and come out honestly only with the dusk? That during the day they make a sham though brave pretence, and after the sun is down their true life begins? Have they the souls of night-things, and is the whole blessed town in the hands of the cats?'

The fancy somehow electrified him with little shocks of shrinking and dismay. Yet, though he affected to laugh, he knew that he was beginning to feel more than uneasy, and that strange forces were tugging with a thousand invisible cords at the very centre of his being. Something utterly remote from his ordinary life, something that had not waked for years, began faintly to stir in his soul, sending feelers abroad into his brain and heart, shaping queer thoughts and penetrating even into certain of his minor actions. Something exceedingly vital to himself, to his soul, hung in the balance.

And, always when he returned to the inn about the hour of sunset, he saw the figures of the townsfolk stealing through the dusk from their shop doors, moving sentry-wise to and fro at the corners of the streets, yet always vanishing silently like shadows at his near approach. And as the inn invariably closed its doors at ten o'clock he had never yet found the opportunity he rather half-heartedly sought to see for himself what account the town could give of itself at night.

'– *à cause du sommeil et à cause des chats*' – the words now rang in his ears more and more often, though still as yet without any definite meaning.

Moreover, something made him sleep like the dead.

III

It was, I think, on the fifth day – though in this detail his story sometimes varied – that he made a definite discovery which increased his alarm and brought him up to a rather sharp climax. Before that he had already noticed that a change was going forward and certain subtle transformations being brought about in his character which modified several of his minor habits. And he had affected to ignore them. Here, however, was something he could no longer ignore; and it startled him.

At the best of times he was never very positive, always negative rather, compliant and acquiescent; yet, when necessity arose he was capable of reasonably vigorous action and could take a strongish decision. The discovery he now made that brought him up with such a sharp turn was that this power had positively dwindled to nothing. He found it impossible to make up his mind. For, on this fifth day, he realized that he had stayed long enough in the town and that for reasons he could only vaguely define to himself it was wiser *and safer* that he should leave.

And he found that he could not leave!

This is difficult to describe in words, and it was more by gesture and the expression of his face that he conveyed to Dr Silence the state of impotence he had reached. All this spying and watching, he said, had as it were spun a net about his feet so that he was trapped and powerless to escape; he felt like a fly that had blundered into the intricacies of a great web; he was caught, imprisoned, and could not get away. It was a distressing sensation. A numbness had crept over his will till it had become almost incapable of decision. The mere thought of vigorous action – action towards escape – began to terrify him. All the currents of his life had turned inwards upon himself, striving to bring to the surface something that lay buried almost beyond reach, determined to force his recognition of something he had long forgotten – forgotten years upon years, centuries almost ago. It seemed as though a window deep within his being would presently open and reveal an entirely new world, yet somehow a world that was not unfamiliar. Beyond that, again, he fancied a great curtain hung; and when that too rolled up he would see still farther into this region and at last understand something of the secret life of these extraordinary people.

'Is this why they wait and watch?' he asked himself with rather a shaking heart, 'for the time when I shall join them – or refuse to join them? Does the decision rest with me after all, and not with them?'

And it was at this point that the sinister character of the adventure first really declared itself, and he became genuinely alarmed. The stability of his rather fluid little personality was at stake, he felt, and something in his heart turned coward.

Why otherwise should he have suddenly taken to walking stealthily, silently, making as little sound as possible, for ever looking behind him? Why else should he have moved almost on tiptoe about the passages of the practically deserted inn, and when he was abroad have found himself deliberately taking advantage of what cover presented itself? And why, if he was not afraid, should the wisdom of staying indoors after sundown have suddenly occurred to him as eminently desirable? Why, indeed?

And, when John Silence gently pressed him for an explanation of these things, he admitted apologetically that he had none to give.

'It was simply that I feared something might happen to me unless I kept a sharp look-out. I felt afraid. It was instinctive,' was all he could say. 'I got the impression that the whole town was after me – wanted me for something; and that if it got me I should lose myself, or at least the Self I knew, in some unfamiliar state of consciousness. But I am not a psychologist, you know,' he added meekly, 'and I cannot define it better than that.'

It was while lounging in the courtyard half an hour before the evening meal that Vezin made this discovery, and he at once went upstairs to his quiet room at the end of the winding passage to think it over alone. In the yard it was empty enough, true, but there was always the possibility that the big woman whom he dreaded would come out of some door, with her pretence of knitting, to sit and watch him. This had happened several times, and he could not endure the sight of her. He still remembered his original fancy, bizarre though it was, that she would spring upon him the moment his back was turned and land with one single crushing leap upon his neck. Of course it was nonsense, but then it haunted him, and once an idea begins to do that it ceases to be nonsense. It has clothed itself in reality.

He went upstairs accordingly. It was dusk, and the oil lamps had not yet been lit in the passages. He stumbled over the uneven surface of the ancient flooring, passing the dim outlines of doors along the corridor – doors that he had never once seen opened – rooms that seemed never occupied. He moved, as his habit now was, stealthily and on tiptoe.

Half-way down the last passage to his own chamber there was a sharp turn, and it was just here, while groping round the walls with outstretched hands, that his fingers touched something that was not wall – something that moved. It was soft and warm in texture, indescribably fragrant, and about the height of his shoulder; and he immediately thought of a furry, sweet-smelling kitten. The next minute he knew it was something quite different.

Instead of investigating, however, – his nerves must have been too overwrought for that, he said, – he shrank back as closely as possible against the wall on the other side. The thing, whatever it was, slipped past him with a sound of rustling and, retreating with light footsteps down the passage behind him, was gone. A breath of warm, scented air was wafted to his nostrils.

Vezin caught his breath for an instant and paused, stock-still, half leaning against the wall – and then almost ran down the remaining distance and entered his room with a rush, locking the door hurriedly behind him. Yet it was not fear that made him run: it was excitement, pleasurable excitement. His nerves were tingling, and a delicious glow made itself felt all over his body. In a flash it came to him that this was just what he had felt twenty-five years ago as a boy when he was in love for the first time. Warm currents of life ran all over him and mounted to his brain in a whirl of soft delight. His mood was suddenly become tender, melting, loving.

The room was quite dark, and he collapsed upon the sofa by the window, wondering what had happened to him and what it all meant. But the only thing he understood clearly in that instant was that something in him had swiftly, magically changed: he no longer wished to leave, or to argue with himself about leaving. The encounter in the passage-way had changed all that. The strange perfume of it still hung about him, bemusing his heart and mind. For he knew that it was a girl who had passed him, a girl's face that his fingers had brushed in the darkness, and he felt in some extraordinary way as though he had been actually kissed by her, kissed full upon the lips.

Trembling, he sat upon the sofa by the window and struggled to collect his thoughts. He was utterly unable to understand how the mere passing of a girl in the darkness of a narrow passage-way could communicate so electric a thrill to his whole being that he still shook with the sweetness of it. Yet, there it was! And he found it as useless to deny as to attempt analysis. Some ancient fire had entered his veins, and now ran coursing through his blood; and that he was forty-five instead of twenty did not matter one little jot. Out of all the inner turmoil and confusion emerged the one salient fact that the mere atmosphere, the merest casual touch, of this girl, unseen, unknown in the darkness, had been sufficient to stir dormant fires in the centre of his heart, and rouse his whole being from a state of feeble sluggishness to one of tearing and tumultuous excitement.

After a time, however, the number of Vezin's years began

to assert their cumulative power; he grew calmer, and when a knock came at length upon his door and he heard the waiter's voice suggesting that dinner was nearly over, he pulled himself together and slowly made his way downstairs into the dining-room.

Every one looked up as he entered, for he was very late, but he took his customary seat in the far corner and began to eat. The trepidation was still in his nerves, but the fact that he had passed through the courtyard and hall without catching sight of a petticoat served to calm him a little. He ate so fast that he had almost caught up with the current stage of the table d'hôte, when a slight commotion in the room drew his attention.

His chair was so placed that the door and the greater portion of the long *salle à manger* were behind him, yet it was not necessary to turn round to know that the same person he had passed in the dark passage had now come into the room. He felt the presence long before he heard or saw any one. Then he became aware that the old men, the only other guests, were rising one by one in their places, and exchanging greetings with some one who passed among them from table to table. And when at length he turned with his heart beating furiously to ascertain for himself, he saw the form of a young girl, lithe and slim, moving down the centre of the room and making straight for his own table in the corner. She moved wonderfully, with sinuous grace, like a young panther, and her approach filled him with such delicious bewilderment that he was utterly unable to tell at first what her face was like, or discover what it was about the whole presentment of the creature that filled him anew with trepidation and delight.

'*Ah, Mamselle est de retour!*' he heard the old waiter murmur at his side, and he was just able to take in that she was the daughter of the proprietress, when she was upon him, and he heard her voice. She was addressing him. Something of red lips he saw and laughing white teeth, and stray wisps of fine dark hair about the temples; but all the rest was a dream in which his own emotion rose like a thick cloud before his eyes and prevented his seeing accurately, or knowing exactly what he did. He was aware that she greeted him with a charming little bow; that her beautiful large eyes looked searchingly into his own; that the perfume he had noticed in the dark passage again assailed his nostrils, and that she was bending a little towards him and leaning with one hand on the table at his side. She was quite close to him – that was the chief thing he knew – explaining that she had been asking after the comfort of her mother's guests, and now was introducing herself to the latest arrival – himself.

'M'sieur has already been here a few days,' he heard the waiter say; and then her own voice, sweet as singing, replied –

'Ah, but M'sieur is not going to leave us just yet, I hope. My mother is too old to look after the comfort of our guests properly, but now I am here I will remedy all that.' She laughed deliciously. 'M'sieur shall be well looked after.'

Vezin, struggling with his emotion and desire to be polite, half rose to acknowledge the pretty speech, and to stammer some sort of reply, but as he did so his hand by chance touched her own that was resting upon the table, and a shock that was for all the world like a shock of electricity, passed from her skin into his body. His soul wavered and shook deep within him. He caught her eyes fixed upon his own with a look of most curious intentness, and the next moment he knew that he had sat down wordless again on his chair, that the girl was already half-way across the room, and that he was trying to eat his salad with a dessert-spoon and a knife.

Longing for her return, and yet dreading it, he gulped

down the remainder of his dinner, and then went at once to his bedroom to be alone with his thoughts. This time the passages were lighted, and he suffered no exciting contretemps; yet the winding corridor was dim with shadows, and the last portion, from the bend of the walls onwards, seemed longer than he had ever known it. It ran downhill like the pathway on a mountain side, and as he tiptoed softly down it he felt that by rights it ought to have led him clean out of the house into the heart of a great forest. The world was singing with him. Strange fancies filled his brain, and once in the room, with the door securely locked, he did not light the candles, but sat by the open window thinking long, long thoughts that came unbidden in troops to his mind.

IV

This part of the story he told to Dr Silence, without special coaxing, it is true, yet with much stammering embarrassment. He could not in the least understand, he said, how the girl had managed to affect him so profoundly, and even before he had set eyes upon her. For her mere proximity in the darkness had been sufficient to set him on fire. He knew nothing of enchantments, and for years had been a stranger to anything approaching tender relations with any member of the opposite sex, for he was encased in shyness, and realized his overwhelming defects only too well. Yet this bewitching young creature came to him deliberately. Her manner was unmistakable, and she sought him out on every possible occasion. Chaste and sweet she was undoubtedly, yet frankly inviting; and she won him utterly with the first glance of her shining eyes, even if she had not already done so in the dark merely by the magic of her invisible presence.

'You felt she was altogether wholesome and good!' queried

the doctor. 'You had no reaction of any sort – for instance, of alarm?'

Vezin looked up sharply with one of his inimitable little apologetic smiles. It was some time before he replied. The mere memory of the adventure had suffused his shy face with blushes, and his brown eyes sought the floor again before he answered.

'I don't think I can quite say that,' he explained presently. 'I acknowledged certain qualms, sitting up in my room afterwards. A conviction grew upon me that there was something about her – how shall I express it? – well, something unholy. It is not impurity in any sense, physical or mental, that I mean, but something quite indefinable that gave me a vague sensation of the creeps. She drew me, and at the same time repelled me, more than – than—'

He hesitated, blushing furiously, and unable to finish the sentence.

'Nothing like it has ever come to me before or since,' he concluded, with lame confusion. 'I suppose it was, as you suggested just now, something of an enchantment. At any rate, it was strong enough to make me feel that I would stay in that awful little haunted town for years if only I could see her every day, hear her voice, watch her wonderful movements, and sometimes, perhaps, touch her hand.'

'Can you explain to me what you felt was the source of her power?' John Silence asked, looking purposely anywhere but at the narrator.

'I am surprised that you should ask me such a question,' answered Vezin, with the nearest approach to dignity he could manage. 'I think no man can describe to another convincingly wherein lies the magic of the woman who ensnares him. I certainly cannot. I can only say this slip of a girl bewitched me, and the mere knowledge that she was living and sleeping in the same house filled me with an extraordinary sense of delight.

'But there's one thing I can tell you,' he went on earnestly, his eyes aglow, 'namely, that she seemed to sum up and synthesise in herself all the strange hidden forces that operated so mysteriously in the town and its inhabitants. She had the silken movements of the panther, going smoothly, silently to and fro, and the same indirect, oblique methods as the townsfolk, screening, like them, secret purposes of her own – purposes that I was sure had *me* for their objective. She kept me, to my terror and delight, ceaselessly under observation, yet so carelessly, so consummately, that another man less sensitive, if I may say so' – he made a deprecating gesture – 'or less prepared by what had gone before, would never have noticed it at all. She was always still, always reposeful, yet she seemed to be everywhere at once, so that I never could escape from her. I was continually meeting the stare and laughter of her great eyes, in the corners of the rooms, in the passages, calmly looking at me through the windows, or in the busiest parts of the public streets.'

Their intimacy, it seems, grew very rapidly after this first encounter which had so violently disturbed the little man's equilibrium. He was naturally very prim, and prim folk live mostly in so small a world that anything violently unusual may shake them clean out of it, and they therefore instinctively distrust originality. But Vezin began to forget his primness after awhile. The girl was always modestly behaved, and as her mother's representative she naturally had to do with the guests in the hotel. It was not out of the way that a spirit of camaraderie should spring up. Besides, she was young, she was charmingly pretty, she was French, and – she obviously liked him.

At the same time, there was something indescribable –

a certain indefinable atmosphere of other places, other times – that made him try hard to remain on his guard, and sometimes made him catch his breath with a sudden start. It was all rather like a delirious dream, half delight, half dread, he confided in a whisper to Dr Silence; and more than once he hardly knew quite what he was doing or saying, as though he were driven forward by impulses he scarcely recognized as his own.

And though the thought of leaving presented itself again and again to his mind, it was each time with less insistence, so that he stayed on from day to day, becoming more and more a part of the sleepy life of this dreamy mediaeval town, losing more and more of his recognizable personality. Soon, he felt, the Curtain within would roll up with an awful rush, and he would find himself suddenly admitted into the secret purposes of the hidden life that lay behind it all. Only, by that time, he would have become transformed into an entirely different being.

And, meanwhile, he noticed various little signs of the intention to make his stay attractive to him: flowers in his bedroom, a more comfortable arm-chair in the corner, and even special little extra dishes on his private table in the dining-room. Conversations, too, with 'Mademoiselle Ilsé' became more and more frequent and pleasant, and although they seldom travelled beyond the weather, or the details of the town, the girl, he noticed, was never in a hurry to bring them to an end, and often contrived to interject little odd sentences that he never properly understood, yet felt to be significant.

And it was these stray remarks, full of a meaning that evaded him, that pointed to some hidden purpose of her own and made him feel uneasy. They all had to do, he felt sure, with reasons for his staying on in the town indefinitely.

'And has M'sieur not even yet come to a decision?' she said softly in his ear, sitting beside him in the sunny yard before *déjeuner*, the acquaintance having progressed with significant rapidity. 'Because, if it's so difficult, we must all try together to help him!'

The question startled him, following upon his own thoughts. It was spoken with a pretty laugh, and a stray bit of hair across one eye, as she turned and peered at him half roguishly. Possibly he did not quite understand the French of it, for her near presence always confused his small knowledge of the language distressingly. Yet the words, and her manner, and something else that lay behind it all in her mind, frightened him. It gave such point to his feeling that the town was waiting for him to make his mind up on some important matter.

At the same time, her voice, and the fact that she was there so close beside him in her soft dark dress, thrilled him inexpressibly.

'It is true I find it difficult to leave,' he stammered, losing his way deliciously in the depths of her eyes, 'and especially now that Mademoiselle Ilsé has come.'

He was surprised at the success of his sentence, and quite delighted with the little gallantry of it. But at the same time he could have bitten his tongue off for having said it.

'Then after all you like our little town, or you would not be pleased to stay on,' she said, ignoring the compliment.

'I am enchanted with it, and enchanted with you,' he cried, feeling that his tongue was somehow slipping beyond the control of his brain. And he was on the verge of saying all manner of other things of the wildest description, when the girl sprang lightly up from her chair beside him, and made to go.

'It is *soupe à l'oignon* today!' she cried, laughing back at him through the sunlight, 'and I must go and see about it. Otherwise, you know, M'sieur will not enjoy his dinner, and then, perhaps, he will leave us!'

He watched her cross the courtyard, moving with all the grace and lightness of the feline race, and her simple black dress clothed her, he thought, exactly like the fur of the same supple species. She turned once to laugh at him from the porch with the glass door, and then stopped a moment to speak to her mother, who sat knitting as usual in her corner seat just inside the hallway.

But how was it, then, that the moment his eye fell upon this ungainly woman, the pair of them appeared suddenly as other than they were? Whence came that transforming dignity and sense of power that enveloped them both as by magic? What was it about that massive woman that made her appear instantly regal, and set her on a throne in some dark and dreadful scenery, wielding a sceptre over the red glare of some tempestuous orgy? And why did this slender stripling of a girl, graceful as a willow, lithe as a young leopard, assume suddenly an air of sinister majesty, and move with flame and smoke about her head, and the darkness of night beneath her feet?

Vezin caught his breath and sat there transfixed. Then, almost simultaneously with its appearance, the queer notion vanished again, and the sunlight of day caught them both, and he heard her laughing to her mother about the *soupe à l'oignon*, and saw her glancing back at him over her dear little shoulder with a smile that made him think of a dew-kissed rose bending lightly before summer airs.

And, indeed, the onion soup was particularly excellent that day, because he saw another cover laid at his small table, and, with fluttering heart, heard the waiter murmur by way of explanation that 'Mamselle Ilsé would honour M'sieur today at *déjeuner*, as her custom sometimes is with her mother's guests.'

So actually she sat by him all through that delirious meal, talking quietly to him in easy French, seeing that he was well looked after, mixing the salad-dressing, and even helping him with her own hand. And, later in the afternoon, while he was smoking in the courtyard, longing for a sight of her as soon as her duties were done, she came again to his side, and when he rose to meet her, she stood facing him a moment, full of a perplexing sweet shyness before she spoke—

'My mother thinks you ought to know more of the beauties of our little town, and *I* think so too! Would M'sieur like me to be his guide, perhaps? I can show him everything, for our family has lived here for many generations.'

She had him by the hand, indeed, before he could find a single word to express his pleasure, and led him, all unresisting, out into the street, yet in such a way that it seemed perfectly natural she should do so, and without the faintest suggestion of boldness or immodesty. Her face glowed with the pleasure and interest of it, and with her short dress and tumbled hair she looked every bit the charming child of seventeen that she was, innocent and playful, proud of her native town, and alive beyond her years to the sense of its ancient beauty.

So they went over the town together, and she showed him what she considered its chief interest: the tumble-down old house where her forebears had lived; the sombre, aristocratic-looking mansion where her mother's family dwelt for centuries, and the ancient marketplace where several hundred years before the witches had been burnt by the score. She kept up a lively running stream of talk about it all, of which he understood not a fiftieth part as he trudged along by her side, cursing his forty-five years and feeling all the yearnings of his early manhood revive and jeer at him. And, as she talked, England and Surbiton seemed very far away indeed, almost in another age of the world's history. Her voice touched something immeasurably old in him, something that slept deep. It lulled the surface parts of his consciousness to sleep, allowing what was far more ancient to awaken. Like the town, with its elaborate pretence of modern active life, the upper layers of his being became dulled, soothed, muffled, and what lay underneath began to stir in its sleep. That big curtain swayed a little to and fro. Presently it might lift altogether. . . .

He began to understand a little better at last. The mood of the town was reproducing itself in him. In proportion as his ordinary external self became muffled, that inner secret life, that was far more real and vital, asserted itself. And this girl was surely the high-priestess of it all, the chief instrument of its accomplishment. New thoughts, with new interpretations, flooded his mind as she walked beside him through the winding streets, while the picturesque old gabled town, softly coloured in the sunset, had never appeared to him so wholly wonderful and seductive.

And only one curious incident came to disturb and puzzle him, slight in itself, but utterly inexplicable, bringing white terror into the child's face and a scream to her laughing lips. He had merely pointed to a column of blue smoke that rose from the burning autumn leaves and made a picture against the red roofs, and had then run to the wall and called her to his side to watch the flames shooting here and there through the heap of rubbish. Yet, at the sight of it, as though taken by surprise, her face had altered dreadfully, and she had turned and run like the wind, calling out wild sentences to him as she ran, of which he had not understood a single word, except that the fire apparently frightened her, and she wanted to get quickly away from it, and to get him away too.

Yet five minutes later she was as calm and happy again as though nothing had happened to alarm or waken troubled thoughts in her, and they had both forgotten the incident.

They were leaning over the ruined ramparts together listening to the weird music of the band as he had heard it the first day of his arrival. It moved him again profoundly as it had done before, and somehow he managed to find his tongue and his best French. The girl leaned across the stones close beside him. No one was about. Driven by some remorseless engine within he began to stammer something – he hardly knew what – of his strange admiration for her. Almost at the first word she sprang lightly off the wall and came up smiling in front of him, just touching his knees as he sat there. She was hatless as usual, and the sun caught her hair and one side of her cheek and throat.

'Oh, I'm so glad!' she cried, clapping her little hands softly in his face, 'so very glad, because that means that if you like me you must also like what I do, and what I belong to.'

Already he regretted bitterly having lost control of himself. Something in the phrasing of her sentence chilled him. He knew the fear of embarking upon an unknown and dangerous sea.

'You will take part in our real life, I mean,' she added softly, with an indescribable coaxing of manner, as though she noticed his shrinking. 'You will come back to us.'

Already this slip of a child seemed to dominate him, he felt her power coming over him more and more; something emanated from her that stole over his senses and made him aware that her personality, for all its simple grace, held forces that were stately, imposing, august. He saw her again moving through smoke and flame amid broken and tempestuous scenery, alarmingly strong, her terrible mother by her side. Dimly this shone through her smile and appearance of charming innocence.

'You will, I know,' she repeated, holding him with her eyes.

They were quite alone up there on the ramparts, and the sensation that she was overmastering him stirred a wild sensuousness in his blood. The mingled abandon and reserve in her attracted him furiously, and all of him that was man rose up and resisted the creeping influence, at the same time acclaiming it with the full delight of his forgotten youth. An irresistible desire came to him to question her, to summon what still remained to him of his own little personality in an effort to retain the right to his normal self.

The girl had grown quiet again, and was now leaning on the broad wall close beside him, gazing out across the darkening plain, her elbows on the coping, motionless as a figure carved in stone. He took his courage in both hands.

'Tell me, Ilsé,' he said, unconsciously imitating her own puffing softness of voice, yet aware that he was utterly in earnest, 'what is the meaning of this town, and what is this real life you speak of? And why is it that the people watch me from morning to night? Tell me what it all means? And, tell me,' he added more quickly with passion in his voice, 'what you really are – yourself?'

She turned her head and looked at him through half-closed eyelids, her growing inner excitement betraying itself by the faint colour that ran like a shadow across her face.

'It seems to me,' – he faltered oddly under her gaze – 'that I have some right to know—'

Suddenly she opened her eyes to the full. 'You love me, then?' she asked softly.

'I swear,' he cried impetuously, moved as by the force of

a rising tide, 'I never felt before – I have never known any other girl who—'

'Then you *have* the right to know,' she calmly interrupted his confused confession, 'for love shares all secrets.'

She paused, and a thrill like fire ran swiftly through him. Her words lifted him off the earth, and he felt a radiant happiness, followed almost the same instant in horrible contrast by the thought of death. He became aware that she had turned her eyes upon his own and was speaking again.

'The real life I speak of,' she whispered, 'is the old, old life within, the life of long ago, the life to which you, too, once belonged, and to which you still belong.'

A faint wave of memory troubled the deeps of his soul as her low voice sank into him. What she was saying he knew instinctively to be true, even though he could not as yet understand its full purport. His present life seemed slipping from him as he listened, merging his personality in one that was far older and greater. It was this loss of his present self that brought to him the thought of death.

'You came here,' she went on, 'with the purpose of seeking it, and the people felt your presence and are waiting to know what you decide, whether you will leave them without having found it, or whether—'

Her eyes remained fixed upon his own, but her face began to change, growing larger and darker with an expression of age.

'It is their thoughts constantly playing about your soul that makes you feel they watch you. They do not watch you with their eyes. The purposes of their inner life are calling to you, seeking to claim you. You were all part of the same life long, long ago, and now they want you back again among them.'

Vezin's timid heart sank with dread as he listened; but the girl's eyes held him with a net of joy so that he had no wish to escape. She fascinated him, as it were, clean out of his normal self.

'Alone, however, the people could never have caught and held you,' she resumed. 'The motive force was not strong enough; it has faded through all these years. But I' – she paused a moment and looked at him with complete confidence in her splendid eyes – 'I possess the spell to conquer you and hold you: the spell of old love. I can win you back again and make you live the old life with me, for the force of the ancient tie between us, if I choose to use it, is irresistible. And I do choose to use it. I still want you. And you, dear soul of my dim past' – she pressed closer to him so that her breath passed across his eyes, and her voice positively sang – 'I mean to have you, for you love me and are utterly at my mercy.'

Vezin heard, and yet did not hear; understood, yet did not understand. He had passed into a condition of exaltation. The world was beneath his feet, made of music and flowers, and he was flying somewhere far above it through the sunshine of pure delight. He was breathless and giddy with the wonder of her words. They intoxicated him. And, still, the terror of it all, the dreadful thought of death, pressed ever behind her sentences. For flames shot through her voice out of black smoke and licked at his soul.

And they communicated with one another, it seemed to him, by a process of swift telepathy, for his French could never have compassed all he said to her. Yet she understood perfectly, and what she said to him was like the recital of verses long since known. And the mingled pain and sweetness of it as he listened were almost more than his little soul could hold.

'Yet I came here wholly by chance—' he heard himself saying.

'No,' she cried with passion, 'you came here because I called to you. I have called to you for years, and you came with the whole force of the past behind you. You had to come, for I own you, and I claim you.'

She rose again and moved closer, looking at him with a certain insolence in the face – the insolence of power.

The sun had set behind the towers of the old cathedral and the darkness rose up from the plain and enveloped them. The music of the band had ceased. The leaves of the plane trees hung motionless, but the chill of the autumn evening rose about them and made Vezin shiver. There was no sound but the sound of their voices and the occasional soft rustle of the girl's dress. He could hear the blood rushing in his ears. He scarcely realized where he was or what he was doing. Some terrible magic of the imagination drew him deeply down into the tombs of his own being, telling him in no unfaltering voice that her words shadowed forth the truth. And this simple little French maid, speaking beside him with so strange authority, he saw curiously alter into quite another being. As he stared into her eyes, the picture in his mind grew and lived, dressing itself vividly to his inner vision with a degree of reality he was compelled to acknowledge. As once before, he saw her tall and stately, moving through wild and broken scenery of forests and mountain caverns, the glare of flames behind her head and clouds of shifting smoke about her feet. Dark leaves encircled her hair, flying loosely in the wind, and her limbs shone through the merest rags of clothing. Others were about her, too, and ardent eyes on all sides cast delirious glances upon her, but her own eyes were always for One only, one whom she held by the hand. For she was leading the dance in some tempestuous orgy to the music of chanting voices, and the dance she led circled about a great and awful Figure on a throne, brooding over the scene through lurid vapours, while innumerable other wild faces and forms crowded furiously about her in the dance. But the one she held by the hand he knew to be himself, and the monstrous shape upon the throne he knew to be her mother.

The vision rose within him, rushing to him down the long years of buried time, crying aloud to him with the voice of memory reawakened. . . . And then the scene faded away and he saw the clear circle of the girl's eyes gazing steadfastly into his own, and she became once more the pretty little daughter of the innkeeper, and he found his voice again.

'And you,' he whispered tremblingly – 'you child of visions and enchantment, how is it that you so bewitch me that I loved you even before I saw?'

She drew herself up beside him with an air of rare dignity.

'The call of the Past,' she said; 'and besides,' she added proudly, 'in the real life I am a princess—'

'A princess!' he cried.

'– and my mother is a queen!'

At this, little Vezin utterly lost his head. Delight tore at his heart and swept him into sheer ecstasy. To hear that sweet singing voice, and to see those adorable little lips utter such things, upset his balance beyond all hope of control. He took her in his arms and covered her unresisting face with kisses.

But even while he did so, and while the hot passion swept him, he felt that she was soft and loathsome, and that her answering kisses stained his very soul. . . . And when, presently, she had freed herself and vanished into the darkness, he stood there, leaning against the wall in a state of collapse, creeping with horror from the touch of her yielding body, and inwardly raging at the weakness that he already dimly realized must prove his undoing.

And from the shadows of the old buildings into which she disappeared there rose in the stillness of the night a singular, long-drawn cry, which at first he took for laughter, but which later he was sure he recognized as the almost human wailing of a cat.

V

For a long time Vezin leant there against the wall, alone with his surging thoughts and emotions. He understood at length that he had done the one thing necessary to call down upon him the whole force of this ancient Past. For in those passionate kisses he had acknowledged the tie of olden days, and had revived it. And the memory of that soft impalpable caress in the darkness of the inn corridor came back to him with a shudder. The girl had first mastered him, and then led him to the one act that was necessary for her purpose. He had been waylaid, after the lapse of centuries – caught, and conquered.

Dimly he realized this, and sought to make plans for his escape. But, for the moment at any rate, he was powerless to manage his thoughts or will, for the sweet, fantastic madness of the whole adventure mounted to his brain like a spell, and he gloried in the feeling that he was utterly enchanted and moving in a world so much larger and wilder than the one he had ever been accustomed to.

The moon, pale and enormous, was just rising over the sea-like plain, when at last he rose to go. Her slanting rays drew all the houses into new perspective, so that their roofs, already glistening with dew, seemed to stretch much higher into the sky than usual, and their gables and quaint old towers lay far away in its purple reaches.

The cathedral appeared unreal in a silver mist. He moved

softly, keeping to the shadows; but the streets were all deserted and very silent; the doors were closed, the shutters fastened. Not a soul was astir. The hush of night lay over everything; it was like a town of the dead, a churchyard with gigantic and grotesque tombstones.

Wondering where all the busy life of the day had so utterly disappeared to, he made his way to a back door that entered the inn by means of the stables, thinking thus to reach his room unobserved. He reached the courtyard safely and crossed it by keeping close to the shadow of the wall. He sidled down it, mincing along on tiptoe, just as the old men did when they entered the *salle à manger*. He was horrified to find himself doing this instinctively. A strange impulse came to him, catching him somehow in the centre of his body – an impulse to drop upon all fours and run swiftly and silently. He glanced upwards and the idea came to him to leap up upon his sill overhead instead of going round by the stairs. This occurred to him as the easiest, and most natural way. It was like the beginning of some horrible transformation of himself into something else. He was fearfully strung up.

The moon was higher now, and the shadows very dark along the side of the street where he moved. He kept among the deepest of them, and reached the porch with the glass doors.

But here there was light; the inmates, unfortunately, were still about. Hoping to slip across the hall unobserved and reach the stairs, he opened the door carefully and stole in. Then he saw that the hall was not empty. A large dark thing lay against the wall on his left. At first he thought it must be household articles. Then it moved, and he thought it was an immense cat, distorted in some way by the play of light and shadow. Then it rose straight up before him and he saw that it was the proprietress.

What she had been doing in this position he could only venture a dreadful guess, but the moment she stood up and faced him he was aware of some terrible dignity clothing her about that instantly recalled the girl's strange saying that she was a queen. Huge and sinister she stood there under the little oil lamp; alone with him in the empty hall. Awe stirred in his heart, and the roots of some ancient fear. He felt that he must bow to her and make some kind of obeisance. The impulse was fierce and irresistible, as of long habit. He glanced quickly about him. There was no one there. Then he deliberately inclined his head toward her. He bowed.

'*Enfin! M'sieur s'est donc décidé. C'est bien alors. J'en suis contente.*'

Her words came to him sonorously as through a great open space.

Then the great figure came suddenly across the flagged hall at him and seized his trembling hands. Some overpowering force moved with her and caught him.

'*On pourrait faire un p'tit tour ensemble, n'est-ce pas? Nous y allons cette nuit et il faut s'exercer un peu d'avance pour cela. Ilsé, Ilsé, viens donc ici. Viens vite!*'

And she whirled him round in the opening steps of some dance that seemed oddly and horribly familiar. They made no sound on the stones, this strangely assorted couple. It was all soft and stealthy. And presently, when the air seemed to thicken like smoke, and a red glare as of flame shot through it, he was aware that some one else had joined them and that his hand the mother had released was now tightly held by the daughter. Ilsé had come in answer to the call, and he saw her with leaves of vervain twined in her dark hair, clothed in tattered vestiges of some curious garment, beautiful as the night, and horribly, odiously, loathsomely seductive.

'To the Sabbath! to the Sabbath!' they cried. 'On to the Witches' Sabbath!'

Up and down that narrow hall they danced, the women on each side of him, to the wildest measure he had ever imagined, yet which he dimly, dreadfully remembered, till the lamp on the wall flickered and went out, and they were left in total darkness. And the devil woke in his heart with a thousand vile suggestions and made him afraid.

Suddenly they released his hands and he heard the voice of the mother cry that it was time, and they must go. Which way they went he did not pause to see. He only realized that he was free, and he blundered through the darkness till he found the stairs and then tore up them to his room as though all hell was at his heels.

He flung himself on the sofa, with his face in his hands, and groaned. Swiftly reviewing a dozen ways of immediate escape, all equally impossible, he finally decided that the only thing to do for the moment was to sit quiet and wait. He must see what was going to happen. At least in the privacy of his own bedroom he would be fairly safe. The door was locked. He crossed over and softly opened the window which gave upon the courtyard and also permitted a partial view of the hall through the glass doors.

As he did so the hum and murmur of a great activity reached his ears from the streets beyond – the sound of footsteps and voices muffled by distance. He leaned out cautiously and listened. The moonlight was clear and strong now, but his own window was in shadow, the silver disc being still behind the house. It came to him irresistibly that the inhabitants of the town, who a little while before had all been invisible behind closed doors, were now issuing forth, busy upon some secret and unholy errand. He listened intently.

At first everything about him was silent, but soon he became aware of movements going on in the house itself. Rustlings and cheepings came to him across that still, moonlit yard. A concourse of living beings sent the hum of their activity into the night. Things were on the move everywhere. A biting, pungent odour rose through the air, coming he knew not whence. Presently his eyes became glued to the windows of the opposite wall where the moonshine fell in a soft blaze. The roof overhead, and behind him, was reflected clearly in the panes of glass, and he saw the outlines of dark bodies moving with long footsteps over the tiles and along the coping. They passed swiftly and silently, shaped like immense cats, in an endless procession across the pictured glass, and then appeared to leap down to a lower level where he lost sight of them. He just caught the soft thudding of their leaps. Sometimes their shadows fell upon the white wall opposite, and then he could not make out whether they were the shadows of human beings or of cats. They seemed to change swiftly from one to the other. The transformation looked horribly real, for they leaped like human beings, yet changed swiftly in the air immediately afterwards, and dropped like animals.

The yard, too, beneath him, was now alive with the creeping movements of dark forms all stealthily drawing towards the porch with the glass doors. They kept so closely to the wall that he could not determine their actual shape, but when he saw that they passed on to the great congregation that was gathering in the hall, he understood that these were the creatures whose leaping shadows he had first seen reflected in the windowpanes opposite. They were coming from all parts of the town, reaching the appointed meeting-place across the roofs and tiles, and springing from level to level till they came to the yard.

Then a new sound caught his ear, and he saw that the windows all about him were being softly opened, and that to each window came a face. A moment later figures began dropping hurriedly down into the yard. And these figures, as they lowered themselves down from the windows, were human, he saw; but once safely in the yard they fell upon all fours and changed in the swiftest possible second into – cats – huge, silent cats. They ran in streams to join the main body in the hall beyond.

So, after all, the rooms in the house had not been empty and unoccupied.

Moreover, what he saw no longer filled him with amazement. For he remembered it all. It was familiar. It had all happened before just so, hundreds of times, and he himself had taken part in it and known the wild madness of it all. The outline of the old building changed, the yard grew larger, and he seemed to be staring down upon it from a much greater height through smoky vapours. And, as he looked, half remembering, the old pains of long ago, fierce and sweet, furiously assailed him, and the blood stirred horribly as he heard the Call of the Dance again in his heart and tasted the ancient magic of Ilsé whirling by his side.

Suddenly he started back. A great lithe cat had leaped softly up from the shadows below on to the sill close to his face, and was staring fixedly at him with the eyes of a human. 'Come,' it seemed to say, 'come with us to the Dance! Change as of old! Transform yourself swiftly and come!' Only too well he understood the creature's soundless call.

It was gone again in a flash with scarcely a sound of its padded feet on the stones, and then others dropped by the score down the side of the house, past his very eyes, all changing as they fell and darting away rapidly, softly, towards the gathering point. And again he felt the dreadful desire to do likewise; to murmur the old incantation, and then drop upon hands and knees and run swiftly for the great flying leap into the air. Oh, how the passion of it rose within him like a flood, twisting his very entrails, sending his heart's desire flaming forth into the night for the old, old Dance of the Sorcerers at the Witches' Sabbath! The whirl of the stars was about him; once more he met the magic of the moon. The power of the wind, rushing from precipice and forest, leaping from cliff to cliff across the valleys, tore him away. . . . He heard the cries of the dancers and their wild laughter, and with this savage girl in his embrace he danced furiously about the dim Throne where sat the Figure with the sceptre of majesty. . . .

Then, suddenly, all became hushed and still, and the fever died down a little in his heart. The calm moonlight flooded a courtyard empty and deserted. They had started. The procession was off into the sky. And he was left behind – alone.

Vezin tiptoed softly across the room and unlocked the door. The murmur from the streets, growing momentarily as he advanced, met his ears. He made his way with the utmost caution down the corridor. At the head of the stairs he paused and listened. Below him, the hall where they had gathered was dark and still, but through opened doors and windows on the far side of the building came the sound of a great throng moving farther and farther into the distance.

He made his way down the creaking wooden stairs, dreading yet longing to meet some straggler who should point the way, but finding no one; across the dark hall, so lately thronged with living, moving things, and out through the opened front doors into the street. He could not believe that he was really left behind, really forgotten, that he had been purposely permitted to escape. It perplexed him.

Nervously he peered about him, and up and down

the street; then, seeing nothing, advanced slowly down the pavement.

The whole town, as he went, showed itself empty and deserted, as though a great wind had blown everything alive out of it. The doors and windows of the houses stood open to the night; nothing stirred; moonlight and silence lay over all. The night lay about him like a cloak. The air, soft and cool, caressed his cheek like the touch of a great furry paw. He gained confidence and began to walk quickly, though still keeping to the shadowed side. Nowhere could he discover the faintest sign of the great unholy exodus he knew had just taken place. The moon sailed high over all in a sky cloudless and serene.

Hardly realizing where he was going, he crossed the open market-place and so came to the ramparts, whence he knew a pathway descended to the high road and along which he could make good his escape to one of the other little towns that lay to the northward, and so to the railway.

But first he paused and gazed out over the scene at his feet where the great plain lay like a silver map of some dream country. The still beauty of it entered his heart, increasing his sense of bewilderment and unreality. No air stirred, the leaves of the plane trees stood motionless, the near details were defined with the sharpness of day against dark shadows, and in the distance the fields and woods melted away into haze and shimmering mistiness.

But the breath caught in his throat and he stood stockstill as though transfixed when his gaze passed from the horizon and fell upon the near prospect in the depth of the valley at his feet. The whole lower slopes of the hill, that lay hid from the brightness of the moon, were aglow, and through the glare he saw countless moving forms, shifting thick and fast between the openings of the trees; while overhead, like leaves driven by the wind, he discerned flying shapes that hovered darkly one moment against the sky and then settled down with cries and weird singing through the branches into the region that was aflame.

Spellbound, he stood and stared for a time that he could not measure. And then, moved by one of the terrible impulses that seemed to control the whole adventure, he climbed swiftly upon the top of the broad coping, and balanced a moment where the valley gaped at his feet. But in that very instant, as he stood hovering, a sudden movement among the shadows of the houses caught his eye, and he turned to see the outline of a large animal dart swiftly across the open space behind him, and land with a flying leap upon the top of the wall a little lower down. It ran like the wind to his feet and then rose up beside him upon the ramparts. A shiver seemed to run through the moonlight, and his sight trembled for a second. His heart pulsed fearfully. Ilsé stood beside him, peering into his face.

Some dark substance, he saw, stained the girl's face and skin, shining in the moonlight as she stretched her hands towards him; she was dressed in wretched tattered garments that yet became her mightily; rue and vervain twined about her temples; her eyes glittered with unholy light. He only just controlled the wild impulse to take her in his arms and leap with her from their giddy perch into the valley below.

'See!' she cried, pointing with an arm on which the rags fluttered in the rising wind towards the forest aglow in the distance. 'See where they await us! The woods are alive! Already the Great Ones are there, and the dance will soon begin! The salve is here! Anoint yourself and come!'

Though a moment before the sky was clear and cloudless, yet even while she spoke the face of the moon grew dark and the wind began to toss in the crests of the plane trees at his feet. Stray gusts brought the sounds of hoarse singing and crying from the lower slopes of the hill, and the pungent odour he had already noticed about the courtyard of the inn rose about him in the air.

'Transform, transform!' she cried again, her voice rising like a song. 'Rub well your skin before you fly. Come! Come with me to the Sabbath, to the madness of its furious delight, to the sweet abandonment of its evil worship! See! the Great Ones are there, and the terrible Sacraments prepared. The Throne is occupied. Anoint and come! Anoint and come!'

She grew to the height of a tree beside him, leaping upon the wall with flaming eyes and hair strewn upon the night. He too began to change swiftly. Her hands touched the skin of his face and neck, streaking him with the burning salve that sent the old magic into his blood with the power before which fades all that is good.

A wild roar came up to his ears from the heart of the wood, and the girl, when she heard it, leaped upon the wall in the frenzy of her wicked joy.

'Satan is there!' she screamed, rushing upon him and striving to draw him with her to the edge of the wall. 'Satan has come. The Sacraments call us! Come, with your dear apostate soul, and we will worship and dance till the moon dies and the world is forgotten!'

Just saving himself from the dreadful plunge, Vezin struggled to release himself from her grasp, while the passion tore at his reins and all but mastered him. He shrieked aloud, not knowing what he said, and then he shrieked again. It was the old impulses, the old awful habits instinctively finding voice; for though it seemed to him that he merely shrieked nonsense, the words he uttered really had meaning in them, and were intelligible. It was the ancient call. And it was heard below. It was answered.

The wind whistled at the skirts of his coat as the air round him darkened with many flying forms crowding upwards out of the valley. The crying of hoarse voices smote upon his ears, coming closer. Strokes of wind buffeted him, tearing him this way and that along the crumbling top of the stone wall; and Ilsé clung to him with her long shining arms, smooth and bare, holding him fast about the neck. But not Ilsé alone, for a dozen of them surrounded him, dropping out of the air. The pungent odour of the anointed bodies stifled him, exciting him to the old madness of the Sabbath, the dance of the witches and sorcerers doing honour to the personified Evil of the world.

'Anoint and away! Anoint and away!' they cried in wild chorus about him. 'To the Dance that never dies! To the sweet and fearful fantasy of evil!'

Another moment and he would have yielded and gone, for his will turned soft and the flood of passionate memory all but overwhelmed him, when – so can a small thing alter the whole course of an adventure – he caught his foot upon a loose stone in the edge of the wall, and then fell with a sudden crash on to the ground below. But he fell towards the houses, in the open space of dust and cobblestones, and fortunately not into the gaping depth of the valley on the farther side.

And they, too, came in a tumbling heap about him, like flies upon a piece of food, but as they fell he was released for a moment from the power of their touch, and in that brief instant of freedom there flashed into his mind the sudden intuition that saved him. Before he could regain his feet he saw them scrabbling awkwardly back upon the wall, as though bat-like they could only fly by dropping from a height, and had no hold upon him in the open. Then, seeing them perched there in a row like cats upon a roof, all dark

313

and singularly shapeless, their eyes like lamps, the sudden memory came back to him of Ilsé's terror at the sight of fire.

Quick as a flash he found his matches and lit the dead leaves that lay under the wall.

Dry and withered, they caught fire at once, and the wind carried the flame in a long line down the length of the wall, licking upwards as it ran; and with shrieks and wailings, the crowded row of forms upon the top melted away into the air on the other side, and were gone with a great rush and whirring of their bodies down into the heart of the haunted valley, leaving Vezin breathless and shaken in the middle of the deserted ground.

'Ilsé!' he called feebly; 'Ilsé!' for his heart ached to think that she was really gone to the great Dance without him, and that he had lost the opportunity of its fearful joy. Yet at the same time his relief was so great, and he was so dazed and troubled in mind with the whole thing, that he hardly knew what he was saying, and only cried aloud in the fierce storm of his emotion. . . .

The fire under the wall ran its course, and the moonlight came out again, soft and clear, from its temporary eclipse. With one last shuddering look at the ruined ramparts, and a feeling of horrid wonder for the haunted valley beyond, where the shapes still crowded and flew, he turned his face towards the town and slowly made his way in the direction of the hotel.

And as he went, a great wailing of cries, and a sound of howling, followed him from the gleaming forest below, growing fainter and fainter with the bursts of wind as he disappeared between the houses.

'It may seem rather abrupt to you, this sudden tame ending,' said Arthur Vezin, glancing with flushed face and timid eyes at Dr Silence sitting there with his notebook, 'but the fact is – er – from that moment my memory seems to have failed rather. I have no distinct recollection of how I got home or what precisely I did.

'It appears I never went back to the inn at all. I only dimly recollect racing down a long white road in the moonlight, past woods and villages, still and deserted, and then the dawn came up, and I saw the towers of a biggish town and so came to a station.

'But, long before that, I remember pausing somewhere on the road and looking back to where the hill-town of my adventure stood up in the moonlight, and thinking how exactly like a great monstrous cat it lay there upon the plain, its huge front paws lying down the two main streets, and the twin and broken towers of the cathedral marking its torn ears against the sky. That picture stays in my mind with the utmost vividness to this day.

'Another thing remains in my mind from that escape – namely, the sudden sharp reminder that I had not paid my bill, and the decision I made, standing there on the dusty highroad, that the small baggage I had left behind would more than settle for my indebtedness.

'For the rest, I can only tell you that I got coffee and bread at a café on the outskirts of this town I had come to, and soon after found my way to the station and caught a train later in the day. That same evening I reached London.'

'And how long altogether,' asked John Silence quietly, 'do you think you stayed in the town of the adventure?'

Vezin looked up sheepishly.

'I was coming to that,' he resumed, with apologetic wrigglings of his body. 'In London I found that I was a whole week out in my reckoning of time. I had stayed over a week in the town, and it ought to have been September 15th, – instead of which it was only September 10th!'

'So that, in reality, you had only stayed a night or two in the inn?' queried the doctor.

Vezin hesitated before replying. He shuffled upon the mat.

'I must have gained time somewhere,' he said at length – 'somewhere or somehow. I certainly had a week to my credit. I can't explain it. I can only give you the fact.'

'And this happened to you last year, since when you have never been back to the place?'

'Last autumn, yes,' murmured Vezin; 'and I have never dared to go back. I think I never want to.'

'And, tell me,' asked Dr Silence at length, when he saw that the little man had evidently come to the end of his words and had nothing more to say, 'had you ever read up the subject of the old witchcraft practices during the Middle Ages, or been at all interested in the subject?'

'Never!' declared Vezin emphatically. 'I had never given a thought to such matters so far as I know—'

'Or to the question of reincarnation, perhaps?'

'Never – before my adventure; but I have since,' he replied significantly.

There was, however, something still on the man's mind that he wished to relieve himself of by confession, yet could only with difficulty bring himself to mention; and it was only after the sympathetic tactfulness of the doctor had provided numerous openings that he at length availed himself of one of them, and stammered that he would like to show him the marks he still had on his neck where, he said, the girl had touched him with her anointed hands.

He took off his collar after infinite fumbling hesitation, and lowered his shirt a little for the doctor to see. And there, on the surface of the skin, lay a faint reddish line across the shoulder and extending a little way down the back towards the spine. It certainly indicated exactly the position an arm might have taken in the act of embracing. And on the other side of the neck, slightly higher up, was a similar mark, though not quite so clearly defined.

'That was where she held me that night on the ramparts,' he whispered, a strange light coming and going in his eyes.

It was some weeks later when I again found occasion to consult John Silence concerning another extraordinary case that had come under my notice, and we fell to discussing Vezin's story. Since hearing it, the doctor had made investigations on his own account, and one of his secretaries had discovered that Vezin's ancestors had actually lived for generations in the very town where the adventure came to him. Two of them, both women, had been tried and convicted as witches, and had been burned alive at the stake. Moreover, it had not been difficult to prove that the very inn where Vezin stayed was built about 1700 upon the spot where the funeral pyres stood and the executions took place. The town was a sort of headquarters for all the sorcerers and witches of the entire region, and after conviction they were burnt there literally by scores.

'It seems strange,' continued the doctor, 'that Vezin should have remained ignorant of all this; but, on the other hand, it was not the kind of history that successive generations would have been anxious to keep alive, or to repeat to their children. Therefore I am inclined to think he still knows nothing about it.

'The whole adventure seems to have been a very vivid revival of the memories of an earlier life, caused by coming directly into contact with the living forces still intense enough to hang about the place, and, by a most singular chance, too, with the very souls who had taken part with him in the events of that particular life. For the mother and daughter who impressed him so strangely must have been leading actors, with himself, in the scenes and practices of witchcraft which at that period dominated the imaginations of the whole country.

'One has only to read the histories of the times to know that these witches claimed the power of transforming themselves into various animals, both for the purposes of disguise and also to convey themselves swiftly to the scenes of their imaginary orgies. Lycanthropy, or the power to change themselves into wolves, was everywhere believed in, and the ability to transform themselves into cats by rubbing their bodies with a special salve or ointment provided by Satan himself, found equal credence. The witchcraft trials abound in evidences of such universal beliefs.'

Dr Silence quoted chapter and verse from many writers on the subject, and showed how every detail of Vezin's adventure had a basis in the practices of those dark days.

'But that the entire affair took place subjectively in the man's own consciousness, I have no doubt,' he went on, in reply to my questions; 'for my secretary who has been to the town to investigate, discovered his signature in the visitors' book, and proved by it that he had arrived on September 8th, and left suddenly without paying his bill. He left two days later, and they still were in possession of his dirty brown bag and some tourist clothes. I paid a few francs in settlement of his debt, and have sent his luggage on to him. The daughter was absent from home, but the proprietress, a large woman very much as he described her, told my secretary that he had seemed a very strange, absent-minded kind of gentleman, and after his disappearance she had feared for a long time that he had met with a violent end in the neighbouring forest where he used to roam about alone.

'I should like to have obtained a personal interview with the daughter so as to ascertain how much was subjective and how much actually took place with her as Vezin told it. For her dread of fire and the sight of burning must, of course, have been the intuitive memory of her former painful death at the stake, and have thus explained why he fancied more than once that he saw her through smoke and flame.'

'And that mark on his skin, for instance?' I inquired.

'Merely the marks produced by hysterical brooding,' he replied, 'like the stigmata of the *religieuses*, and the bruises which appear on the bodies of hypnotized subjects who have been told to expect them. This is very common and easily explained. Only it seems curious that these marks should have remained so long in Vezin's case. Usually they disappear quickly.'

'Obviously he is still thinking about it all, brooding, and living it all over again,' I ventured.

'Probably. And this makes me fear that the end of his trouble is not yet. We shall hear of him again. It is a case, alas! I can do little to alleviate.'

Dr Silence spoke gravely and with sadness in his voice.

'And what do you make of the Frenchman in the train?' I asked further – 'the man who warned him against the place, *à cause du sommeil et à cause des chats*? Surely a very singular incident?'

'A very singular incident indeed,' he made answer slowly, 'and one I can only explain on the basis of a highly improbable coincidence—'

'Namely?'

'That the man was one who had himself stayed in the

town and undergone there a similar experience. I should like to find this man and ask him. But the crystal is useless here, for I have no slightest clue to go upon, and I can only conclude that some singular psychic affinity, some force still active in his being out of the same past life, drew him thus to the personality of Vezin, and enabled him to fear what might happen to him, and thus to warn him as he did.

'Yes,' he presently continued, half talking to himself, 'I suspect in this case that Vezin was swept into the vortex of forces arising out of the intense activities of a past life, and that he lived over again a scene in which he had often played a leading part centuries before. For strong actions set up forces that are so slow to exhaust themselves, they may be said in a sense never to die. In this case they were not vital enough to render the illusion complete, so that the little man found himself caught in a very distressing confusion of the present and the past; yet he was sufficiently sensitive to recognize that it was true, and to fight against the degradation of returning, even in memory, to a former and lower state of development.

'Ah yes!' he continued, crossing the floor to gaze at the darkening sky, and seemingly quite oblivious of my presence, 'subliminal up-rushes of memory like this can be exceedingly painful, and sometimes exceedingly dangerous. I only trust that this gentle soul may soon escape from this obsession of a passionate and tempestuous past. But I doubt it, I doubt it.'

His voice was hushed with sadness as he spoke, and when he turned back into the room again there was an expression of profound yearning upon his face, the yearning of a soul whose desire to help is sometimes greater than his power.

STEPHEN VINCENT BENÉT

THE KING OF
THE CATS

'BUT, MY *DEAR*,' said Mrs Culverin, with a tiny gasp, 'you can't actually mean — a *tail!*'

Mrs Dingle nodded impressively. 'Exactly. I've seen him. Twice. Paris, of course, and then, a command appearance at Rome – we were in the Royal box. He conducted – my dear, you've never heard such effects from an orchestra – and, my dear,' she hesitated slightly, 'he conducted *with it.*'

'How perfectly fascinating. Too horrid for words!' said Mrs Culverin in a dazed but greedy voice. 'We *must* have him to dinner as soon as he comes over – he is coming over, isn't he?'

'The twelfth,' said Mrs Dingle with a gleam in her eyes. 'The New Symphony people have asked him to be guest-conductor for three special concerts – I do hope you can dine with *us* some night while he's here – he'll be very busy, of course – but he's promised to give us what time he can spare—'

'Oh, thank you, dear,' said Mrs Culverin, abstractedly, her last raid upon Mrs Dingle's pet British novelist still fresh in her mind. 'You're always so delightfully hospitable – but you mustn't wear yourself out – the rest of us must do *our* part – I know Henry and myself would be only too glad to—'

'That's very sweet of you, darling.' Mrs Dingle also remembered the larceny of the British novelist. 'But we're just going to give Monsieur Tibault – sweet name, isn't it! They say he's descended from the Tybalt in "Romeo and Juliet" and that's why he doesn't like Shakespeare – we're just going to give Monsieur Tibault the simplest sort of time – a little reception after his first concert perhaps. He hates,' she looked around the table, 'large, mixed parties. And then, of course, his – er – little idiosyncrasy—' she coughed delicately. 'It makes him feel a trifle shy with strangers.'

'But I don't understand yet, Aunt Emily,' said Tommy Brooks, Mrs Dingle's nephew. 'Do you really mean this Tibault bozo has a tail? Like a monkey and everything?'

'Tommy dear,' said Mrs Culverin, crushingly, 'in the first place, Monsieur Tibault is not a bozo – he is a very distinguished musician – the finest conductor in Europe. And in the second place—'

'He has,' Mrs Dingle was firm. 'He has a tail. He conducts with it.'

'Oh, but honestly!' said Tommy, his ear pinkening. 'I mean – of course, if you say so, Aunt Emily, I'm sure he has – but still, it sounds pretty steep, if you know what I mean! How about it, Professor Tatto?'

Professor Tatto cleared his throat. 'Tck,' he said, putting his fingertips together cautiously, 'I shall be very anxious to see this Monsieur Tibault. For myself, I have never observed a genuine specimen of *homo caudatus*, so I should be inclined to doubt, and yet . . . In the Middle Ages, for instance, the belief in men – er – tailed or with caudal appendages of some sort, was both widespread and, as far as we can gather, well founded. As late as the eighteenth century, a Dutch sea-captain with some character for veracity recounts the discovery of a pair of such creatures in the island of Formosa. They were in a low state of civilization, I believe, but the appendages in question were quite distinct. And in 1860, Dr Grimbrook, the English surgeon, claims to have treated no less than three African natives with short but evident tails – though his testimony rests upon his unsupported word.

After all, the thing is not impossible, though doubtless unusual. Web feet – rudimentary gills – these occur with some frequency. The appendix we have with us always. The chain of our descent from the ape-like form is by no means complete. For that matter,' he beamed around the table, 'what can we call the last few vertebrae of the normal spine but the beginnings of a concealed and rudimentary tail? Oh, yes – yes – it's possible – quite – that in an extraordinary case – a reversion of type – a survival – though, of course—'

'I told you so,' said Mrs Dingle triumphantly. '*Isn't* it fascinating? Isn't it, Princess?'

The Princess Vivrakanarda's eyes, blue as a field of lark-spur, fathomless as the centre of heaven, rested lightly for a moment on Mrs Dingle's excited countenance.

'Ve-ry fascinating,' she said, in a voice like stroked, golden velvet. 'I should like – I should like ve-ry much to meet this Monsieur Tibault.'

'Well, *I* hope he breaks his neck!' said Tommy Brooks, under his breath – but nobody ever paid much attention to Tommy.

Nevertheless as the time for M. Tibault's arrival in these States drew nearer and nearer, people in general began to wonder whether the Princess had spoken quite truthfully – for there was no doubt of the fact that, up till then, she had been the unique sensation of the season – and you know what social lions and lionesses are.

It was, if you remember, a Siamese season, and genuine Siamese were at quite as much of a premium as Russian accents had been in the quaint old days when the Chauve-Souris was a novelty. The Siamese Art Theatre, imported at terrific expense, was playing to packed houses. *Gushuptzgu*, an epic novel of Siamese farm life, in nineteen closely-printed volumes, had just been awarded the Nobel prize.

Prominent pet-and-newt dealers reported no cessation in the appalling demand for Siamese cats. And upon the crest of this wave of interest in things Siamese, the Princess Vivra-kanarda poised with the elegant nonchalance of a Hawaiian water-baby upon its surfboard. She was indispensable. She was incomparable. She was everywhere.

Youthful, enormously wealthy, allied on one hand to the Royal Family of Siam and on the other to the Cabots (and yet with the first eighteen of her twenty-one years shrouded from speculation in a golden zone of mystery), the mingling of races in her had produced an exotic beauty as distinguished as it was strange. She moved with a feline, effortless grace, and her skin was as if it had been gently powdered with tiny grains of the purest gold – yet the blueness of her eyes, set just a trifle slantingly, was as pure and startling as the sea on the rocks of Maine. Her brown hair fell to her knees – she had been offered extraordinary sums by the Master Barbers' Protective Association to have it shingled. Straight as a waterfall tumbling over brown rocks, it had a vague perfume of sandalwood and suave spices and held tints of rust and the sun. She did not talk very much – but then she did not have to – her voice had an odd, small, melodious huskiness that haunted the mind. She lived alone and was reputed to be very lazy – at least it was known that she slept during most of the day – but at night she bloomed like a moonflower and a depth came into her eyes.

It was no wonder that Tommy Brooks fell in love with her. The wonder was that she let him. There was nothing exotic or distinguished about Tommy – he was just one of those pleasant, normal young men who seem created to carry on the bond business by reading the newspapers in the University Club during most of the day, and can always be relied upon at night to fill an unexpected hole in a dinner-party.

It is true that the Princess could hardly be said to do more than tolerate any of her suitors – no one had ever seen those aloofly arrogant eyes enliven at the entrance of any male. But she seemed to be able to tolerate Tommy a little more than the rest – and that young man's infatuated day-dreams were beginning to be beset by smart solitaires and imaginary apartments on Park Avenue, when the famous M. Tibault conducted his first concert at Carnegie Hall.

Tommy Brooks sat beside the Princess. The eyes he turned upon her were eyes of longing and love, but her face was as impassive as a mask, and the only remark she made during the preliminary bustlings was that there seemed to be a number of people in the audience. But Tommy was relieved, if anything, to find her even a little more aloof than usual, for, ever since Mrs Culverin's dinner-party, a vague disquiet as to the possible impression which this Tibault creature might make upon her had been growing in his mind. It shows his devotion that he was present at all. To a man whose simple Princetonian nature found in 'Just a Little Love, a Little Kiss', the quintessence of musical art, the average symphony was a positive torture, and he looked forward to the evening's programme itself with a grim, brave smile.

'Ssh!' said Mrs Dingle, breathlessly. 'He's coming!' It seemed to the startled Tommy as if he were suddenly back in the trenches under a heavy barrage, as M. Tibault made his entrance to a perfect bombardment of applause.

Then the enthusiastic noise was sliced off in the middle and a gasp took its place – a vast, windy sigh, as if every person in that multitude had suddenly said, 'Ah'. For the papers had not lied about him. The tail was there.

They called him theatric – but how well he understood the uses of theatricalism! Dressed in unrelieved black from head to foot (the black dress-shirt had been a special token of

Mussolini's esteem), he did not walk on, he strolled, leisurely, easily, aloofly, the famous tail curled nonchalantly about one wrist – a suave, black panther lounging through a summer garden with that little mysterious weave of the head that panthers have when they pad behind bars – the glittering darkness of his eyes unmoved by any surprise or elation. He nodded, twice, in regal acknowledgement, as the clapping reached an apogee of frenzy. To Tommy there was something dreadfully reminiscent of the Princess in the way he nodded. Then he turned to his orchestra.

A second and louder gasp went up from the audience at this point, for, as he turned, the tip of that incredible tail twined with dainty carelessness into some hidden pocket and produced a black baton. But Tommy did not even notice. He was looking at the Princess instead.

She had not even bothered to clap, at first, but now – he had never seen her moved like this, never. She was not applauding, her hands were clenched in her lap, but her whole body was rigid, rigid as a steel bar, and the blue flowers of her eyes were bent upon the figure of M. Tibault in a terrible concentration. The pose of her entire figure was so still and intense that for an instant Tommy had the lunatic idea that any moment she might leap from her seat beside him as lightly as a moth, and land, with no sound, at M. Tibaut's side to – yes – to rub her proud head against his coat in worship. Even Mrs Dingle would notice in a moment.

'Princess—' he said, in a horrified whisper, 'Princess—'

Slowly the tenseness of her body relaxed, her eyes veiled again, she grew calm.

'Yes, Tommy?' she said, in her usual voice, but there was still something about her . . .

'Nothing, only – oh, hang – he's starting!' said Tommy, as M. Tibault, his hands loosely clasped before him, turned and *faced* the audience. His eyes dropped, his tail switched once impressively, then gave three little preliminary taps with his baton on the floor.

Seldom has Gluck's overture to 'Iphigenie in Aulis' received such an ovation. But it was not until the Eighth Symphony that the hysteria of the audience reached its climax. Never before had the New Symphony been played so superbly – and certainly never before had it been led with such genius. Three prominent conductors in the audience were sobbing with the despairing admiration of envious children towards the close, and one at least was heard to offer wildly ten thousand dollars to a well-known facial surgeon there present for a shred of evidence that tails of some variety could by any stretch of science be grafted upon a normally decaudate form. There was no doubt about it – no mortal hand and arm, be they ever so dexterous, could combine the delicate elan and powerful grace displayed in every gesture of M. Tibault's tail.

A sable staff, it dominated the brasses like a flicker of black lightning; an ebon, elusive whip, it drew the last exquisite breath of melody from the woodwinds and ruled the stormy strings like a magician's rod. M. Tibault bowed and bowed again – roar after roar of frenzied admiration shook the hall to its foundations – and when he finally staggered, exhausted, from the platform, the president of the Wednesday Sonata Club was only restrained by force from flinging her ninety thousand dollar string of pearls after him in an excess of aesthetic appreciation. New York had come and seen – and New York was conquered. Mrs Dingle was immediately besieged by reporters, and Tommy Brooks looked forward to the 'little party' at which he was to meet the new hero of the hour with feelings only a little less lugubrious than those that would have come to him just before taking his seat in the electric chair.

The meeting between his Princess and M. Tibault was worse and better than he expected. Better because, after all, they did not say much to each other – and worse because it seemed to him, somehow, that some curious kinship of mind between them made words unnecessary. They were certainly the most distinguished-looking couple in the room, as he bent over her hand. 'So darlingly foreign, both of them, and yet so different,' babbled Mrs Dingle – but Tommy couldn't agree.

They were different, yes – the dark, lithe stranger with the bizarre appendage tucked carelessly in his pocket, and the blue-eyed, brown-haired girl. But that difference only accentuated what they had in common – something in the way they moved, in the suavity of their gestures, in the set of their eyes. Something deeper, even, than race. He tried to puzzle it out – then, looking around at the others, he had a flash of revelation. It was as if that couple were foreign, indeed – not only to New York but to all common humanity. As if they were polite guests from a different star.

Tommy did not have a very happy evening, on the whole. But his mind worked slowly, and it was not until much later that the mad suspicion came upon him in full force.

Perhaps he is not to be blamed for his lack of immediate comprehension. The next few weeks were weeks of bewildered misery for him. It was not that the Princess's attitude towards him had changed – she was just as tolerant of him as before, but M. Tibault was always there. He had a faculty of appearing, as out of thin air – he walked, for all his height, as lightly as a butterfly – and Tommy grew to hate the faintest shuffle on the carpet that announced his presence.

And then, hang it all, the man was so smooth, so infernally, unrufflably smooth! He was never out of temper, never embarrassed. He treated Tommy with the extreme of urbanity, and yet his eyes mocked, deep-down, and Tommy could do nothing. And, gradually, the Princess became more and more drawn to this stranger, in a soundless communion that found little need for speech – and that, too, Tommy saw and hated, and that, too, he could not mend.

He began to be haunted not only by M. Tibault in the flesh, but by M. Tibault in the spirit. He slept badly, and when he slept, he dreamed – of M. Tibault, a man no longer, but a shadow, a spectre, the limber ghost of an animal whose words came purringly between sharp little pointed teeth. There was certainly something odd about the whole shape of the fellow – his fluid ease, the mould of his head, even the cut of his fingernails – but just what it was escaped Tommy's intensest cogitation. And when he did put his finger on it at length, at first he refused to believe.

A pair of petty incidents decided him, finally against all reason. He had gone to Mrs Dingle's, one winter afternoon, hoping to find the Princess. She was out with his aunt, but was expected back for tea, and he wandered idly into the library to wait. He was just about to switch on the lights, for the library was always dark even in summer, when he heard a sound of light breathing that seemed to come from the leather couch in the corner. He approached it cautiously and dimly made out the form of M. Tibault, curled up on the couch, peacefully asleep.

The sight annoyed Tommy so that he swore under his breath and was back near the door on his way out, when the feeling we all know and hate, the feeling that eyes we cannot see are watching us, arrested him. He turned back –

M. Tibault had not moved a muscle of his body to all appearance – but his eyes were open now. And those eyes were black and human no longer. They were green – Tommy could have sworn it – and he could have sworn that they had no bottom and gleamed like little emeralds in the dark. It only lasted a moment, for Tommy pressed the light-button automatically – and there was M. Tibault, his normal self, yawning a little but urbanely apologetic, but it gave Tommy time to think. Nor did what happened a trifle later increase his peace of mind.

They had lit a fire and were talking in front of it – by now Tommy hated M. Tibault so thoroughly that he felt that odd yearning for his company that often occurs in such cases. M. Tibault was telling some anecdote and Tommy was hating him worse than ever for basking with such obvious enjoyment in the heat of the flames and the ripple of his own voice.

Then they heard the street-door open, and M. Tibault jumped up – and jumping, caught one sock on a sharp corner of the brass firerail and tore it open in a jagged flap. Tommy looked down mechanically at the tear – a second's glance, but enough – for M. Tibault, for the first time in Tommy's experience, lost his temper completely. He swore violently in some spitting, foreign tongue – his face distorted suddenly – he clapped his hand over his sock. Then, glaring furiously at Tommy, he fairly sprang from the room, and Tommy could hear him scaling the stairs in long, agile bounds.

Tommy sank into a chair, careless for once of the fact that he heard the Princess's light laugh in the hall. He didn't want to see the Princess. He didn't want to see anybody. There had been something revealed when M. Tibault had torn that hole in his sock – and it was not the skin of a man. Tommy had caught a glimpse of – black plush. Black velvet. And then had come M. Tibault's sudden explosion of fury. Good *Lord* – did the man wear black velvet stockings under his ordinary socks? Or could he – could he – but here Tommy held his fevered head in his hands.

He went to Professor Tatto that evening with a series of hypothetical questions, but as he did not dare confide his real suspicions to the Professor, the hypothetical answers he received served only to confuse him the more. Then he thought of Billy Strange. Billy was a good sort, and his mind had a turn for the bizarre. Billy might be able to help.

He couldn't get hold of Billy for three days and lived through the interval in a fever of impatience. But finally they had dinner together at Billy's apartment, where his queer books were, and Tommy was able to blurt out the whole disordered jumble of his suspicions.

Billy listened without interrupting until Tommy was quite through. Then he pulled at his pipe. 'But, my dear *man*—' he said, protestingly.

'Oh, I know – I know—' said Tommy, and waved his hands, 'I know I'm crazy – you needn't tell me that – but I tell you, the man's a cat all the same – no, I don't see how he could be, but he is – why, hang it, in the first place, everybody knows he's got a tail!'

'Even so,' said Billy, puffing. 'Oh, my dear Tommy, I don't doubt you saw, or think you saw, everything you say. But, even so—' He shook his head.

'But what about those other birds, werewolves and things?' said Tommy.

Billy looked dubious. 'We-ll,' he admitted, 'you've got me there, of course. At least – a tailed man *is* possible. And the yarns about werewolves go back far enough, so that – well, I wouldn't say there aren't or haven't been werewolves – but then I'm willing to believe more things than most people.

333

But a were-cat – or a man that's a cat and a cat that's a man – honestly, Tommy—'

'If I don't get some real advice I'll go clean off my hinge. For Heaven's sake, tell me something to *do*!'

'Lemme think,' said Billy. 'First, you're pizen-sure this man is—'

'A cat. Yeah,' and Tommy nodded violently.

'Check. And second – if it doesn't hurt your feelings. Tommy – you're afraid this girl you're in love with has – er – at least a streak of – felinity – in her – and so she's drawn to him?'

'Oh, Lord, Billy, if I only knew!'

'Well – er – suppose she really is, too, you know – would you still be keen on her?'

'I'd marry her if she turned into a dragon every Wednesday!' said Tommy, fervently.

Bill smiled. 'H'm,' he said, 'then the obvious thing to do is to get rid of this M. Tibault. Lemme think.'

He thought about two pipes full, while Tommy sat on pins and needles. Then, finally, he burst out laughing.

'What's so darn funny?' said Tommy, aggrievedly.

'Nothing, Tommy, only I've just thought of a stunt – something so blooming crazy – but if he is – h'm – what you think he is – it *might* work—' And, going to the book-case, he took down a book.

'If you think you're going to quiet my nerves by reading me a bedtime story—'

'Shut up, Tommy, and listen to this – if you really want to get rid of your feline friend.'

'What is it?'

'Book of Agnes Repplier's. About cats. Listen.'

' "There is also a Scandinavian version of the ever famous story which Sir Walter Scott told to Washington Irving,

334

which Monk Lewis told to Shelley and which, in one form or another, we find embodied in the folklore of every land" – now, Tommy, pay attention – "the story of the traveller who saw within a ruined abbey, a procession of cats, lowering into a grave a little coffin with a crown upon it. Filled with horror, he hastened from the spot; but when he had reached his destination, he could not forbear relating to a friend the wonder he had seen. Scarcely had the tale been told when his friend's cat, who lay curled up tranquilly by the fire, sprang to its feet, cried out, 'Then I am the King of the Cats!' and disappeared in a flash up the chimney."

'Well?' said Billy, shutting the book.

'By gum!' said Tommy, staring. 'By gum! Do you think there's a chance?'

'*I* think we're both in the booby-hatch. But if you want to try it—'

'Try it! I'll spring it on him the next time I see him. But – listen – I can't make it a ruined abbey—'

'Oh, use your imagination! Make it Central Park – any-where. Tell it as if it happened to you – seeing the funeral procession and all that. You can lead into it somehow – let's see – some general line – oh, yes – "Strange, isn't it, how fact so often copies fiction. Why, only yesterday—" See?'

'Strange, isn't it, how fact so often copies fiction,' repeated Tommy dutifully. 'Why, only yesterday—'

'I happened to be strolling through Central Park when I saw something very odd.'

'I happened to be strolling through – here, gimme that book!' said Tommy, 'I want to learn the rest of it by heart!'

Mrs Dingle's farewell dinner to the famous Monsieur Tibault, on the occasion of his departure for his Western tour, was looked forward to with the greatest expectations. Not only would everybody be there, including the Princess

Vivrakanarda, but Mrs Dingle, a hinter if there ever was one, had let it be known that at this dinner an announcement of very unusual interest to Society might be made. So everyone, for once, was almost on time, except for Tommy. He was at least fifteen minutes early, for he wanted to have speech with his aunt alone. Unfortunately, however, he had hardly taken off his overcoat when she was whispering some news in his ear so rapidly that he found it difficult to understand a word of it.

'And you mustn't breathe it to a soul!' she ended, beaming. 'That is, not before the announcement – I think we'll have *that* with the salad – people never pay very much attention to salad—'

'Breathe what, Aunt Emily?' said Tommy, confused.

'The Princess, darling – the dear Princess and Monsieur Tibault – they just got engaged this afternoon, dear things! Isn't it *fascinating*?'

'Yeah,' said Tommy, and started to walk blindly through the nearest door. His aunt restrained him.

'Not there, dear – not in the library. You can congratulate them later. They're just having a sweet little moment alone there now—' And she turned away to harry the butler, leaving Tommy stunned.

But his chin came up after a moment. He wasn't beaten yet.

'Strange, isn't it, how often fact copies fiction?' he repeated to himself in dull mnemonics, and, as he did so, he shook his fist at the library door.

Mrs Dingle was wrong, as usual. The Princess and M. Tibault were not in the library – they were in the conservatory, as Tommy discovered when he wandered aimlessly past the glass doors.

He didn't mean to look, and after a second he turned away. But that second was enough.

Tibault was seated in a chair and she was crouched on a stool at his side, while his hand, softly, smoothly, stroked her brown hair. Black cat and Siamese kitten. Her face was hidden from Tommy, but he could see Tibault's face. And he could hear.

They were not talking, but there was a sound between them. A warm and contented sound like the murmur of giant bees in a hollow tree – a golden, musical rumble, deep-throated, that came from Tibault's lips and was answered by hers – a golden purr.

Tommy found himself back in the drawing-room, shaking hands with Mrs Culverin, who said, frankly, that she had seldom seen him look so pale.

The first two courses of the dinner passed Tommy like dreams, but Mrs Dingle's cellar was notable, and by the middle of the meat course, he began to come to himself. He had only one resolve now.

For the next few moments he tried desperately to break into the conversation, but Mrs Dingle was talking, and even Gabriel will have a time interrupting Mrs Dingle. At last, though, she paused for breath and Tommy saw his chance.

'Speaking of that,' said Tommy, piercingly, without knowing in the least what he was referring to, 'Speaking of that—'

'As I was saying,' said Professor Tatto. But Tommy would not yield. The plates were being taken away. It was time for salad.

'Speaking of that,' he said again, so loudly and strangely that Mrs Culverin jumped and an awkward hush fell over the table. 'Strange, isn't it, how often fact copies fiction?' There, he was startled. His voice rose even higher. 'Why, only today I was strolling through—' and, word for word, he repeated his lesson. He could see Tibault's eyes glowing at him, as he described the funeral. He could see the Princess, tense.

He could not have said what he had expected might happen when he came to the end; but it was not bored silence, everywhere, to be followed by Mrs Dingle's acrid, 'Well, Tommy, is that *quite* all?'

He slumped back in his chair, sick at heart. He was a fool and his last resource had failed. Dimly he heard his aunt's voice, saying, 'Well, then—' and realized that she was about to make the fatal announcement.

But just then Monsieur Tibault spoke.

'One moment, Mrs Dingle,' he said, with extreme politeness, and she was silent. He turned to Tommy.

'You are – positive I suppose, of what you saw this afternoon, Brooks?' he said, in tones of light mockery.

'Absolutely,' said Tommy sullenly. 'Do you think I'd—'

'Oh, no, no, no,' Monsieur Tibault waved the implication aside, 'but – such an interesting story – one likes to be sure of the details – and, of course, you *are* sure – *quite* sure – that the kind of crown you describe was on the coffin?'

'Of course,' said Tommy, wondering, 'but—'

'Then I'm the King of the Cats!' cried Monsieur Tibault in a voice of thunder, and, even as he cried it, the houselights blinked – there was the soft thud of an explosion that seemed muffled in cotton-wool from the minstrel gallery – and the scene was lit for a second by an obliterating and painful burst of light that vanished in an instant and was succeeded by heavy, blinding clouds of white, pungent smoke.

'Oh, those *horrid* photographers,' came Mrs Dingle's voice in a melodious wail. 'I *told* them not to take the flashlight picture till dinner was over, and now they've taken it *just* as I was nibbling lettuce!'

Someone tittered a little nervously. Someone coughed. Then, gradually the veils of smoke dislimned and the green-and-black spots in front of Tommy's eyes died away.

They were blinking at each other like people who have just come out of a cave into brilliant sun. Even yet their eyes stung with the fierceness of that abrupt illumination and Tommy found it hard to make out the faces across the table from him.

Mrs Dingle took command of the half-blinded company with her accustomed poise. She rose, glass in hand. 'And now, dear friends,' she said in a clear voice, 'I'm sure all of us are very happy to—' Then she stopped, open-mouthed, an expression of incredulous horror on her features. The lifted glass began to spill its contents on the tablecloth in a little stream of amber. As she spoke, she had turned directly to Monsieur Tibault's place at the table – and Monsieur Tibault was no longer there.

Some say there was a bursting flash of fire that disappeared up the chimney – some say it was a giant cat that leaped through the window at a bound, without breaking the glass. Professor Tatto puts it down to a mysterious chemical disturbance operating only over M. Tibault's chair. The butler, who is pious, believes the devil in person flew away with him, and Mrs Dingle hesitates between witchcraft and a malicious ectoplasm dematerializing on the wrong cosmic plane. But be that as it may, one thing is certain – in the instant of fictive darkness which followed the glare of the flashlight, Monsieur Tibault, the great conductor, disappeared forever from mortal sight, tail and all.

Mrs Culverin swears he was an international burglar and that she was just about to unmask him, when he slipped away under cover of the flashlight smoke, but no one else who sat at that historic dinner-table believes her. No, there are no sound explanations, but Tommy thinks he knows, and he will never be able to pass a cat again without wondering.

Mrs Tommy is quite of her husband's mind regarding

cats – she was Gretchen Woolwine, of Chicago – for Tommy told her his whole story, and while she doesn't believe a great deal of it, there is no doubt in her heart that one person concerned in the affair was a *perfect* cat. Doubtless it would have been more romantic to relate how Tommy's daring finally won him his Princess – but, unfortunately, it would not be veracious. For the Princess Vivrakanarda, also, is with us no longer. Her nerves, shattered by the spectacular denouement of Mrs Dingle's dinner, required a sea-voyage, and from that voyage she has never returned to America.

Of course, there are the usual stories – one hears of her, a nun in a Siamese convent, or a masked dancer at Le Jardin de ma Soeur – one hears that she has been murdered in Patagonia or married in Trebizond – but, as far as can be ascertained, not one of these gaudy fables has the slightest basis of fact. I believe that Tommy, in his heart of hearts, is quite convinced that the sea-voyage was only a pretext, and that by some unheard-of means, she has managed to rejoin the formidable Monsieur Tibault, wherever in the world of the visible or the invisible he may be – in fact, that in some ruined city or subterranean palace they reign together now, King and Queen of all the mysterious Kingdom of Cats. But that, of course, is quite impossible.

URSULA K. LE GUIN

SCHRÖDINGER'S CAT

AS THINGS APPEAR to be coming to some sort of climax, I have withdrawn to this place. It is cooler here, and nothing moves fast.

On the way here I met a married couple who were coming apart. She had pretty well gone to pieces, but he seemed, at first glance, quite hearty. While he was telling me that he had no hormones of any kind, she pulled herself together, and by supporting her head in the crook of her right knee and hopping on the toes of the right foot, approached us shouting, 'Well what's *wrong* with a person trying to express themselves?' The left leg, the arms, and the trunk, which had remained lying in the heap, twitched and jerked in sympathy. 'Great legs,' the husband pointed out, looking at the slim ankle. 'My wife has great legs.'

A cat has arrived, interrupting my narrative. It is a striped yellow tom with white chest and paws. He has long whiskers and yellow eyes. I never noticed before that cats had whiskers about their eyes; is that normal? There is no way to tell. As he has gone to sleep on my knee, I shall proceed.

Where?

Nowhere, evidently. Yet the impulse to narrate remains. Many things are not worth doing, but almost anything is worth telling. In any case, I have a severe congenital case of *Ethica laboris puritanica*, or Adam's Disease. It is incurable except by total decapitation. I even like to dream when asleep, and to try and recall my dreams: it assures me that

I haven't wasted seven or eight hours just lying there. Now here I am, lying, here. Hard at it.

Well, the couple I was telling you about finally broke up. The pieces of him trotted around bouncing and cheeping, like little chicks, but she was finally reduced to nothing but a mass of nerves: rather like fine chicken-wire, in fact, but hopelessly tangled.

So I came on, placing one foot carefully in front of the other, and grieving. This grief is with me still. I fear it is part of me, like foot or loin or eye, or may even be myself: for I seem to have no other self, nothing further, nothing that lies outside the borders of grief.

Yet I don't know what I grieve for: my wife? my husband? my children, or myself? I can't remember. Most dreams are forgotten, try as one will to remember. Yet later music strikes the note and the harmonic rings along the mandolin-strings of the mind, and we find tears in our eyes. Some note keeps playing that makes me want to cry; but what for? I am not certain.

The yellow cat, who may have belonged to the couple that broke up, is dreaming. His paws twitch now and then, and once he makes a small, suppressed remark with his mouth shut. I wonder what a cat dreams of, and to whom he was speaking just then. Cats seldom waste words. They are quiet beasts. They keep their counsel, they reflect. They reflect all day, and at night their eyes reflect. Overbred Siamese cats may be as noisy as little dogs, and then people say, 'They're talking,' but the noise is farther from speech than is the deep silence of the hound or the tabby. All this cat can say is meow, but maybe in his silences he will suggest to me what it is that I have lost, what I am grieving for. I have a feeling that he knows. That's why he came here. Cats look out for Number One.

It was getting awfully hot. I mean, you could touch less and less. The stove-burners, for instance; now I know that stove-burners always used to get hot, that was their final cause, they existed in order to get hot. But they began to get hot without having been turned on. Electric units or gas rings, there they'd be when you came into the kitchen for breakfast, all four of them glaring away, the air above them shaking like clear jelly with the heatwaves. It did no good to turn them off, because they weren't on in the first place. Besides, the knobs and dials were also hot, uncomfortable to the touch.

Some people tried hard to cool them off. The favorite technique was to turn them on. It worked sometimes, but you could not count on it. Others investigated the phe- nomenon, tried to get at the root of it, the cause. They were probably the most frightened ones, but man is most human at his most frightened. In the face of the hot stove-burners they acted with exemplary coolness. They studied, they observed. They were like the fellow in Michelangelo's *Last Judgment*, who has clapped his hands over his face in horror as the devils drag him down to Hell – but only over one eye. The other eye is busy looking. It's all he can do, but he does it. He observes. Indeed, one wonders if Hell would exist, if he did not look at it. However, neither he, nor the people I am talking about, had enough time to do much about it. And then finally of course there were the people who did not try to do or think anything about it at all.

When the water came out of the cold-water taps hot one morning, however, even people who had blamed it all on the Democrats began to feel a more profound unease. Before long forks and pencils and wrenches were too hot to handle without gloves; and cars were really terrible. It was like open- ing the door of an oven going full blast, to open the door of your car. And by then, other people almost scorched your fingers off. A kiss was like a branding iron. Your child's hair flowed along your hand like fire.

Here, as I said, it is cooler, and, as a matter of fact, this animal is cool. A real cool cat. No wonder it's pleasant to pet his fur. Also he moves slowly, at least for the most part, which is all the slowness one can reasonably expect of a cat. He hasn't that frenetic quality most creatures acquired – all they did was ZAP and gone. They lacked presence. I suppose birds always tended to be that way, but even the humming-bird used to halt for a second in the very center of his metabolic frenzy, and hang, still as a hub, present, above the fuchsias – then gone again, but you knew something was there besides the blurring brightness. But it got so that even robins and pigeons, the heavy impudent birds, were a blur, and as for swallows, they cracked the sound barrier. You knew of swallows only by the small, curved sonic booms that looped about the eaves of old houses in the evening.

Worms shot like subway trains through the dirt of gardens, among the writhing roots of roses.

You could scarcely lay a hand on children, by then: too fast to catch, too hot to hold. They grew up before your eyes.

But then, maybe that's always been true.

I was interrupted by the cat, who woke and said meow once, then jumped down from my lap and leaned against my legs diligently. This is a cat who knows how to get fed. He also knows how to jump. There was a lazy fluidity to his leap, as if gravity affected him less than it does other creatures. As a matter of fact there were some localized cases, just before I left, of the failure of gravity; but this quality in the cat's leap was something quite else. I am not yet in such a state of confusion that I can be alarmed by grace. Indeed, I found it reassuring. While I was opening a can of sardines, a person arrived.

Hearing the knock, I thought it might be the mailman. I miss mail very much, so I hurried to the door and said, 'Is it the mail?' A voice replied, 'Yah!' I opened the door. He came in, almost pushing me aside in his haste. He dumped down an enormous knapsack he had been carrying, straightened up, massaged his shoulders, and said, 'Wow!'

'How did you get here?'

He stared at me and repeated, 'How?'

At this my thoughts concerning human and animal speech recurred to me, and I decided that this was probably not a man, but a small dog. (Large dogs seldom go yah, wow, how, unless it is appropriate to do so.)

'Come on, fella,' I coaxed him. 'Come, come on, that's a boy, good doggie!' I opened a can of pork and beans for him at once, for he looked half starved. He ate voraciously, gulping and lapping. When it was gone he said 'Wow!' several times. I was just about to scratch him behind the ears when he stiffened, his hackles bristling, and growled deep in his throat. He had noticed the cat.

The cat had noticed him some time before, without interest, and was now sitting on a copy of *The Well-Tempered Clavier* washing sardine oil off its whiskers. 'Wow!' the dog, whom I had thought of calling Rover, barked.

'Wow! Do you know what that is? *That's Schrödinger's Cat!*'

'No it's not; nor any more; it's my cat,' I said, unreasonably offended.

'Oh, well, Schrödinger's dead, of course, but it's his cat. I've seen hundreds of pictures of it. Erwin Schrödinger, the great physicist, you know. Oh, wow! To think of finding it here!'

The cat looked coldly at him for a moment, and began to wash its left shoulder with negligent energy. An almost religious expression had come into Rover's face. 'It was meant,' he said in a low, impressive tone. 'Yah. It was *meant*. It can't be a mere coincidence. It's too improbable. Me, with the box; you, with the cat; to meet – here – now.' He looked up at me, his eyes shining with happy fervor. 'Isn't it wonderful?' he said. 'I'll get the box set up right away.' And he started to tear open his huge knapsack.

While the cat washed its front paws, Rover unpacked. While the cat washed its tail and belly, regions hard to reach gracefully, Rover put together what he had unpacked, a complex task. When he and the cat finished their operations simultaneously and looked at me, I was impressed. They had come out even, to the very second. Indeed it seemed that something more than chance was involved. I hoped it was not myself.

'What's that?' I asked, pointing to a protuberance on the outside of the box. I did not ask what the box was as it was quite clearly a box.

'The gun,' Rover said with excited pride.

'The gun?'

'To shoot the cat.'

'To shoot the cat?'

'Or to *not shoot* the cat. Depending on the photon.'

'The photon?'

'Yah! It's Schrödinger's great Gedankenexperiment. You see, there's a little emitter here. At Zero Time, five seconds after the lid of the box is closed, it will emit one photon. The photon will strike a half-silvered mirror. The quantum mechanical probability of the photon passing through the mirror is exactly one-half, isn't it? So! If the photon passes through, the trigger will be activated and the gun will fire.

If the photon is deflected, the trigger will not be activated and the gun will not fire. Now, you put the cat in. The cat is in the box. You close the lid. You go away! You stay away! What happens?' Rover's eyes were bright.

'The cat gets hungry?'

'The cat gets shot – or not shot,' he said, seizing my arm, though not, fortunately, in his teeth. 'But the gun is silent, perfectly silent. The box is soundproof. There is no way to know whether or not the cat has been shot, until you lift the lid of the box. There is NO way! Do you see how central this is to the whole of quantum theory? Before Zero Time the whole system, on the quantum level or on our level, is nice and simple. But after Zero Time the whole system can be represented only by a linear combination of two waves. We cannot predict the behavior of the photon, and thus, once it has behaved, we cannot predict the state of the system it has determined. We cannot predict it! God plays dice with the world! So it is beautifully demonstrated that if you desire certainty, any certainty, you must create it yourself!'

'How?'

'By lifting the lid of the box, of course,' Rover said, looking at me with sudden disappointment, perhaps a touch of suspicion, like a Baptist who finds he has been talking church matters not to another Baptist as he thought, but a Methodist, or even, God forbid, an Episcopalian. 'To find out whether the cat is dead or not.'

'Do you mean,' I said carefully, 'that until you lift the lid of the box, the cat has neither been shot nor not been shot?'

'Yah!' Rover said, radiant with relief, welcoming me back to the fold. 'Or maybe, you know, both.'

'But why does opening the box and looking reduce the system back to one probability, either live cat or dead cat?

Why don't we get included in the system when we lift the lid of the box?'

There was a pause. 'How?' Rover barked, distrustfully.

'Well, we would involve ourselves in the system, you see, the superposition of two waves. There's no reason why it should only exist *inside* an open box, is there? so when we came to look, there we would be, you and I, both looking at a live cat, and both looking at a dead cat. You see?'

A dark cloud lowered on Rover's eyes and brow. He barked twice in a subdued, harsh voice, and walked away. With his back turned to me he said in a firm, sad tone, 'You must not complicate the issue. It is complicated enough.'

'Are you sure?'

He nodded. Turning, he spoke pleadingly. 'Listen. It's all we have – the box. Truly it is. The box. And the cat. And they're here. The box, the cat, at last. Put the cat in the box. Will you? Will you let me put the cat in the box?'

'No,' I said, shocked.

'Please. Please. Just for a minute. Just for half a minute! Please let me put the cat in the box!'

'Why?'

'I can't stand this terrible uncertainty,' he said, and burst into tears.

I stood some while indecisive. Though I felt sorry for the poor son of a bitch, I was about to tell him, gently, No; when a curious thing happened. The cat walked over to the box, sniffed around it, lifted his tail and sprayed a corner to mark his territory, and then lightly, with that marvelous fluid ease, leapt into it. His yellow tail just flicked the edge of the lid as he jumped, and it closed, falling into place with a soft, decisive click.

'The cat is in the box,' I said.

'The cat is in the box,' Rover repeated in a whisper, falling to his knees. 'Oh, wow. Oh, wow. Oh, wow.'

There was silence then: deep silence. We both gazed, I afoot, Rover kneeling, at the box. No sound. Nothing happened. Nothing would happen. Nothing would ever happen, until we lifted the lid of the box.

'Like Pandora,' I said in a weak whisper. I could not quite recall Pandora's legend. She had let all the plagues and evils out of the box, of course, but there had been something else, too. After all the devils were let loose, something quite different, quite unexpected, had been left. What had it been? Hope? A dead cat? I could not remember.

Impatience welled up in me. I turned on Rover, glaring. He returned the look with expressive brown eyes. You can't tell me dogs haven't got souls.

'Just exactly what are you trying to prove?' I demanded.

'That the cat will be dead, or not dead,' he murmured submissively. 'Certainty. All I want is certainty. To know for *sure* that God *does* play dice with the world!'

I looked at him for a while with fascinated incredulity. 'Whether he does, or doesn't,' I said, 'do you think he's going to leave you a note about it in the box?' I went to the box, and with a rather dramatic gesture, flung the lid back. Rover staggered up from his knees, gasping, to look. The cat was, of course, not there.

Rover neither barked, nor fainted, nor cursed, nor wept. He really took it very well.

'Where is the cat?' he asked at last.

'Where is the box?'

'Here.'

'Where's here?'

'Here is now.'

351

'We used to think so,' I said, 'but really we could use larger boxes.'

He gazed about him in mute bewilderment, and did not flinch even when the roof of the house was lifted off just like the lid of a box, letting in the unconscionable, inordinate light of the stars. He had just time to breathe, 'Oh, wow!'

I have identified the note that keeps sounding. I checked it on the mandolin before the glue melted. It is the note A, the one that drove the composer Schumann mad. It is a beautiful, clear tone, much clearer now that the stars are visible. I shall miss the cat. I wonder if he found what it was we lost.

ANGELA CARTER

PUSS-IN-BOOTS

FIGARO HERE; Figaro, there, I tell you! Figaro upstairs, Figaro downstairs and – oh, my goodness me, this little Figaro can slip into my lady's chamber smart as you like at any time whatsoever that he takes the fancy for, don't you know, he's a cat of the world, cosmopolitan, sophisticated; he can tell when a furry friend is the Missus' best company. For what lady in all the world could say 'no' to the passionate yet *toujours discret* advances of a fine marmalade cat? (Unless it be her eyes incontinently overflow at the slightest whiff of fur, which happened once, as you shall hear.)

A tom, sirs, a ginger tom and proud of it. Proud of his fine, white shirtfront that dazzles harmoniously against his orange and tangerine tessellations (oh! what a fiery suit of lights have I); proud of his bird-entrancing eye and more than military whiskers; proud, to a fault, some say, of his fine, musical voice. All the windows in the square fly open when I break into impromptu song at the spectacle of the moon above Bergamo. If the poor players in the square, the sullen rout of ragged trash that haunts the provinces, are rewarded with a hail of pennies when they set up their makeshift stage and start their raucous choruses; then how much more liberally do the citizens deluge me with pails of the freshest water, vegetables hardly spoiled and, occasionally, slippers, shoes and boots.

Do you see these fine, high, shining leather boots of mine? A young cavalry officer made me the tribute of, first one; then, after I celebrate his generosity with a fresh obbligato, the moon no fuller than my heart – whoops! I nimbly spring aside – down comes the other. Their high heels will click like castanets when Puss takes his promenade upon the tiles, for my song recalls flamenco, all cats have a Spanish tinge although Puss himself elegantly lubricates his virile, muscular, native Bergamasque with French, since that is the only language in which you can purr.

'*Merrrrrrrrrrci!*'

Instanter I draw my new boots on over the natty white stockings that terminate my hinder legs. That young man, observing with curiosity by moonlight the use to which I put his footwear, calls out: 'Hey, Puss! Puss, there!'

'At your service, sir!'

'Up to my balcony, young Puss!'

He leans out, in his nightshirt, offering encouragement as I swing succinctly up the façade, forepaws on a curly cherub's pate, hindpaws on a stucco wreath, bring them up to meet your forepaws while, first paw forward, hup! on to the stone nymph's tit; left paw down a bit, the satyr's bum should do the trick. Nothing to it, once you know how, rococo's no problem. Acrobatics? Born to them; Puss can perform a back somersault whilst holding aloft a glass of vino in his right paw and *never spill a drop*.

But, to my shame, the famous death-defying triple somersault *en plein air*, that is, in middle air, that is, unsupported and without a safety net, I, Puss, have never yet attempted though often I have dashingly brought off the double tour, to the applause of all.

'You strike me as a cat of parts,' says this young man when I'm arrived at his windowsill. I made him a handsome genuflection, rump out, tail up, head down, to facilitate his friendly chuck under my chin; and, as involuntary free gift, my natural, my habitual smile.

For all cats have this particularity, each and every one,

from the meanest alley sneaker to the proudest, whitest she that ever graced a pontiff's pillow – we have our smiles, as it were, painted on. Those small, cool, quiet Mona Lisa smiles that smile we must, no matter whether it's been fun or it's been not. So all cats have a politician's air; we smile and smile and so they think we're villains. But, I note, this young man is something of a smiler hisself.

'A sandwich,' he offers. 'And, perhaps, a snifter of brandy.'

His lodgings are poor, though he's handsome enough and even *en déshabillé*, nightcap and all, there's a neat, smart, dandified air about him. Here is one who knows what's what, thinks I; a man who keeps up appearances in the bedchamber can never embarrass you out of it. And excellent beef sandwiches; I relish a lean slice of roast beef and early learned a taste for spirits, since I started life as a wine-shop cat, hunting cellar rats for my keep, before the world sharpened my wits enough to let me live by them.

And the upshot of this midnight interview? I'm engaged, on the spot, as Sir's valet: *valet de chambre* and, from time to time, his body servant, for, when funds are running low, as they must do for every gallant officer when the pickings fall off, he pawns the quilt, doesn't he. Then faithful Puss curls up on his chest to keep him warm at night. And if he don't like me to knead his nipples, which, out of the purest affection and the desire – ouch! he says – to test the retractability of my claws, I do in moments of absence of mind, then what other valet could slip into a young girl's sacred privacy and deliver her a billet-doux at the very moment when she's reading her prayerbook with her sainted mother? A task I once or twice perform for him, to his infinite gratitude.

And, as you will hear, brought him at last to the best of fortunes for us all.

So Puss got his post at the same time as his boots and I dare say the Master and I have much in common for he's proud as the devil, touchy as tin-tacks, lecherous as liquorice and, though I say it as loves him, as quick-witted a rascal as ever put on clean linen.

When times were hard, I'd pilfer the market for breakfast – a herring, an orange, a loaf; we never went hungry. Puss served him well in the gaming salons, too, for a cat may move from lap to lap with impunity and cast his eye over any hand of cards. A cat can jump on the dice – he can't resist to see it roll! poor thing, mistook it for a bird; and, after I've been, limp-spined, stiff-legged, playing the silly buggers, scooped up to be chastised, who can remember how the dice fell in the first place?

And we had, besides, less . . . gentlemanly means of main-tenance when they closed the tables to us, as, churlishly, they sometimes did. I'd perform my little Spanish dance while he went around with his hat: *olé!* But he only put my loyalty and affection to the test of this humiliation when the cup-board was as bare as his backside; after, in fact, he'd sunk so low as to pawn his drawers.

So all went right as ninepence and you never saw such boon companions as Puss and his master; until the man must needs go fall in love.

'Head over heels, Puss.'

I went about my ablutions, tonguing my arsehole with the impeccable hygienic integrity of cats, one leg stuck in the air like a ham bone; I choose to remain silent. Love? What has my rakish master, for whom I've jumped through the win-dow of every brothel in the city, besides haunting the virginal back garden of the convent and god knows what other goat-ish errands, to do with tender passion?

'And she. A princess in a tower. Remote and shining as Aldebaran. Chained to a dolt and dragon-guarded.'

I withdrew my head from my privates and fixed him with my most satiric smile; I dared him warble on in *that* strain.

'All cats are cynics,' he opines, quailing beneath my yellow glare.

It is the hazard of it draws him, see.

There is a lady sits in a window for one hour and one hour only, at the tenderest time of dusk. You can scarcely see her features, the curtains almost hide her; shrouded like a holy Image, she looks out on the piazza as the shops shut up, the stalls go down, the night comes on. And this is all the world she ever sees. Never a girl in all Bergamo so secluded except, on Sundays, they let her go to Mass, bundled up in black, with a veil on. And then she is in the company of an aged hag, her keeper, who grumps along grim as a prison dinner.

How did he see that secret face? Who else but Puss revealed it?

Back we come from the tables so late, so very late at night we found, to our emergent surprise that all at once it was early in the morning. His pockets were heavy with silver and both our guts sweetly a-gurgle with champagne, Lady Luck had sat with us, what fine spirits were we in! Winter and cold weather. The pious trot to church already with little lanterns through the chill fog as we go ungodly rolling home.

See, a black barque, like a state funeral; and Puss takes it into his bubbly-addled brain to board her. Tacking obliquely to her side, I rub my marmalade pate against her shin; how could any duenna, be she never so stern, take offence at such attentions to her chargeling from a little cat? (As it turns out, this one: *attishooo!* does.) A white hand fragrant as Arabia descends from the black cloak and reciprocally rubs behind his ears at just the ecstatic spot. Puss lets rip a roaring purr, rears briefly on his high-heeled boots; jig with joy and pirouette with glee – she laughs to see and draws her veil aside. Puss glimpses high above, as it were, an alabaster lamp lit behind by dawn's first flush: her face.

And she smiling.

For a moment, just that moment, you would have thought it was May morning.

'Come along! Come! Don't dawdle over the nasty beast!' snaps the old hag, with the one tooth in her mouth, and warts; she sneezes.

The veil comes down; so cold it is, and dark, again.

It was not I alone who saw her; with that smile he swears she stole his heart.

Love.

I've sat inscrutably by and washed my face and sparkling dicky with my clever paw while he made the beast with two backs with every harlot in the city, besides a number of good wives, dutiful daughters, rosy country girls come to sell celery and endive on the corner, and the chambermaid who strips the bed, what's more. The Mayor's wife, even, shed her diamond earrings for him and the wife of the notary unshuffled her petticoats and if I could, I would blush to remember how her daughter shook out her flaxen plaits and jumped in bed between them and she not sixteen years old. But never the word, 'love', has fallen from his lips, nor in nor out of any of these transports, until my master saw the wife of Signor Panteleone as she went walking out to Mass, and she lifted up her veil though not for him.

And now he is half sick with it and will go to the tables no more for lack of heart and never even pats the bustling rump of the chambermaid in his new-found maudlin celibacy, so we get our slops left festering for days and the sheets filthy and the wench goes banging about bad-temperedly with her broom enough to fetch the plaster off the walls.

I'll swear he lives for Sunday morning, though never before was he a religious man. Saturday nights, he bathes himself punctiliously, even, I'm glad to see, washes behind his ears, perfumes himself, presses his uniform so you'd think he had a right to wear it. So much in love he very rarely panders to the pleasures, even of Onan, as he lies tossing on his couch, for he cannot sleep for fear he miss the summoning bell. Then out into the cold morning, harking after that black, vague shape, hapless fisherman for his sealed oyster with such a pearl in it. He creeps behind her across the square; how can one so amorous bear to be so inconspicuous? And yet, he must; though, sometimes, the old hag sneezes and says she swears there is a cat about.

He will insinuate himself into the pew behind milady and sometimes contrive to touch the hem of her garment, when they all kneel, and never a thought to his orisons; she is the divinity he's come to worship. Then sits silent, in a dream, till bed-time; what pleasure is his company for me?

He won't eat, either. I brought him a fine pigeon from the inn kitchen, fresh off the spit, *parfumé avec* tarragon, but he wouldn't touch it so I crunched it up, bones and all, performing, as ever after meals, my meditative toilette, I pondered, thus: one, he is in a fair way to ruining us both by neglecting his business; two, love is desire sustained by unfulfilment. If I lead him to her bedchamber and there he takes his fill of her lily-white, he'll be right as rain in two shakes and next day tricks as usual.

Then Master and his Puss will soon be solvent once again.

Which, at the moment, very much not, sir.

This Signor Panteleone employs, his only servant but the hag, a kitchen cat, a sleek, spry tabby whom I accost. Grasping the slack of her neck firmly between my teeth, I gave her the customary tribute of a few firm thrusts of my striped loins and, when she got her breath back, she assured me in the friendliest fashion the old man was a fool and a miser who kept herself on short commons for the sake of the mousing and the young lady a soft-hearted creature who smuggled breast of chicken and sometimes, when the hag-dragon-governess napped at midday, snatched this pretty kitty out of the hearth and into her bedroom to play with reels of silk and run after trailed handkerchiefs, when she and she had as much fun together as two Cinderellas at an all-girls' ball.

Poor, lonely lady, married so young to an old dodderer with his bald pate and his goggle eyes and his limp, his avarice, his gore belly, his rheumaticks, and his flag hangs all the time at half-mast indeed; and jealous as he is impotent, tabby declares – he'd put a stop to all the rutting in the world, if he had his way, just to certify his young wife don't get from another what she can't get from him.

'Then shall we hatch a plot to antler him, my precious?'

Nothing loath, she tells me the best time for this accomplishment should be the one day in all the week he forsakes his wife and his counting-house to ride off into the country to extort more grasping rents from starveling tenant farmers. And she's left all alone, then, behind so many bolts and bars you wouldn't believe; all alone – but for the hag!

Aha! This hag turns out to be the biggest snag; an iron-plated, copper-bottomed, sworn man-hater of some sixty bitter winters who – as ill luck would have it – shatters, clatters, erupts into paroxysms of the *sneeze* at the very glimpse of a cat's whisker. No chance of Puss worming his winsome way into *that* one's affections, nor for my tabby neither! But, oh my dear, I say; see how my ingenuity rises to the challenge ... So we resume the sweetest part of our conversation in the dusty convenience of the coalhole and she promises me, least she can do, to see the fair, hitherto-inaccessible one gets a letter safe if I slip it to her and slip it to her forthwith I do, though somewhat discommoded by my boots.

He spent three hours over his letter, did my master, as long as it takes me to lick the coaldust off my dicky. He tears up half a quire of paper, splays five pen-nibs with the force of his adoration: 'Look not for any peace, my heart; having become a slave to this beauty's tyranny, dazzled am I by this sun's rays and my torments cannot be assuaged.' *That's* not the high road to the rumpling of the bedcovers; she's got *one* ninny between them already!

'Speak from the heart,' I finally exhort. 'And all good women have the missionary streak, sir; convince her her orifice will be your salvation and she's yours.'

'When I want your advice, Puss, I'll ask for it,' he says; all at once hoity-toity. But at last he manages to pen ten pages; a rake, a profligate, a card-sharper, a cashiered officer well on the way to rack and ruin when first he saw, as if it were a glimpse of grace, her face . . . his angel, his good angel, who will lead him from perdition.

Oh, what a masterpiece he penned!

'Such tears she wept at his addresses!' says my tabby friend.

'Oh, Tabs, she sobs – for she calls me "Tabs" – I never meant to wreak such havoc with a pure heart when I smiled to see a booted cat! And put his paper next to her heart and swore it was a good soul that sent her his vows and she was too much in love with virtue to withstand him. If, she adds, for she's a sensible girl, he's neither old as the hills nor ugly as sin, that is.'

An admirable little note the lady's sent him in return, per

Figaro here and there; she adopts a responsive yet uncom-
promising tone. For, says she, how can she usefully discuss
his passion further without a glimpse of his person?

He kisses her letter once, twice, a thousand times; she
must and will see me! I shall serenade her this very evening!

So, when dusk falls, off we trot to the piazza, he with an
old guitar he pawned his sword to buy and most, if I may
say so, outlandishly rigged out in some kind of vagabond
mountebank's outfit he bartered his gold-braided waistcoat
with poor Pierrot braying in the square for, moon-struck
zany, lovelorn loon he was himself and even plastered his face
with flour to make it white, poor fool, and so ram home his
heartsick state.

There she is, the evening star with the clouds around her;
but such a creaking of carts in the square, such a clatter and
crash as they dismantle the stalls, such an ululation of ballad-
singers and oration of nostrum-peddlers and perturbation
of errand boys that though he wails out his heart to her:
'Oh, my beloved!' why she, all in a dream, sits with her gaze
in the middle distance where there's a crescent moon stuck
on the sky behind the cathedral pretty as a painted stage,
and so is she.

Does she hear him?

Not a grace-note.

Does she see him?

Never a glance.

'Up you go, Puss; tell her to look my way!'

If rococo's a piece of cake, that chaste, tasteful, early Palladian stumped many a better cat than I in its time. Agility's
not in it, when it comes to Palladian, daring alone will carry
the day and, though the first storey's graced with a hefty
caryatid whose bulbous loincloth and tremendous pects facilitate the first ascent, the Doric column on her head proves

a horse of a different colour, I can tell you. Had I not seen my precious Tabby crouched in the gutter above me keening encouragement, I, even I, might never have braved that flying, upward leap that brought me, as if Harlequin himself on wires, in one bound to her windowsill.

'Dear god!' the lady says, and jumps. I see she, too, ah, sentimental thing! clutches a well-thumbed letter. 'Puss-in-boots!'

I bow her with a courtly flourish. What luck to hear no sniff or sneeze; where's hag? A sudden flux sped her to the privy – not a moment to lose.

'Cast your eye below,' I hiss. 'Him you know of lurks below, in white with the big hat, ready to sing you an evening ditty.'

The bedroom door creaks open, then, and: whee! through the air Puss goes, discretion is the better part. And, for both their sweet sakes I did it, the sight of both their bright eyes inspired me to the never-before-attempted, by me or any other cat, in boots or out of them – the death-defying triple somersault!

And a three-storey drop to ground, what's more; a grand descent.

Only the merest trifle winded. I'm proud to say, I neatly land on all my fours and Tabs goes wild, huzzah! But has my master witnessed my triumph? Has he, my arse. He's tuning up that old mandolin and breaks, as down I come, again into his song.

I would never have said, in the normal course of things, his voice would charm the birds out of the trees, like mine; and yet the bustle died for him, the homeward-turning costers paused in their tracks to hearken, the preening street girls forgot their hard-edged smiles as they turned to him and some of the old ones wept, they did.

365

Tabs, up on the roof there, prick up your ears! For by its power I know my heart is in his voice.

And now the lady lowers her eyes to him and smiles, as once she smiled at me.

Then, bang! a stern hand pulls the shutters to. And it was as if all the violets in all the baskets of all the flower-sellers drooped and faded at once; and spring stopped dead in its tracks and might, this time, not come at all; and the bustle and the business of the square, that had so magically quieted for his song, now rose up again with the harsh clamour of the loss of love.

And we trudge drearily off to dirty sheets and a mean supper of bread and cheese, all I can steal him, but at least the poor soul manifests a hearty appetite now she knows he's in the world and not the ugliest of mortals; for the first time since that fateful morning, sleeps sound. But sleep comes hard to Puss tonight. He takes a midnight stroll across the square, soon comfortably discusses a choice morsel of salt cod his tabby friend found among the ashes on the hearth before our converse turns to other matters.

'Rats!' she says. 'And take your boots off, you uncouth bugger; those three-inch heels wreak havoc with the soft flesh of my underbelly!'

When we'd recovered ourselves a little, I ask her what she means by those 'rats' of hers and she proposes her scheme to me. How my master must pose as a *rat-catcher* and I, his ambulant marmalade rat-trap. How we will then go kill the rats that ravage milady's bedchamber, the day the old fool goes to fetch his rent, and she can have her will of the lad at leisure for, if there is one thing the hag fears more than a cat, it is a rat and she'll cower in a cupboard till the last rat is off the premises before she comes out. Oh, this tabby one, sharp as a tack is she; I congratulate her ingenuity with a few affectionate cuffs round the head and home again, for breakfast, ubiquitous Puss, here, there and everywhere, who's your Figaro?

Master applauds the rat ploy; but, as to the rats themselves; how are they to arrive in the house in the first place? he queries.

'Nothing easier, sir; my accomplice, a witty soubrette who lives among the cinders, dedicated as she is to the young lady's happiness, will personally strew a large number of dead and dying rats she has herself collected about the bedroom of the said ingénue's duenna, and, most particularly, that of the said ingénue herself. This to be done tomorrow morning, as soon as Sir Pantaloon rides out to fetch his rents. By good fortune, down in the square, plying for hire, a rat-catcher! Since our hag cannot abide either a rat or a cat, it falls to milady to escort the rat-catcher, none other than yourself, sir, and his intrepid hunter, myself, to the site of the infestation.

'Once you're in her bedroom, sir, if *you* don't know what to do, then I can't help you.'

'Keep your foul thoughts to yourself, Puss.'

Some things, I see, are sacrosanct from humour.

Sure enough, prompt at five in the bleak next morning, I observe with my own eyes the lovely lady's lubberly husband hump off on his horse like a sack of potatoes to rake in his dues. We're ready with our sign: SIGNOR FURIOSO, THE LIVING DEATH OF RATS; and in the leathers he's borrowed from the porter, I hardly recognize him myself, not with the false moustache. He coaxes the chambermaid with a few kisses – poor, deceived girl! love knows no shame – and so we install ourselves under a certain shuttered window with the great pile of traps she's lent us, the sign of our profession, Puss perched atop them bearing the humble yet determined look of a sworn enemy of vermin.

We've not waited more than fifteen minutes – and just as well, as many rat-plagued Bergamots approach us already and are not easily dissuaded from employing us – when the front door flies open on a lusty scream. The hag, aghast, flings her arms round flinching Furioso; how fortuitous to find him! But, at the whiff of me, she's sneezing so valiantly, her eyes awash, the vertical gutters of her nostrils aswill with snot, she barely can depict the scenes inside, rattus domesticus dead in her bed and all; and worse! in the Missus' room.

So Signor Furioso and his questing Puss are ushered into the very sanctuary of the goddess, our presence announced by a fanfare from her keeper on the nose harp. *Attishhoooo!!!*

Sweet and pleasant in a morning gown of loose linen, our ingénue jumps at the tattoo of my boot heels but recovers instantly and the wheezing, hawking hag is in no state to sniffle more than: 'Ain't I seen that cat before?'

'Not a chance,' says my master. 'Why, he's come but yesterday with me from Milano.'

So she has to make do with that.

My Tabs has lined the very stairs with rats; she's made a morgue of the hag's room but something more lively of the lady's. For some of her prey she's very cleverly not killed but crippled; a big black beastie weaves its way towards us over the turkey carpet, Puss, pounce! Between screaming and sneezing, the hag's in a fine state, I can tell you, though milady exhibits a most praiseworthy and collected presence of mind, being, I guess, a young woman of no small grasp so, perhaps, she has a sniff of the plot already.

My master goes down on hands and knees under the bed.

'My god!' he cries. 'There's the biggest hole, here in the wainscoting, I ever saw in all my professional career! And there's an army of black rats gathering behind it, ready to storm through! To arms!'

But, for all her terror, the hag's loath to leave the Master and me alone to deal with the rats; she casts her eye on a silver-backed hairbrush, a coral rosary, twitters, hovers, screeches, mutters until milady assures her, amidst scenes of rising pandemonium:

'I shall stay here myself and see that Signor Furioso doesn't make off with my trinkets. You go and recover yourself with an infusion of friar's balsam and don't come back until I call.'

The hag departs; quick as a flash, la belle turns the key in the door on her and softly laughs; the naughty one.

Dusting the slut-fluff from his knees, Signor Furioso now stands slowly upright; swiftly, he removes his false moustache, for no element of the farcical must mar this first, delirious encounter of these lovers, must it. (Poor soul, how his hands tremble!)

Accustomed as I am to the splendid, feline nakedness of my kind, that offers no concealment of that soul made manifest in the flesh of lovers, I am always a little moved by the poignant reticence with which humanity shyly hesitates to divest itself of its clutter of concealing rags in the presence of desire. So, first, these two smile, a little, as if to say 'How strange to meet you here!' uncertain of a loving welcome, still. And do I deceive myself, or do I see a tear a-twinkle in the corner of his eye? But who is it steps towards the other first? Why, she; women, I think, are, of the two sexes, the more keenly tuned to the sweet music of their bodies. (A penny for my foul thoughts, indeed! Does she, that wise, grave personage in the negligee, think you've staged this grand charade merely in order to kiss her hand?) But, then – oh, what a pretty blush! steps back; now it's his turn to take two steps forward in the saraband of Eros.

I could wish, though, they'd dance a little faster; the hag

will soon recover from her spasms and shall she find them in flagrante?

His hand, then, trembling, upon her bosom; hers, initially more hesitant, sequentially more purposeful, upon his breeches. Then their strange trance breaks; that sentimental havering done, I never saw two fall to it with such appetite. As if the whirlwind got into their fingers, they strip each other bare in a twinkling and she falls back on the bed, shows him the target, he displays the dart, scores an instant bullseye. Bravo! Never can that old bed have shook with such a storm before. And their sweet choked mutterings, poor things: 'I never...' 'My darling...' 'More...' And etc. etc. Enough to melt the thorniest heart.

He rises up on his elbows once and gasps at me: 'Mimic the murder of the rats, Puss! Mask the music of Venus with that clamour of Diana!'

A-hunting we shall go! Loyal to the last, I play catch as catch can with Tab's dead rats, giving the dying the *coup de grâce* and baying with resonant vigour to drown the extravagant screeches that break forth from that (who would have suspected?) more passionate young woman as she comes off in fine style. (Full marks, Master.)

At that, the old hag comes battering at the door. What's going on? Whyfor the racket? And the door rattles on its hinges.

'Peace!' cries Signor Furioso. 'Haven't I just now blocked the great hole?'

But milady's in no hurry to don her smock again, she takes her lovely time about it; so full of pleasure gratified her languorous limbs you'd think her very navel smiled. She pecks my master prettily thank-you on the cheek, wets the gum on his false moustache with the tip of her strawberry tongue and sticks it back on his upper lip for him, then lets her wardress into the scene of the faux carnage with the most modest and irreproachable air in the world.

'See! Puss has slaughtered all the rats.'

I rush, purring proud, to greet the hag; instantly, her eyes o'erflow.

'Why the bedclothes so disordered?' she squeaks, not quite blinded yet by phlegm, and chosen for her post from all the other applications on account of her suspicious mind, even (oh, dutiful) when in *grande peur des rats*.

'Puss had a mighty battle with the biggest beast you ever saw upon this very bed; can't you see the bloodstains on the sheets? And now, what do we owe you, Signor Furioso, for this singular service?'

'A hundred ducats,' says I, quick as a flash, for I know my master, left to himself, would like an honourable fool, take nothing.

'That's the entire household expenses for a month!' wails avarice's well-chosen accomplice.

'And worth every penny! For those rats would have eaten us out of house and home.' I see the glimmerings of sturdy backbone in this little lady. 'Go, pay them from your private savings that I know of, that you've skimmed off the house-keeping.'

Muttering and moaning but nothing for it except to do as she is bid; and the furious Sir and I take off a laundry basket full of dead rats as souvenir – we drop it, plop! in the nearest sewer. And sit down to one dinner honestly paid for, for a wonder.

But the young fool is off his feed again. Pushes his plate aside, laughs, weeps, buries his head in his hands and, time and time and time again, goes to the window to stare at the shutters behind which his sweetheart scrubs the blood away and my dear Tabs rests from her supreme exertions. He sits, for a while, and scribbles; rips the page in four, hurls it aside. I spear a falling fragment with a claw. Dear God, he's took to writing poetry.

'I must and will have her for ever,' he exclaims.

I see my plan has come to nothing. Satisfaction has not satisfied him; that soul they both saw in one another's bodies has such insatiable hunger no single meal could ever appease it. I fall to the toilette of my hinder parts, my favourite stance when contemplating the ways of the world.

'How can I live without her?'

You did so for twenty-seven years, sir, and never missed her for a moment.

'I'm burning with the fever of love!'

Then we're spared the expense of fires.

'I shall steal her away from her husband to live with me.'

'What do you propose to live on, sir?'

'Kisses,' he said distractedly. 'Embraces.'

'Well, you won't grow fat on that, sir; though *she* will. And then, more mouths to feed.'

'I'm sick and tired of your foul-mouthed barbs, Puss,' he snaps. And yet my heart is moved, for now he speaks the plain, clear, foolish rhetoric of love and who is there cunning enough to help him to happiness but I? Scheme, loyal Puss, scheme!

My wash completed, I step out across the square to visit that charming she who's wormed her way directly into my own hitherto-untrammelled heart with her sharp wits and her pretty ways. She exhibits warm emotion to see me; and, oh! what news she has to tell me! News of a rapt and personal nature, that turns my mind to thoughts of the future, and, yes, domestic plans of most familial nature. She's saved me a pig's trotter, a whole entire pig's trotter the Missus smuggled to her with a wink. A feast! Masticating, I muse.

372

'Recapitulate,' I suggest, 'the daily motions of Sir Panta-loon when he's at home.'

They set the cathedral clock by him, so rigid and so regular his habits. Up at the crack, he meagrely breakfasts off yesterday's crusts and a cup of cold water, to spare the expense of heating it up. Down to his counting-house, counting out his money, until a bowl of well-watered gruel at midday. The afternoon he devotes to usury, bankrupting, here, a small tradesman, there, a weeping widow, for fun and profit. Dinner's luxurious, at four; soup, with a bit of rancid beef or a tough bird in it – he's an arrangement with the butcher, takes unsold stock off his hands in return for a shut mouth about a pie that had a finger in it. From four-thirty until five-thirty, he unlocks the shutters and lets his wife look out, oh, don't I know! while hag sits beside her to make sure she doesn't smile. (Oh, that blessed flux, those precious loose minutes that set the game in motion!)

And while she breathes the air of evening, why, he checks up on his chest of gems, his bales of silk, all those treasures he loves too much to share with daylight and if he wastes a candle when he so indulges himself, why, any man is entitled to one little extravagance. Another draught of Adam's ale healthfully concludes the day; up he tucks besides Missus and, since she is his prize possession, consents to finger her a little. He palpitates her hide and claps her flanks: 'What a good bargain!' Alack, can do no more, not wishing to profligate his natural essence. And so drifts off to sinless slumber amid the prospects of tomorrow's gold.

'How rich is he?'

'Croesus.'

'Enough to keep two loving couples?'

'Sumptuous.'

Early in the uncandled morning, groping to the privy

bleared with sleep, were the old man to place his foot upon the subfusc yet volatile fur of a shadow-camouflaged young tabby cat –

'You read my thoughts, my love.'

I say to my master: 'Now, you get yourself a doctor's gown, impedimenta all complete or I'm done with you.'

'What's this, Puss?'

'Do as I say and never mind the reason! The less you know of why, the better.'

So he expends a few of the hag's ducats on a black gown with a white collar and his skull cap and his black bag and, under my direction, makes himself another sign that announces, with all due pomposity, how he is Il Famed Dottore: *Aches cured, pains prevented, bones set, graduate of Bologna, physician extraordinary.* He demands to know, is she to play the invalid to give him further access to her bedroom?

'I'll clasp her in my arms and jump out of the window; we too shall both perform the triple somersault of love.'

'You just mind your own business, sir, and let me mind it for you after my own fashion.'

Another raw and misty morning! Here in the hills, will the weather ever change? So bleak it is, and dreary; but there he stands, grave as a sermon in his black gown and half the market people come with coughs and boils and broken heads and I dispense the plasters and the vials of coloured water I'd forethoughtfully stowed in his bag, he too *agitato* to sell for himself. (And, who knows, might we not have stumbled on a profitable profession for future pursuit, if my present plans miscarry?)

Until dawn shoots his little yet how flaming arrow past the cathedral on which the clock strikes six. At the last stroke, that famous door flies open once again and – *eeeeeeeeeeeech!* the hag lets rip.

374

'Oh, Doctor, oh, Doctor, come quick as you can; our good man's taken a sorry tumble!'

And weeping fit to float a smack, she is, so doesn't see the doctor's apprentice is most colourfully and completely furred and whiskered.

The old booby's flat out at the foot of the stair, his head at an acute angle that might turn chronic and a big bunch of keys, still, grinned in his right hand as if they were the keys to heaven marked: *Wanted on voyage*. And Missus, in her wrap, bends over him with a pretty air of concern.

'A fall—' she begins when she sees the doctor but stops short when she sees your servant, Puss, looking as suitably down-in-the-mouth as his chronic smile will let him, humping his master's stock-in-trade and hawing like a sawbones. 'You, again,' she says, and can't forbear to giggle. But the dragon's too blubbered to hear.

My master puts his ear to the old man's chest and shakes his head dolefully; then takes the mirror from his pocket and puts it to the old man's mouth. Not a breath clouds it. Oh, sad! Oh, sorrowful!

'Dead, is he?' sobs the hag. 'Broke his neck, has he?'

And she slyly makes a little grab for the keys, in spite of her well-orchestrated distress; but Missus slaps her hand and she gives over.

'Let's get him to a softer bed,' says Master.

He ups the corpse, carries it aloft to the room we know full well, bumps Pantaloon down, twitches an eyelid, taps a kneecap, feels a pulse.

'Dead as a doornail,' he pronounces. 'It's not a doctor you want, it's an undertaker.'

Missus has a handkerchief very dutifully and correctly to her eyes.

'You just run along and get one,' she says to hag. 'And then

I'll read the will. Because don't think he's forgotten you, thou faithful servant. Oh, my goodness, no.'

So off goes hag; you never saw a woman of her accumulated Christmases spring so fast. As soon as they are left alone, no trifling, this time; they're at it, hammer and tongs, down on the carpet since the bed is *occupé*. Up and down, up and down his arse; in and out, in and out her legs. Then she heaves him up and throws him on the back, her turn at the grind, now, and you'd think she'll never stop.

Toujours discret, Puss occupies himself in unfastening the shutters and throwing the windows open to the beautiful beginning of morning in whose lively yet fragrant air his sensitive nostrils catch the first and vernal hint of spring. In a few moments, my dear friend joins me. I notice already – or is it only my fond imagination? – a charming new *portliness* in her gait, hitherto so elastic, so spring-heeled. And there we sit upon the windowsill like the two genii and protectors of the house; ah, Puss, your rambling days are over. I shall become a hearthrug cat, a fat and cosy cushion cat, sing to the moon no more, settle at last amid the sedentary joys of a domesticity we two, she and I, have so richly earned.

Their cries of rapture rouse me from this pleasant reverie.

The hag chooses, *naturellement*, this tender if outrageous moment to return with the undertaker in his chiffoned topper, plus a brace of mutes black as beetles, glum as bailiffs, bearing the elm box between them to take the corpse away in. But they cheer up something wonderful at the unexpected spectacle before them and he and she conclude their amorous interlude amidst roars of approbation and torrents of applause.

But what a racket the hag makes! Police, murder, thieves! Until the Master chucks her purseful of gold back again, for a gratuity. (Meanwhile, I note that sensible young woman, mother-naked as she is has yet the presence of mind to catch hold of her husband's key ring and sharply tug it from his sere, cold grip. Once she's got the keys secure, she's in charge of all.)

'Now, no more of your nonsense!' she snaps to hag. 'If I hereby give you the sack, you'll get a handsome gift to go along with you for now' – flourishing the keys – 'I am a rich widow and here' – indicating to all my bare yet blissful master – 'is the young man who'll be my second husband.'

When the governess found Signor Panteleone had indeed remembered her in his will, left her a keepsake of the cup he drank his morning water from, she made not a squeak more, pocketed a fat sum with thanks and, sneezing, took herself off with no more cries of 'murder' neither. The old buffoon briskly bundled in his coffin and buried; Master comes into a great fortune and Missus rounding out already and they as happy as pigs in plunk.

But my Tabs beat her to it, since cats don't take much time about engendering; three fine, new-minted ginger kittens, all complete with snowy socks and shirtfronts, tumble in the cream and tangle Missus's knitting and put a smile on every face, not just their mother's and proud father's for Tabs and I smile all day long and, these days, we put our hearts in it.

So may all your wives, if you need them, be rich and pretty; and all your husbands, if you want them, be young and virile; and all your cats as wily, perspicacious and resourceful as:

PUSS-IN-BOOTS.

STEVEN MILLHAUSER

CAT 'N' MOUSE

THE CAT IS CHASING the mouse through the kitchen: between the blue chair legs, over the tabletop with its red-and-white-checkered tablecloth that is already sliding in great waves, past the sugar bowl falling to the left and the cream jug falling to the right, over the blue chair back, down the chair legs, across the waxed and butter-yellow floor. The cat and the mouse lean backward and try to stop on the slippery wax, which shows their flawless reflections. Sparks shoot from their heels, but it's much too late: the big door looms. The mouse crashes through, leaving a mouse-shaped hole. The cat crashes through, replacing the mouse-shaped hole with a larger, cat-shaped hole. In the living-room they race over the back of the couch, across the piano keys (delicate mouse tune, crash of cat chords), along the blue rug. The fleeing mouse snatches a glance over his shoulder, and when he looks forward again he sees the floor lamp coming closer and closer. Impossible to stop – at the last moment he splits in half and rejoins himself on the other side. Behind him the rushing cat fails to split in half and crashes into the lamp: his head and body push the brass pole into the shape of a trombone. For a moment the cat hangs sideways there, his stiff legs shaking like the clapper of a bell. Then he pulls free and rushes after the mouse, who turns and darts into a mousehole in the baseboard. The cat crashes into the wall and folds up like an accordion. Slowly he unfolds, emitting accordion music. He lies on the floor with his chin on his upraised paw, one eyebrow lifted high in disgust, the claws of his other forepaw tapping the floorboards. A small piece of plaster drops on his head. He raises an outraged eye. A framed painting falls heavily on his head, which plunges out of sight between his shoulders. The painting shows a green tree with bright red apples. The cat's head struggles to rise, then pops up with the sound of a yanked cork, lifting the picture. Apples fall from the tree and land with a thump on the grass. The cat shudders, winces. A final apple falls. Slowly it rolls toward the frame, drops over the edge, and lands on the cat's head. In the cat's eyes, cash registers ring up NO SALE.

The mouse, dressed in a bathrobe and slippers, is sitting in his plump armchair, reading a book. He is tall and slim. His feet rest on a hassock, and a pair of spectacles rest on the end of his long, whiskered nose. Yellow light from a table lamp pours onto the book and dimly illuminates the cozy brown room. On the wall hang a tilted sampler bearing the words HOME SWEET HOME, an oval photograph of the mouse's mother with her gray hair in a bun, and a reproduction of Seurat's *Sunday Afternoon* in which all the figures are mice. Near the armchair is a bookcase filled with books, with several titles visible: *Martin Cheddarwit*, Gouda's *Faust*, *The Memoirs of Anthony Edam*, *A History of the Medicheese*, the sonnets of Shakespaw. As the mouse reads his book, he reaches without looking toward a dish on the table. The dish is empty: his fingers tap about inside it. The mouse rises and goes over to the cupboard, which is empty except for a tin box with the word CHEESE on it. He opens the box and turns it upside down. Into his palm drops a single tooth-pick. He gives it a melancholy look. Shaking his head, he returns to his chair and takes up his book. In a bubble above his head a picture appears: he is seated at a long table covered with a white tablecloth. He is holding a fork upright in one fist and a knife upright in the other. A mouse butler dressed in tails sets before him a piece of cheese the size of a wedding cake.

From the mousehole emerges a red telescope. The lens looks to the left, then to the right. A hand issues from the end of the telescope and beckons the mouse forward. The mouse steps from the mousehole, collapses the telescope, and thrusts it into his bathrobe pocket. In the moonlit room he tiptoes carefully, lifting his legs very high, over to the base of the armchair. He dives under the chair and peeks out through the fringe. He emerges from beneath the armchair, slinks over to the couch, and dives under. He peeks out through the fringe. He emerges from beneath the couch and approaches the slightly open kitchen door. He stands flat against the doorjamb, facing the living-room, his eyes darting left and right. One leg tiptoes delicately around the jamb. His stretched body snaps after it like a rubber band. In the kitchen he creeps to a moonlit chair, stands pressed against a chair leg, begins to climb. His nose rises over the tabletop: he sees a cream pitcher, a gleaming knife, a looming pepper mill. On a breadboard sits a wedge of cheese. The mouse, hunching his shoulders, tiptoes up to the cheese. From a pocket of his robe he removes a white handkerchief that he ties around his neck. He bends over the cheese, half closing his eyes, as if he were sniffing a flower. With a crashing sound the cat springs onto the table. As he chases the mouse, the tablecloth bunches in waves, the sugar bowl topples, and waterfalls of sugar spill to the floor. An olive from a fallen cocktail glass rolls across the table, knocking into a cup, a saltshaker, a trivet: the objects light up and cause bells to ring, as in a pinball machine. On the floor a brigade of ants is gathering the sugar: one ant catches the falling grains in a bucket, which he dumps into the bucket of a second ant, who dumps the sugar into the bucket of a third ant, all the way across the room, until the last ant dumps it into a waiting truck. The cat chases the mouse over the blue chair back, down the chair legs, across the waxed floor. Both lean backward and try to stop as the big door comes closer and closer.

The mouse is sitting in his armchair with his chin in his hand, looking off into the distance with a melancholy expression. He is thoughtful by temperament, and he is distressed at the necessity of interrupting his meditations for the daily search for food. The search is wearying and absurd in itself, but is made unbearable by the presence of the brutish cat. The mouse's disdain for the cat is precise and abundant: he loathes the soft, heavy paws with their hidden hooks, the glinting teeth, the hot, fish-stinking breath. At the same time, he confesses to himself a secret admiration for the cat's coarse energy and simplicity. It appears that the cat has no other aim in life than to catch the mouse. Although the faculty of astonishment is not highly developed in the mouse, he is constantly astonished by the cat's unremitting enmity. This makes the cat dangerous, despite his stupidity, for the mouse recognizes that he himself has long periods when the cat fades entirely from his mind. Moreover, despite the fundamental simplicity of the cat's nature, it remains true that the cat is cunning: he plots tirelessly against the mouse, and his ludicrous wiles require in the mouse an alert attention that he would prefer not to give. The mouse is aware of the temptation of indifference; he must continually exert himself to be wary. He feels that he is exhausting his nerves and harming his spirit by attending to the cat; at the same time, he realizes that his attention is at best imperfect, and that the cat is thinking uninterruptedly, with boundless energy, of him. If only the mouse could stay in his hole, he would be happy, but he cannot stay in his hole, because of the need to find cheese. It is not a situation calculated to produce the peace of mind conducive to contemplation.

The cat is standing in front of the mousehole with a hammer in one hand and a saw in the other. Beside him rests a pile of yellow boards and a big bag of nails. He begins furiously hammering and sawing, moving across the room in a cloud of dust that conceals him. Suddenly the dust clears and the cat beholds his work: a long, twisting pathway that begins at the mousehole and passes under the couch, over the back of the armchair, across the piano, through the kitchen door, and onto the kitchen table. On the tablecloth, at the end of the pathway, is a large mousetrap on which sits a lump of cheese. The cat tiptoes over to the refrigerator, vanishes behind it, and slyly thrusts out his head: his eyes dart left and right. There is the sound of a bicycle bell: *ring ring*. A moment later the mouse appears, pedaling fiercely. He speeds from the end of the pathway onto the table. As he screeches to a stop, the round wheels stretch out of shape and then become round again. The mouse is wearing riding goggles, a riding cap, and gloves. He leans his bicycle against the sugar bowl, steps over to the mousetrap, and looks at it with interest. He steps onto the mousetrap, sits down on the brass bar, and puts on a white bib. From a pocket of his leather jacket he removes a knife and fork. He eats the cheese swiftly. After his meal, he replaces the knife and fork in his pocket and begins to play on the mousetrap. He swings on a high bar, hangs upside down by his legs, walks the parallel bars, performs gymnastic stunts. Then he climbs onto his bicycle and disappears along the pathway, ringing his bell. The cat emerges from behind the refrigerator and springs onto the table beside the mousetrap. He frowns down at the trap. From the top of his head he plucks a single hair: it comes loose with the sound of a snapping violin string. Slowly he lowers the hair toward the mousetrap. The hair touches the spring. The mousetrap remains motionless. He presses the spring with a spoon. The mousetrap remains motionless. He bangs the spring with a sledgehammer. The mousetrap remains motionless. He looks at the trap with rage. Cautiously he reaches out a single toe. The mousetrap springs shut with the sound of a slammed iron door. The cat hops about the table holding his trapped foot as the toe swells to the size of a lightbulb, bright red.

The cat enters on the left, disguised as a mouse. He is wearing a blond wig, a nose mask, and a tight black dress slit to the thigh. He has high and very round breasts, a tiny waist, and round, rolling hips. His lips are bright red, and his black lashes are so tightly curled that when he blinks his eyes the lashes roll out and snap back like window shades. He walks slowly and seductively, resting one hand on a hip and one hand on his blond hair. The mouse is standing in the mousehole, leaning against one side with his hands in his pockets. His eyes protrude from their sockets in the shape of telescopes. In the lens of each telescope is a thumping heart. Slowly, as if mesmerized, the mouse sleepwalks into the room. The cat places a needle on a record, and rumba music begins to play. The cat dances with his hands clasped behind his neck, thrusting out each hip, fluttering his long lashes, turning to face the other way: in the tight black dress, his twitching backside is shaped like the ace of spades. The mouse faces the cat and begins to dance. They stride back and forth across the room, wriggling and kicking in step. As they dance, the cat's wig comes loose, revealing one cat ear. The cat dances over to a bearskin rug and lies down on his side. He closes his long-lashed eyes and purses his red, red lips. The mouse steps up to the cat. He reaches into his pocket, removes a cigar, and places it between the big red lips. The cat's eyes open. They look down at the cigar, look up, and look down again. The cat removes the cigar and stares at it. The cigar explodes. When the smoke clears, the cat's face is black. He gives a strained, very white smile. Many small lines appear in his teeth. The teeth crack into little pieces and fall out.

The cat is lying on his back in his basket in the kitchen. His hands are clasped behind his head, his left knee is raised, and his right ankle rests sideways on the raised knee. He is filled with rage at the thought of the mouse, who he knows despises him. He would like to tear the mouse to pieces, to roast him over a fire, to plunge him into a pan of burning butter. He understands that his rage is not the rage of hunger and he wonders whether the mouse himself is responsible for evoking this savagery, which burns in his chest like indigestion. He despises the mouse's physical delicacy, his weak arms thin as the teeth of combs, his frail, crushable skull, his fondness for books and solitude. At the same time, he is irritably aware that he admires the mouse's elegance, his air of culture and languor, his easy self-assurance. Why is he always reading? In a sense, the mouse intimidates the cat: in his presence, the cat feels clumsy and foolish. He thinks obsessively about the mouse and suspects with rage that the mouse frequently does not think about him at all, there in his brown room. If the mouse were less indifferent, would he burn with such hatred? Might they learn to live peacefully together in

the same house? Would he be released from this pain of out-
rage in his heart?

The mouse is standing at his workbench, curling the eyelashes of a mechanical cat. Her long black hair is shiny as
licorice; her lips look like licked candy. She is wearing a tight
red dress, black fishnet stockings, and red high heels. The
mouse stands the mechanical cat on her feet, unzips the back
of her dress, and winds a big key. He zips up the dress
and aims her toward the mousehole. In the living-room, the
mechanical cat struts slowly back and forth; her pointy
breasts stick out like party hats. The cat's head rises over the
back of the armchair. In his eyes appear hearts pierced by
arrows. He slithers over the chair and slides along the floor
like honey. When he reaches the strutting cat, he glides to
an upright position and stands mooning at her. His heart is
thumping so hard that it pushes out the skin of his chest with
each beat. The cat reaches into a pocket and removes a straw
boater, which he places on his head at a rakish angle. He
fastens at his throat a large polka-dot bow tie. He becomes
aware of a ticking sound. He removes from his pocket a
round yellow watch, places it against his ear, frowns, and
returns it to his pocket. He bends close to the face of the cat
and sees in each of her eyes a shiny round black bomb with
a burning fuse. The cat turns to the audience and then back
to the dangerous eyes. The mechanical cat blows up. When
the smoke clears, the cat's fur hangs from him in tatters,
revealing his pink flesh and a pair of polka-dot boxer shorts.

Outside the mousehole, the cat is winding up a mouse that
exactly resembles the real mouse. The mechanical mouse
is wearing a bathrobe and slippers, stands with hands in
pockets, and has a pair of eyeglasses perched at the end of its

388

nose. The cat lifts open the top of the mouse's head, which is attached in the manner of a hinged lid. He inserts a sizzling red stick of dynamite and closes the lid. He sets the mouse in front of the hole and watches as it vanishes through the arched opening. Inside, the mouse is sitting in his chair, reading a book. He does not raise his eyes to the visitor, who glides over with its hands in its pockets. Still reading, the mouse reaches out and lifts open the head of his double. He removes the sizzling dynamite, thrusts it into a cake, and inserts the cake into the mouse's head. He turns the mechanical mouse around and continues reading as it walks out through the arch. The cat is squatting beside the hole with his eyes shut and his fingers pressed in his ears. He opens his eyes and sees the mouse. His eyebrows rise. He snatches up the mouse, opens its head, and lifts out a thickly frosted cake that says HAPPY BIRTHDAY. In the center of the cake is a sizzling red stick of dynamite. The cat's fur leaps up. He takes a tremendous breath and blows out the fuse with such force that for a moment the cake is slanted. Now the cat grins, licks his teeth, and opens his jaws. He hears a sound. The cake is ticking loudly: *tock tock, tock tock.* Puzzled, the cat holds it up to one ear. He listens closely. A terrible knowledge dawns in his eyes.

The cat rides into the living-room in a bright yellow crane. From the boom hangs a shiny black wrecking ball. He drives up to the mousehole and stops. He pushes and pulls a pair of levers, which cause the wrecking ball to be inserted into a gigantic rubber band attached to a gigantic slingshot. The rubber band stretches back and back. Suddenly it releases the shiny black ball, which smashes into the wall. The entire house collapses, leaving only a tall red chimney standing amid the ruins. On top of the chimney is a stork's nest, in which a stork sits with a fishing pole. He is wearing a blue baseball cap. Below, in the rubble, a stirring is visible. The cat rises unsteadily, leaning on a crutch. His head is covered with a white bandage that conceals an eye; one leg is in a cast and one arm in a sling. With the tip of his crutch, he moves away a pile of rubble and exposes a fragment of baseboard. In the baseboard we see the unharmed mousehole. Inside the mousehole, the mouse sits in his chair, reading a book.

The mouse understands that the clownishly inept cat has the freedom to fail over and over again, during the long course of an inglorious lifetime, while he himself is denied the liberty of a single mistake. It is highly unlikely, of course, that he will ever be guilty of an error, since he is much cleverer than the cat and immediately sees through every one of his risible stratagems. Still, might not the very knowledge of his superiority lead to a relaxation of vigilance that will prove fatal, in the end? After all, he is not invulnerable; he is invulnerable only insofar as he is vigilant. The mouse is bored, deeply bored, by the ease with which he outwits the cat; there are times when he longs for a more worthy enemy, someone more like himself. He understands that his boredom is a dangerous weakness against which he must perpetually be on his guard. Sometimes he thinks, If only I could stop watching over myself, if only I could let myself go! The thought alarms him and causes him to look over his shoulder at the mousehole, across which the shadow of the cat has already fallen.

The cat enters from the left, carrying a sack over one shoulder. He sets the sack down beside the mousehole. He unties a rope from the neck of the sack, plunges both hands in, and carefully lifts out a gray cloud. He places the cloud in the

390

air above the mousehole. Rain begins to fall from the cloud, splashing down in great drops. The cat reaches into the sack and removes some old clothes. He swiftly disguises himself as a peddler and rings the mouse's bell. The mouse appears in the arched doorway, leaning against the side with his arms folded across his stomach and his ankles crossed as he stares out at the rain. The cat removes from the sack an array of mouse-size umbrellas, which he opens in turn: red, yellow, green, blue. The mouse shakes his head. The cat removes from the sack a yellow slicker, a pair of hip boots, a fishing rod and tackle box. The mouse shakes his head. The cat removes a red rubber sea horse, a compressed-air tank, a diving bell, a rowboat, a yacht. The mouse shakes his head, steps into his house, and slams the door. He opens the door, hangs a sign on the knob, and slams the door again. The sign reads NOT HOME. The rain falls harder. The cat steps out from under the cloud, which rises above his head and begins to follow him about the room. The storm grows worse: he is pelted with hailstones the size of golf balls. In the cloud appear many golfers, driving golf balls into the room. Forked lightning flashes; thunder roars. The cat rushes around the room trying to escape the cloud and dives under the couch. His tail sticks out. Lightning strikes the tail, which crackles like an electric wire. The couch rises for an instant, exposing the luminous, electrified cat rigid with shock; inside the cat's body, with its rim of spiked fur, his blue-white skeleton is visible. Now snow begins to fall from the cloud, and whistling winds begin to blow. Snow lies in drifts on the rug, rises swiftly up the sides of the armchair, sweeps up to the mantelpiece, where the clock looks down in terror and covers its eyes with its hands. The cat struggles slowly through the blizzard but is soon encased in snow. Icicles hang from his chin. He stands motionless, shaped like a cat struggling

391

forward with bent head. The door of the mousehole opens and the mouse emerges, wearing earmuffs, scarf, and gloves. The sun is shining. He begins shoveling a path. When he comes to the snow-cat, he climbs to the top of his shovel and sticks a carrot in the center of the snowy face. Then he climbs down, steps back, and begins throwing snowballs. The cat's head falls off.

The cat is pacing angrily in the kitchen, his hands behind his back and his eyebrows drawn down in a V. In a bubble above his head a wish appears: he is operating a circular saw that moves slowly, with high whining sounds, along a yellow board. At the end of the board is the mouse, lying on his back, tied down with ropes. The image vanishes and is replaced by another: the cat, wearing an engineer's hat, is driving a great train along a track. The mouse is stretched across the middle of the track, his wrists fastened to one rail and his ankles to the other. Sweat bursts in big drops from the mouse's face as the image vanishes and is replaced by another: the cat is turning a winch that slowly lowers an anvil toward the mouse, who is tied to a little chair. The mouse looks up in terror. Suddenly the cat lets go of the crank and the anvil rushes down with a whistling sound as the winch spins wildly. At the last moment, the mouse tumbles away. The anvil falls through the bubble onto the cat's head.

The cat understands that the mouse will always outwit him, but this tormenting knowledge serves only to inflame his desire to catch the mouse. He will never give up. His life, in relation to the mouse, is one long failure, a monotonous succession of unspeakable humiliations; his unhappiness is relieved only by moments of delusional hope, during which he believes, despite doubts supported by a lifetime of bitter experience, that at last he will succeed. Although he knows that he will never catch the mouse, who will forever escape into his mousehole a half inch ahead of the reaching claw, he also knows that only if he catches the mouse will his wretched life be justified. He will be transformed. Is it therefore his own life that he seeks, when he lies awake plotting against the mouse? Is it, when all is said and done, himself that he is chasing? The cat frowns and scratches his nose.

The cat stands before the mousehole holding in one hand a piece of white chalk. On the blue wall he draws the outline of a large door. The mousehole is at the bottom of the door. He draws the circle of a doorknob and opens the door. He steps into a black room. At the end of the room stands the mouse with a piece of chalk. The mouse draws a white mousehole on the wall and steps through. The cat kneels down and peers into the mousehole. He stands up and draws another door. He opens the door and steps into another black room. At the end of the room stands the mouse, who draws another mousehole and steps through. The cat draws another door, the mouse draws another mousehole. Faster and faster they draw: door, hole, door, hole, door. At the end of the last room, the mouse draws on the wall a white stick of dynamite. He draws a white match, which he takes in his hand and strikes against the wall. He lights the dynamite and hands it to the cat. The cat looks at the white outline of the dynamite. He offers it to the mouse. The mouse shakes his head. The cat points to himself and raises his eyebrows. The mouse nods. The stick of dynamite explodes.

The cat enters on the left, wearing a yellow hard hat and pushing a red wheelbarrow. The wheelbarrow is piled high with boards. In front of the mousehole, the cat puts down the handles of the barrow, pulls a hammer and saw from the pile of boards, and thrusts a fistful of black nails between his teeth. He begins sawing and hammering rapidly, moving from one end of the room to the other as a cloud of dust conceals his work. Suddenly the dust clears and the cat beholds his creation: he has constructed a tall guillotine, connected to the mousehole by a stairway. The blue-black glistening blade hangs between posts high above the opening for the head. Directly below the opening, on the other side, stands a basket. On the rim of the basket the cat places a wedge of cheese. The cat loops a piece of string onto a lever in the side of the guillotine and fastens the other end of the string to the wedge of cheese. Then he tiptoes away with hunched shoulders and vanishes behind a fire shovel. A moment later, the mouse climbs the stairs onto the platform of the guillotine. He stands with his hands in the pockets of his robe and contemplates the blade, the opening for the head, and the piece of cheese. He removes from one pocket a yellow package with a red bow. He leans over the edge of the platform and slips the loop from the lever. He thrusts his head through the head hole, removes the piece of cheese from the rim of the basket, and sets the package in its place. He ties the string to the package, slides his head back through the hole, and fits the loop of the string back over the lever. From his pocket he removes a large pair of scissors, which he lays on the platform. He next removes a length of rope, which he fastens to the lever so that the rope hangs nearly to the floor. On the floor he stands cross-ankled against the wheel of the barrow, eating his cheese. A moment later, the cat leaps onto the platform. He looks up in surprise at the unfallen blade. He crouches down, peers through the head hole, and sees the yellow package. He frowns. He looks up at the blade. He looks at the yellow package. Gingerly he reaches a paw through the opening and snatches it back. He frowns at the string. A cunning look comes into his eyes. He notices the pair of scissors, picks them up, and cuts the string. He waits, but nothing happens. Eagerly he thrusts his head through the opening and reaches for the package. The mouse, eating his cheese with one hand, lazily tugs at the rope with the other. The blade rushes down with the sound of a roaring train; a forlorn whistle blows. The cat tries to pull his head out of the hole. The blade slices off the top half of his head, which drops into the basket and rolls noisily around like a coin. The cat pulls himself out of the hole and stumbles about until he falls over the edge of the platform into the basket. He seizes the top of his head and puts it on like a hat. It is backward. He straightens it with a half turn. In his hand he sees with surprise the yellow package with the red bow. Frowning, he unties it. Inside is a bright red stick of dynamite with a sizzling fuse. The cat looks at the dynamite and turns his head to the audience. He blinks once. The dynamite explodes. When the smoke clears, the cat's face is black. In each eye a ship cracks in half and slowly sinks in the water.

The mouse is sitting in his chair with his feet on the hassock and his open book facedown on his lap. A mood of melancholy has invaded him, as if the brown tones of his room had seeped into his brain. He feels stale and out of sorts: he moves within the narrow compass of his mind, utterly devoid of fresh ideas. Is he perhaps too much alone? He thinks of the cat and wonders whether there is some dim and distant possibility of a connection, perhaps a companionship. Is it possible that they might become friends? Perhaps he could teach the cat to appreciate the things of the mind, and learn from the cat to enjoy life's simpler pleasures. Perhaps the cat, too, feels an occasional sting of loneliness. Haven't they much in common, after all? Both are bachelors, indoor sorts, who enjoy the comforts of a cozy domesticity; both are secretive; both take pleasure in plots and schemes. The more the mouse pursues this line of thought, the more it seems to him that the cat is a large, soft mouse. He imagines the cat with mouse ears and gentle mouse paws, wearing a white bib, sitting across from him at the kitchen table, lifting to his mouth a fork at the end of which is a piece of cheese.

The cat enters from the right with a chalkboard eraser in one hand. He goes over to the mousehole, bends down, and erases it. He stands up and erases the wall, revealing the mouse's home. The mouse is sitting in his chair with his feet on the hassock and his open book facedown on his lap. The cat bends over and erases the book. The mouse looks up in irritation. The cat erases the mouse's chair. He erases the hassock. He erases the entire room. He tosses the eraser over his shoulder. Now there is nothing left in the world except the cat and the mouse. The cat snatches him up in a fist. The cat's red tongue slides over glistening teeth sharp as ice picks. Here and there, over a tooth, a bright star expands and contracts. The cat opens his jaws wider, closes his eyes, and hesitates. The death of the mouse is desirable in every way, but will life without him really be pleasurable? Will the mouse's absence satisfy him entirely? Is it conceivable that he may miss the mouse, from time to time? Is it possible that he needs the mouse, in some disturbing way?

As the cat hesitates, the mouse reaches into a pocket of his robe and removes a red handkerchief. With swift circular strokes he wipes out the cat's teeth while the cat's eyes watch in surprise. He wipes out the cat's eyes. He wipes out the cat's whiskers. He wipes out the cat's head. Still held in the cat's fist, he wipes out the entire cat, except for the paw holding him. Then, very carefully, he wipes out the paw. He drops lightly down and slaps his palms together. He looks about. He is alone with his red handkerchief in a blank white world. After a pause, he begins to wipe himself out, moving rapidly from head to toe. Now there is nothing left but the red handkerchief. The handkerchief flutters, grows larger, and suddenly splits in half. The halves become red theater curtains, which begin to close. Across the closing curtains, words write themselves in black script: THE END.

ACKNOWLEDGMENTS

ALICE ADAMS: 'The Islands' from *The Stories of Alice Adams* by Alice Adams. Reprinted by permission of International Creative Management, Inc. Copyright © 2002 by Alice Adams. 'The Islands' from *The Stories of Alice Adams* by Alice Adams, copyright © 2002 by The Estate of Alice Adams Linenthal. Used by permission of Alfred A. Knopf, a division of Random House, Inc.

STEPHEN VINCENT BENÉT: 'The King of the Cats', copyright © 1928 by Stephen Vincent Benét; copyright renewed © 1957 by Rosemary Carr Benét. Used by permission of Brandt & Hochman Literary Agents, Inc.

MAEVE BRENNAN: 'I See You, Bianca', copyright © 2000 by The Estate of Maeve Brennan from *The Rose Garden* by Maeve Brennan. Reprinted by permission of Counterpoint.

ITALO CALVINO: 'The Garden of Stubborn Cats' from *Marcovaldo or The Seasons in the City* by Italo Calvino, copyright © 1963 by Giulio Einaudi editore s.p.a., Torino, English translation by William Weaver copyright © 1983 by Harcourt, Inc. and Martin Secker and Warburg Limited, reprinted by permission of Harcourt, Inc.

'The Garden of Stubborn Cats' from *Marcovaldo* by Italo Calvino, published by Vintage Books. Reprinted by permission of The Random House Group Limited and the Wylie Agency as representatives of the Estate of Italo Calvino.

ANGELA CARTER: 'Puss-in-Boots' taken from *The Bloody Chamber* by Angela Carter. Copyright © 1979 Angela Carter. Reproduced by permission of The Estate of Angela Carter, c/o Rogers, Coleridge & White Ltd., 20 Powis Mews, London W11 1JN.

WALTER DE LA MARE: 'Broomsticks' by Walter de la Mare, reprinted with permission from The Literary Trustees of Walter de la Mare and The Society of Authors as their representative.

NEIL GAIMAN: 'The Price' from *Smoke and Mirrors* (pp. 49–56) by Neil Gaiman. Copyright © 1999 by Neil Gaiman. Reprinted by permission of HarperCollins Publishers.

'The Price' from *Smoke and Mirrors* by Neil Gaiman. Reproduced by permission of Headline Publishing Group Limited.

PATRICIA HIGHSMITH: 'Ming's Biggest Prey' from *The Selected Stories of Patricia Highsmith* by Patricia Highsmith. Copyright © 2001 by The Estate of Patricia Highsmith. Used by permission of W. W. Norton & Company, Inc.

Patricia Highsmith's *Selected Stories* published by W. W. Norton & Company, New York. Copyright © 1993 Diogenes Verlag AG, Zürich, Switzerland.

URSULA K. LE GUIN: 'Schrödinger's Cat' by Ursula K. Le Guin. Copyright © 1974, 2002 by Ursula K. Le Guin; first appeared in *Universe 5*; from *The Compass Rose*; reprinted by permission of the author and the author's agents, the Virginia Kidd Agency, Inc. and MBA Literary Agents, London.

FRITZ LEIBER: 'Space-Time for Springers' from *Gummitch and Friends* by Fritz Leiber. Reprinted with permission from Richard Curtis Associates, Inc., on behalf of the Estate of Fritz Leiber.

DORIS LESSING: 'An Old Woman and Her Cat' from *The Temptation of Jack Orkney and Other Stories* by Doris Lessing. Copyright © 1972 Doris Lessing. Reprinted by kind permission of Jonathan Clowes Ltd., London, on behalf of Doris Lessing.

STEVEN MILLHAUSER: 'Cat 'n' Mouse' from *Dangerous Laughter* by Steven Millhauser. Reprinted by permission of International Creative Management, Inc. Copyright © 2008 by Steven Millhauser.

'Cat 'n' Mouse' from *Dangerous Laughter: Thirteen Stories* by Steven Millhauser, copyright © 2008 by Steven Millhauser. Used by permission of Alfred A. Knopf, a division of Random House, Inc.

DAMON RUNYON: 'Lillian' from *Guys and Dolls* by Damon Runyon, copyright © 2008 by American Rights Management Co., LLC. Used by permission of Viking Penguin, a division of Penguin Group (USA) Inc.

P. G. WODEHOUSE: 'Cats Will Be Cats' from *Mulliner Nights* by P. G. Wodehouse. Copyright © P. G .Wodehouse. Reproduced by permission of the Estate of P. G. Wodehouse c/o Rogers, Coleridge & White Ltd., 20 Powis Mews, London W11 1JN.